Di Morrissey is one of Australia's most successful writers. She began writing as a young woman, training and working as a journalist for Australian Consolidated Press in Sydney and Northcliffe Newspapers in London. She has worked in television in Australia and Hawaii and in the USA as a presenter, reporter, producer and actress. After her marriage to a US diplomat, Peter Morrissey, she lived in Singapore, Japan, Thailand, South America and Washington. Returning to Australia, Di continued to work in television before publishing her first novel in 1991.

Di has a daughter, Dr Gabrielle Hansen, and her children, Sonoma Grace and Everton Peter, arc Di's first grandchildren. Di's son, Dr Nicolas Morrissey, is a lecturer in South East Asian Art History and Buddhist Studies at the University of Georgia, USA.

Di and her partner, Boris Janjic, divide their time between Byron Bay and the Manning Valley in New South Wales when not travelling to research her novels, which are all inspired by a particular landscape.

www.dimorrissey.com

Di Morrissey

The Plantation

MACMILLAN

Pan Macmillan Australia

First published in Macmillan in 2010 by Pan Macmillan Australia Pty Limited
1 Market Street, Sydney

National Library of Australia
cataloguing-in-publication data:

Morrissey, Di

The plantation / Di Morrissey.

ISBN 978-1-4050-3998-7 (pbk.)

A823.3

Internal illustrations by Yeong Seak Ling
Typeset in 12.5/15 pt Sabon by Post Pre-press Group
Printed in Australia by McPherson's Printing Group

To my late uncles: Jim Revitt, ABC Radio and TV foreign correspondent in Malaysia between 1968 and 1970, who always inspired, mentored and watched over me and hoped I'd write this book. And Ron Revitt, my 'big brother', who made me laugh, teased me, shared dreams and taught me to see the world through the eyes of an artist. May they both rest peacefully where we were all born, in the Manning Valley, NSW.

And to my new grandson, Everton Peter Hansen, who has come into my life to bring us joy.

Acknowledgments

THANKS TO . . .

My darling Boris who shares my life and whom I love so much.

My daughter, Dr Gabrielle (Morrissey) Hansen, for her advice and love and the gift of her growing family, especially the precious Sonoma.

My son, Dr Nick Morrissey (and his beautiful Mimi), who first suggested I write about Malaysia. Congratulations on your appointment to the faculty of the University of Georgia, I'm very proud of you.

Josephine De Freitas (and the wonderful Philip) for her memories of growing up on a plantation in Malaysia.

Huge thanks to Martin Bek-Nielsen for his time and hospitality at United Plantation.

To Liz Adams, my incomparable editor, who is more friend as well as advisor and life coach!

Liz Foster for her calm efficiency. And to copy editor Rowena Lennox for her unerring eye.

To Christopher Jonach, pilot extraordinaire!

To my publisher, James Fraser, and everyone at Pan Macmillan, love and thanks.

To my lawyer Ian Robertson with affection and admiration.

And to all those friends and advisors in Australia and Malaysia, including: James Ritchie, Dato' Wong Sulong, Harold Speldewinde, PT (Puvi) Singam, Aidi Bin Abdullah, Lawrence Cheah, Barry Wain, Alison Fraser and Narelle McMurtrie at the Bon Ton Resort, Langkawi Island.

Prologue

Sarawak, 1960

IT WAS THE DUSTED light, sifting from the rainforest canopy that captivated her. In the green illumination the skyscraper trees, living columns bound in twisted vines, towered above the forest floor. Silence prevailed.

The woman, dressed in sturdy cotton slacks and shirt with camera and notebook at the ready, sat comfortably on the layer of rotting leaves where a seed sprouted at the base of a venerable tree. She no longer felt a stranger in this jungle nor was she afraid of being here alone.

She stared upwards to where, far above the floor of the forest, giant ferns, orchids and lichen proliferated on the trees, seeking a place in the sunlight. She still marvelled at the hundred shades of green; the variations of leaf shapes; fruits and seeds ripening to the moment of bursting; and the platoons of insects, birds and animals, small and large, busy at their daily task of survival.

She waited and listened for the faint shudder of branches, the rustle of leaves, the cracking of a small branch high above, that would announce the arrival of those she hoped to see. But the sounds that came to her were unexpected. They came from closer to the river, near the small trail that lead from the camp of tents and palm huts. She waited, holding her breath, thinking perhaps that it was one of the creatures she was yet to see, or perhaps a wandering pygmy rhino, a sun bear or a wild boar.

Then, through the trees, she saw silent movement and glimpsed the shape of two men. One was European, the other a shorter, darker man with the distinctive hair and profile that signalled that he was indigenous, but he was no one she recognised from the local Iban tribe.

She was about to rise to her feet when her attention was caught by the rattling of swaying treetops.

The two men also stopped, startled by the sound, and gazed upwards as a female orangutan, an infant clinging to her, swung to the next tree.

Thrilled by their arrival, the woman jumped to her feet, but then she stopped in horror.

The European was lifting a rifle, looking through its sights as he aimed skywards. The other man lifted the blow pipe he was carrying, ready to let loose a poison dart.

In Malay she shouted, 'Stop! What are you doing?'

The men spun in shock and the orangutan and infant crashed through the trees out of sight.

The European, startled and angry, shouted at her. 'Get away. What are you doing here?'

The woman strode forward, avoiding roots, pushing vines and branches aside as she made her way towards the men. 'I am from Camp Salang. Who are you? You can't shoot orangutans! They're such beautiful creatures.'

'Who said we are shooting apes? We are hunting for food. Mind your own business, lady.'

She stopped, unnerved by his hostile, threatening manner. She saw the local man moving away, and in seconds he was out of sight. The European moved his rifle menacingly while he stared at her, before he quickly followed his companion into the jungle.

Feeling shaken, the peace and solitude of her surroundings broken by the presence of the two men, she began to retrace her steps. As she approached the small jungle camp carved from the forest at the edge of the river, she saw activity on the tiny landing as the klotok, the village longboat, prepared to head downriver to trade for supplies. Behind it was moored the motor boat she and her husband had travelled in to reach this remote place. She walked on to where he was talking with the village headman. She spoke quietly to her husband, and his reaction was one of surprise and worry.

As soon as he could politely conclude his business, the two of them set off with one of the Iban from the longhouse to the place where she had confronted the two men. The tribesman, so at home in this jungle, moved easily, but the husband and wife soon became breathless as they struggled to keep up. The young man quickly lengthened the distance between them. Through the trees in the dim light they saw that he had stopped and had bent down.

The woman reached him first and let out a cry. Stumbling, her hand to her mouth, she turned away to her husband. He reached the scene and opened his arms to his stricken wife, shielding her from the terrible sight before them.

A tangled pile of matted orange fur was covered in blood. The stomach of the creature had been gutted but what distressed them even more was that her head, feet and hands had been roughly hacked off.

'Where's her baby?' whispered the woman.

The young man lifted his shoulders and, looking at her husband, said, 'Gone, tuan. Sold for money.'

'Poachers. How utterly senseless.'

His wife buried her face in his shirt as he stroked her hair. 'You start back, dear. Leonard and I will bury the poor creature,' he said.

'How I wish we could catch these people. It's too distressing,' said his wife through her tears. 'It's just too hard. I want to leave here.'

I

Brisbane, 2009

THE RAIN FELL IN sheets that sliced across the windscreen and shone in the lights of oncoming cars. Julie Reagan was glad she had known these suburban streets all her life as she turned into a driveway which ran with the deluge from the summer storm. She pulled up in front of a beautiful big old house, set high on stumps to allow the cooling air to flow beneath the solid wooden floors. The house was encircled by a wide verandah accessed by sandstone steps and atop its pitched roof sat a small, ornate turret. The old Queenslander had an imperious air, perched above the other nearby homes, with its sweeping views from the verandah, the colonnades of which were smothered in the bright yellow flowers of an alamanda vine.

The young woman turned up the collar of her cotton jacket before racing across the sodden lawn, under a dripping poinciana tree, up the steps and onto the front verandah. She stepped out of her shoes and shook the drips from her hair and shirt. She knew her shoulder-length brown hair was starting to curl in the warm dampness.

Julie opened the carved white front door with its panels of stained glass and paused to hear the news on the TV in the sitting room and inhale the toasty, cheesy smell of something that her mother was cooking. The long, airy hallway with its polished wooden floor, the white wooden fretwork, the floral pattern in the pressed-metal ceilings and the carpet runner that had belonged to her great grandmother – everything was familiar to her.

Bayview had originally been bought by her great grandparents more than one hundred years ago. Her grandmother, Margaret, had lived here and now her parents. Her mother Caroline said that although old Queenslanders were expensive to maintain, she had no wish to give up the comfortable and gracious home where little had changed since she was a schoolgirl. For Julie, the house had always been a constant in her life and, while she valued her career, social life and independence, the idea of not having this wonderful family home was inconceivable.

'Mum? It's me.'

'In the kitchen, Jules.'

'Not watching the news?'

'Listening from here. I had to get this out of the oven. Nothing special but as your father is going to be late I've indulged myself.' Caroline Reagan looked at her thirty-two-year-old daughter standing in the doorway and her heart warmed at the sight of her. She saw her regularly but occasionally, like now, she paused and couldn't help but think of what a lovely looking girl Julie was, with her thick, wavy hair, bright blue eyes, firm square jaw and large, happy mouth. But there was also something else about Julie that Caroline hoped others, meeting her for the first time, would also notice. There was a calmness, strength and warmth that radiated from her even before she spoke.

Caroline turned her attention to the dinner plates. 'Do you want to stay and eat?'

Julie dropped into her family home a couple of times a week and knew that it wasn't necessary to stand on ceremony, for her mother was always happy to feed her. Her parents' fridge was always full of tasty leftovers or the makings of a quick meal.

'I wasn't, but it smells good and that rain is atrocious. So I'll wait for awhile, if that's okay?'

'Do stay, sweetie. I've been hoping you'd call by.'

'Oh, why is that?' Julie could tell from her voice that Mother Had News. 'Heard from Adam and Heather lately?' Julie's mother was always hoping that Julie's married brother in South Australia would announce the imminent arrival of a baby.

'Yes. But nothing really exciting to report. Oh, they've found some fabulous old recycled timbers which they're going to use in their renovations, but no big news to speak of.'

Julie smiled to herself. It mightn't be news in big letters to her mother but she could imagine how pleased Adam must have been at finding a treasure for the mud brick home he and Heather were creating in the Adelaide Hills. 'So what news do you have?'

'I'll tell you in a minute. Pour us a small drink. How's work?' asked her mother.

'The same. Hectic. Trying to help get some new companies on the map is always hard.'

'Well, I guess that's what a marketing consultant gets paid to do. Give them good advice.' Her mother wiped her hands on a tea towel and led the way into the living room as Julie followed her with two glasses of chilled white wine.

7

Caroline turned off the TV and settled herself on the sofa. 'We'll eat in a minute. It's just macaroni and cheese and a little salad. I want you to read this first.' She handed Julie a letter from the coffee table.

Julie put down her glass. 'Is it from someone you know?'

'No. But it's an interesting letter.'

Julie scanned the letterhead of one of Queensland's universities and noted the signature, Dr David Cooper. Intrigued, she read the letter slowly.

Dear Mrs Reagan,
I hope you don't mind my contacting you, but I am an associate professor in the Department of Anthropology, currently researching the Iban people of Borneo with a special focus on the changes to their methods of agriculture, social structure and lifestyle given their loss of habitat and resettlement from their previous existence as jungle and river dwellers in Sarawak. In the course of my research in Malaysia I came across a small book, My Life with the Headhunters of Borneo *by Bette Oldham, which was published in the seventies, and in which she recounts a period of time spent with a local group of Iban in Sarawak. The author was, I believe, your aunt.*

I would, of course, very much like to know more about Bette Oldham and her work. If you can help me at all, I'd very much appreciate it. I can be contacted at the above address or email, or phone.
Yours sincerely,
Dr David Cooper

'Good grief!' exclaimed Julie. 'Is this the Aunt Bette that Gran was always so critical of? Did you know that Aunt Bette lived with the headhunters of Borneo? It sounds amazing.'

'Mother always said that her sister was wild and had shamed the family,' said Caroline. 'But I had no idea that she'd done anything like that.'

'And Gran never told you anything?'

'First I've heard of it.'

'Do you remember Aunt Bette?' asked Julie.

'Vaguely, when I was very little and still lived in Malaya, before Mother moved back here.'

Julie was thoughtful. 'Well, Gran hardly ever mentioned her sister to me but if she did she always called her names like, "my dreadful sister" or "the horrendous one". There didn't seem to be much love there.'

'No, there certainly wasn't. Funny that this David Cooper should raise the subject of Aunt Bette. To be honest, I rarely think about our family in Malaya. Malaysia, as it is now,' said Caroline.

'Not surprising. We tend to get wrapped up in the immediate day-to-day stuff, don't we,' said Julie. 'Are you going to contact him about Bette?'

'No. What can I say? I hardly remember her and Mother clearly disliked her so much that she could barely bring herself to talk about her.'

'I'd like to know how this David Cooper tracked us down. Now, can we eat? I'm starving.' Julie folded the letter and slipped it into her pocket.

It wasn't until several days later that Julie had a few moments free to pull David Cooper's letter from her handbag and then ring the phone number he'd given.

'Dr Cooper? This is Julie Reagan. You wrote to my mother Caroline about my Great Aunt Bette . . .'

'Indeed! How wonderful to hear back from you so quickly. Your aunt seemed to be quite a remarkable woman, if the book is anything to go by. I'd really like to learn more about her. May I ask if she's still alive?'

'Actually, I have no idea. I'd be surprised if she were,

9

as she'd be quite old. But I have to tell you that although she was my grandmother's sister, they were estranged, so I know nothing about her at all and my mother barely remembers her. That's why we were intrigued to hear of her book. Is it possible to get a copy of it?'

'I doubt it. I knew of the existence of the book and I've been trawling the net for over a year looking for it. I was elated when I found it in the Sarawak museum shop in Kuching. You're welcome to borrow my copy. It's a slim volume but quite insightful.'

'Yes, I'd like that. Tell me, how did you track down my mother?'

'It wasn't very difficult at all. You see there is a dedication in the front of the book to Philip Elliott at the Utopia plantation in Malaysia. I contacted the plantation, it's well known, and his sons Shane and Peter, your cousins who run it. They gave me your mother's address. They did mention to me that they had never met your mother,' he added.

'That's true,' said Julie. 'My grandmother and my mother returned to live in Brisbane after the war, but Uncle Philip stayed on with my grandfather on the plantation, in Malaysia. So my mother has spent most of her life here, which is why she won't be of much help to you, I'm afraid.'

'I appreciate your contacting me. My email address is on the letter. Just in case anything does come up, or your mother recalls anything,' said David.

'I don't think she will. As I said, my mother left Malaya when she was very young and she had little contact with that side of the family, except for birthday and Christmas cards and that sort of thing.'

'That's a pity. I enjoy Malaysia so I try to find as many reasons as possible to go there.'

'Are you investigating the headhunters too?' asked Julie. He sounded youngish and she imagined he was probably a bit stuffy.

David chuckled. 'Yes, I've done a lot of research on the Iban tribespeople in particular. Borneo is pretty amazing. I've adopted several orangutans in a sanctuary because their habitat, like that of the indigenous people, is threatened. So I use both these reasons to keep going back as much as I can. If you ever plan a trip there let me know and I'll pass on some tips and contacts.'

'Thank you, but that's not on my agenda at the moment. Good luck with your research.'

'Many thanks. Julie, was it?'

'Yes. And you're happy to lend me the book?'

'Of course. What's your address and email?'

She told him. 'Good bye, Dr Cooper.'

'Please, call me David. Good bye, Julie.'

She hung up and hoped he would remember to lend them the copy of her great aunt's book. Bette Oldham had started to fascinate her.

When Julie dropped in to see her parents the following Saturday, she found her mother sitting on the floor of the sewing room. It had been her great grandmother's sewing room, but Margaret and now Caroline, who didn't sew, used it as their storeroom, library and everything else room. To Julie's surprise, her mother was surrounded by a box, a dog-eared expanding file and a pile of photo albums.

'What on earth are you doing?'

'Hello, Jules. Come and join me. This is all quite interesting.' Caroline raised her voice over the rumble of her husband's lawnmower outside. 'As you know, I've never been one for raking over the past, but the letter I got from David Cooper gave me pause for thought. I don't remember much about the family plantation in Malaysia. I remember some chairs under an enormous rain tree and Mother serving tea on a white wicker table, but not much else, so I thought I'd look through Mother's old photos to see if anything else jogged my memory.'

'Looks like a rain tree here,' said Julie as she picked up several photographs and flipped through them. 'Is this Gran? Done up to the nines. Who are these people? Looks like they're at the races.'

'That's my father Roland, I recognise the moustache,' said Caroline.

'There are several local people in the group. An Indian and a Chinese man. And here . . . Is that . . . ?' Julie peered closer.

'Yes, that's Bette. Defying convention – no hat or gloves, just an umbrella to keep off the sun.'

'She's very pretty. Gran is smartly dressed, but Bette looks more natural.'

'Her hair looks like yours,' commented Caroline. 'Mother had fine hair and always wore it tightly waved or pinned up. Bette looks more casual, doesn't she?'

'I wish I'd known them when they were young. The only thing I really know about Great Aunt Bette is that she disgraced the family in some terrible way. I've never asked what she did that so upset Gran. Do you know what it was, Mum?'

'Oh yes. Bette, according to my mother, ran off and married a Chinaman,' said Caroline. 'Actually, the way Mother talked, it sounded as if the devil himself had cast a spell on her sister.'

'That must have stirred things up at the time. When was it?' asked Julie.

'Oh, after the war, but I don't know the details because Mother was so angry about her sister's behaviour and the disgrace she said it brought to the family – I learned not to raise the subject.'

Julie continued to shuffle through the pictures. 'These photos are amazing. Must have been an incredible time before the war. All the gentlemen in white suits and Panama hats, all quite like the raj, isn't it?'

'Planters and memsahibs, I suppose. I just love the way everybody dressed up,' said Caroline. 'It was a different life and Mother fitted right in. All those airs and graces.' She studied a photo and then handed it to Julie.

'Look, just Mother and Bette, the two sisters. Do you see what I see?'

Julie glanced at the formally posed portrait of the two women, then looked at Caroline – her hair pulled back into a youthful ponytail, her peaked eyebrows, firm upper lip and pointed chin – looking for a resemblance. She studied the face of the younger Bette with her loose hair, sparkling thick-lashed eyes, wide smiling mouth and square face. 'Oh my gosh! I look like her! And you look like Gran. I remember how alike you were. I've never seen photos of Great Aunt Bette before.'

'You've taken after the pretty one,' said her mother.

'Mum, you're stunning. I always thought I had the prettiest mother at school,' said Julie quickly. She meant it.

'Thank you, darling. But I think that Bette looks like one of those women who would always look terrific no matter what – without make-up, first thing in the morning, when they're sick or tired. Mother and I scrubbed up okay after we'd done what Dad calls "the face painting".' She smiled at Julie. 'You look gorgeous all the time whether you're trying or not.'

'I hope when I make an effort I look a bit better than when I've just fallen out of bed,' said Julie. Then she added, 'Y'know what, Mum? I think you do know a lot more than you realise. Gran must have told you a lot of stories about the old days.'

'Oh, she did indeed. I have every chapter and verse of her life before the war. And there are letters in that

13

shoebox that she wrote to her parents describing married life in Malaya,' said Caroline.

'Well, then! You could tell that anthropologist fellow heaps!' exclaimed Julie.

'But they're personal things, dear. He wouldn't be interested in that.'

'So how come you didn't know about Great Aunt Bette and the jungle people? asked Julie.

'Mmm. Well, that book was written long after Mother and I had left Malaya and, as I've already said, Mother only mentioned Bette to criticise her. "That terrible woman, that disgrace to the family", that sort of thing.'

'That was an odd sort of arrangement, wasn't it, with you and Gran here in Brisbane, and your father and brother Philip in Malaya,' said Julie

'We didn't really think of it like that. When Mother wanted to come back to live in Brisbane, Philip was in boarding school in England – he was ten years older than me – so he stayed there and I came here. Then, when he left school, he wanted to stay in Malaysia with Father. So I never really got to know him. Of course, I have Mother's version of events, but there are probably a few missing pieces to the story.'

'Do you think that the war had anything to do with the split in the family?'

'I don't know. Probably not. I think that Father spent most of the war in India, while Mother saw it out in Brisbane. But they both went back to Malaya afterwards, otherwise I wouldn't have been born. But that doesn't tell us anything more about Bette, does it?'

'Maybe David Cooper knows something more. I mean he knew to look for her book, didn't he?'

'I thought he was researching the native people of Borneo, not our family!' said Caroline.

'I know but it mightn't hurt to meet him. He did

promise to loan me the copy of Bette's book. I sent him an email.'

Caroline shrugged. 'Well, ask him over for a cup of tea. He might like to look at some of these pictures. I wish Mother had written names on the back of these photos, at least!' she said in exasperation. 'Who are they all?'

Julie watched as David Cooper got out of his car, then stopped and looked at her mother's home. He walked across the lawn to gaze up into the thick arms of the poinciana tree and then turned to admire the view across Moreton Bay. He was perhaps in his late thirties, medium build, with his hair a bit long so that it flopped near his dark glasses. He wore jeans that had been pressed, a short-sleeved lemon shirt and he carried a small package. As he headed towards the front steps, Julie came out onto the verandah to greet him.

'Hi, I'm Julie. You like our view?'

'It's a stunning old place. Nice to know there are still some around in such good condition, though not too many are as beautiful as this. Hello, I'm David.' He stepped onto the verandah beside her and Julie realised he was taller than she'd thought. She took his outstretched hand and shook it. He handed her the package.

'The book. As promised.'

'Thank you, we'll return it as soon as Mum and I have read it.'

'No, please keep it. I've photocopied what I need and I think that the original should be with Bette's family.'

'Well, thank you. Come on in. My mother has made a cake in your honour.'

'I'm impressed. How nice.'

Julie smiled and opened the front door. 'Mum isn't known for her baking skills, so it's an easy pineapple cake.'

'Sounds great.'

Caroline was putting a jug of water on the table on the back verandah. 'Hello, nice to meet you. I'm Caroline Reagan. Would you prefer tea, coffee, iced tea?'

'Iced tea sounds great.' David Cooper glanced around at the cool, casual surrounds with the cane furniture, bright cushions and a climbing creeper screening the lush private garden. 'This reminds me of the tropics and the colonial planters' homes.'

'It's not intended. This house was here in this style long before my mother ever heard of Malaya,' said Caroline. 'Do sit down and tell me about yourself.'

'I'll get the iced tea,' said Julie, leaving David Cooper to her mother's gentle inquisition. When she returned the two of them were talking animatedly. Caroline smiled as Julie put down glasses and poured the iced tea over fresh mint leaves.

'Did you know David's family come from Brisbane? I believe that I could have played tennis against his mother when I was at school,' said Caroline.

'Really? Did you grow up here?' Julie asked David.

'I did. But I went to ANU to do my degree. I hated the cold in Canberra, so I'm glad to get back here to work.' He took the glass of iced tea she handed to him. 'I suppose the climate's another reason I like South East Asia, too.'

'Can you tell us a little more about your project and how you stumbled across my aunt?' asked Caroline.

'It was serendipity, I suppose. I knew of the existence of her book for some time through references to it in other works, but I was so pleased when I found a copy of it in Kuching and, as I told Julie, it had a dedication that led me to your family's plantation, Utopia, and then to you. Shane and Peter, your cousins, were very hospitable,' he added.

'Oh, can I see the book?' asked Caroline. She began

to leaf through the small book, glancing at the print and examining the photos. 'This looks really interesting.'

'Your aunt seems to have had a great affinity and understanding of the Iban people in Sarawak. The stories of expatriate observers, even if they are not trained anthropologists, can tell us a lot about the living conditions and habits of indigenous people. They certainly add an extra dimension to my research. And Bette was a wonderful observer.'

'Mum was born on Utopia,' said Julie for something to say as her mother looked thoughtful.

'Have you been there? asked David.

'No,' replied Julie. 'I've never really thought about it. What's Malaysia like?'

'You should go and see it for yourself,' said David quietly.

'Maybe I will,' said Julie lightly, but giving the impression she had little intention of doing so. 'More tea?'

'Thanks, but no. The cake was delicious, thank you, Mrs Reagan.'

'You're welcome, and do call me Caroline.' Caroline took his hand as he rose. 'But wait, I've been thinking. Did Julie tell you I've been going through a lot of my mother's letters and photographs and there are a couple there of Bette, taken before the war. Perhaps you'd like to see them?'

'I'd love to put a face to the book!'

'Be a dear and clear the cake and cups would you please, Jules,' asked Caroline, as she led David Cooper along the verandah to the French doors of her storeroom.

Julie was kept busy for the next two weeks travelling interstate for a new client who was expanding his company from a vineyard into a hospitality venue. It had been interesting travelling through the wine country of Victoria but she was glad to be back in sunny Brisbane. As she drove home from the airport she couldn't help comparing the openness of the Victorian countryside to the clutter of the apartment complexes now cramming the skyline around Brisbane.

She was renting a little old-fashioned house, hidden in a lush, overgrown garden, in what had once been a modest family suburb. While her mother's house, Bayview, was grander and larger, there were similarities in the breezy white wooden Queenslander she rented.

Julie pulled into her rickety carport beneath a large mango tree. She often imagined the people who had lived in this house sitting on their front steps, chatting to their neighbours in similar houses. Now her house seemed an anachronism, with a split-level modern glass and chrome house on one side, and a block of six units overshadowing her on the other. Every day the street was busy and lined with cars as parking was at a premium; the many flats and units that had sprung up never provided enough parking places. She turned her gaze away from all the new buildings and opened the door of her little cottage.

The light on the answering machine was blinking and her mother's voice echoed around Julie's tiny bright kitchen.

'Hope your trip went well, Jules. When you have a minute, come over and have dinner. Dad and I have some news we need to talk to you about. We're fine, but it's ghastly council stuff. Bye, darling.'

Her parents were preparing dinner when Julie arrived the following evening.

'Dad's got the barbecue going. So good to see you,'

said Caroline, kissing Julie on the cheek. 'I do wish Adam was here, but perhaps we'll chat to him later.'

'What's going on?' asked Julie.

'It's just unbelievable. Here, read this letter from the council.' Her mother pushed a letter towards her but before Julie could open it, Caroline was heatedly explaining its contents. 'They want to resume this area for a bypass! Have you ever heard of anything so ridiculous? Imagine knocking down beautiful homes for a bypass!'

'What do you mean, knock down? Not this house? They couldn't,' said Julie. 'Let me see the letter.'

'It's true, isn't it, Paul? Ask your father,' said Caroline as Paul Reagan walked into the kitchen.

He ran his fingers through his hair. 'Well, it sounds like that's the idea. Nothing's really definite, yet, though.'

Julie skimmed the letter. 'It's outrageous. We have to stop this at once. Obviously these so-called planners have never set foot in these streets and seen the homes that are around here or they'd never mark them for demolition.'

'This was a beautiful suburb in Grandma's day. And it's even more so now,' said her mother.'

'No one builds houses like this any more, that's for sure,' added her father.

'Have you talked to Adam? What did he say?' asked Julie.

'No, not yet. You know your brother, he'll just say that we should wait and see, nothing may come of it,' sighed Caroline.

'Yes, I guess so,' said Julie. 'He's never been one to make an instant decision. Well, we can't take that chance. Have you talked to the neighbours?'

'They're obviously not happy either,' said her father.

'We need to get everyone together and make a plan to oppose this,' said Julie firmly. 'Let's make some tea, Mum, sit down and start nutting out a few ideas.'

'There, I told you Julie would come up with something,' said Caroline, looking slightly cheered.

Julie was still making notes on how to oppose the council's plans, when David Cooper rang her the next day.

'Hello, did you enjoy your great aunt's book?'

'To tell you the truth, I haven't had a chance to look at it yet, I've been so busy. Mum's had her head in it, though.'

'I've found out a little more information, in case you and your mother are interested,' he said.

'I'm sure Mum would be, but we're a bit distracted at the moment. We're fighting the local council's plans to rip down our house,' said Julie.

'What! Your grandmother's house? That's ridiculous. Why on earth would they want to do that?'

'Actually, it was my great grandmother's house, too. They want to put in a bypass to ease traffic flow away from the CBD or something,' said Julie. 'It's crazy.'

David Cooper paused. 'Er, run that by me again. Surely putting in such a road in your neighbourhood would mean pulling down a lot of historic homes?'

'Obviously. The authorities must have some idea what these older homes are like. They must know that most were built over a hundred years ago. And they only have to look at them to know that they are not dilapidated old heaps with bad plumbing and peeling paint,' said Julie. 'Mum's organising a committee to fight the bypass.'

'Would she like some help? I'm pretty good at researching and I might be able to find enough information on the history and heritage value of the neighbourhood to stop the road. I'd hate to see such beautiful homes, indeed streets and suburbs, desecrated,' said David.

'That's the word all right. Desecrated. Ripping up

beautiful old houses is desecration. Look, any help would be appreciated. Could you come along to our neighbourhood meeting tonight? It's down the road from Mum's place. Seven pm.'

'Of course. Can I meet you at your mother's so you can show me where to go?'

'Yes, and thanks a lot. We really appreciate your help.' An academic, good at research who could sift through relevant information, would be very useful, thought Julie, glad that they'd met David Cooper. 'Thanks, Great Aunt Bette,' she said to herself.

The neighbourhood meeting was informal but passionate. Two dozen families gathered in the back garden of one of the threatened homes, that had also been in the same family for generations. Caroline and another resident were elected spokespersons and they directed their comments to the council representative, Fred Louden, who'd come along to hear their concerns. David Cooper sat in the background with a digital recorder and a notebook, which had prompted Fred Louden to ask, with some concern, if David was from the media. When David said he was a friend of the Reagans, Louden gave him an affable smile and took his seat.

Caroline read aloud the letter they'd all received and, keeping her voice calm, said, 'We all seem in agreement as to what this letter is saying: that the council is considering moving ahead with a plan to resume a section of our neighbourhood to create a road bypass to skirt this area, to facilitate traffic flow and allow for the easy implementation of future infrastructure.' She paused before adding, 'Whatever that actually means. Hopefully Mr Louden will be able to enlighten us.'

But when Fred Louden rose to speak, he talked in

such broad and general terms – about the growth of Brisbane and the need for residents to make sacrifices and of course there would be adequate compensation – that no one present was any clearer about the council's plans. Caroline then asked for comments and questions from the floor and there was suddenly an outburst of grievances. David Cooper scribbled faster as the complaints grew louder.

'Mr Louden, has anyone in council or the roads department walked around here and seen just where your proposed bypass will be?' demanded one woman. 'Have they seen the lovely homes and gardens that will be lost?'

'Of course not!' exclaimed another. 'They've just looked at a map and seen how close we are to the city and they think that because these places were built a hundred years ago they're falling down! Well, they're not. These are people's homes and we're proud of them.'

'What about our local shops and the school and the library?' called another. 'How are our kids going to get around a great bloody bypass to get to school?'

'Are the school and library going to be moved, too?' asked another.

Fred Louden kept his head down, apparently making notes, and his answers were bland and soothing, telling the audience nothing.

David caught Julie's eye and she went and sat beside him.

'You might want to ask about what reports and studies have been done or what they plan to do,' David suggested. 'Environmental impact studies, noise issues, visual impairment and so on.'

'Those are all part of the feasibility study,' replied Fred Louden smoothly as he closed his notebook. 'Obviously there's a lot more to be done before any definite decision is made and Council is committed to community consultation, so thank you for inviting me. I have another meeting to attend and I'm sure you have matters to discuss among yourselves.'

After Louden left, the room was buzzing.

'So, what did we make of that?' asked Caroline.

'Not a lot, it seems,' said Julie. 'We have to plan a response.'

'Lets chain ourselves to our front gates with placards, "We're Not Going Anywhere" and call in the media,' was one suggestion.

'What about the National Trust? Can these homes be classified heritage so they can't be touched?' asked someone else.

Caroline looked at her husband. 'We did talk about that once, but it put too many restrictions on what alterations and changes we could do to the house.'

'Not that we've ever made any structural changes, or want to. No one would ever dream of altering such a classic building,' said Paul.

'Look, I think playing to the media might come in handy but I also think we have to have a more thorough plan of attack,' said Julie. 'We don't want to sound like an elitist mob who don't want our beautiful homes to be demolished. It's not just the old houses, gardens and trees here, it's hard to see just what we or anybody else will be gaining. Is a bypass really needed in this particular area?'

'I think you need to get some professional advice from engineers, environmentalists and specialists in noise pollution and visual impact, and advice about the possible inconvenience to health and lifestyle this bypass is going to cause, as well as other practical aspects,' said David. 'And I'm sure the council cost estimates are ballpark, so you need to find out just what such an undertaking might cost, and what its cost to the ratepayers will be. That might give us some ammunition.'

'That sort of research will be expensive. We need a fighting fund,' said Caroline. There was an immediate enthusiastic burst of chatter. Raising money was an easier idea to grapple with than the proposed destruction of their homes.

'Thanks for your suggestions, David,' said Julie.

'It's my home town, too,' said David. 'I don't live in this area but I'd hate to see a cement swathe cut through here. And I don't think it would serve much purpose. Actually, it seems to me to be rather an odd place to put a bypass. Maybe you need someone to do a report on traffic projections, too. I can give you a few contacts if you like. We can keep in touch by email.'

'Fantastic. I think a lot of people here think they just have to jump up and down on TV and get the local paper involved and Council will back down. But it's not as simple as that,' said Julie. 'You need a few good arguments as well.'

'Don't underestimate people power. Getting attention is one thing, but you're right, you have to be prepared to have a strong case. It could even go to court,' said David. 'It's lucky that we live in a democracy. In some countries you'd have no say at all. The government would just start digging and building.'

After the meeting the residents dispersed into the night, still angry about the proposed destruction of their houses, but at least optimistic that they could do something to prevent it.

It was late, so Julie decided to stay the night at her parents' house. She loved sleeping in her old turret bedroom at the top of the house, still filled with her childhood books and toys. She said goodnight and climbed the narrow stairs. From the dormer window she could see the moon shining over the sleeping suburb. All was still and quiet, save for the occasional swoop of a fruit bat in the backyard trees. In the distance glimmered the expanse of Moreton Bay, where her father had taught her to sail a small Flying Ant.

She dropped her gaze to the front garden. The top of the poinciana tree was almost level with the roof, the lawn around it deep in shadow. She remembered the old swing that had once been there. The ropes had been replaced when Julie was a toddler, but she recalled its solid seat of smooth wood that her grandfather, or possibly her great grandfather, had made. This was a house and garden filled with nostalgia. Her earliest memories were of being in this house and she assumed that it was the same for her mother and grandmother.

Julie closed her eyes, feeling the brush of the balmy warm air, and tried to imagine the sounds of children's laughter, the gentle murmur of adults taking tea or drinks in the garden, the firm fall of footsteps along the broad verandah, the clatter and crunch of stones in the driveway where cars, maybe a horse-drawn cart, or carriages, had pulled up to the front entrance. The tall hedges and tropical shrubs shielded the house from the neighbours who had also surrounded themselves with lush green oases.

Julie opened her eyes and smiled to herself as she felt a rush of emotion, and knew there was no way she could allow this house or any of the others to be clawed and chewed up by the steel jaws of machinery ripping along the wide, quiet sweep of the street atop the hill. She was about to turn away and go to bed when a flicker, a flutter of paleness, caught her eye. She leaned further out of the window, straining to see into the garden shadows.

Was it a white cat? No, too big.

Her imagination was playing tricks with her. Too much thinking about the past, she decided. For if she didn't know better, the shadows beneath the poinciana seemed to hold the shape of a woman. Some instinct told Julie to just be still and absorb the scene. The sepia photographs in the albums that her mother had shown her sprang to her mind. The shadow looked like a woman from an era of drifting soft muslin, upswept hair, parasols and white buckled shoes. It was almost as though her great grandmother had reappeared in the garden she'd created and loved.

Suddenly a breeze sprang up, the leaves of the tree shook and the shadow was gone. The lawn beneath the tree was dark and empty.

Julie drew the curtain across the small window and lay on her bed, making a promise to herself that she would help fight to save this home, not just for herself, but for the others who came from an era when life was very different.

In the morning, as her mother buttered toast, Julie said, 'I had a sort of dream last night that Great Grandmother was on the lawn, under the tree. I'm sure that if we try really hard, we'll be able to save the house.'

'Well, I'm sure you're right, darling. David seemed to have some good advice.' Caroline put the toast beside Julie's boiled egg.

'Yes, we'll have to pick his brains.' Julie dipped a bit of toast into the soft yolk. 'I was thinking about all the memories this house holds for us . . . my great grandmother, Gran, you, me . . . What are your special memories?'

Caroline shrugged. 'Oh, goodness. I remember how happy my grandparents were to have Mother and me living here. That's after my parents separated. I'm not sure that Mother was all that happy then.'

'But why? Gran loved this place so much,' said Julie.

'Yes, she did. She was very proud of the garden, too. But – it's funny – occasionally Mother would say that her time in Malaya as a bride before the war was the happiest time of her life.'

'So why did she live in Brisbane?' asked Julie.

'I'm not really sure. Sometimes I got the impression that the reason she left Malaya was as much to do with Bette as it was with Father.'

Julie had a sudden thought and her eyes widened. 'Mum! Your father didn't have an affair with Bette did he?'

Caroline vehemently shook her head. 'No, of course not.'

'So why did she come back to Australia?' asked Julie.

'I really can't tell you. That was a closed topic. But I did get snippets of Mother's story and one day, when I was about fifteen, she actually decided to tell me the story of how she met my father and her early years with him,' said Caroline. 'It was a long time ago, but I'll try to remember what she said if you'd like to hear it?'

'I would,' said Julie, helping herself to more toast and waiting expectantly.

2

The Mediterranean Sea, 1937

THE YOUNG WOMAN CLUTCHED her large circular straw hat, the salty breeze causing the soft voile of her dress to cling to her legs and outline her trim figure. The older woman beside her, dressed in a sensible cotton skirt and cork-soled shoes with a large hat tied under her chin, pointed to several sheltered deck chairs.

'Why don't we sit down, out of the wind? We've walked around the deck at least three times.'

The young woman glanced behind her. 'I was hoping we might see that nice Mr Elliott again. I've heard that his father owns a plantation in Malaya. It sounds very interesting and romantic.'

'Margaret Oldham, you're impossible. I'm sure you'll see him this evening since we've been invited to join the captain's table and I believe he has, too. And we have weeks more at sea before we reach Brisbane. So I'm sure you'll meet lots of other nice young men.'

Adelaide Monkton sat on one of the vacant deck chairs, smoothed a light blanket over her skirt and opened the small book of poetry she'd been carrying. She'd had a very interesting tour of Europe and England these past several months, but accompanying the much younger Miss Oldham had been tiring.

The twenty-one-year-old Margaret was energetic, overly so, Adelaide thought, and at times she could be a bit too forward, a bit too keen to look for the company of young men rather than learning about the culture of the Old World. While Margaret was a well-raised young lady, who'd been to one of Brisbane's most prestigious schools, Adelaide Monkton had decided there was something of a rebellious streak in her youthful charge. Where Margaret's friends and contemporaries were demure, Margaret was rather forthright. Perhaps it was her tall, straight-backed figure, no doubt learned in classes devoted to deportment, but Margaret could appear slightly imperious even for a twenty-one year old.

Was her manner due to the subtle sense of entitlement that was bred into girls from well-to-do families in the small social sphere from where she came, wondered Adelaide? Certainly, she recalled that when they had been introduced into high society in London, Margaret had been unfazed and seemed to fit in perfectly well. Margaret had been seen as a good sport and referred to as that 'rather fun Australian gel'. Adelaide also noted that Margaret's vowels had now taken on what Brisbane would consider to be a rather toffy accent. Yes, Adelaide would be glad to hand Margaret back to her parents so she could enjoy some leisurely pursuits.

Margaret sat back in her deck chair and closed her eyes, enjoying the warmth of the sun, completely unaware that her travelling companion had been analysing her. But soon Margaret, who was quickly bored, got up. 'I think I'll go and get ready for luncheon. Shall I see you in our cabin?'

'Yes, I'll be down shortly. This is jolly pleasant.' Adelaide folded her hands, one finger marking the page she was reading, and closed her eyes.

Margaret took a circuitous route to the cabin she shared with her chaperone. Winifred, Margaret's mother, had declined to take her elder daughter to England since she was not fond of travel. Moreover her younger daughter Bette was in her final year of school and so she had entrusted her elder daughter to an old family friend. The two of them had been away for more than nine months and were now on the final voyage home.

Margaret went into the first class lounge on A deck and then through the music room and peeped into the closed glass doors of the smoke room, which was a reproduction of an old baronial hall complete with a huge fireplace with a large crest above it. Beside the fireplace was a suit of armour and a small museum of medallions and some artifacts that had belonged to Bonnie Prince Charlie. Continuing down the swirl of the red carpeted staircase with its art deco design and fittings, she paused at the small birdcage French lift. It descended to the indoor swimming pool that designer Miss Elsie Mackay had modelled after Roman baths with marble pillars and elaborate mosaic tiles. Adelaide permitted Margaret to bathe there during the sessions set aside for lady swimmers. Adelaide said that it was a more discreet activity than the playful pool games and social activities of the outdoor pool on B Deck.

Back outside on B deck, Margaret pulled off her hat and leaned against the railing, watching the wash of blue water foam away from the curve of the ship's white hull. On the breeze she heard a burst of laughter, so she went around the corner of a lifeboat to the games deck and saw that there was an energetic game of deck quoits in progress. She recognised some of the younger set, especially the tall figure of Roland Elliott. She stopped to watch, clapping as the game came to an end.

Roland Elliott, dressed in tropical whites, looking flushed but pleased to be on the winning team, came over to her. 'Hello, Miss Oldham, how cool you look. Jolly hot work out here.' His accent placed him squarely in a box marked English Public School.

'It looks a lot of fun. You played awfully well,' said Margaret.

'Would you like to join us after lunch for a second tournament challenge?' he asked. 'Just for fun, nothing too serious.'

'You look as though you play very seriously,' said Margaret.

He gave a slight shrug. 'My father tells me that if you do something, do it to the best of your ability.'

'I've never played quoits, but I'd love to try,' said Margaret, thinking that it couldn't be very hard to throw a rope ring over a spike.

'Excellent. We assemble up here in the late afternoon when the sun is off this deck. Say around four?'

'Wonderful. I'll see you here.'

'Deck sports? Sounds exhausting,' said Adelaide. 'I'll come and watch.'

'You don't have to, if you don't want to. It's a nice young crowd, I'll be fine.'

Adelaide Monkton hesitated. 'If you're sure. Tonight might be a late evening. We're the second sitting. I'd quite like a longish nap.'

Margaret thought about what to wear for the deck

quoits. While she was not beautiful, she was attractive and made the most of her patrician looks, having an eye for the clothes that suited her tall figure. She settled on loose, wide-legged trousers, sandshoes, a navy-and-white striped maillot top and the perky white sunshade she used for tennis.

Arriving on deck she found two other girls in shorts and another who wore a long skirt and a halter-neck top. Already their fair skin had turned a blushing pink and, with several more weeks at sea, Margaret imagined they'd be having trouble with sunburn.

'I'm from Queensland, I'm used to the sun,' she told one of the girls.

'You're so lucky. I'm dreading the Australian sunshine in one way but it will be nice to get away from the rain. We've had a dreadful winter.'

'Do you all know each other, or have you met on board?' asked Margaret, wondering at the camaraderie of the group.

'Our families are friends, and those two chaps know each other from school,' answered one of the English roses.

The game got underway and Margaret was elated at being on Roland Elliott's team. He was tall, tanned and handsome. He had a pencil-thin moustache, just like Ronald Coleman, and was older and more sophisticated than the chinless wonders she'd met in England. He seemed to be a person who radiated natural authority, which she found quite attractive. Their team won the best of three matches.

He shook her hand. 'Well done, partner. You had some good throws there.'

'No, that was luck,' said Margaret lightly and he laughed.

As they walked to a table on the verandah terrace,

where jugs of iced water and cool handcloths were set out, Margaret thought that the two of them made a handsome pair. Both were tall, athletic looking, with similar colouring, and fine fair hair.

'I say, is everybody coming for sundowner stengahs? We can meet in the bar off the music room,' said Roland as the group prepared to leave the deck.

'It sounds delightful. What exactly is a stengah?' asked Margaret.

'You Australians! It's whisky and water. But you could have something else. A G and T, or a BGA, a gimlet, that sort of thing,' said Roland. 'Gin and tonic, brandy ginger ale, gin and lime,' he added.

'Oh, of course. I'd love to. I believe we're seated together at dinner.'

'Good show. See you later then.' He strode away.

That evening Adelaide watched Margaret pat her hair into place and smooth the bias-cut satin evening gown with its ruched bodice. Diamanté buckles held the straps at her shoulders. Adelaide handed her a finely embroidered shawl, as much for modesty as warmth.

'You'll need this. I'm glad you've met some nice sociable young people.'

'Not that young, Adelaide. They're a very sophisticated group. Mostly English and Scottish. Mr Elliott must be at least thirty-two.'

'I'll meet you in the first class dining lounge when the gong goes for dinner,' said Adelaide as Margaret twirled out of the cabin.

It was the same group in the bar that she'd met at deck quoits as well as some other couples she'd seen at the pool. Everybody was smartly dressed. Margaret felt they all looked as though they had posed for a magazine advertisement for an expensive cigarette or vermouth, where gentlemen in dinner jackets and women in clinging movie-star gowns smoked cigarettes with an ivory holder and held martini glasses.

Roland, who was dressed in a faultlessly tailored dinner jacket, lifted a glass of champagne from a tray a waiter proffered, and handed it to Margaret, taking a whisky for himself. 'Shall we sit down?' He indicated the comfortable cane table and chairs beneath a string of coloured lights.

She noticed that he sat carefully, so as not to crease his trousers.

He raised his glass, 'Cheers, Margaret.' He sipped his drink then drew a silver cigarette case from his jacket and took out a cigarette, tapping it lightly on the lid before snapping open a matching lighter. 'Oh, sorry, do you?' he held out the silver case.

'No, thank you,' said Margaret. 'Though I do indulge on occasion.' This was true, but she had done it more to annoy her mother and Adelaide since she didn't particularly like the taste of cigarettes.

'Do you make the trip to the Far East regularly?' asked Margaret.

'It depends. My grandparents are quite elderly, and Mother has been staying with them in Kent, looking after them. I've just been to visit the three of them.'

'Will you be staying in Malaya?' asked Margaret.

He raised an eyebrow slightly. 'Of course. My family owns a rubber plantation called Utopia. It's my home. I was born there and, apart from boarding school and Cambridge, I've always lived there.' He blew a thin spiral of smoke. 'But you're right, I have made this voyage – port out, starboard home – to England and back several times.'

'Do you have a lot of friends in England?' asked Margaret, trying to imagine what his life must be like, split between two countries.

'Oh, most certainly. Of course, other friends are scattered, in Singapore, all over Malaya and India, but that's the nature of the empire. Some of them work in the Civil Service, others are plantation managers and so forth. Surely none of this interests you.' He spoke mildly but the look he gave her was probing.

But Margaret was interested in anything that Roland said. 'Oh it does! It sounds fascinating. Adventuresome and, well, an interesting life. Not like my boring existence in Brisbane.'

He gave a half smile. 'It isn't boring in Malaya. It's often quite adventuresome, as you put it, though some adventures aren't always welcome. Life is what you make of it, *n'est ce pas?*' He stubbed out his cigarette. 'Another champagne?'

'Why not? Thank you.' Margaret let her wrap drop from her bare shoulders and sat back in her chair. 'It's going to be hard to settle down at home after this trip. I've discovered I love travelling. It can be so stimulating. It's been a bit tiresome having Miss Monkton along looking after me, but my parents insisted.'

'Quite right. Perhaps you could plan another trip. When we get to Port Said, you'll find that interesting, I'm sure. I know Colombo jolly well, too, if you would let me show it to you. With Miss Monkton, of course. I'm leaving the ship there, but we would have some time to sightsee before this ship continues on to Singapore. Perhaps we could organise something.'

'Oh, so you're disembarking at Colombo. I wouldn't like to impose on your time . . .'

He gave an airy wave with his cigarette. 'I'd be delighted. You won't have much time there, but we can make the most of it.'

Margaret was sorry that he wouldn't be travelling all the way to Australia, but she flashed him a dazzling smile, thinking that she would just have to make the most of every minute.

'That would be wonderful. Adelaide is a bit nervous about venturing ashore in some of these places. But I'm sure you know the very best sights.' She smiled, hoping that Roland Elliott would take her out on her own and not with his group of friends.

'There's the dinner gong,' said Roland standing and holding out his hand to help Margaret from the chair.

'Thank you for the champagne,' said Margaret.

'My pleasure.' He gave a nod and a warm smile as they walked together into the dining room.

Adelaide and Margaret had both been impressed by the decorations in the grand dining room. Candles glowed above epergnes filled with fresh roses from the coldroom. The crystal glassware sparkled and the dinner service with the shipping company's crest was edged in gold. In the centre of the room a vaulted skylight surrounded by delicate plasterwork was supported by columns wound with gauzy drapery and clusters of leaves.

Margaret was escorted to the captain's table by Roland, while a stiffly attired ship's officer escorted Adelaide. The men at the table rose while the ladies were seated. Having met the captain already at his cocktail reception, both ladies were at ease as they were introduced to the other guests at the table. After a few pleasantries, the men quickly dominated the conversation.

When Margaret was finally asked by the man on her right about where she'd been and what her future plans were, she answered quietly, 'Miss Monkton and I have been touring Europe, which has been most interesting. My trip was a twenty-first birthday present from my parents. I'm returning home to Brisbane now. I haven't made any specific plans, but I would like to travel some more.'

Adelaide blinked at this. It was the first time she'd heard Margaret's wish for further travel.

'Jolly good idea to travel before settling down,' agreed another woman at the table.

Margaret added politely, 'I'm looking forward to seeing Port Said and especially Colombo. Mr Elliott has offered to show me some of the sights there.'

'Keep away from those thieving markets,' advised the captain. 'And be careful about buying precious stones. Many can be fakes, you understand.'

Roland smiled at Margaret. 'Perhaps there will be time to take a trip to Kandy, the old Sinhalese capital. See some of the exotic Buddhist temples.'

'How exotic?' asked Adelaide with a faint frown. 'I hear some of those places, well, the carvings, can be somewhat explicit. Maybe they are not suitable for a young lady.'

'There's always the Cinnamon Gardens,' suggested one of the women at the table.

'Yes, good idea,' agreed Roland and turned to Adelaide. 'Have you seen much of the Far East, Miss Monkton?'

'No, I prefer the culture of Europe,' replied Adelaide.

'You should go out to Malaya. You'll find it frightfully interesting,' said the captain cheerfully. 'Isn't that so, Mr Elliott?'

'Is that where you live?' asked Adelaide.

The captain gave a hearty laugh. 'By Jove, yes. These young chaps are making their fortune in rubber, isn't that so?' he boomed.

'Some do,' said Roland, modestly.

'Which rubber estate are you on?' asked one of the men, a retired colonel travelling to Australia to visit his aged sister.

'The plantation's called Utopia and it's in Perak state,

37

which I must admit can still be a bit wild,' said Roland before he changed the subject, asking the captain about his sea-going adventures.

Adelaide glanced at Margaret as she finished her dessert and thought to herself, 'Well, Mr Elliott will be out of the running now.' She couldn't see Margaret anywhere near a jungle.

But Margaret's interest in the charming Roland Elliott didn't wane at all. In fact most afternoons while Adelaide took her afternoon rest, the pair could be found sitting on the upper deck verandah, Margaret drinking American-style ice cream sodas while Roland contented himself with tea.

She asked him many questions about his life in Malaya, trying to understand exactly what he did and how a plantation worked. She found all of his answers interesting, even when he talked about the daily muster, the need to keep a close eye on the native workers, the problems with up-country estates, the communist troublemakers, the drop in tin prices, the idea of turning some of the rubber estate over to oil palms, and the renewed interest in rubber as the effects of the Depression eased. However, what Margaret really wanted to know about was his social life. Did he have a special lady friend?

In the ship's library she'd found an autobiography of a British planter who'd been in Malaya in the early 1900s and he had not been shy in writing about the charms of the local women in the brothels. Margaret wondered if Roland knew about this side of life in Malaya. But while she asked a lot of pleasant and superficial questions, she was having trouble scratching beneath the debonair veneer Roland Elliott presented.

Later she broached the subject with Adelaide. 'Why do you think Mr Elliott hasn't married? Do you think he has some native paramour?'

Adelaide was shocked. 'Margaret! What do you know – or care – about such matters? It's none of your business. I suggest you take less interest in a gentleman who's shortly going to be leaving the ship, and whom you will never see again.'

Privately, Adelaide too had wondered why Mr Elliott was still unattached since he came from such a good background and was evidently well off. But he was courteous and affable so she supposed there was no harm in Margaret indulging in a small shipboard flirtation. Nonetheless Adelaide was aware of her responsibility in keeping an eye on her young charge.

Even though Roland talked a lot about his life in Malaya and his family, Margaret managed to keep her end of the conversation up too, as she described her life in Queensland. She told him how her father had taught her and her sister to sail a small wooden, single-sail dinghy on Moreton Bay and described the Great Barrier Reef, which she had seen when the family had holidayed in the Whitsunday Islands.

Roland and Margaret became something of a pair at the social events on board, dancing under the stars at pool deck soirees and at the jazz and tea dances in the ballroom. They played deck tennis and quoits regularly and occasionally made a foursome at cards in the writing room. Margaret now became a fixture at the outdoor pool on B Deck where she sunbathed while Roland and his friends played a version of water polo in the pool. He laughingly admitted Margaret could probably outswim him, but said that he preferred to watch her lounging in a deck chair.

'You're pretty as a picture, sunbaking,' he said.

For Margaret it was a glorious time. She felt she'd been given membership to a glamorous club, where everyone was her best friend, where she was admired and flattered and waited upon, where days were frittered away between music and laughter and dances. She knew she was falling in love with Roland as they meandered the quiet decks in the moonlight, pausing to watch the phosphorescence in the sea before he kissed her sweetly.

Adelaide noted Margaret's possessive arm linked through Roland's, the closeness as they sat together in earnest conversation, sometimes broken by Margaret's trilling laugh.

'Just enjoy the voyage,' advised Adelaide. 'But don't get your hopes up that anything will come of this friendship.'

Margaret was cosseted in the world of the shipboard routine sprinkled with starry nights, an ocean breeze, and the warmth of Roland's arms about her as they danced or kissed. Together they played and sang and enjoyed the frivolous fun of fancy dress balls, games, quiz nights and an hilarious talent contest. The outside world was excluded as the days at sea rolled on.

Roland and Margaret and three other couples had become good friends. They toured Port Said together, shopping in the marketplace and the bazaar, and ended up in a club of dubious repute where they ate strange spicy food with their fingers and were entertained by a bellydancer. But while Margaret acted with worldly sophistication she found it all rather tawdry and intimidating and clung to Roland like a limpet.

Adelaide watched the transformation in Margaret, who had always been so independent and outspoken. She started to become attentive to Roland's every word as he held forth. Adelaide also observed the blossoming shipboard romances among the other couples and, in a quiet moment, mentioned it to her friend, the purser.

The purser smiled and shrugged. 'Happens every voyage. Can't blame these young fellows. Usually the young men are under contract, so they aren't allowed to marry until they've put in several years work out in the East. So when the companies they work for allow them to settle down, they begin courting in earnest. There's not much opportunity for wife hunting in the colonies so if they don't find a wife on home leave they meet her on board ship. Many of these young women are known as the fishing fleet travelling to the East, looking for suitable husbands.'

'I suppose so. It just seems, well, rather calculated,' said Adelaide.

'Ah, aided and abetted by the moonlight, the stars and the sea. It's a time without cares. There'll be long and lonely hours for some of these chaps stationed out in the hills and jungles. And it's not without its dangers. These fellows can tell some terrifying stories. Not the sort of thing they want the ladies to hear,' added the purser.

'And do these shipboard liaisons last?' wondered Adelaide.

'I believe so. I've seen couples meet and sail back on home leave a few years later with youngsters in tow,' said the purser.

While Adelaide found Roland Elliott to be very polite and eligible, she couldn't imagine Margaret being happy living so far away from Australia and her family in what could be very primitive and isolated conditions. Adelaide knew from experience that, whatever Margaret might say, her young charge wouldn't like life in a foreign place surrounded by smells, filth and strange customs. But she bit her tongue and waited, knowing that the situation would resolve itself when Roland left the ship at Colombo.

Any disappointment Margaret felt about Roland she kept to herself. When she awoke one morning to find the ship engines stilled, she looked out the porthole, and exclaimed to Adelaide, 'We're in Colombo! Oh, how romantic. Look, palm trees and a beach!'

Adelaide squeezed beside Margaret. 'What a lovely looking place. Is that a fort or something?'

'Oh, look at all those little boats, how sweet,' said Margaret.

'Yes, very colourful. All selling something no doubt.'

Margaret dressed quickly and hurried onto the deck to find Roland at the railing as the liner passed the breakwater. The ship was greeted by a flotilla of small, makeshift craft carrying excited children and adults holding up their wares.

'Goodness me, how do some of those things stay afloat?' she exclaimed. 'Wouldn't catch me in one of them. What are they selling?'

'Everything you don't need but will be enticed to buy – from a fan, a necklace, a basket, to a piece of silk,' laughed Roland.

'Oh, they're coming on board!' She grasped Roland's hand. 'They've climbed up the side just like monkeys! And what's that smell?' Margaret wrinkled her nose.

'Cinnamon most likely, my dear.' Roland reached into his pocket and held up a coin, calling out to the young men and boys all shouting and waving to the passengers from the water below. As soon as the coin left Roland's hand, the children dived into the waters of the harbour until, triumphant, one boy surfaced with the penny clenched between his teeth. Other passengers began throwing coins, taking photos and enjoying the entertainment. Roland took Margaret's arm. 'Come on, let's see if the snake charmer has appeared on deck.'

They found a small crowd around a dark-skinned man wearing what looked to Margaret to be a length of bright cloth knotted like a baby's nappy. He was cajoling everyone for coins to be thrown on a mat in front of his lidded basket.

'Is there really a snake in there?' whispered Margaret.

'There certainly is – a dangerous cobra,' said Roland with a grin.

As the man removed the basket lid and began playing a reedy flute, a snake, a curved hood over its head, swayed from the basket.

Margaret clutched Roland's arm. 'I hope it doesn't come out!'

There were squeals and laughter as the snake rose up, swaying to the music. 'These Hindu magic men are pretty amazing with their tricks,' said Roland.

Margaret merely nodded and kept hold of his arm.

The performance over, Roland announced that he was going down to breakfast. Margaret agreed to go with him even though she'd had a quick tea and toast with Adelaide earlier in their cabin.

'What is there to do here?' she asked.

'I promised to show you around, so let me surprise you,' said Roland. 'I'll organise to have my luggage taken ashore. It won't take long. We should get away as soon as we can to go to Kandy, the old capital, which is in the highlands and is much cooler. And tonight, before the ship sails, I'd like to take you to dinner. Just us. Would you like that?'

They exchanged a long glance and then Margaret nodded. 'It sounds lovely.' She was determined not to show him how sad she was at the thought of their imminent parting. She'd quickly learned that Roland was a no nonsense sort of a man who was uncomfortable around sentiment and emotions. She was determined not to be the sort of woman he'd referred to as 'those teary little idiots who fall apart and get flustered at the smallest matter. I like strong women who are capable and who don't make a fuss'.

Adelaide had debated with herself about going with them, but she didn't like the smells of Colombo and had decided that the two were unlikely to come to any harm since Roland seemed familiar with the place. She would stay on board the ship.

Roland had hired a car and driver, as had several others from the ship, and they all headed to the ancient Sinhalese capital. In the cool hills their first stop was at the Temple of the Tooth, the name of which Margaret found amusing, until she saw the beautiful old carved temple set beside a lake and surrounded by dark green hills.

'All this for a tooth relic?'

'The Lord Buddha's tooth, my dear,' said Roland. 'This is a very sacred place.'

'Well, it's certainly a beautiful setting. And the town is quite agreeable. Far fewer beggars.'

'The last of the Sinhalese kings built Lake Bogambara from a paddy field in the early 1800s,' said Roland. 'Quite a feat. Jolly peaceful place, isn't it.'

From the temple they went to the lake to watch the elephants and their handlers bathe in the water. After a light lunch at the elegant Queen's Hotel, which impressed Margaret with its grandeur, they drove back to Colombo.

'I'll come back to the ship at sunset with a driver,' Roland told Margaret.

Margaret watched him as he strode away, realising how much she was going to miss him.

She dressed with great care that evening, changing her mind several times before settling on a soft muslin print dress that, while demure, floated around her figure in alluring folds. She wished she had luxuriant hair like her sister Bette's, but she pinned up her own, curling the front and sides in tight wisps in the manner of glamorous movie stars like Janet Gaynor and Jean Arthur.

Roland was waiting at the bottom of the gangplank

dressed in a white dinner jacket and black trousers. The driver behind him held open the car door.

'Where are we going?' asked Margaret.

He took her hand. 'Mount Lavinia. Dinner on the hotel terrace, which overlooks a very pretty beach.'

'It sounds lovely. You know this place well.'

'I've been here a few times. My father has several business acquaintances in Ceylon. Actually, that's why I've had to disembark here, to meet with one of them who's in tea.'

'Oh, I see. Adelaide said to say goodbye from her.'

'Could you tell her from me that it's been a pleasure to have met her and I hope that the rest of her voyage is enjoyable.' He held Margaret's hand and kissed her fingertips. 'I hope you will remember this evening.'

'Oh, I will,' she said.

Roland pointed out the sights of Colombo as they drove along the coast road, the leaning coconut palms etched against the molten sunset.

Margaret felt devastated. Roland was more than a shipboard dinner companion and dance partner. He was the most fascinating man she had ever met. She liked hearing him discuss the politics of the empire, the future of plantation commodities, the problems and disasters of the native staff, and the vicissitudes of cricket matches at 'The Dog' with the other men. Roland always seemed very knowledgeable and secure in his position in the fraternity of planters, civil servants, military and business people and he was certainly far more sophisticated than any other man who'd paid her attention.

Roland lifted his stengah and touched the edge of her champagne glass. 'Here's to meeting a very special young woman.'

'I've so enjoyed meeting you too, Roland.' She wanted to say more but couldn't think what to say without getting teary or appearing clingy.

'I'd like you to know that I've enjoyed your company more than I can say, Margaret. More than I have with anyone else. You'll be in my thoughts for a long time to come.'

'Mine too,' said Margaret.

'Then perhaps you might consider this.' He reached into his pocket and took out a small velvet box and placed it in front of her. 'Margaret, would you do me the honour of becoming my wife?'

Margaret gasped and her hand shook as she put down her glass and opened the little box. Nestled inside was a ring, a sky-blue stone surrounded by diamonds. 'Oh, Roland. It's beautiful. Of course, oh yes. Yes, I'd love to marry you.'

'Excellent.' He took the ring and put it on her finger and leaned across and kissed her softly. 'Then it's settled. I hope you like it,' he added as Margaret held out her hand to admire the ring. 'It's a jolly good Ceylon sapphire, perfect, just like you.'

'It's really beautiful. And it's special because of our being here, isn't that so?'

'I thought so. Now, my dear, let's order dinner. We do have quite a few things to discuss. Naturally I will write to your father and formally ask him for your hand in marriage. Have to do the right thing.'

'Will we get married in Brisbane?'

''Fraid not. I've just had my leave. No, you'll have to come to Kuala Lumpur. Any problem with that?'

Margaret gulped. She would have liked a wedding at home with all her friends and family to show off her handsome husband but instead she said, 'I'm sure my mother will come. But Father runs a business, so taking time away might be difficult. And Bette is still at school.'

'You'll work things out. We can discuss plans later. You'll have to book a passage up to Singapore as soon as you can.'

'So then a wedding in three or four months?' asked Margaret feeling quite breathless, already wondering how she could get a wedding dress made and a trousseau together so quickly.

Roland earnestly began to explain how their life would revolve around Utopia, the family plantation. He talked of the obligations and tribulations, but also of the community of workers, which he called the plantation estate 'family'.

'It will be quite different from your life in Australia,' he said. 'But there is a wonderful social life, even in our isolated area, and an excellent social scene in Penang and KL when we go there.' He patted her hand. 'I know you'll get on with everyone and you'll handle the climate much better than the English wives do, coming from Queensland,' he said confidently.

So it was decided. Winifred, Margaret's mother, would accompany her daughter to Kuala Lumpur, where the wedding would take place at St Mary's Church. A passage on a P&O steamer was booked to Singapore. From there, they would take the coastal steamship to Port Swettenham and then the local train would take them to Kuala Lumpur where Roland would meet them. The wedding would take place a week later.

Roland's father, Eugene, would attend the wedding, but his mother, Charlotte, was still in England. Because Margaret's father was unable to be there, Roland suggested that Dr Hamilton, the Scottish doctor in Perak and a great friend of the Elliotts, could give her away.

There was much fussing over Margaret's trousseau. Winifred fretted that Margaret's clothes might not be considered as stylish and as up to date as some of the clothes that came from Europe or London, but in one of his weekly letters, Roland offered some advice.

'My dear, the tailors in Malaya are excellent. Bring some pictures from ladies' magazines and have them copy them. They can make them cheaply and quickly.'

'He may be right. Why don't you take some lengths of good fabric,' suggested her mother.

Fine table linens and some favourite pieces of family silver were given to Margaret for her glory box, and Winifred offered to send her anything else she might need in the coming months, which she couldn't obtain 'up there'.

Roland made all the arrangements for the wedding and reception, which he hoped would meet with their approval.

'St Mary's is an impressive church, and jolly handy to The Dog. That's what we call the Selangor Club.'

'I do hope that the Peninsula Hotel which Roland has organised for the reception is adequate, not a rowdy sort of place,' worried Winifred.

Margaret was swept up in the whole idea of being a wife and living on an exotic plantation, which she described in extravagant detail to her friends. When her mother asked which country they might eventually end up in, especially if children came along, Margaret ignored the question.

'Why, we have the best of all worlds, surely. Roland has family in England, his parents in Malaya and my family here.'

Winifred looked sad. 'I fear your family here will be at the bottom of the list. But never mind, so long as you are happy, comfortable and healthy, that's all I ask.'

'Mother, don't be silly. Of course we'll come and visit. Lots of times,' said Margaret, although she was unsure how often this would be. Roland had mentioned a trip back to England every couple of years or so.

*

Margaret embraced her father and sister at the station at Roma Street before she and her mother alighted the Sydney-bound train. In Sydney they would board their liner. It wasn't until the train had left the station and gathered speed that it occurred to Margaret that she was leaving her home and family and had no idea when she might see them again. She was glad that her mother was travelling with her, though she did suspect she'd be looking after Winifred more than the other way around. Winifred was not much of a traveller.

'I do hope Ted will manage,' said Winifred, dabbing at her eyes as she waved goodbye to her husband and younger daughter.

'Bette will keep an eye on him. They'll be fine. Now, Mother, I need you to be strong. You're supposed to be helping me, the nervous bride,' said Margaret, not looking the least bit concerned or nervous.

'Yes, dear. You're right,' sighed her mother. 'It just seems such a big step. Marriage. A strange country. Different sort of people.' She struggled to smile. 'Well, at least I'll know where you are, and you can explain it all to us when you write.'

'That's right. Now let's make the most of the trip. The voyage will be fun and very relaxing for you. A real holiday,' said Margaret.

When the time came to disembark, Winifred eyed the Singapore River, crowded with all manner of strange small craft as well as ships and freighters. In front of the godowns and warehouses was stacked all kinds of cargo. On the wharves, among the crush of people, Chinese coolies in their peaked hats carried poles weighed down with heavy baskets, while Indian porters pushed barrows laden with luggage and trishaw drivers touted for business.

Sauntering Europeans in starched uniforms or linen suits stood out as they carefully escorted well-dressed women who carried umbrellas to ward off the sun. As Margaret watched from the deck, she saw many of them nodding and exchanging greetings.

Winifred fanned herself and wondered what kind of a world they'd come to and how she'd cope with it all, even for a short time.

Margaret seemed quite calm amidst all the chaos and, helped by the purser, found an Indian taxi driver. 'He's honest and reliable, miss. He will take you to the dock where the Straits Steamship leaves for Port Swettenham and help you with your luggage, which has gone ahead.'

They set off, the taxi nosing its way through the crowd of trishaws, drays, carts, pedestrians and cars.

When they arrived at the dock from where the Straits Steamship was leaving, Margaret whispered to her mother, 'Honest, my foot. I think he's taken us in a very circuitous way.'

'Never mind, dear, just pay him what he asks and let's find our belongings,' said Winifred, feeling faint.

'You'll feel better after a good rest. Our steamship leaves at four this afternoon for Port Swettenham, and then it's just a short train trip to Kuala Lumpur in the morning. We're very lucky that the arrival of our P&O ship coincided with the departure of the coastal vessel, so we don't have to wait around in Singapore,' said Margaret.

'Yes, but all the same this travelling is so tiresome,' said Winifred. 'But I must say you've handled everything splendidly, Margaret. I really am impressed with the way you've managed all this. Such a pity Roland couldn't meet us.'

'He'll meet us at the railway station in Kuala Lumpur as planned, Mother.'

Their cabin on the small Straits Steamship was comfortable, and the officers and other passengers on board were very friendly. When it became known Margaret was travelling to her wedding, toasts were made and best wishes exchanged. The two women slept well, the sensation of being at sea was familiar and after a hearty breakfast they docked at Port Swettenham at eight. Margaret had arrived on the mainland of Malaya.

Margaret and Winifred looked through the train window at the busy port as it pulled out of the station. Soon they were in the countryside. The scenery changed to one of villages with red-roofed shops, their colourful goods displayed outside and their signs written in Chinese characters. They passed bright green rice fields, small towns, a sweep of jungle with glimpses of thatched huts, a man on a bicycle wearing a sarong, a woman carrying baskets and children playing near a river. Stray chickens pecked by the side of a red dirt road. The larger towns were crowded with trishaws, bicycles and cars. Laden drays and carts were pulled by horses, buffalo and oxen. To Winifred it all seemed dirty and smelly, but Margaret didn't seem to care.

Margaret knew that her mother was bothered by these scenes and she put any disquiet she might have felt herself to one side and maintained a positive outlook. She assumed that she would rarely, if ever, mingle in the squalid areas the train passed through, for Roland had given her the impression of a grand lifestyle, although he had been honest about their comparative isolation.

It was with great relief that, as the train steamed into the station at Kuala Lumpur, Margaret spotted the tall figure of Roland waiting on the platform. She pointed him out to her mother. He looked very smart in a white linen suit, holding his solar topee.

Doors banged and before the hissing rush of steam from the engine had dissipated, Margaret had stepped down from the train, waving a lace-edged handkerchief to her husband-to-be.

He reached her and kissed her cheek, smiling broadly. 'Margaret, it's wonderful to see you. I'd almost forgotten how pretty you are.' Nodding to the Indian standing behind him, he said, 'Hamid, get the memsahib's luggage and take it to the car.' He stepped forward and helped Winifred down from the train.

'My, what a trip. It's so good to be here at last,' she said. 'Oh, this is an impressive railway station,' she added, gazing up at the soaring ceiling and grand entrance.

'Roland, this is my mother, Mrs Oldham.'

'I'm so pleased to meet you, Mrs Oldham. I hope your journey was not too tiresome.'

'It was not too terrible, I suppose. But please, not Mrs Oldham, call me Mother, or Winifred.'

'How far away is the hotel where we're staying?' asked Margaret.

'Very close, it's the Station Hotel. It's a great old place. I think you'll enjoy it. Hamid will bring the car.'

'Look at those little contraptions that those men are pedalling. Like the ones we saw in Singapore,' said Margaret, looking at the little canopied bicycles lined up in front of the station.

'Are they safe?' asked Winifred doubtfully as Roland, Margaret's arm tucked in his, led them towards the car.

'Trishaws are a form of transport you'll have to try,' said Roland. 'They'll get through the traffic faster than a car. Ah, there's Hamid with Father's automobile now.'

Safely in the hotel, Margaret and Winifred settled themselves at a table and ordered tea and dainty sandwiches on a terrace facing a lush garden. Mother and daughter exchanged a glance as two Chinese waiters in crisp uniforms with brass buttons hovered close by, ready to pour milk and pass sugar.

'I don't imagine I'll be living in such grand circumstances,' sighed Margaret. 'But it's very nice to know there are places like this we can enjoy. Roland says there are some excellent hotels around the country and the E&O Hotel in Penang is right on the sea.'

'Yes, but how often will you get away from the plantation?' asked Winifred. 'It sounds like his work keeps him very busy.'

Margaret ignored this remark and began discussing the wedding.

'I do hope Roland has thought to engage a photographer,' she said.

'Indeed I have,' said Roland, as he joined them, removing his hat and sitting down. 'I've taken advice from some of the ladies who know about these sorts of things.'

'Well, Mother, now we're here, I think we can look after any other details,' said Margaret briskly.

'I'm sure you're most capable, my dear,' said Roland with a smile. 'But things are done a bit differently out here in the East, so I hope you'll listen to the good advice from the other mems. Now, after you've settled in your rooms and rested, we shall meet for drinks and over dinner I'll explain all the other plans to you.'

'And can we see the church and reception place? We also have a few last minute purchases,' began Margaret.

Roland held up his hand. 'All in good time. We can start tomorrow, eh?'

'If you don't mind too much, I think I'd like to stay in my hotel room tonight. I'm feeling quite tired. I'll have something sent up for dinner. Besides, I'm sure you two would like to be alone,' said Winifred. 'You must have a lot to catch up on.'

'Thank you, Mother,' said Margaret demurely.

Roland glanced at his watch. 'I have some brief business to attend to while I'm in KL, but I shall tap on your door at five pm.' He leaned over, kissed Margaret's cheek and headed to the hotel foyer, nodding to an acquaintance as he passed.

That evening, Hamid drove Roland and Margaret to a small European restaurant on a street filled with eateries. At one end of the street were stalls where hawkers cooked over open fires in sizzling woks. There were local family-style restaurants, a tea house and at the other end of the street where the food places stopped, were some large Chinese homes squatting behind stone and wire fences.

'This is a decent neighbourhood. The proprietors of the place where we are going to eat are Dutch, so I think you'll like the food. You might not take to the local spices straight away,' he said.

'I thought we'd go to your club,' said Margaret, thinking the restaurant rather plain and old fashioned.

'I'd rather we take your mother there for lunch tomorrow. Then I'll take you to the Peninsula Hotel. The manager there will meet you and you can inspect the menu for the wedding reception, that sort of thing. Are you still tired from your journey?'

'Yes, it has been quite a trip. Mother is very glad to be staying in one place for awhile and pleased to be having a tray sent to her room tonight.'

Margaret was pleasantly surprised by the dinner. She enjoyed the food and the attentive service from the couple who owned the restaurant and the fuss they made over meeting Roland's fiancée. Being with Roland felt strange in a way but she began to revel in her role and looked forward to her new status as his wife. Studying him across the table as he chatted, she felt as though she was looking at him for the first time, and she tried to imagine what it would be like to spend the rest of her life with this handsome and sophisticated man.

On the way home she leaned her head against his shoulder in the Oldsmobile, as Hamid nosed through the streets still busy with activity.

'So many people, whole families, all out eating on the street, in eating houses. Do they do that all the time?' she asked.

'Many of them do. It's easier and cheaper, generally,' he answered. 'And eating is a very social occupation in the East . . . By Jove, what's happening up ahead?' He spoke rapidly to Hamid, who pulled over.

There was a fire glowing and clusters of people, some of them shouting. Two large Sikh police officers were waving back the crowd.

'Oh my goodness, has there been an accident?' asked Margaret.

'Wait here in the car. I will investigate.' Roland got out of the car.

'Do be careful, Roland.'

The crowd had swelled and seemed to be moving down the street towards the car. Roland stopped a young man as he ran past and spoke to him. The frightened young man pointed behind him to the crowd outside a house where a fire was burning.

'What is happening, Hamid?' Margaret asked the driver.

Hamid shrugged. 'I don't know, mem. Some trouble.'

Margaret got out of the car and hurried after Roland, ignoring Hamid's shouts. As she got closer she could see in front of the doorway of a small house the smouldering remains of some kind of vehicle. But she stopped in shock as, from an alley beside the house, a small Malay man came running, wielding what looked to Margaret like a huge knife. The crowd suddenly parted. Women were screaming and running. The man with the parang stopped as he saw the two policemen and Roland. Even at a distance the sight of the near-naked man holding the large machete in such a threatening manner was very frightening to Margaret. In the glow of the firelight he looked quite crazy and he was shouting incoherently.

'Roland!' she cried.

Furiously Roland turned around and hurried back to her. 'I told you to stay in the car. The man is crazy and he's likely to start slashing at anyone. Go. Now.' He gave her a firm shove.

Margaret was stunned, shocked as much by Roland's brusque manner as by the scene before her. Suddenly the crazed man lunged towards the crowd. Margaret ran. When she reached the car, Hamid quickly opened the door. From there she could see one of the policemen suddenly grab the man from behind, forcing him to drop the weapon. The other policeman was brandishing what looked like a thick wooden stick, hitting the man about the shoulders.

Shaking, Margaret huddled in the corner of the car. The romantic evening was spoiled and suddenly she realised she was in a strange place that had lost its benign novelty. She felt that there was another current here. The mixture of faces and nationalities and the way the people had looked, the fear in their eyes, unsettled her.

Roland spoke to Hamid and got in beside Margaret.

'Sorry I shouted at you but anything could have happened back there. The man went amok. It happens for no reason that anyone knows. These fellows just explode, grab a weapon and threaten to murder anyone in their way. And they do, which is why I wanted you out of sight.'

'Sorry, Roland. I was so afraid for you.'

'Don't worry about me, darling, I can look after myself. Hotel, please, Hamid.'

'Does this happen often?' asked Margaret wondering how safe she'd be in the streets.

'No, not very often. It's mainly Malays, it's as though they just can't cope any more and they go crazy, almost inviting someone to kill them. A dark streak in their normally sunny nature.'

'Amok, is no good, sahib,' said Hamid. 'I think maybe a riot. Chinese people.'

'Riots?' said Margaret, her voice rising.

'There, there. Calm down, dear. There was a clash, a strike over wages last month. An isolated incident caused by some communists.' He smiled. 'Nothing like this happens out at peaceful Utopia.'

'But if it's in their character . . .' Margaret had a sudden vision of being alone in a house when a native suddenly had one of these wild turns.

'You will be safe, Margaret. I'll see to that at all times. But perhaps it might be better not to mention this incident to your mother. Tomorrow at lunch, when you see the old Spotted Dog, you'll enjoy it more.'

'Oh, the Selangor Club. Yes, Roland,' said Margaret, too exhausted to argue.

The tall Sikh doorman at the hotel gave Margaret a small bow. 'Did memsahib have a very excellent evening?'

Margaret gave him a withering look as the door closed behind her. 'Not exactly.'

In the morning Winifred put Margaret's pale demeanour down to tiredness.

'Well, this is all very exciting, isn't it? My daughter getting married. It's really coming home to me that you are,' said Winifred effusively.

'Yes, Mother. Me too.' She picked up her handbag. 'It will be interesting to discover why this Selangor Club is known as The Dog. Sounds a bit of a worry, really. Not quite where I'd envisioned socialising. But they seem to do things quite differently out here in the East.'

Winifred folded her gloved hands over the clasp on her handbag, looking rather pleased with herself. 'I know the story. One of the ladies I've been talking to in the hotel lobby told me.'

'So what is it?' asked Margaret politely.

'There are several different stories, but the most popular version is actually about dogs. Those black and white dalmatian dogs were popular pets back in the old days, and as pets weren't allowed into the club, everyone let their dogs roam around that green field in front of the building . . .'

'It's called the padang,' Margaret interrupted, glad that she'd absorbed one local fact.

'And a well-known lady had her two dalmatians wait for her at the bottom of the club steps every day when she came into the Selangor Club. So the club became known as "The Spotted Dog",' finished Winifred.

'Better dogs than tigers, I suppose,' said Margaret. 'Actually Roland told me this club is quite exclusive.'

'Now when you write and tell me you had lunch at The Dog, I'll know just where you mean,' said Winifred.

'Well, I'm still glad we're having our reception at the Peninsula Hotel. I can't see invitations for a reception at "The Dog" sounding very smart,' said Margaret, causing her mother to raise an eyebrow at her daughter's new-found grand airs.

3

ON THE GREEN PADANG, manicured to perfection, a cricket game was in progress. The faint thwack of leather on willow echoed in the long bar of the Selangor Club where Roland, dressed in his formal wedding suit, was enjoying a quick drink with his best man, Gilbert Mason before walking to St Mary's Church.

In their hotel, Winifred was checking Margaret's gown as the two Chinese 'wedding ladies', recommended by the district officer's wife, fussed around her.

'You look beautiful, Margaret. I'm so glad we chose this Du Barry pattern. It's elegant, not too formal. And you can take the train off and make a few changes and wear it as an evening gown.'

'You look lovely too, Mother. I love your hat. I must get more hats, one needs them in this climate.'

'This dress has been beautifully made, and in such a short time, too,' said Winifred, fingering Margaret's cream silk-satin gown in the latest fashion. 'Now, let's put your veil on.'

The two wedding ladies attached the floor-length silk tulle veil to Margaret's waved hair, which was pinned up and topped with a small pearl tiara. Then they carefully turned down the short veil to cover Margaret's face.

Winifred held her daughter's bridal bouquet, made up of magnificent tropical lilies, ginger flowers and orchids, while Margaret held her skirt above her satin shoes as she made her way to the waiting car with Thelma, the district officer's daughter who was her bridesmaid and carried the long train of her dress.

Dr Hamilton, who had agreed to give Margaret away, was waiting by the car, resplendent in a white jacket with a small red rose boutonniere. He bowed and held out his arm. 'You look stunning, dear girl. Extremely elegant. What a striking pair you and Roland will make. Are you nervous?'

'Not at all,' said Margaret firmly. 'This is very kind of you, Dr Hamilton.'

'I feel for your father. Difficult to miss your first daughter's wedding.'

'There will be plenty of photographs and he still has the opportunity to give away my sister when the time comes. Is everything ready at the church?' asked Margaret.

But Winifred's eyes misted as she thought of what her husband was missing and how proud he would be of his elder child if he could see her now.

Dr Hamilton took Winifred's arm. 'Please, don't concern yourself. Roland is a superb organiser, Mrs Oldham. You look spiffing too. You and Thelma can ride together in this car and Margaret and I will be behind you.'

Roland and his friend Gil were already waiting in

St Mary's, as the cars drew up in front. Roland, slicky groomed, his pencil-thin moustache neatly trimmed, hair freshly cut, nails buffed and wearing a wide, approving smile on his face, watched Margaret make her way down the aisle. He told her later that with her height, the little tiara and the train, she had looked very regal and beautiful.

After the ceremony, the newlyweds, friends and family posed outside the church for photographs. More pictures were taken outside the elegant Peninsula Hotel before the bridal party was ushered into the formal ballroom for their reception. Winifred was surprised at the large number of guests and found herself seated next to Roland's father.

Eugene Elliott was a courtly, if rather formal, sort of gentleman, stiff, precise and proper. He did not indulge in small talk but launched into quite complicated details in response to Winifred's simple question, 'How did you get into rubber, Mr Elliott?'

'The British were growing cocoa and coffee in Malaya but a disease swept through and wiped out many of their crops, so a few chaps started looking about to start anew. They'd been living in the East and made a fair fist of it so weren't about to settle back in the Old Dart.'

'Oh dear,' said Winifred as she sipped on her brown windsor soup. 'So what happened?'

'About sixty years ago some chap smuggled rubber tree seeds out of Brazil, rather naughty of him. Brought them to Kew Gardens in London and some of the saplings were sent to Ceylon and Malaya, to see what they'd do. The resident of Perak was something of an amateur botanist and encouraged some of the planters to switch their empty plantations over to rubber. We had all those unemployed Ceylonese workers hanging about, so we had a workforce and cleared land. So rubber took off in Malaya, especially with the need for pneumatic tyres for motor

61

cars. I established my own plantation – Utopia – about forty years ago. Couldn't help but make money in those days. Been a few ups and downs since then, but we're very proud of what we've done.'

'And you've been here ever since?' said Winifred, beginning to get an inkling of how deep Roland's roots were in Malaya.

Dr Hamilton, on the other side of Winifred, had been listening to Eugene and interjected, 'It's not a place one leaves easily, Mrs Oldham. The East gets a hold of you, as your daughter will discover. But it's especially so for the menfolk. It's a lifestyle. Friendships are forged in difficult conditions and the community unites because of the unique circumstances in which people find themselves.'

'It's a way of life we've created, and we enjoy our successes and triumphs in business, on the sporting field and we also share our tribulations. The esprit de corps is very strong,' said Eugene. 'And because most of the Europeans are scattered about we tend to make the most of social occasions. So this is a very happy day for our families.' He raised his empty glass. 'Boy!' A waiter was instantly at his side, replenishing his drink and Dr Hamilton's.

Winifred was impressed by the calibre of the guests at the reception. The district officer, his wife and their daughter, Thelma, were there. Winifred had been introduced to planters and representatives from both the great trading firms of Bousteads and Guthries, as well as members of the Malayan Civil Service and she was quite surprised to see a few well dressed Chinese there also.

When she questioned Dr Hamilton about their presence, he replied, 'This isn't India, you know. We like to mix with the other races and some of these fellows are quite good chaps. Shrewd business people.'

As the afternoon wore on, Winifred became bemused by the steady drinking and uninhibited dancing. Everyone seemed to be having a fine time. And she had been twirled around the dance floor several times, by Roland, Gilbert, Eugene and Dr Hamilton.

Margaret was also enjoying every moment, every compliment and every friendly promise of invitations to meet to show her the ropes. Roland danced with her superbly, kissing her cheek and whispering in her ear, making her blush. She was reluctant to leave the party when her mother tapped her on the shoulder, suggesting it was time that she retired and changed into her going-away outfit.

With Winifred's help Margaret put on a pale-blue linen suit, a small hat and grey-heeled shoes. She carried soft grey gloves and a matching handbag. Her small suit-case, packed with clothes for her honeymoon, was already in the boot of the car when she returned to the reception room. Margaret and Roland were swept up in rounds of farewells.

'Oh, Mother, are you sure you'll be all right here on your own?' asked Margaret, as she embraced Winifred.

Dr Hamilton took Winifred's arm. 'She'll be right as rain, dear girl. We're all off to a splendid dinner and during the next week I shall escort her anywhere she wishes, around the city,' he said.

'Oh, that won't be necessary,' began Winifred.

'Nonsense. The DO's wife has invited us all over for luncheon tomorrow. I shall collect you at noon,' said the kindly doctor.

'And we'll be back in time to drive you to Port Swettenham for the boat home,' Margaret assured her mother.

Dr Hamilton turned to the newlyweds and gave Margaret a comforting smile. 'Now, off you two go.'

Margaret kissed her mother and in a shower of coloured rice and flower petals she and Roland got into the gleaming Studebaker that Roland had borrowed from a friend and they drove away. The wedding guests then adjourned to the long bar of the nearby Selangor Club.

Roland took Margaret's hand. 'Just the two of us. You looked so beautiful at the wedding. I was proud of you.'

Margaret leaned her head against the back of the car seat and smiled contentedly.

In the still, burning light that marked the end of her wedding day, Margaret gazed at the passing scenes of rural simplicity as they left the city behind and entered the lush countryside on the way to the dark, steep hills of their destination. In kampongs, she glimpsed children playing in a river where women washed their long black hair, the coloured fabric of their sarongs clinging wetly to their lithe frames. An unattended fruit stall, a bicycle lying on its side beneath trees, the lazy smoke of a cooking fire indicated the slowing of the day. Preparations for evening were unfolding. The long fingers of slanting rays were reflected in the still pools of the rice paddies, which were neatly dissected by mounds of raised red soil lying in mathematical precision.

The car began to climb the hills, though it seemed briefly to Margaret that they were sinking, shrinking into night, flattened by a sky alight with the glowing first stars. The trees reached upwards, dark fingers pointed to the heavens, and the headlights of the car danced from side to side as they curved their way up the steepening mountain.

Margaret sat in silence, her eyes closed, holding her husband's hand.

'Here we are. The Gap,' said Roland. 'Did you sleep, Margaret?'

'No. I think I'm overexcited, it's been a big day.'

He kissed her quickly, murmuring, 'And it's not over yet.' Then added as he opened the door, 'A relaxing drink, a small snack. I'm peckish. I didn't eat enough today. Too busy socialising. Come along, Margaret.'

The sprawling government rest house was welcoming, but scarcely what Margaret considered to be elegant. Then she realised that it was simply a stopover that supplied basic accommodation, a dining room, a verandah and a bar.

'We could spend the night here if you're not feeling up to any more travel,' said Roland looking at her pale face. 'It isn't particularly smart but it's comfortable and hospitable. We have to wait here for the road ahead to open. There's only a single lane into the hills and this is the changeover point.'

'You mean cars can travel only in one direction on the road?' asked Margaret.

'Yes, this final ascent to the peak is narrow so there's a timetable to allow cars to go up or cars to go down. But not at the same time.' He laughed.

Margaret decided that she didn't want to spend her honeymoon night here as it was not at all romantic. So she sipped her tea as Roland hugged a brandy and chatted with several other travellers who were also heading to Fraser's Hill.

And then the road was opened, and they were back in the car as part of a small procession making its way in single file to the popular hill town. The road was narrow and dark. Margaret saw lights from scattered bungalows, an illuminated sign here and there and a small village square surrounded by solid buildings. Then she sighed with relief as finally the car tyres crunched on the gravel driveway under the portico of Ye Olde Smokehouse Hotel.

A servant opened the car door and Margaret shivered in the surprisingly chill air. The mock Tudor building had ivy climbing the walls and boxes beneath its diamond-paned windows were filled with flowers. Mr MacAllister, the manager, welcomed them effusively and showed them into a small lounge room where the décor was a homage to bonnie Scotland – the cushions and a sofa were upholstered in the Fraser tartan. A fire burned and Margaret suddenly felt as though she was in the Scottish Highlands again.

'Welcome, Mr Elliott and Mrs Elliott. Please enjoy a drink while your luggage is taken to your room. Would you like a bath drawn, sir?'

Roland turned to Margaret. 'Would you care for a relaxing bath, my dear? I will be up shortly. Unless you care to join me here for a nightcap?'

'A hot bath sounds wonderful. You won't be long, Roland?'

'Not at all. I'll let you settle while I catch up on the district news with Mr MacAllister.'

Their host bowed slightly. 'This is my wife, Janet. She will show to you to your room and provide anything you need. I look forward to seeing you tomorrow, Mrs Elliott.'

'Thank you.' Margaret followed Mrs MacAllister up the stairs feeling incredibly pleased at being called Mrs Elliott.

The time at Fraser's Hill passed too quickly for Margaret. It took a little while to adjust to the lack of privacy caused by living with a man and being together twenty-four hours a day. But Roland was kind and attentive and obviously very pleased with his young and attractive wife. Margaret was glad she'd been a virgin on her wedding night but, while Roland was a considerate and gentle lover, Margaret was yet to really experience the wild, passionate elation from sex that she'd read about in novels. She responded with what she hoped was satisfactory ardour to Roland's lovemaking but couldn't help feeling relieved when it was over.

Margaret revelled in the cool climate. Roland was an

early riser, so, before breakfast, they took a walk around the grounds of the hotel while the mist still shrouded the thickly wooded hillsides. After a traditional English breakfast they went out into the bright morning armed with binoculars and a field guide to watch birds.

'The highlands are famous for the birdlife,' said Roland. 'The hornbill, an extraordinary looking bird, is quite something. Magnificent colours and a huge curved beak. Supposed to be good luck if we spot one.'

Margaret had never been particularly interested in birds but found she quite enjoyed the meandering walks along the tiny trails in the forest. Sometimes they passed Indian girls carrying produce or clean laundry up to the other hotels and occasionally they came upon a neat bungalow that was both fenced and guarded.

'A lot of banks, companies and wealthy business people have bungalows up here. It gets very busy and very social as people come up from the coast to escape the heat,' said Roland. 'Cameron Highlands is becoming popular too. It's bigger and has tea plantations in the area.'

On their walks they sometimes came across a group of English schoolgirls who attended St Margaret's Anglican Boarding School at Fraser's Hill and they would exchange pleasantries with their teacher. Margaret thought it must be a lovely place to go to school and the girls would have the benefit of being close to their families. Better, she thought, than being sent to school in England.

After their post-luncheon nap, they took tea with scones and strawberry jam on the terrace each afternoon. Their cosy room was furnished with rattan chairs and chintz curtains. There was a small fireplace in their sitting room, which they found blazing each night when they came up after dinner.

They met several other couples and played cards and joined in a games night, but Roland preferred to have his pre-dinner stengah by the fire and talk local politics and business with the other men. Margaret read the women's magazines that had been sent out from London and thought perhaps she'd better purchase some books to take to the plantation. When she mentioned that to Roland he nodded.

'Yes, we already have an arrangement with the KL Book Club. When we next get to KL, you should pop in and introduce yourself to Mrs Nicky. She's the new secretary.'

'A library? But how often will I be able to visit it?' said Margaret.

'The Kuala Lumpur Book Club was set up thirty or more years ago for planters in remote outstations and books are mailed to them. Mrs Nixon, that's her proper name, will send you books so you should chat to her about what you like.'

'I'll do that,' said Margaret, knowing that she would have lots of time on her hands. Roland had told her that there was house staff at the plantation. The routine had already been established by Eugene and Charlotte, Roland's mother, so Margaret would need to do little to maintain her new home.

One morning in the breakfast room, as Roland heaped marmalade on to his toast, he said, 'I've made plans to play golf today with a few chaps, so I'm afraid you'll be on your own for a bit. Do you mind?'

Margaret tried not to show her disappointment. 'Oh. Of course not, Roland. Who are you playing with? Maybe I could get together with their wives.' She didn't really want him to go off and leave her, but she knew they were probably influential people.

'Ah, mmm, perhaps. I think two of them have their wives with them, and the other fellow is unmarried. I only met them briefly, though we have mutual acquaintances, as one does out here.'

'Quite,' said Margaret, who'd already been impressed with the important people that Roland knew and, indeed, had invited to their wedding. How easily he befriended people who seemed to be in high positions. 'Are they staying here at the Smokehouse?'

'No. One is at Maxwell's, the others are in a company bungalow. You saw the chaps in here having dinner last night. They're high up in the Civil Service.'

'Oh. The ones you had a drink with after I went upstairs to bed,' said Margaret pointedly.

'You didn't mind, old girl, did you? It's rather how it is, we fellows learn an awful lot about things on these social occasions.'

'As women do, too, when they get together,' said Margaret. While she might be impressed by the important people Roland associated with, she didn't want to be dismissed as a frivolous young bride who didn't know how to mingle.

'Ah yes, but we men talk about important matters. It pays to keep a handle on people's movements, plantings, prices, what the locals are up to in various districts.' He cut the last of his toast into neat squares, popped them into his mouth and looked at his wife. 'If you'd rather I didn't go, tell me now and we'll plan our day.' He looked as though he had suddenly realised that it might not be the done thing to abandon his new wife on their honeymoon.

Margaret didn't want to upset him but neither did she want him slipping back into his old bachelor habits of doing as he pleased with friends and acquaintances. 'No, really, Roland. I want you to play golf. I'm sure you don't have the opportunity very often. This is your time to relax as well,' said Margaret in a tone of voice designed to show Roland that she was miffed by his plans, which would cause him to cancel the game and spend the day with her.

Roland, however, took her words at face value.

'Excellent, then. I'll chat to the fellows and see what their wives are up to during the day.'

'Please, don't force my company on them if they have other plans,' said Margaret quickly. 'I'm quite sure I can entertain myself. Or I'll read a book and relax.'

'That's the spirit.' He leaned over and took her hand. 'Margaret, you do understand, when we get to Utopia I will be returning to my work and all that that entails. I want you to be part of it but I can't be at your side all the time as we are now. The women, the mems, they have to fend for themselves a lot of the time. Of course you'll have house staff, but you will be left on your own a lot. It will be a different life for you.'

'Roland! I understand that,' said Margaret lightly. 'Which is why I want to make the most of our honeymoon. While I have you all to myself,' she added coquettishly.

He gave a big smile. 'Is that an invitation?' He kissed her hand. 'Tonight. A romantic dinner and time to ourselves in our room, in front of the fire, a bottle of MacAllister's best champagne. How does that sound?'

'Lovely.'

'Right. I'd better get going and find the set of clubs MacAllister promised me. Are you coming or do you want something else?'

'I might have another pot of tea,' said Margaret.

Roland signalled to the waiter, who hurried to the table. 'Another tea for memsahib.'

Then he was gone and Margaret was left alone feeling faintly irritated.

'Earl Grey?' enquired the waiter.

'No, English Breakfast,' said Margaret, sounding quite waspish.

Shortly afterwards, Margaret received a message from the two wives of Roland's golfing partners to say that they would like her to join them for luncheon at the

Broadstairs' bungalow. A driver would be sent to fetch her from the Smokehouse at noon.

Before getting ready for lunch and with time to kill, Margaret decided to go for a walk by herself in the woods surrounding the nearby golf course. Armed with Roland's binoculars and a walking stick she borrowed from the hotel, she set out. It was a longish walk but she found a small trail and saw it heading up toward a peak that she thought would give her an expansive view of the area.

As she wandered along the path, the trees became denser, blocking the sunlight. An occasional side trail led away from the track she was on. She assumed they led to private bungalows or were short cuts used by the hotel staff. Everything was quiet, save for the swishing flight of an occasional bird.

She stopped to gaze up into the trees when she heard a rustling in the treetops and to her surprise saw through the binoculars, a round-faced monkey staring at her as curiously as she was looking at it. As she put the binoculars down, the monkey swung away with a high-pitched shriek that startled dozens of other monkeys, and all of them raced and called through the trees.

Margaret was quite elated by the sight, and continued on along the path, which was now less well marked as it dipped down before curving upwards again, towards the peak.

It was like being in a dark-green cavern, and she was glad when she found herself in a small clearing where a break in the trees gave a full vista of the hills on the other side. This seemed to be far more rugged country and, while she assumed there must be some small villages hidden away somewhere, she could see nothing but jungle. These were not the benign slopes accommodating the bungalows, hotels, shops and landscaped gardens planted with familiar trees, where she and Roland had walked. Through the binoculars she could see, stretched out before her, an endless tangle of tall trees, choked with vines and ferns. Suddenly the talk she had heard about tigers and wild animals became very real. Here was a different part of the country. It was untamed and appeared suddenly threatening. She felt a long way from the suburbs of Brisbane.

She turned and walked back the way she'd come, hurrying slightly. But as she came to where a small track branched away from the main one, she stopped in shock. Straddling her path was a giant lizard, scaly, prehistoric, stone-cold eyes observing her, tongue flicking. Margaret's hand flew to her mouth. She'd seen small lizards in her mother's garden, but this was a monster and it did not appear to want to move. It continued to block her way.

Margaret was not going to go near the creature. Its claws splayed from it's gnarled feet making it look dangerous. Swiftly she glanced around and took another side path, thinking that it would either join the main trail or end up at someone's bungalow, or at one of the scattered clusters of houses where the locals lived. But after following this narrow track for some time and not finding her way back to the golf course, Margaret realised she was lost. Where this path went, she had no idea.

She was hot, perspiring with fear as much as from the claustrophobic heat. She imagined that she could hear rustling and noises in the undergrowth and the more she hurried the more she stumbled over roots and stones, her breath coming in short gasps. She glanced at her watch and realised that it was already noon and the car would be at the hotel to take her to the pre-arranged luncheon.

She stopped to catch her breath, her hand on her heaving chest, trying to think calmly. No one would know where she was, but her disappearance would certainly raise the alarm. Roland could be gone till late afternoon, playing golf, and not give her a thought. These scenarios played out in her mind, although she was more overwhelmed by the embarrassment of her misadventure than anything else.

She set off again and couldn't stop the tears that flowed down her face. She had a terrible feeling she was walking in circles, for everything looked the same. To her eyes there were no identifiable landmarks. Then she heard a movement behind her. She stopped, closing her eyes, not daring to look, waiting for whatever creature that was there to pounce on her.

'Mem?'

She spun around to see a barefoot Malay wearing a checked sarong topped with a khaki jumper and carrying a long knife.

'Oh. Oh dear,' said Margaret recalling how Malays could sometimes run amok.

The man looked puzzled. 'Mem, kamu sesat?'

'I don't understand,' said Margaret fearfully. 'I was near the golf club, but I changed trails and . . .' Seeing his uncomprehending expression, she used her walking stick as a golf club and swung it awkwardly.

On her second swing there was a flicker in the man's eyes. He pointed in the direction opposite to the way she was headed. 'Nanti saya tunjuk jalan.' He turned and trotted away from her, signalling her to follow.

For a moment she hesitated, wondering if she should trust the short, brown-skinned man with the large bush knife. Then, drawing herself up, Margaret strode after him, even though he was going in the opposite direction to where she thought they should go. Suddenly she recognised where she was. She saw in the distance a green fairway and a fluttering flag on a green.

The man stopped and pointed with his parang.

'Oh, I see it. Oh, thank you, thank you so much.' She started to run towards the golf course, then turned

73

to thank the man again, but he had disappeared. As she approached the clubhouse she could see a group of men gathered in front of it, including Roland and a man in a khaki uniform who was obviously a policeman.

She hurried forward, trying to maintain her dignity.

'There she is! Oh my Lord. Margaret! Where have you been? We were about to send out a search party!' Roland came towards her.

'I'm so terribly sorry. I went for a bit of an explore and I got lost, I'm afraid.' She smiled, putting on a brave face. 'I'm sorry if I've inconvenienced everyone . . .'

Roland put his arm around her. 'Are you all right, my dear? This has been such a worry. You can't just walk off into the jungle on your own.'

'I hadn't planned to, Roland. I got lost, but here I am.'

He smiled at the police inspector and shook his hand. 'All's well that ends well, eh? Frightfully sorry for the call out. My wife has found her own way back.'

'I'm pleased you're all right, Mrs Elliott. I know you are a newcomer, but this is not England. You can't walk unattended in these forests. I'm surprised you didn't run into any of the Orang Asli, the local tribesmen.' The inspector gave a brief salute. 'Happy to be of service, Mr and Mrs Elliott.'

'Oh, how embarrassing,' said Margaret. 'And those ladies, I'm dreadfully sorry to miss their luncheon.'

One of Roland's golfing partners stepped forward and held out his hand. 'I'm Reginald Broadstairs, Mrs Elliott. My wife was expecting you for luncheon and it was she who raised the alarm when no one could find you.'

'Please thank her. Very silly of me, I know. I was trying to get to the peak for the view, and this giant lizard appeared and gave me such a fright, I turned around and took the wrong path and . . .'

'It's fine, Margaret. You did jolly well to find your

way back,' said Roland. 'You probably saw an iguana. Those big ones can look very fearsome.'

'I will telephone my wife and tell her all is well,' said Broadstairs. 'Would you like to go over to my bungalow? The ladies will still be there.'

'I'd rather not if you don't mind,' said Margaret. 'I'm not properly dressed and I feel a little shaken. Please extend my apologies and hopefully we can reciprocate the hospitality.' Margaret glanced at Roland.

'Of course. Why don't you all come to dinner tonight at the Smokehouse, Broadstairs? I'll let MacAllister know,' said Roland.

'Splendid idea,' said Broadstairs.

'Did you finish your game?' Margaret asked Roland sheepishly.

'No, we didn't, I'm afraid.'

'Oh, it's my fault I do so apologise to you all. Please, all of you go and finish your game. If you can just arrange a car to take me back . . .'

'Are you sure, my dear? I hate to let these fellows down.'

'I insist. I'll take a bath and a rest and see you all this evening.' She gave the men a wan smile.

'Righto, you can use my driver,' said Broadstairs.

'I suggest we go straight to the twelfth hole. It won't take us long to finish,' said the man partnering Broadstairs.

By the time Roland returned to their room, Margaret had bathed, dressed, eaten a sandwich, taken a nap and collected herself. She was almost ready to laugh off the episode. Roland gave her a big hug and she could smell whisky on his breath, but she was pleased that he seemed so loving and wasn't at all cross with her for spoiling his golf game.

'Well, aren't you the talk of the club! Everyone agrees it's very easy to get lost on those trails, but you found your way out, no hysterics, no tears. Quite a feat, darling. But please, it is dangerous. You have to take care.' He gave her a big smile. 'Next time you go out walking, stick to the paths and take someone with you. I shouldn't have left you alone. I am so sorry.'

While Margaret was quietly pleased by his contrition, she said graciously, 'Please, Roland. Don't be sorry. I'm upset I spoiled your game of golf with those important people.'

Roland pulled off his jacket and loosened his shirt. 'Oh, stuff and nonsense. Father has had dealings with Broadstairs' firm, but he and those other fellows are a bit stuffy. And my game was dreadfully off today. So I should have listened and stayed here with you.' He reached for her. 'Shall we have a cuddle before we go out?'

Margaret stood up. 'Didn't you say six pm to meet everyone? By the time you're bathed and dressed . . . Shall I meet you downstairs? I was going to walk around the garden.'

'Don't stray too far!' he said. And they both laughed.

But Margaret was unsettled. She hoped that when she got to the security of Utopia she would feel safer because the vastness, the strangeness of this landscape, its people, its culture felt very alien.

When they finally arrived at Utopia, after farewelling Winifred in Kuala Lumpur, it was dark. Roland had suggested that Winifred might like to travel further, perhaps going as far as Bangkok, before returning to Australia. But Winifred had no desire to travel on her own, and, she suspected, she would have had her fill of the exotic East by the time Roland and Margaret had returned from their honeymoon. The darkness was almost physical; damp, pressing and enveloping. Margaret had been asleep and barely took in the glow of lights, the murmur of voices, even when Roland helped her from the car while issuing instructions to the people who had met them.

A light shrouded with small flying insects hung by the front door under a portico. Eugene stood at the door as she went up the steps to the front entrance.

'Welcome, my dear Margaret, welcome. This is an unholy hour to arrive, Roland.'

'I know, Father. Margaret is weary. I made a call at Tanjung Estate and saw Sidney Baker. You know how he loves to chat. He's had a few problems but I'll go into that later. Do you want some supper, Margaret dear?'

'No, I'd just like to fall into bed if that's possible. Start afresh in the morning.' Margaret noticed the heavy, dark wooden furniture in the entrance, but she was simply too tired to be curious about her surroundings, although the house had appeared large and impressive.

'Kim has made up the guestroom for you both here. I thought it easier,' said Eugene.

'Thank you, Father. Very thoughtful. Good evening, Kim. Margaret, this is Kim, our amah, who'll show you to our room.'

A Chinese woman, smiling broadly, hands clasped in front of her crisp white tunic came forward. 'Hello, mem. Kim happy for Mr Roland. Very good, very good.'

'Kim, when you've shown the mem to the guestroom bring her some tea,' said Roland. 'I'll have your suitcase sent in, Margaret. I'll be there shortly after I have a chat with Father.'

'I'll be asleep, I'm sure. Goodnight, Mr Elliott. Thank you.'

'See you in the morning, my dear.'

Margaret followed the amah down a hallway to a

large room furnished with two single beds, a large closet and a dressing table. The room had big windows but the shutters were closed. The furniture in the room was made from rattan with faded print cushions. A large fan spun lazily overhead. Kim began to pull down the mosquito nets which were suspended from the ceiling, and tuck them around the beds.

A large bowl and china jug filled with water sat on a dresser. Margaret poured some water from the jug into the bowl, splashed her face and fell into bed.

In the morning when she awoke, Roland was already up. She had no sooner opened the shutters to the bright morning when Kim tapped at the door.

'Mem wish tea? Warm bath?'

'A bath would be lovely. Where's the bathroom?'

'Kim do.'

Margaret followed Kim down the hallway to a large, white bathroom where a bath stood in the middle of the room. It was filled with tepid water. Kim spread a towel on a chair and indicated the soap and washer and left Margaret staring around the spartan room. The starkness, indeed plainness, of the interior of the house surprised Margaret. She had the impression it would be far grander, which made her wonder about the bungalow that had been built a couple of years before for Roland and in which they would both now live.

Dressed and refreshed Margaret found Roland and his father sitting at a glass-topped cane dining table in a room that overlooked the garden. Both men rose.

'Sorry, we've started breakfast without you. How did you sleep?' asked Roland, kissing her.

'Didn't hear a thing.' Margaret gazed around the simple room that had ceiling fans, a wooden floor and two well-worn comfortable lounges as well as the dining chairs and table. A dart board and games table were at the far end of the room. Palms and tropical plants in pots stood along its length, protected from the sun by bamboo blinds.

An elderly Chinese man, dressed in a navy cotton jacket with short sleeves and matching pants, placed a bowl of porridge and a plate of toast before her. 'Tea, mem? Or mem take coffee?'

'This is Ho, Father's houseboy,' said Roland.

'Tea, thank you, Ho,' said Margaret, somewhat startled that such an elderly man should be referred to as a houseboy.

'Ho runs this household with an iron fist. Been with Father for years,' said Roland. 'Darling, I'm just about to go to a section of the estate with Father, then I'll be back and we can go over to our house and you can start settling in.'

'Won't keep him long, Margaret. He's got a little catching up to do. After your breakfast take a stroll around Charlotte's garden. She's very proud of it and I've been trying to maintain it while she's been away,' said Eugene, rising. Ho immediately stepped forward to hold the chair for him and push it back under the table as Eugene walked away.

'How is Mrs Elliott?' asked Margaret unsure how to refer to her mother-in-law since they'd never met. 'And her mother?'

'It's difficult, of course. Charlotte is being brave,' said Eugene.

'Have some fruit from mother's garden. The papaya is excellent,' said Roland as he, too, stood, kissed her quickly and followed Eugene out of the room.

Margaret turned to find Ho smiling at her expectantly. 'Yes, please. We call it pawpaw at home, and I love it. And more tea, please.'

After eating breakfast, Margaret returned to the guest-room to fetch her sunhat and found that her bed had been made and that everything had been tidied and her suitcase repacked.

She decided to explore the house before heading into the garden. There was a formal lounge room and a bar room hung with some photographs of cricket teams. The room led to a dining room, with a teak dining setting and beside it was another room, which looked to be Eugene's office. On its walls were the stuffed heads of various animals, including boars and deer. Further down the corridor was the master bedroom with a small dressing room beside it. To one side of the shaded verandah was a sleep-out, which was clearly used for casual accommodation. Behind the dining room Margaret could see a small detached building. When she reached it she discovered it was the kitchen. It contained a large wood-fired stove, a long wooden table and a sink, as well as a large pantry. A Chinese man dressed in cotton pants and a loose singlet was chopping vegetables on a heavy wooden block. He looked up in surprise as Margaret entered. Suddenly, Kim appeared from what appeared to be the laundry and the servants' quarters.

'Sorry, mem. You want something? I get,' said Kim, ushering Margaret from what was clearly the servants' domain.

'No, thank you. I was just looking for the way to the garden.'

'I show. Follow me.' Kim showed her the door leading into the back garden.

'Thank you.' Margaret wandered across the grass to a fenced area where there were colourful shrubs, two large flowering trees, several pawpaw trees and a kitchen garden. What caught her attention were some stakes tied to a fence. These supported huge stands of flame and coral coloured miniature orchids. Winifred would have admired them as she had several orchids in pots that she prized and which she nurtured carefully. These orchids, however, looked to be growing untended and in great profusion.

The kitchen and the servants' quarters were screened from the house and garden by a bamboo fence. Through the fence she could see a metal washing tub, several pails, a large pottery pitcher and a rough outdoor fireplace with a large shallow pan on top, like she'd seen the hawkers use. There were several rope chairs and two tiny rooms which she thought must house some of the domestic staff. Washing was hanging on a rope line. Margaret doubted if this was the sort of place where a mem would spend any time.

She turned away and walked around the house to the front driveway where Eugene's black Oldsmobile was parked beneath the portico of plastered stone pillars supporting a tiled roof, covered in a rampant flowering vine. The exterior of the house was high, and its timber and stone gave it a stately appearance.

Lush plants grew under the side of the portico. The driveway leading to the house wound around a small circular garden before joining a narrow dirt road. There was no fence, front gate or demarcation between the house and the red laterite road lined on either side by palm trees. In the distance she could see thickly forested hills. As Margaret turned down the road she saw, for the first time, a section of young rubber trees.

An Indian who had been tending the garden stood and gave her a swift salute. 'Memsahib require car?'

'No, thank you. I'm just walking.'

He shook his head from side to side. 'No good memsahib walk. Very hot. Many snakes.'

'Snakes? Oh, I see. Thank you.' She turned back towards the house.

The gardener crouched back down to the small border of flowers.

Margaret sat on the verandah and fanned herself. All the staff had asked if they could help her and they had been very respectful. Margaret was enchanted. Clearly while Charlotte Elliott was away, Margaret was the 'boss mem'. No one at home in Brisbane would ever imagine living with so many servants.

She jumped up as she heard Roland's Bedford truck returning.

He took off his hat and wiped his face with his handkerchief. 'Right, Mrs Elliott, shall we go and inspect our house? I've asked Hamid to take our things over there. Then later this afternoon when it starts to cool, we'll go for a bit of a tour about the rest of the place.' He kissed her. 'I know this might seem strange and difficult but our bungalow will be your own domain to make of what you will.' He put his arm about her shoulders as they walked indoors.

'This place is rather, well, old looking. Outdated,' said Margaret. 'I suppose older people don't like change.'

'Well, that's part of it. But Margaret, we've just come through the Depression when rubber prices were at rock bottom. It was a struggle for us just to keep the plantation viable. So there's been no money for what Father would consider frivolous things. My mother certainly understood that whenever there was spare cash, it was put straight back into the business. Things are picking up now and because my parents were frugal and hung on through the bad times, they were able to come out way ahead. Actually we have been able to expand our operation because we bought up a lot of estates around here from other families and companies that couldn't make a go of things in the last few years.'

'So you actually expanded Utopia during the Depression?' asked Margaret, impressed with the Elliotts' business acumen.

Roland nodded. 'Yes, I'll show you later. For now

let's drive over to our house. Can I carry you over the threshold?'

Margaret was glad that their bungalow was some distance from the main house. On the way there, they passed worksheds housing equipment, lean-tos sheltering seedlings and a collection of rough shacks of woven palm leaves, which was where some of the rubber tappers lived. All around, stretched the pale-green lines of the rubber trees.

'There's a local village of sorts not far away where a lot of the Indian tappers live. I'll explain the workings of the plantation to you another time,' said Roland.

When Margaret saw her new home, so unadorned, so basic, so . . . words failed her. By local standards it was new, only two years old, but there had been no attention given to a garden, not even pot plants. She dreaded to think what it would be like inside. The one redeeming feature, which gave the house some identity, was a massive nipa palm growing close to the front step, its fronds spreading into a thick green fan. The house itself was a wooden construction set up high with a wide verandah all around. It reminded Margaret slightly of a small Queenslander.

'It needs a garden,' she managed to say.

'There's a kitchen patch out the back. Greens and things. Ask the gardener and he'll do whatever you want out the front here.'

And with that, Roland swept Margaret up in his arms, marched up the front steps and deposited her on the verandah.

'This looks like a pleasant area to sit,' said Margaret noting the old-style planters' chairs, wicker table, a rack overflowing with newspapers and a drinks trolley. As the bungalow was on a rise, the view from the verandah across the sea of ribbed rows of rubber trees to the hills was quite spectacular.

She tried to hide her disappointment as she went from room to room realising how very simple it all was. Indeed the kitchen out the back was so primitive that the stove appeared to be a converted kerosene tin. She was relieved she wouldn't have to work with it.

'Where's the toilet and bathroom?' asked Margaret.

'Thunder box, I'm afraid. It gets emptied every day.' Roland opened a small door and Margaret felt the sultry outside air hit her as she gaped in shock.

The bathroom was an unlined wooden cubicle with a section of the floor made up of slats a few inches apart, just wide enough for snakes to come in, Margaret thought grimly. A huge ceramic jar stood beside a tin bathtub. There was a dipper made from half a coconut shell hanging beside it.

'No hot water, I'm afraid,' said Roland cheerfully. 'You ladle the cold water from the Shanghai jar over yourself. It's always cold, so you'll find it refreshing. The amah will get you some hot water if you want a warm bath.'

The bungalow had three bedrooms, and like the main bungalow, there was a sleep-out with several bamboo stretcher beds, their feet in saucers of kerosene.

'Keeps the ants and bugs off,' explained Roland. 'Sometimes people stop over when travelling round the district. Dr Hamilton, the DO and his wife, if she's with him, stay at the big house of course.'

Their bedroom was furnished simply, but there was a big mosquito net over a solid carved Chinese bed. A standing mirror, a dressing table with a small vase of fresh flowers, an armoire and an ornate chest at the foot of the bed made up the rest of the furniture. The windows had shutters without curtains, the floorboards were bare but painted cream and there was a small, attractive Indian rug.

The lounge room and dining room were combined,

making one big space with lots of chairs and a long table. It was not the cosiness that Margaret was used to and compared with the ornaments, knick-knacks, decorative items and personal touches jammed into Winifred's house, this looked very spacious and uncluttered.

'It's a nice big space, and cool,' said Margaret.

'Oh, I'm sure you'll give this place the homey touch,' said Roland. Then he added seriously, 'But some things will have to wait. I'm sure we can manage quite well for the time being, don't you? If you need anything for entertaining just borrow it from the big house. Come and meet Ah Kit, our houseboy. He'll run everything, but keep an eye on the other servants and make sure they don't rob us too much.' He lowered his voice. 'And don't be too cosy with them. Pleasant but firm. You understand how it is.'

'Er, yes. I suppose so,' said Margaret.

Ah Kit was Chinese, younger than Eugene's houseboy, possibly the same age as Roland, with bright, inquisitive dark eyes and a quick smile. He wore what was obviously the local uniform of white tunic and black pants. He bowed and said, 'I am very happy to work for you, mem.'

'Thank you,' said Margaret.

'You want tea? Ah Kit learn what mem like, no like.'

'In a little while, Ah Kit. I'll show the mem around,' said Roland. As they walked away, he said to Margaret, 'You'll have to instruct him on the way you like things done, he's very quick to learn.'

'Does he cook as well?' asked Margaret.

'No, Cookie does that. Cookie's Malay and a Muslim so he won't touch any pork. Sometimes he has disagreements with the others about cooking utensils, which have been used to cook pork with, and so on. You'll get the hang of it all. Come on, let's go for a drive and I'll show you some of the better divisions.'

Margaret recalled the big distances and the wide open

spaces of Queensland but, even so, the size of the sections of the plantation surprised her. Roland drove her past mile after mile of avenues of rubber trees where occasionally he would stop and inspect some of the trees or chat to the working tappers.

'Don't get out of the car, you're not wrapped up,' advised Roland. 'The mosquitoes among these trees are vicious.'

Margaret had noticed that the workers wore long sleeves and pants, or saris topped with cotton shirts. They all wore hats with scarves wrapped around their faces as they worked. Many wore cotton gloves and now she knew why.

'The tapping is done in the early hours of the morning while it's still cool,' explained Roland as they drove. 'The tappers cut into the bark in a spiral on one side and the latex bleeds down into the cup. Once the sun is up the latex congeals and stops flowing so after midday the cups are collected, which is what is happening now. Later, the opposite side of the tree is cut, while the other side heals.'

'And what happens to the latex?' asked Margaret.

'It's poured into moulds, smoked and dried and then rolled into rubber sheets for export. A lot of our rubber was on that steamship that runs between Port Swettenham and Singapore,' said Roland.

It was a strange and eerie world that Roland inhabited, thought Margaret as she watched him shrug into his cotton jacket and don a solar topee, which had a kind of veil attached. He wrapped it around his face to protect himself from the mosquitoes. If the mosquitoes are really this bad, thought Margaret, perhaps I'd better take quinine each day as Eugene has suggested so that I don't get malaria. And she'd better speak to Roland about getting some kind of screen for their bedroom windows as a mosquito had been trapped in the netting the previous night.

Two or three days later she again went out with Roland. She watched him walk the length of one row of rubber trees, disappearing into the shadowy green light. He seemed to enjoy the conformity, the neat exactness of the rows of trees and Margaret wondered if he'd played with tin soldiers as a boy, lining them up in serried ranks.

'Sorry, dear, hope you're not bored coming out here again. But if I don't check, the workers get sloppy with their cuts and either they don't cut deep enough to get the latex, or they go too deeply and kill the tree. I'll take you down to the river now. You'll like that,' said Roland, flinging his hat on to the seat of the Bedford truck.

'Have you ever got lost?' asked Margaret. 'Everything looks the same.'

He stared at her in surprise then laughed. 'Gosh, no. I know every tree. I've been around this estate ever since I could walk!'

Margaret was pleasantly surprised when they came to the river. They drove past the smoke house where the latex was made, a workshop and a small factory, which was really just a shed shaded by an attap with open sides where the latex was rolled out and stacked ready to be sent downriver. They came to a solid wharf that looked as though it had been built many years before. The river-bank had been cleared except for a few shady trees, and nearby was a small locked storehouse.

'That's where we keep all the goods that come up here by boat. It's always locked, although Ho has a key if we need to replenish household supplies. Possibly we could also let Ah Kit have one too, so that you can get anything you need. Once a month the workers can buy their bulk rice and sugar and other basics from here, too.'

'The river is pretty,' said Margaret looking at the

broad brown sweep of water, bordered by thick jungle that came to the water's edge on the other side. 'Can we take a trip down it sometime? Do you have a boat?'

'There are several longboats, small praus and a motor launch upriver, near the village. We'll organise a picnic and a river trip. Get the social club together for an outing. Be good for everyone to meet you.'

'What sort of club is it?' asked Margaret.

'Basically, our neighbours and friends have a club-house, about half an hour's or so drive from here. We get together regularly for tennis and cards, tiffin, stengahs, that sort of thing. A break from the routine.'

'It's sounds fun,' said Margaret enthusiastically.

'It is, rather. Sometimes we also go to each other's plantations or have swimming parties. There's also a lodge in the hills we can use.'

'What's the lodge like?'

Roland smiled. 'Father built it years ago with some of his friends. Carved it out of the jungle. They built a very simple bungalow but it can sleep ten people or so if they want to stay over when they go out hunting. Wait till you see it.'

'Hunting animals, you mean? Like tigers? Deer? Pigs?'

He nodded. 'Yes, Father's a pretty good shot. Good fishing in the headwaters, too.'

'It all sounds exciting,' said Margaret, pleased at the idea of socialising.

'Before we head back, I'd like to show you another rather special place. It's a bit a drive, I'm afraid.'

Margaret nodded. 'Lead on,' she said.

As Roland drove into the hills surrounding Utopia, Margaret looked down into the jungle-clad ravine. He pointed out landmarks and talked of how his father, Eugene, had come as a young man to establish a plantation in such rugged country.

'Tiger country. All kinds of wild animals used to come

around at night. That's one reason why the houses are built on stilts. There weren't the roads, rough as they are, that are here now. I'll show you the lodge one day. It's basic, but quite an adventure. And it can be rather fun if we go with good friends.'

His voice was filled with enthusiasm and he sounded almost excited. Usually Roland was reserved but now she was seeing a different side to him. 'You sound like you enjoy that sort of thing. I don't think it's something ladies would care to do,' said Margaret rather primly. 'Hunting and roughing it, I mean.'

'My Lord, Margaret, my mother used to enjoy it. No airs and graces, a chance to look after ourselves as we only have basic staff and a couple of natives to help with the hunting. Some of the women are very good shots. You can see photographs of them in Father's study.'

Margaret didn't answer, but looked again at the wilderness around them, finding it difficult to comprehend that this was her new home.

Soon the jungle gave way again to the neat rows of rubber trees, and Roland drove to a rise and stopped the truck. From this spot the 360 degree view took in the great scope of Utopia. But what interested Margaret more was that up here, on the top of the hill so far from any civilisation, stood a small white church.

'What's the church here for? It's miles from anywhere. Who would come here for services?'

'My father built this for my mother, a sentimental gesture. It's for our family and friends to use on occasion. My mother always hoped I'd get married here.'

'Oh, for goodness' sake, I'm glad we didn't! No one would come way out here!' said Margaret. 'And who would conduct the ceremony?'

'The clergy come around regularly and conduct services here. Our neighbours come, as well.'

'It's a nice idea, I suppose, but I'm very glad we were married in KL,' said Margaret firmly.

'Come and have a look around,' said Roland. 'My father wants to be buried here. Mother is in England caring for her own parents but she'll eventually come back here to enjoy her final years with Father at Utopia.'

'Ugh. How morbid. Perhaps we should go and visit her in Kent. I'd love to meet her,' said Margaret.

'Let's settle into life out here first,' said Roland. 'And you have just been to Europe. Most people wait till a child or two arrives before making the pilgrimage back home.' His tone was final.

Margaret didn't reply as Roland went to open the little church door and show her inside. But a trip back to England to meet his mother sounded rather like a good idea. She was sure that she would be able to persuade him, eventually.

Within two weeks Margaret had settled into the plantation routine and had taken to running the household as a small fiefdom, as though she'd done it all her life. Roland slipped from bed while it was still dark to take the muster, leaving her to sleep until Ah Kit tapped on the door and brought her a tray with a pot of tea and a slice of bread and butter. While Margaret sipped her tea, hot water was brought in and poured into the water pitcher so that she could bathe in warm water. She found that in the hot and humid climate, she changed clothes several times a day, but whatever she dropped was picked up and returned fresh and ironed the next morning.

When Roland returned later in the morning their hot breakfast of toast, eggs, smoked fish or kedgeree and fruit was ready. He then bathed and changed and returned to work, reappearing after midday. Sometimes they lunched with Roland's father at the big house where they were seated in the dining room and served a three-course meal. Margaret paid attention to the menu so she could ask her cook to prepare similar dishes – chicken à la king, steak and kidney pudding, mulligatawny soup. Sometimes there was a visitor passing through and one day she was thrilled to see Dr Hamilton, who had called on Eugene before heading up-country.

'Have you heard from your lovely mother?' asked Dr Hamilton. 'We had a splendid time in KL while you were at Fraser's. I'm sorry I didn't get to see her before she left. Had a bit of an emergency at the hospital, if I remember correctly.'

'Mother is settling back in at home and sends her best wishes to you,' said Margaret.

'And how are you settling in, my dear?' asked the kindly doctor.

'Everything is wonderful. I feel very spoiled. I'm learning the household and other duties,' she answered.

'A tip, don't tread on the houseboy's toes, they like everything to remain status quo,' said the doctor. 'But you mustn't let the others think they can raid the larder either, if you know what I mean. There is always a bit of leniency, a closed eye here and there, which they consider their right and due, but if they think they can hoodwink you, they will.'

'Oh, Roland has taught me that and I'm not about to be taken advantage of, or thought of as a softie,' said Margaret firmly, and the doctor patted her shoulder.

'Excellent. You'll fit in marvellously. I'm looking forward to our tennis tournament. All meant to be fun, but those devils take it frightfully seriously. I'm the umpire.'

'That's at the Stevenson's place, isn't it,' said Margaret.

'Right. Jolly nice setup they have. Excellent court. Two weeks after your little boating extravaganza, I hear. Sorry I can't make that, have to get around the district, you know.'

*

Dearest Mother, Dad and Bette,

Where has the time gone? Surprisingly the weeks have flown by and I thought I might find time hanging heavily on my hands. Far from it! Since I last wrote I feel I have settled into our bungalow and my trunks have arrived and been unpacked so I feel a lot more comfortable with some of my things around me.

Roland and his father have been busy getting a shipment of rubber ready to send down to Singapore but we still find time to enjoy the best part of the day together – a G & T for me and Roland's stengah on the verandah at sunset. Cookie makes delicious 'nibbles kechil' (that means small eats) and we share our news.

There was much excitement last Friday when a snake was found curled up around the Shanghai pitcher in the laundry. It was a huge thing, brightly coloured, and I believe quite dangerous. But the gardener dispatched it with a parang – those lethal large knives they carry to clear the jungle. I do feel I am getting a little more used to the idea of wildlife being about, though in the rubber trees one sees mainly birds, but you hear the monkeys shrieking at night. Sometimes we go over to the big house for drinks and dinner with Roland's father and he does enjoy telling me stories of his hunting trips – and has the trophies to prove it! The jungle is all around us so who knows what creatures could be lurking. While the plantation has been cut from mostly secondary jungle, I always have the feeling that if the plantation was not maintained and the jungle kept back, we'd be swallowed up in no time and who would know we were ever here? But of course I wouldn't say that to Roland. The Elliotts have worked so hard to establish Utopia.

Hamid, my father-in-law's driver, has taken us into Slim River several times which is quite some distance away, an hour or more, but it's been very interesting to see this little town, which is very colourful and filled with stalls and local food places. Roland loves to eat the local snacks like murtabak, which is like an apple turn-over but filled with spiced meat and egg with pickles and cucumber to accompany it. I ate a very tasty ikan baka – a grilled local fish. As you can see I'm learning quite a few Malay words. The servants speak far too fast and sing-song for me at present, but I'm getting the hang of it!

Roland knows of a wonderful waterfall and hot springs in the area, but he says that it's very difficult to get to them.

I have even started a garden plan. When we visit other plantations – such fun – I come back with an armful of cuttings. Some of the gardens around the old established bungalows are very charming and things grow very quickly here. Our English friends are always amazed at how fast plants pop up.

Dr Hamilton stopped in for lunch last week and sent his best wishes. And I played tennis with the DO's wife, whom you met at my wedding and she asked to be remembered to you and hoped you and Father would take a trip here to see us in the not too distant future!

Give Bette my congratulations on her exam results and her art classes sound most intriguing.

The houseboy has just brought me afternoon tea and truly exquisite scones. Cookie is a very deft baker! And no, I don't feel too spoiled as I'm doing my bit and Roland is very pleased that the house runs so smoothly. But I have to admit, I am getting very used to the luxury of help and having no nasty domestic chores at all to do! Don't forget the coloured buttons to match that piece of material I sent you, please, Mother. There's an excellent tailor in Slim River and I'm having a light silk suit made for the races coming up. It will be a really big do in KL. Roland will

combine it with business but we are looking forward to a
few days in the city with friends.
Signing off for now,
Your affectionate daughter,
Margaret

Margaret wrote home weekly, in great detail, about her activities. But the next week her letter home had only one piece of exciting news – she was expecting a baby.

4

Port Swettenham, 1940

THE PORT WAS BUSY. Exports of rubber, copra, pineapples
and wood from the large trading houses were swung in
giant nets onto the decks of the cargo ships. Incoming goods
were offloaded. The passengers on board the steamer from
Singapore stood at the railing, watching the activity on the
dock, seeking familiar faces as they waited for the gangplank to be raised and permission given to go ashore.

Roland stood head and shoulders above the rest of
the crowd on the dock, dressed in his high-collared, white
suit. He waved to Margaret, who was holding their son
Philip's hand as the two year old jumped up and down at
the excitement of it all. Holding the boy's other hand was
Margaret's sister, Bette.

Although there was a family resemblance, Bette dif-
fered from her sister in that she was shorter and curvier

with long, thick hair which the breeze blew about her shoulders. Bette wore a sundress and looked younger than her twenty years. Margaret was wearing a smart suit and a small jaunty hat. Margaret usually tended to dress rather formally, especially since discovering the local tailor with his swathes of Indian silks and Egyptian fine cottons. She ordered fashion magazines that arrived regularly and designs from them were quickly copied by her tailor. Margaret acknowledged that she sometimes overdressed, but she felt that there was a standard to maintain in being Mrs Roland Elliott of Utopia plantation, especially as their busy social life seemed to demand an up-to-date wardrobe. It was an indulgence she said was justified and she rarely asked for anything for the house any more after an initial flurry of curtain and cushion making. Even the baby's room had been kept somewhat basic. Margaret, however, did not extend the same restraint to her garden, which she loved. She had designed it herself and made sure that it was attended each day by the gardener. It had started to look quite beautiful.

The gangplank was in place and Roland smiled as he watched his son drop his mother's hand and dart between adults, dragging Bette with him as he forged his way to the bottom.

Roland caught him and swung him high in the air. 'Hello, young man. My, how you've grown! Did you miss your papa?'

In reply the little boy flung his arms around Roland's neck, squeezing him tight.

Roland held out his hand to Bette. 'Lovely to meet you, Bette. How was the trip?'

'Wonderful. I'm so excited to be here. I think Philip has missed you.' She turned to look for Margaret. 'I must help Margie. Goodness knows where our bags have gone.'

'They'll be fine. Despite the apparent chaos, there is

a system to all this. Hamid will sort out things. Hello, my dear.' He untangled Philip and balanced him on his hip as Margaret caught up with them. He embraced Margaret and kissed her lightly on the mouth. 'Good trip? The boy was good?'

'Spoiled rotten. But everyone thought him splendid. It will be good to get him back into a routine at home, though. Three months in Brisbane was too long to be away. I certainly missed the amah's help,' she added. 'You've met Bette?'

'Yes. We can talk in the car. Hamid will get the luggage. Let's get out of this crush. This must be a bit overwhelming for you, Bette.' Roland led the way with Philip now riding on his shoulders.

'I'm so excited to be here. This is so exotic,' said Bette. 'All the hustle and bustle, not as big as Singapore, but just as colourful.'

Roland glanced at her bright eyes and happy smile as she gazed about. 'There's lots more to see. Let's start with a cold drink before we start our journey,' he said. Margaret linked her arm through Roland's as they walked along the dock.

'How was everything in Brisbane? Your family is well? They must have enjoyed having Philip around. We all missed having him about the place here.'

'He was the centre of attention. But it's been tiring managing him on my own. Bette helped of course. Mother enjoyed the bedtime story and cooked him cakes and biscuits. The activity helped keep Father distracted. He pours over the newspapers and listens to the radio all the time. He's terribly concerned about the war in Europe, as is everyone else at home.'

Roland glanced back at Bette. 'Yes. It's very worrying.'

'But surely we're fine here. The war will never touch Malaya,' said Margaret firmly.

Roland didn't look as convinced as his wife, but turned to Bette. 'So this is your birthday trip? The war in Europe certainly changed any plans you might have had about going there, like Margaret did.'

'Oh, I wouldn't have gone to Europe anyway. I've wanted to come here, to the East, for ages. Margaret's letters home make it sound so fascinating.'

'Then we'll try our best to keep you entertained,' said Roland.

'You don't have to do that. I'm quite good at entertaining myself,' said Bette cheerfully.

'She wants to go into the jungle,' said Margaret with a small smile. 'I've told her that's a foolish idea. She'll understand why when she gets there.'

'We've invited some of the neighbours over for a big curry tiffin on Sunday, to meet Bette and welcome you home. The club hasn't been as much fun these past few months without you, and I've been losing badly at bridge without my best partner.'

'You play bridge now?' Bette asked. 'How clever of you, Margie.'

'One has to keep one's end up. It's very popular here.'

Bette sat in the back of the Oldsmobile with Margaret and Philip.

'There's not a lot to see,' warned Margaret. 'Endless jungle, plantations and a few villages. A small town or two.'

'But that's exactly what I want to see,' said Bette. 'I've brought my sketchpads and watercolours. I just know I'm going to love being here.' She glanced at her sister. 'Thanks so much for inviting me. And you too, Roland.'

'It's lovely for Margaret to have your company. And fun for Philip.' He glanced back at the boy. 'You going to show Aunt Bette your favourite toys, eh, young man?'

'Bet-Bet . . . play,' said Philip enthusiastically.

'Oh goody,' said Bette. 'Do you have any pets?'

'Ah, that's a moot point,' smiled Roland.

'Roland, I asked you to get rid of those animals while we were away,' said Margaret.

'It's tricky to boss a macaque around,' said Roland.

'A who?' asked Bette.

'A very mischievous monkey. Don't encourage them, they become pests,' said Margaret.

'Did you have pets when you grew up here?' Bette asked Roland as they drove along the old trunk road towards Slim River.

'I certainly did. I even kept a python for awhile, until feeding it became an issue and Mother made me release it.'

'Ugh. There are enough animals in the wild without encouraging them around the house,' said Margaret.

'What fun,' said Bette.

'Are you always so enthusiastic about things?' Roland asked Bette with a smile.

Before Bette could answer, Margaret chipped in, 'Mother calls her our little Miss Sunshine. I call her Pollyanna. Really, if Bette can find a good side to a bad situation she will.'

Bette merely smiled and began asking Roland questions about the plantation. How was the rubber collected, what did the workers do, where did they come from, how did they live? She asked how and why Roland's father had come to Malaya. What was his childhood like at Utopia? Would Philip have the same experiences?

Margaret closed her eyes and Philip put his head in her lap and slept. But Margaret was listening to the long exchanges between Roland and Bette and learned more about her husband's history than she'd known previously.

Bette kept in the background when they arrived at Utopia. Everyone was fussing over Philip, who raced around. Eugene kissed Margaret on the cheek before she introduced him to her sister.

'Very nice to meet you, young lady. I hope you enjoy your stay with us,' he said, rather formally.

But Bette's effusive and genuine responses soon had the old man smiling broadly.

Margaret called Philip from Kim's embrace. 'Bette, this is Roland's old amah. She thinks she owns Roland, and now, I suspect that she thinks the same about Philip. We'll take you over to our bungalow so that you can settle in. We'll see Mr Elliott again later for drinks at sunset.'

'Really? How lovely.'

At Margaret and Roland's bungalow, Ah Kit showed Bette to her room while Margaret went to inspect her garden and Philip trailed behind his father. When Bette had washed and changed her travelling clothes, she stood on the verandah looking out at the view.

Margaret joined her and sat down in one of the wicker chairs, sighing. 'Really, these people do let things go the minute your back is turned. I've lost several shrubs. And the weeds! Thankfully the kitchen garden seems all right. I suspect Cookie keeps an eye on that because vegetables are more useful than flowers.'

Bette turned to her sister. 'Margie, this is magical. Magnificent. Out there . . . total jungle up on those hills. It's such a wildly romantic setting.'

'Wild is right,' said Margaret. 'I've had one experience wandering through the forest. No more. And I was close to civilisation, but I still felt ill at ease.'

'I'd so love to get out there. Do you think Roland could arrange it? You wrote about the hunting trips he and his father used to make . . .'

'Bette! You don't know how to use a gun.'

'I don't mean to go shooting. Just to go and see the wilderness, experience it all. I'd love to sketch the jungle and the birds and other wildlife, and scenes in the villages, like those we passed.'

'They're called kampongs. Whatever for? Just relax, Bette. You'll find there are plenty of other things to do here. We'll go to our club, at least a couple of times each week for tennis and cards, and there will be lots of parties at the other plantations. There are heaps of single men for you to meet, but you must be careful and not get too carried away with all the attention. Be guided by Roland as to whom is suitable,' advised Margaret.

'I'm not looking for a husband!' exclaimed Bette. 'I'll just hang around Eugene. I bet he has a million stories.'

'Mr Elliott,' said Margaret firmly. 'Bette, don't get carried away. It's not becoming to be so gung-ho. This is, after all, just a pocket, an oasis, if you like, of civilisation in a very primitive setting.'

'That's what I like,' said Bette. 'I should have been a Victorian lady explorer.'

'What rubbish,' said Margaret. 'Why don't you have a rest before we go to the big house for drinks.'

'I'd rather take a walk around the garden with Philip. You said that he had a swing, didn't you?'

'Well, don't get all hot and bothered before we go over to the big house,' said Margaret.

Within days, word had spread through the district among the single assistant plantation managers, army officers and young men from the civil service of the arrival of a pretty, single young woman. Attendance at the club swelled. Bette was in demand as a partner for tennis, card games and dances. She was squired around the district to picnics, into Slim River, and on other sightseeing forays by a series of young men. Everyone seemed to find her delightful company, with her ready laugh and happy nature.

Margaret was pleased that her sister was so popular, but she was also protective. Roland was amused and enjoyed teasing Bette about the young men who had found their way to Utopia, but he was careful to pay attention to make sure that the men were the right type.

Bette told Margaret how much she enjoyed being with her and doing things together that they hadn't done since they were children. Their age difference and the fact that Margaret had left home while Bette was still at school hadn't given them a chance to be young women together. Now, dressing for the rounds of social events, even casual occasions, Margaret remembered the rainy days she and Bette had spent playing dress-ups in Winifred's cast-off clothes. Bette also reminded Margaret about the board games they'd played on Sunday evenings and when she found an old collection of Roland's puzzles and games in a bookcase, she suggested that they teach Philip a simple game like snakes and ladders.

'Oh, he's far too young. He'd rather play marbles with the amah,' replied Margaret.

'I just thought it would be fun to play a game with him. Like we used to. Remember rainy days and Sunday nights after dinner?'

'Yes. Try it if you want to. I have some crochet I want to do this afternoon.'

So Bette played with Philip at the table on the verandah, teaching him numbers and colours and letting him draw pictures with her. Just the same, she had to admit that Philip seemed just as happy playing with Ah Min, his amah, and even the laundry girl. Indeed, it seemed that there was little for Margaret to do with Philip, except to kiss him in the morning and before bed at night.

As Bette's visit lengthened, it became clear to both Margaret and Roland that, as well as being the party-loving sister from Australia, she had a serious side to her nature. They both found Bette very self-possessed. She liked her own company as well as being sociable. It was at these times that she stole away with her sketchbook to sit quietly and draw scenes, people and daily life around the plantation.

Bette had also taken to walking to Eugene's big house, when invited, rather than driving there with Margaret and Roland. She said that she found the twenty minute walk along the narrow dirt road through trees and cleared ground always interesting.

But the river soon became her favourite place and whenever Eugene or Roland had to go to the smokehouse where the latex was processed, or the supply store, they'd take Bette with them. She'd sit in the shade, on the riverbank with her drawing book, and do charcoal or finely detailed pencil sketches.

Once, when she walked further along the bank, she saw a crocodile surface in the middle of the river and then drift on the current, like a knotted old log, its eyes focused on her. She hurried back towards the wharf and told Roland.

'I told you not to go too far downstream. A child from one of the villages was taken a few weeks ago,' he said.

'Margaret said there was a swimming spot somewhere. Is that safe?' asked Bette.

'It's a bit of a trek upriver. Dad had a pagar set up in the river for swimming where a lodge had already been built. A pagar is an area fenced off by bamboo so you're protected from the crocs. Quite a nice spot. The grass is cut down by the riverbank, and there are big shady trees. Great place to escape the heat. I haven't taken Philip there yet. Maybe it's time I did an inspection in the area, as we're now experimenting with palm oil and we've got a new assistant manager in that section. The pagar's out in the middle of the jungle because not much of the land has been cleared, so the accommodation at the lodge is very basic, just a big verandah and half-a-dozen or so beds.'

'Sounds exciting. I'd love to do that.'

Roland floated the idea past Margaret but she wasn't keen on going up-country just then because of the forthcoming Penang race meeting.

'We'll definitely do it before you go back to Australia. We still have a couple of months to get to the pool, but Margaret's right. Penang first. You'll enjoy that, too. Interesting old city,' said Roland.

Bette had never been to the races before, so had no comparison, but it didn't matter because she found the whole day utterly fascinating and fun. Margaret seemed more interested in people and the new Penang Turf Club than in the horses. Everyone was dressed smartly, even flamboyantly, and was out to have a good time. Roland and Eugene seemed to know everyone and there was a lot of socialising in the clubhouse and on the terrace and lawns before each race.

Roland introduced Bette and Margaret to a striking looking Chinese couple, Tony Tsang and his beautiful wife Mai Ling. Both were quite tall, very attractive and dressed immaculately. Tony Tsang wore a white suit and his wife was in a silk cheongsam. Her sleek dark hair was pulled up into a chignon held up with a jewelled pin and she wore exquisite jewellery of jade and diamonds.

'Tony and I were at university together,' said Roland.

'And you live in Penang? asked Bette.

'I'm in the family business,' said Tony.

'He's the smart one. Sits in an office and doesn't have to trudge around plantations,' said Roland affably.

Later, Roland explained to Margaret and Bette that Tony and Mai Ling came from what were known as Peranakan families. Their ancestors had come to the Malaccan Straits from China in the seventeenth and eighteenth centuries and, because they were now born locally and weren't new immigrants, they were called Peranakan.

The men were referred to as baba, while the women were called nyonya. This community was very loyal to the British, because the law and order the British imposed on the colony meant that their livelihoods were secure, but they also adopted some of the ways and dress of the Malays. The basis of their wealth came originally from the sea trade their ancestors had established throughout South East Asia and many of the families were very wealthy. Mai Ling was a nyonya from a rich family that originally came from Hokkien. Tony's family were among those Straits elite who decided that the best way forward for their families was to have their sons educated in England, and Tony had made his family very proud by winning a scholarship to Cambridge. He was, Roland assured the sisters, a very progressive businessman.

'He certainly must be,' said Margaret, quietly to Bette, 'if Mai Ling's beautiful jewellery is anything to go by.'

'Malaya is certainly a mix of races, isn't it, Roland?' commented Bette.

Coming from an Anglo Saxon middle-class background, with little exposure to such diversity, Bette found it all fascinating and exotic. 'I mean, there are native Malays, the Chinese, the Tamils from India who work on the plantation and Europeans. Your plantation seems to be a microcosm of this mix. Where do your workers come from?'

'Heavens, Margaret, your sister is inquisitive. You never asked me these kinds of questions. Well, there is a household hierarchy. The Chinese houseboy, Ah Kit is number one in my house. The amahs are also Chinese. They are usually single women who devote themselves to the family. Kim, my old amah, still works for Father. Ah Min, Philip's amah, is relatively young. Most of the menial work is done by Indians. The coolies who work on our plantation are Tamils while our guards tend to be

Sikhs. The majority of Europeans have Malays as drivers, but Father would never have anyone except Hamid. I grew up with him and we used to play together when we were young.'

'So loyalty is a two-way street,' said Bette, thoughtfully.

The Tsangs had several horses running and they invited the sisters to go and see their stables. Margaret, who was sitting with a group of ladies dressed in hats, gloves and very high heels, sipping champagne beneath a vine covered trellis at the edge of a terrace, accepted the invitation and the two followed the Tsangs to the stables.

'Do you ride?' Tony asked the two women.

'I had lessons when I was young, in my pony club phase,' said Bette. 'But I haven't had the opportunity since then. Actually, I'd rather like to try again.'

'It's quite popular here. There are a lot of equestrian clubs in the highlands where it's cool for the horses. Tony and Roland are excellent riders and polo players,' said Mai Ling in a very clipped British accent.

'I'd love to watch them some time,' said Bette.

'Me too,' said Margaret. 'I had no idea that Roland was a good rider.'

'Well, we'll have to arrange an exhibition for you ladies,' said Tony Tsang. 'Now I think I'll place a bet or two. Have to show my faith in my own horses, right?'

That evening after the races, Bette, the Elliotts and their friends dined at the E&O hotel. The elegant white building on the seafront was packed with partygoers, formally dressed and enjoying the opulent surroundings. Seated on the terrace verandah under a starry sky as the moon rose over the fronds of tall palm trees, the water lapping against the seawall, Bette whispered to Margaret, 'This is so romantic. It's like a scene in a film at the pictures!'

Margaret gave a satisfied smile. 'This is life out here. We're very lucky.'

Seated around a large round table, their group was served lavish food, including strawberries flown in from Australia and French champagne. After covering the race day events, the talk turned to the war in Europe.

Lighting a cigar, one of the well-known rubber planters commented, 'The Nazi invasion of France has been a disaster. I would love to go and fight for England but, of course, we have to stay to make sure that the rubber production continues.'

'It must be dreadful living at home now. Of course, it is much worse in France and the Low Countries. No one would want to see their country invaded,' replied a woman opposite Margaret.

'Did you hear how Peggy Harrison went to England to get her children out? They had to travel across the Atlantic to Canada on a blacked-out ship, and then set out to Vancouver by train and then take another ship across the Pacific to get to Malaya. It was very brave,' said the planter's wife.

'Of course, it must be awful for those parents who can't get their school children out of England,' said another of the guests.

'I'm afraid that Charlotte is still there,' said Eugene. 'I would so love her to come here where it's safe, but she has to stay with her parents. She can hardly leave them at a time like this.'

'I'm not that sure that we are all that safe,' said Roland.

His comments were immediately howled down.

'Who are we going to fight in Malaya?' asked a red-faced man sitting next to Bette. 'It won't be the Germans.'

Roland gave him a quizzical look. 'I think that we'll have trouble with the Japanese.'

'Nonsense, old boy. Everyone knows that the Japanese are short-sighted. They won't be able to see us. And besides, their planes are rubbish, can't fly,' boomed one of them, setting off a ripple of laughter round the table.

'Well,' said Roland. 'The Japanese have been very aggressive in China. They want to expand their empire, reach the oil in the Dutch East Indies and what's to stop them?'

One of the women scoffed at the suggestion. 'What about the British Navy? Everyone knows that we will be protected because the rubber supplies have to be maintained. Lord knows it's about time that we started to make some money out of rubber. The last few years have been lean and now the war has meant that the good times are here for us, finally.'

Margaret was somewhat irked by Roland's remarks. As far as she was concerned, they were all doing their bit for the war effort in England and Roland should not be making such unsettling comments. She was knitting like mad. In fact, in Perak, there was a network of knitters and several hundred garments had already been created and sent to England for the soldiers.

'We're doing our bit,' she said.

'That's true,' replied another woman. 'The Patriotic Fund organises lots of mah jong parties and afternoon teas to raise money, but I think that the administration should be looking at doing more to defend us, if the need arose.'

'The Chinese community has raised a lot of money, too. It's not just the British who are doing the right thing,' commented Tony Tsang.

Roland began to look exasperated. 'Look, I know that a lot of what I'm saying isn't generally accepted because the authorities are often busy covering up things that they don't want made public, but there are suspicious things happening. I have heard, more than once, that the Japanese have been measuring our beaches, swamps and jungles for some time. Why would they do that?'

'Who knows?' replied the planter beside Margaret. 'But our enemy is Germany, not the Japs and, as my wife says, we've got the navy.'

'Well,' said Roland. 'I don't think that's enough. I think we need professional troops on the ground, a lot more than the volunteers that we have training now. If you ask me, we're all too complacent and sometime in the near future we're going to be very sorry that we have been.'

Margaret attempted to change the conversation. 'Oh, Roland, you really are a wet blanket. We've had a wonderful day and we're here with good friends, can't you think of something happier to talk about?'

Roland gave a small shrug and smiled at his wife. 'Tell me, what plans have you got for tomorrow?'

'Yes, Margaret, what are we doing?' asked Bette.

Margaret and several ladies had planned to go shopping the following day and Bette agreed to go along.

'Though I'm more interested in seeing the city than the markets and the jewellers and tailors,' Bette confided to Eugene Elliott.

'Then come with me, dear girl. I'm visiting a few old friends, a few business calls in George Town. You're quite welcome.'

'I won't be in the way?'

Eugene shook his head. 'I'll enjoy your company. You might want to bring that sketchbook of yours.'

When Margaret heard of their plan she decided to join them too, as she said to Bette, 'He is my father-in-law.'

And so the sisters were shown parts of the old capital that even Margaret, who had been to Penang a few times, didn't know existed. Bette was intrigued by Eugene's intimate knowledge of George Town.

'Penang was part of the kingdom of Kedah but became a British trading post in the late eighteenth century when

Captain Light landed at the fort and claimed the island for the East India Company,' Eugene told them, as Hamid drove along Light Street. 'The story goes that, to clear the land, he had a canon filled with coins and fired it into the jungle. In the rush to find the coins the natives cut down the jungle in record time and so George Town was founded. See that little fenced-off corner under the frangipani trees? That's where Light's buried. The Christian cemetery. Looks a bit neglected, I'm afraid.'

'This doesn't look as organised, or planned, as Singapore,' said Bette. 'I like the way the streets spill out in every direction.'

'A lot of the streets were allotted to particular groups: the Chinese traders, the Eurasians, Europeans, Indians, and later Armenians, Achenese and Sumatrans. And you see their cultures in the street. You could spend a day going around to the various temples, mosques and churches,' said Eugene.

'I do hope I can come back here,' said Bette. 'I could walk and walk and walk.'

'And you must stop and try all the different foods, so you can keep walking,' said Eugene.

'I don't think I'd like to do that,' said Margaret. 'Surely food cooked on the footpath can't be very hygienic.'

Bette laughed. 'Oh, Margie, where's your spirit of adventure? It sounds like fun.'

Eugene spoke to Hamid, who nodded and turned down a side street.

'Just going to take a small detour,' said Eugene.

They stopped in a narrow street filled with intriguing shops. Eugene got out and went over to a leather shop. He greeted the owner who was standing outside smoking and the two women looked at the small display in the window. Beaded and embroidered shoes and slippers were lined up.

'Look, Margaret, those are the pretty shoes I've seen the Chinese women wear with their cheongsams.'

'The Malay women wear them with their sarong kebayas. You know, some of the Chinese women also wear the sarong kebayas,' said Margaret authoritatively.

'They're just lovely shoes,' said Bette.

'Come inside,' said Eugene as the shop owner hurried ahead, treating Eugene with deference.

'You like see shoes?' The owner bowed to the sisters.

'Show him your foot, Bette,' said Eugene.

Bette was startled as the owner pulled out some larger sized shoes wrapped in brown paper. 'Oh, look at these scuffs!' She fingered the little green silk slip-on sandals, beaded and embroidered with a flower pattern. 'Aren't they beautiful.'

'Try them on,' said Eugene.

'Have leather sole, very strong,' said the shop owner.

'They're gorgeous,' said Bette reaching for her change purse in her bag. 'I must buy them.'

Eugene stopped her hand. 'Allow me this small indulgence. Charlotte is also very fond of these shoes, and they will be something nice for you to take back to Brisbane.' He reached into his pocket as the shopkeeper spoke in rapid Chinese. He may have been trying to negotiate a price, though it seemed to Margaret, he wasn't trying very hard. Clearly he wanted to please Eugene.

'Show them the old shoes,' Eugene instructed.

The shopkeeper pulled out a box and unwrapped some tissue paper to show the women a pair of the tiniest brocade boots they'd ever seen. Each was the length of the palm of Margaret's hand, laced up with leather shoelaces and made with a leather sole.

'They look like doll's shoes,' said Bette.

'This cobbler's shop has been making shoes for the bound feet of Chinese ladies for more than a century,' said

Eugene. 'Terrible practice. Supposed to make the women more attractive, but the bones of the feet were broken and the foot was kept bound so that it couldn't grow. So cruel.'

After they returned to the hotel and the sisters had thanked Eugene for the outing, Margaret listened in silence while Bette told Roland how much they'd enjoyed their morning with Eugene.

'Father has certainly taken to you, Bette. As everyone has. The Oldham girls are quite a hit out here. And how did you enjoy it, Margaret, dear?' asked Roland.

She shrugged. 'Well, I can't say that I was as enthusiastic as Bette. I don't really like those pokey little Chinese shops. I thought it was nice of your father to buy Bette those slippers. He must have known the shopkeeper quite well, because I could tell that the Chinaman didn't want to take any money. Anyway, this afternoon we're off with some of my friends. The Penang girls have such beautiful bungalows. One of them has a beach house at Batu Ferrinhgi. Sounds divine. Roland, perhaps that might be something we could look into – a beach house.'

'No time for beach holidays, my dear. And Utopia's too far away from Penang. We have places where we can relax closer to home.'

'It's not very social,' said Margaret.

'You mean the pagar and jungle cabin you told me about?' said Bette. 'That sounds fun. I mean really exciting and different. Why don't we do that, Margie?' asked Bette.

'I have a small child, Bette. I don't think it's safe to take him out where there are wild animals and unfriendly natives,' retorted Margaret.

'Oh, come on, dear. Philip adores getting out.'

'Roland! It's jungle! With marauding killer beasts of all descriptions,' said Margaret. 'It isn't like a walk in the botanic gardens.'

112

Roland shrugged. 'My son will have to learn to deal with these things. Just as I did.'

'We'll all be there to keep an eye on him. I'd so like to go and see some of the up-country areas,' pleaded Bette. 'It might be my only opportunity, Margie. Oh Lord, there seems so much I haven't seen of this country and time is running out.'

'I always need to go and check out the areas mapped for the expansion of the plantation, talk to the local people, so we might as well all go,' said Roland. 'You ladies could be quite comfortable for a few days if we go up to the pagar. It would certainly give Bette a sense of the real bush country,' said Roland. 'It's still very tribal.'

Margaret rolled her eyes. 'Tribal! That's the last thing we want to see. Headhunters and scary animals. If I had my own transport, I could go where I wanted. I could take Bette to much more interesting places. Like Ipoh.'

Neither Bette nor Roland leapt at the idea.

'Isn't Ipoh a big tin city? I've just been to a city,' said Bette. 'I didn't come all this way to go to the pictures and sit in shops and hotels,' she said, adding carefully, 'Even though I've loved Penang.'

'You'd be surprised by what's in Ipoh. But it's all a moot point as we have no means of getting there. It's simply too hard to get Roland to take us as he's busy and I really can't ask Mr Elliott if we can borrow Hamid and his car all the time. There just has to be a solution.'

No more was said until Gilbert, Roland's friend who'd been best man at the wedding, called in at Utopia.

'I'm going down to look at a small estate. It's a holding that went bankrupt. I bought it from some ex-army officer who was given a land grant after the Great War, and couldn't make a go of it.'

'There are not enough big plantations and I think that too many of those individual holdings are too small

113

to really work, especially when times are tough,' said Roland. 'That's why many are selling out to concerns like ours. As you know, we've amalgamated a few of these small estates into one large outlying division that we're trying to turn over to oil palm.'

'Experimenting, eh?' said Gilbert.

'I think we should be expanding our horizons. Father's not so keen. Wants to hold off until the war situation has sorted itself out, and he might be right in that.'

Over tiffin, they talked about the fun they'd had in Penang at the races and Bette added how much she'd loved the city, saying that she would like to explore it some more. 'Margaret wants to take me to see Ipoh and Taiping as well.'

'Many more interesting places to go than those,' said Gilbert.

'Bette wants to go up-country. See the wildlife,' said Roland.

'That sounds good. Do you still have that old lodge and pagar your father built upriver? That'd be the place to go,' said Gilbert. 'Bette would enjoy that.'

'I suppose we could go,' said Margaret. 'But I'd still like to take her around a bit more. I so wish we had another car.' She sighed. 'I've asked Roland for one for ages, so that I can be independent, but you know how everything that is earned is ploughed back into the plantation.'

Before Roland could say anything, Gilbert slapped his knee. 'By Jove, Henderson's going to Australia. His wife has a bee in her bonnet about the Japs making some sort of a move here, so he's selling off everything. First to go is his wife's car, a Baby Austin Tourer. Nifty little thing. Perfectly good nick, I believe, and he'll take whatever he can get for it.'

Margaret's eyes lit up. 'Oh, Roland! Couldn't we buy it? Think how much easier it would be for Bette and I to get around!'

'We could have all kinds of little adventures, Margaret!' added Bette.

Gilbert laughed. 'Your little adventures could get you into a spot of bother. Can't have two ladies taking off on their own into the wilds.'

'Not the wilds,' protested Margaret, but her eyes were shining as she looked at Roland.

'I'll think about it,' he said.

'Well, if Bette is so keen to see up-country, why don't we take her up to the pagar? Bit of a picnic, a swim. Stay a couple of nights. Be a nice break for me before I have to head back,' said Gilbert.

'Oh, Gilbert, what a wonderful idea,' said Bette. 'How about it, Margaret?'

They set off early the following morning, after Roland had done the six am muster of the plantation workers. Roland was looking forward to seeing how the palm oil on the newest part of the plantation was progressing but for the others the expedition was an exciting break, and they were all cheery as they set off.

They travelled in the big Oldsmobile with Roland driving, Gilbert beside him and Bette and Margaret in the back with Philip between them. They sang songs and Gilbert taught the sisters a Malay song.

'How come you know so much?' Bette asked him. 'You haven't been out here very long, have you?'

'I like to spend time with the local families. It helps to keep the workers on side and makes running the plantation smoother. Most of the coolies like to stay put and send back money to their families in India or China, so I like to make it easy for them to do so.'

'Maybe if they had better facilities and it felt more like they were putting down roots they'd be happier,' said Bette.

Gilbert glanced at her. 'I say, that's quite perceptive.'

'Do you like working here?' asked Bette.

115

'When Roland suggested I apply to manage a plantation I thought it would be fun, but the work can be quite punishing. You're on call every day from dawn until dark. Unless it rains. Don't you love waking to the sound of torrential rain, Roland?' Gilbert grinned.

'It's a lovely sound,' agreed Bette.

'No, he means he can sleep in,' said Margaret. 'Too wet to tap the trees.'

'So what does an assistant manager do? Are you out in the field all day?' asked Bette. Gilbert was younger than Roland. While his family lived in England and had no holdings in Malaya, and he knew nothing about rubber, he had decided to take the job that Roland had suggested because it sounded so interesting and challenging.

'Dawn to dusk,' he said. 'Checking on the slashing, clearing, planting and tapping that the coolies do on the plantation. And that's before we get to sell the stuff. And there always seems to be some hullabaloo happening between the different tappers, coolies and their families. Accidents, fights, sickness. Still, it's never dull. And I rather like exploring my divisions. Quite pretty country. We have a lot of streams running down from the jungle. Rugged though. I'm lucky, too. The manager's a good chap, lets me get away a bit.'

Margaret glanced at Bette and nudged her, indicating Gilbert with a questioning look. Bette smiled and shook her head. But they both stifled a giggle.

Roland drove the car steadily towards the hills, and then turned off and headed along a cleared grassy track towards the river. At the water's edge beside a small kampong was a boat landing. From one of the huts came a Malay, who took them over to a long open wooden boat with an exposed engine in its centre.

'How far are we going in that boat?' asked Bette as they walked over to it.

'Not very far. It's the best way to get to the pagar,' said Roland. 'Usually when we come up here we drive along the road through the plantation, but it's much longer and not very interesting.'

'I have to say that this looks fun. Just as well we brought sunhats.'

'We have umbrellas, too, if you want them,' said Roland.

'Come on, Philip, let's go and see the boat,' said Margaret.

'I don't suppose there is a problem with crocodiles,' said Bette, remembering her earlier encounter.

'No, it's fine,' said Roland. He spoke to the boatman, and another bare-chested man, wearing a checked cotton baju, sauntered over to them. Roland had them both unload the car and pile their belongings into the boat. Then he explained, 'We're leaving the car here. It'll be safe with the villagers.'

The man in the baju nodded. 'Yes, tuan.'

They all enjoyed chugging through the thick brown water, the wind in their faces, hats protecting them from the sun. Passing a village at the water's edge they waved to the children, who waved back. As they got near to where the jungle grew close to the river's edge, the water became clearer. The boatman angled the boat towards the bank and rounding a bend they came to a cleared area under shady trees. There was an attap hut with a verandah and a thatched lean-to over a large table. Next to the landing bamboo poles jutted above the surface of the water and made a fence that staked out the swimming area.

'This is just beautiful,' said Bette to Margaret.

The boatman, helped by Roland and Gilbert, hauled out the picnic baskets and cotton bags containing their clothes and put them in the shade of the table, while Roland opened up the little hut.

117

'Basic change room, a water jar to rinse off, and thunder box.'

'I'm going in for a swim! Coming Philip?' Bette pulled off her sundress, which she'd worn over her swimming costume.

'I'll be there in a minute, too. I'm going to change in the hut,' said Margaret.

Holding Philip's hand, Bette walked to the water's edge and peered into the cool clear water. 'Looks safe enough. It certainly looks refreshing.'

Gilbert came up behind them, and swung Philip onto his shoulders. 'Come on, young man, let's jump in!'

'Be careful,' called Margaret as she followed them to the river.

Gilbert waded in and with Philip clinging to his back, arms tight around his neck, he swam out into the river, followed closely by Bette.

'This is glorious! Come on in, Marg!' shouted Bette.

Roland soon joined them, and they all splashed and played and Philip, now feeling brave, tried to swim, but needed a lot of help. Everyone applauded his efforts.

On the bank the boatman had started a small fire and began cooking savoury meat on skewers, turning the sizzling meat and dribbling peanut and coconut sauce over them.

While Margaret and Roland dried Philip, Bette and Gilbert spread towels and sarongs on the grass and dried off in the sun.

'They seem to be getting on well,' Margaret said quietly to Roland. 'Do you think they like each other? I mean, are they attracted to each other?'

'Early days, dear girl.'

'Wouldn't it be nice if Bette met someone and stayed out here. It would be lovely to have some of my family around,' said Margaret.

'Well, there's been no shortage of interested chaps,' said Roland. 'But Gilbert still has a couple more years of his contract to run before the company will let him get married.'

'I think that's such a dreadful restriction,' said Margaret. 'I can't believe that companies dictate when their employees can get married.'

'Not really. It's sensible. Men have to prove that they have what it takes to work on a plantation before a company goes to the expense of paying a wife's fare out here. The single men can be flexible and live in pretty basic accommodation. That changes when they get married, so companies have to make sure the chaps are the right sort. It's paying one's dues, as Father says.'

Margaret watched Gilbert and Bette lying side by side and talking. 'Perhaps I'd better make Bette aware of his situation before she falls too heavily for him,' murmured Margaret.

'I don't think she's very serious about anyone . . . she just loves being here, though I have to admit she's the perfect kind of a girl to fit in out here. Like you.' He gave her a quick kiss and picked up Philip. 'Come on, soldier, let's go eat. I'm starving.'

They sat on the grass in the shade eating the satay sticks with their fingers.

The next two days were ones they all remembered for the rest of their lives. Roland was right. The lodge that Eugene had built years before was only basic, but the setting was perfect.

Local villagers cooked them curries, rice and fish. They had pineapples, bananas and papaya for breakfast. With simple food and simple surroundings, the lazy days passed gently. Swimming, afternoons spent sleeping in a hammock, playing board games and talking into the night by kerosene lamplight, sharing a bottle of whisky, and sometimes just sitting in companionable silence. Philip slept curled between his mother and father under the cloud of mosquito net. Bette tried to stay awake as long as she could, listening to the night sounds of the forest.

Both women enjoyed Gilbert's company. They found him amusing and easy going. Because he was Roland's friend, he seemed to treat Bette as though she was the younger sister of his best friend's wife, and as a result Bette relaxed and didn't worry about what sort of impression she was making or how she looked. Margaret also eschewed make-up and didn't fuss about what she wore. The two sisters dressed in sarongs over shorts and swimsuits and found they were reminiscing and laughing more than they ever had. Everyone felt comfortable in each other's company.

On their third morning, Roland announced that he'd better to do some work. 'Sorry, but I did come up here to see how the new palm oil plantation is going. Who wants to come along?'

Everyone was lazing along the verandah so there wasn't an immediate flurry of interest.

'Gilbert and I were just about to hike down to where one of the villagers told us there's a little waterfall,' said Bette.

'Who's managing the place for you?' asked Gilbert.

'Smedley-Smith. Frightfully good chap. I'm very pleased with him. It's his first contract, but he's made some remarkable advances for us,' said Roland.

'He mightn't take too kindly to my arriving with you unannounced. Really none of my business,' said Gilbert.

'All right, Gil. You stay with Bette and find the waterfall. I'll take Margaret and Philip with me.' He turned to Margaret. 'You haven't been up to the place for awhile. I think you'll be impressed with what he's done.'

Margaret smiled to her husband as they took the boat back to the small kampong where they had left the Oldsmobile. 'Nice manoeuvre, dear. Leaving them alone in a romantic spot. I wonder how Bette feels about that.'

'Gilbert is a gentleman, she'll be safe as houses.'

'Hmm. We'll see. Well it's up to Bette.'

'Gil's a good chap, but do you really think that your parents would like Bette to end up in Malaya, too?'

As Margaret got into the car, she remembered her mother had joked that she hoped Bette wouldn't fall for some planter fellow too, so she let the subject drop and concentrated on trying to stay comfortable on the bone jarring road. Philip bounced, enjoying the ride.

Roland drove past the deep dark rows of the oil palms arching towards each other, making long dark tunnels. Mounds of large red prickly nuts were heaped at regular intervals along the ground. Roland stopped, got out and picked up several of the nuts to check them and got back into the car. Then he turned off the dirt track and drove slowly up and down through some of the avenues of trees.

'Hmm. It's well cleared and maintained. Smedley-Smith is doing a good job. We'll drive by the bungalow. He's probably there having lunch and might welcome some company. Gets lonely up here by oneself.'

'It's rather basic housing,' commented Margaret as she saw the small bungalow. A not very successful attempt had been made to establish a garden.

As they walked towards the house, a lanky young man wearing a khaki shirt over a sarong came out to meet them.

'Ha, Mr Elliott, you've arrived. What a pleasant surprise. Excuse my dress, I was having a rest before the afternoon inspection. Please, come in and make yourself comfortable while I change. Tea? Or a soft drink?'

'Ask your boy to get us some ginger beer, and we'll sit on the verandah,' said Roland.

Margaret knew how fortunate they were to be living at Utopia, and not in a tiny house like this, equipped only with simple rattan furniture, and no trimmings, in absolutely the middle of nowhere. She heard glasses rattling, and while Roland was showing Philip a small gecko that was clinging to one of the chick blinds, Margaret went inside.

A pretty, young Malay girl came towards her with a tray of glasses and a large bottle of ginger beer and pieces of fresh lime. To Margaret's surprise the girl handed her the tray and scurried out of the room as Smedley-Smith reappeared in a planter's cotton suit, buttoned to the neck, and leather shoes.

Margaret returned to the verandah, but despite the lowered blinds and fan, she was hot as she listened to the two men talking about the plantation, while Philip was clearly bored.

'I'm very hot here. I'll take a little stroll outside under the trees. Come on, Philip,' she said.

It wasn't long until Roland emerged from the bungalow, followed by Smedley-Smith, who had donned a solar topee. The assistant manager shook Margaret's hand and said goodbye to both the Elliotts, before jumping on an ancient bicycle and pedalling away along the rutted plantation paths.

'That was all very satisfactory,' said Roland as they drove away.

'Roland! You have to get rid of that young man. It's disgusting.'

'What do you mean? The fact we caught him having an afternoon nap? No harm in that. In fact, I think it's a good idea.'

'No. That young Malay girl. She's living with him,' said Margaret.

122

'Nonsense. That's not on. Not allowed. She's just a housegirl from the local kampong.'

'She might be. But she's also living there,' said Margaret firmly. 'When I was walking outside I passed his bedroom and I saw her clothes in there. When I asked her why they were there, she got very embarrassed and ran away.'

Roland paused. 'Well, it's not an uncommon situation, Margaret. It gets pretty lonely way out here. Hard for a young man to be on his own all the time.'

'Then why do all the big companies forbid their single white staff from fraternising with local women? If Smedley-Smith was working for one of them and they found out what he was doing they'd ship him home. Anyway, what would your father say if he knew?'

'He wouldn't like it,' admitted Roland. 'But we are a family concern and I can bend the rules a bit.'

'Your father wouldn't. He'll send him off once he knows,' said Margaret.

'Margaret, Father is not going to know. Smedley-Smith is an excellent worker and I simply can't replace him. There's a war on in Europe, in case you've forgotten, so where do I get someone else to take his place?'

Margaret stared at Roland. 'So you're going to let this situation persist? And are you telling me not to say anything about it?'

'Yes, I am. I have to be practical.'

Margaret was quiet a moment then said briskly, 'Well, if that's the way it is, I'll strike a bargain with you. I won't mention this situation to your father . . . but in exchange I think you should get me that Baby Austin car that Gilbert told you about.'

'Margaret! That's blackmail,' exploded Roland but just the same he sounded amused by her cheek as they got into the car.

Margaret stared out the window. 'I'm so looking

forward to driving Bette around and showing her a few new places in my own car.'

Roland said, 'Well, I hope you girls enjoy Ipoh.'

When they pulled up back at the lodge, Margaret marched up the front steps and stopped as she saw Bette stretched out on a sarong on the floor of the verandah in her swimsuit and Gilbert bending over her, his face close to her bare leg.

'What on earth is going on?' she demanded.

Gilbert straightened up and held up a jar. 'Leeches, I'm afraid. We're covered in them.'

'Ugh. I hate those things,' said Margaret.

'I'll get the salt,' said Roland. 'That gets rid of them.'

True to his word, Roland bought the Baby Austin Tourer for Margaret, and Gilbert drove it to Utopia from Kuala Lumpur.

'I'll drive Gilbert back up to KL in the Oldsmobile, as we have to attend a planters' meeting,' Roland told Margaret.

'Roland, the car is gorgeous. It will be so useful, thank you, darling,' said Margaret, experimenting with the fold-down roof.

'A deal's a deal,' grinned Roland. 'Father agreed, when I told him that I'd bought it. Said he didn't want women stranded here with no transport, especially as I'm moving around a lot more these days.'

'Gilbert, can you entertain Bette? I won't be long. I just want to savour my independence and get used to driving the car before I take passengers.'

'I love the shape and the open roof. It can fit four passengers, too,' exclaimed Bette as Margaret took the key from Gilbert.

'It's been checked out, and it's as sound as a bell. I had

no trouble driving it here,' said Gilbert. 'So, Roland, we'll leave early tomorrow morning for the meeting then?'

'Yes. And thanks for bringing the car. Bette, make sure Margaret doesn't drive too far until she's familiar with it,' said Roland.

'She's a good driver. What meeting are you going to?' asked Bette. 'Aren't you going too, Margaret?'

'I don't think Margaret would be all that interested. My friends are telling me there is talk of Malays in the countryside aligning themselves with the communists,' said Roland. 'These communists are a loose, somewhat unstructured group and usually they have been in the big towns. Communist alliances in the countryside will destabilise the local communities and plantations, so there's an extraordinary meeting of the Planters' Association to see what can be done about it. With the war favourably affecting exports, we have to make sure that these communist groups don't upset the applecart.'

Bette stared at Roland in alarm. 'So it could be trouble for the plantation, then?'

'I shouldn't think so, but best to be on top of things,' said Gilbert.

'I still think we should have a few more precautions in place other than what the government here is doing,' said Roland.

Gilbert wrapped his arm around Bette's shoulder. 'Keep smiling, Bette. Next time I come back what say we go into Taiping for a day, go to the pictures, have a slap-up meal?'

'Sounds fun. I'll look forward to it.'

'Well, I'm taking the car for a drive around the estate. See you in half an hour,' said Margaret gaily, as she drove off in her little Austin Tourer over the bumpy roads of the plantation.

*

The two men left for Kuala Lumpur early the next morning and Margaret insisted on driving her new car over to show Eugene.

'I know you like walking over there, Bette, but come with me for a change. You must know every tree on the estate by now.'

'Not quite, but I do enjoy the silence and the smells and the scenery.'

'Well, I think it's time for a sisterly talk. What do you think about Gilbert?'

'That's a pretty direct question. Let me see,' Bette replied. 'He's a nice man. I think he would be steady and reliable. He's quietly amusing, too. Different from other men I know who always laugh uproariously at their own jokes. Gil is not too competitive, either. He's a good tennis player, but he seems happy to fool around and make me laugh and he lets me win. I like that.'

'I hate it when people hold back and don't play properly,' said Margaret.

'Yes, and then you hate it when you don't win against them. Margie, you're way too competitive, sometimes. I think I like Gil because he's a bit like me and doesn't take everything too seriously.'

As soon as she could organise it, Margaret drove Bette to Taiping and they spent a day there, shopping and seeing Margaret's friends for lunch before returning to Utopia. Margaret was thrilled with her independence and had the gardener polish her car each day.

Bette had by now become known to many of the plantation workers as she took her drawing book into the avenues of rubber trees to sketch scenes and people. Margaret thought Bette's fascination with the workers odd but, nevertheless, she supplied her sister with clothes to protect her from the mosquitoes. Bette drew the tappers working and sometimes walked back with them through the rubber trees to their kampongs. She had also started doing a series of sketches of two pretty Indian women tappers.

She had initially befriended one of the young women after she'd watched her packing up her bicycle at the edge of the section near a little roadside altar. Bette studied her carefully as the woman removed her long-sleeved cotton jacket, gloves and her hat and, finally, unwound the scarf from about her head, revealing her pretty face. The girl then gave another female worker a ride home on her bicycle and the two smiled and nodded at Bette, chattering and giggling as they headed back to their kampong on the wobbly old bicycle. The next day Bette asked the women if she could sketch them and they agreed.

When she showed the sketches of the two women to Margaret and Roland, both had to admit that Bette's work was enchanting and that she'd captured the life of the plantation workers very well. So one morning when Margaret asked her if she wanted to go into Slim River with her in the Baby Austin, Bette, who was getting ready to go and sketch, said, 'Can you manage without me? I really want to finish these sketches of the two Indian girls.'

'I can't imagine why you want to draw them. It's so muggy and bug-ridden down there,' said Margaret. 'I'll be back just after lunch. Philip is with Ah Min.'

'I'll make sure I'm back in time to have lunch with him,' said Bette.

Margaret waved happily to Bette as she sailed off in her beautiful Austin Tourer, enjoying her new found independence and feeling that life was just wonderful.

*

Several hours later, Margaret awoke in what was clearly a hospital bed with her anxious sister sitting beside her.

'Oh, Margaret, thank heavens you've woken up. You have given us such a fright.'

'What happened? Where am I?'

'You're in the hospital at Tanjong Malim and you've broken your leg rather badly, I'm afraid.'

'Where's Roland? Is Philip all right?'

'Roland's on his way back from KL. He won't be long, and I left Philip with his amah. He's fine.'

'How did you find me?'

'That's a bit of a story. When you hadn't returned by mid afternoon, I began to worry. Roland and Eugene were in Kuala Lumpur and while I thought you might have got delayed shopping or run into a friend, I decided to go over to Mr Elliott's place and see Ho, who I thought was the most senior person left on the estate. When I told him that I was worried, he looked very concerned.

'"Mem, maybe mem Elliott had accident." I thought this was a bit dramatic, but it wouldn't hurt to check, so I rang the police station at the district headquarters.'

'So you spoke to Alan Williams, the police commander, did you?'

'No, he wasn't there, so things got a bit more complicated and it took a while to speak to someone who understood what I was saying. Eventually, with Ho's help, I managed to explain to him that I was worried about you and he grasped what I was saying. He then asked me if I was coming there and I said, no I was just looking for you. Had he heard if you had broken down? But he kept on insisting that I had to come there. Finally he said, "Mem, you must come at once. Mem's car, it run into bad buffalo and fall over. Mem, she go to hospital in Tanjong Malim."'

'So how did you get here? There's only the Bedford truck left, and no one can drive that.'

128

'Yes, I found that out when I asked Ho. He assured me that only Roland, Eugene and Hamid could drive it. But I can drive, so I collected some toiletries and a change of clothes for you, made sure Ah Kit understood what was going on. I spoke to Ah Min and gave Philip a hug and told him that I was going to see his mummy and that he was to be a good boy and I'd be back soon. I have to say that truck is very difficult to drive. I don't think the gears work very well, but here I am. Tell me what happened to you, if you're up to it.'

The hospital halls echoed, rubber-soled shoes squeaked and there was the unmistakable smell of disinfectant. Margaret's leg was in traction and there was a bandage around her head, but she managed to smile wanly at her sister.

'I don't really know. I was happily driving along, past a kampong, when a great water buffalo seemed to leap out at me and the next thing I know, I'm here. How's my beautiful little car?'

Just then one of the doctors walked into the room.

'Is she all right? Doctor, this is my sister, how is she?' asked Bette anxiously.

'I'm Dr Singh, I'm afraid your sister has a very badly broken leg and a fractured ankle.'

'Why has she a bandage on her head?' asked Bette nervously, stroking Margaret's hand.

'She hit her head on the windscreen and she has some cuts, which have required some stitches, but they are not serious.' He smiled at Margaret. 'You are very lucky, Mrs Elliott. Your injuries could have been much worse.'

Roland and Eugene arrived at the hospital later.

'I shouldn't have let you talk me into that car. I feel that this is all my fault.'

129

'Don't be silly, Roland,' said Margaret. 'It was the stupid buffalo. I'll be all right.'

Roland called in another doctor from Kuala Lumpur for a second opinion. He was assured that Dr Singh had done all the right things but that Margaret would have to spend quite some time in the hospital in traction.

As Margaret grew stronger there was a constant stream of visitors who brought food, champagne, flowers and chocolates along with magazines newly arrived from Australia.

Philip visited frequently and was fascinated by the contraption suspending his mother's leg. Margaret was glad she'd joined the KL Book Club, as she now had time to read while trapped in bed. The hospital was clean and well run and the staff were friendly and seemed to Margaret to be fairly capable. Her private room was basic, with just a large fan and shuttered windows that overlooked a garden, and she was very bored.

After several weeks Margaret was well enough to go home, but she was still in plaster and she could only just manage to move on crutches. She had a long list of instructions from Dr Singh about rest and not overdoing things. While she was pleased to return to the plantation, she found everything difficult and told Bette that she felt clumsy, awkward and ugly.

'Nonsense, Margie. You're managing very well. And thank goodness you have your amah, the houseboy and so many people to help you! Imagine if this had happened when you and Philip were in Brisbane!' said Bette.

Margaret grabbed Bette's hand. 'It's still hard. I need you around to help me, Bette. I hate this. I feel like an old lady. I'm bored, too. I can't play tennis and it's so hard to get around anywhere. I can't even get to the club. You must stay on. You're so good with Philip. Roland is away so much these days. All this war talk is driving me silly. Come on, entertain me, let's play cards.'

'Well, you know my ticket's booked to go home next month,' said Bette, but seeing Margaret's anguished and pleading expression, she added, 'I'll speak to Roland. Father and Mother might be disappointed, but I'm sure they'd want me to stay and help out.' She patted her sister's hand.

Margaret lay her head against the back of the rattan chair on the verandah, her leg on an ottoman, her eyes closed, looking pained. 'Thank you, Bette. It's not as if you have anything pressing back at home, anyway.'

Roland was grateful to Bette when she told him she would stay on at Margaret's request and would postpone her journey home.

'Margaret needs a lot of attention while she is still incapacitated, Bette. I will send a telegram to your parents, to let them know your change of plan. We should follow it up with a letter to tell them not to worry about Margaret. Anyway, I think your father will be relieved that his daughters are sitting out these troubles in a peaceful place like Utopia.'

Margaret was pleased and seemed to cheer up once she was sure Bette was staying. She gave her a bright smile. 'And staying on will give you a chance to see more of Gilbert, won't it?'

5

Brisbane, 2009

IT WAS SUNNY AND clear, with just enough breeze to keep things cool for the crowd who swelled and then lingered at the fundraising fete run by the Campaign Against the Bypass Committee. Julie and her mother watched from the front verandah of their home, where tables and chairs were set for tea, scones and cakes. At the bottom of the front steps, under a shady awning, was a small bar where cold drinks were sold. Dotted all around the garden under colourful umbrellas were stalls selling everything from home-made jams and pickles to craft items, plants, a white elephant stall, books and odds and ends. Scattered throughout the garden were games such as hoopla, lucky dips, a chocolate wheel and a mini fun fair.

Julie was amazed at the transformation of her mother's garden. A whole team of neighbours and friends had come together for this day, which would be the start of many events to raise money for a serious cause – to stop the council wiping out an area of beautiful old homes. But despite the seriousness of the purpose, the atmosphere was light-hearted, as though everyone had come to a party.

'The more money we can put in the kitty to fight the council, the better,' said Caroline.

'The more people that come and see what a special place this is, the better too, I suppose,' said Julie. 'Not just our house, but the whole area. Then they'll understand why it's so important to preserve it.'

Caroline gave her daughter a big smile. 'I'd better go, it's my turn to man the chocolate wheel. Have you heard about that fortune teller? Her tent has quite a queue now!'

'Fortune teller? That's Mrs Godden from the pharmacy,' said Julie.

Caroline shrugged. 'Maybe, but people are saying it's uncanny what she knows.'

'Perhaps I should see her and find out what's going to happen with the council. Could save a lot of time and effort.'

'And miss all this fun!' laughed Caroline as the two women walked down into the garden.

Julie watched David Cooper try his luck at the hoopla. She couldn't help but smile at the anthropologist who was wearing a check shirt with the sleeves rolled up and slacks. He was the only male in sight not in shorts. Julie walked across the lawn to join him.

A neighbour stopped Julie. 'This is a wonderful event. Such fun, and so good to see the community working together. We simply can't let that dreadful bypass go through. You've done a wonderful job.'

'Thank my mother. She's pulled all this together,' said Julie. In fact she'd been amazed at how Caroline had taken on all the work with her small committee. Julie had helped with the promotion of the fete, but had been too busy at work to do as much as she'd have liked. Caroline had run things marvellously.

'This place is so beautiful. It makes you realise how much work and history are in the old gardens in this neighbourhood,' added the woman.

'Exactly. My great grandmother Winifred helped plant this. She was a keen gardener like her mother. But both my grandmother and Mum have worked hard to maintain it,' answered Julie.

David Cooper turned from the hoopla stall and smiled as Julie approached. 'I've just donated some money to the cause. I didn't win a thing.'

'It's going well, isn't it? Mum and her mates have done a brilliant job.'

'You certainly got the word out there,' said David.

'There's still a long way to go,' said Julie. 'We need to raise a heap more money to make our voice heard and get support from other parts of the city, not just locally. People must realise that these beautiful old homes and gardens are worth preserving.'

'True. You don't want to come across just as "Not in my Backyarders." I've been looking at the ramifications of this bypass and if it's established it could set a precedent for other parts of Brisbane,' said David.

'That's the message we have to get across,' said Julie firmly.

As they walked through the crowded garden, David was thoughtful. 'It's interesting that the council has gone very quiet on the matter. They say they are consulting.'

'Consulting with whom? Not with any of us,' said Julie.

'Want to try one of those home-made fruit punch drinks? Looks very delicious,' said David, stopping by a stall that was selling freshly squeezed juices made from mangoes and other tropical fruit piled in baskets. As they sipped their smoothies and watched groups of people chatting and enjoying themselves with their friends and families, Julie said, 'If what you say is right, and the council has gone quiet, maybe putting the bypass on the back burner until things quieten down, perhaps I could leave town for a short break.'

'I suppose so,' said David. 'I'll have to leave Brisbane, too. Work calls, but I don't think anyone will consider us deserters. Where're you going?'

'Malaysia.'

'What? Really!' David looked elated. 'My stamping ground. Have I piqued your interest?'

'In a way, yes. Actually, I suppose I thought of this trip because of you,' began Julie.

'You won't regret it!' broke in David, now quite excited. 'You must let me show you around . . .'

'Hang about,' laughed Julie. 'I've been asked to stay with my cousins at Utopia plantation.'

'Shane and Peter Elliott?'

'That's right. After you met them and asked them about Bette's book, they wrote to us, inviting us to go and visit. My parents don't want to go right now, but my mother has been telling me stories about my grandmother's time in Malaya when she went there as a bride. Gran told Mum that they were the happiest years of her life.'

'Then do you have any idea why your Aunt Bette would write a book on the Iban?'

'No, none at all, because by then my grandmother wasn't speaking to her.'

'So it's a mystery?' asked David.

'Yes, Gran wouldn't tell Mum about anything after the war broke out in Malaya. The story just kind of stops. So now I'm curious about the family plantation and I'm also rather intrigued by Bette, though I doubt I'll find out much more about her.'

'Knowing what she wrote, she must have been quite adventurous. An interesting woman. It's a shame you didn't know her. What was your grandmother like?'

'Ever since I can remember, my grandmother lived in this house. She was a strong, forthright kind of person, not sentimental or soft. I don't know anything about her sister. Gran rarely mentioned her, except to be critical, and to murmur darkly that she'd gone off and married a Chinaman. But I really want to go and see the place where my mother was born.'

'It's odd that one half of your family stayed put in Brisbane while the other half stayed in Malaysia.'

'It's how things worked out, I suppose. But because this side of the family have lived here in Brisbane for so long, I have such a strong sense of family tradition and history for this place, which is why I couldn't bear to see this house bulldozed.'

'I don't know how many of the old houses round here have had four generations of the one family living in them,' said David. 'But even if a new family has just moved in, they must appreciate the style, the beauty and history of these houses. They don't build them like this any more. What are your plans for Malaysia? I'd like to help, if I can.'

Emails flew back and forth between the cousins in Malaysia and Brisbane. Shane, the older brother, seemed to be the main contact and he wrote, if somewhat formally, to Julie giving her information about travel, some history of the plantation and what she might expect.

We are very much in a work routine here but of course we would hope to be able to take you around the district and show you some of the places with which our grandparents were connected. However,

136

there are no 'bright lights' near us, so perhaps you might like to arrange to see other parts of Malaysia while you're here. My brother and I will be happy to meet you in KL and drive you back to Utopia. I have made arrangements for you to stay in the main guesthouse near to us. It will be a chance for us to exchange information about our families and we look forward to meeting you!

'Are you sure you won't come with me, Mum?' persisted Julie. 'This is where you were born and where your mother spent her early married life.'

'No, darling, not at the moment. I really want to stay on top of the bypass business. And I think you need a holiday, I can't remember when you last had a proper break. Are you going to meet up with David and get him to show you around a bit? He seems very knowledgeable about the country.'

'I don't really know. Perhaps we'll hook up at some stage,' said Julie.

'David's work sounds interesting,' said Caroline. 'He was telling me that he's involved in several different projects up there.'

'You've seen a lot more of him than I have these past few weeks,' said Julie.

'Don't forget, if it wasn't for David's research you wouldn't have become interested in Utopia and meeting your cousins,' Caroline reminded her.

'That's the thing, Mum. I don't know all that much about our family connection to the plantation. I think it's odd that Gran never spoke to me about it and she hardly talked to you about it at all. I just sense that there's a story behind it,' said Julie.

'Well, I have to agree. It would be interesting to find out what your cousins know,' said Caroline.

Despite what she said to Caroline, Julie did agree with her mother that it would be wise to pick David Cooper's brain, so she accepted an invitation from him to go to dinner for a briefing on her trip.

'I understand that you want to see Utopia but, if you have the opportunity, you have to see some other places. Malaysia's such an intriguing place. It's made up of several states and every state is a little bit different – and proud of it. I'm sure your cousins will show you around,' he said over a pre-dinner drink.

'They sound very hospitable but I think they are very bound up in running Utopia, so I don't want them to feel obliged to drop everything for me.'

'I wish I could visit their plantation again. You know, you can't help but see palm oil estates everywhere you go, but most of the big companies are very protective, in fact almost secretive, about what they're doing. They're not tourist stops, that's for sure.'

'You sound critical,' said Julie.

'Julie, palm oil is such a contentious subject. There's so much of it in our food. Do you know that you ate about ten kilos of palm oil last year and you probably weren't even aware because often it's not labelled? Not just that, palm oil plantations are causing havoc for the wildlife and forests. While Utopia is trying to be a modern, sustainable plantation, it's still in a business that causes deforestation, which destroys animal habitat. It's not just the big mammals that are becoming rarer, but because palm oil is a monoculture, the plantations don't provide enough variety of foods for the smaller wildlife, like birds and insects, and they are disappearing fast, too. Many plantations have displaced the indigenous population, and the rapid expansion of them is frequently related to government corruption.'

Julie stared at David in astonishment. 'Is this what your work, your research, entails?'

'It's part of it. I am trying to find out as much as I can about the indigenous tribes, like the Iban, before their traditional lifestyle is gone for good. It's not just tigers and orangutans that are losing their habitat and dying out. It's people as well.'

'I thought there were sanctuaries for the orangutans,' said Julie. She didn't quite know what to think about David's passionate outburst. And she was surprised at her own, suddenly defensive, feelings about Utopia because it was part of her family history and heritage.

David must have sensed her shift in mood. 'Look, I suppose the plantations that moved from rubber to palm oil aren't as bad as those where old-growth forests are being cut down to establish palm oil plantations, because the damage to the natural vegetation has already been done. And you're right, there are places on the island of Borneo that provide sanctuary, whereby if the mother orangutans are killed, the babies, if they have been lucky enough to be found, can go to a care centre. But there's little chance of them ever being released back into the wild because of the lack of safe habitats.'

'That's sad,' said Julie. 'I'd like to go and see some orangutans.'

'That's easy to organise,' said David. 'Now, what are you going to order?'

Julie's parents took her to Brisbane airport.

Caroline hugged her. 'Darling, just have fun. I hope you enjoy your cousins but remember, they lead a very different life from you.'

'Yes, that's true. I just feel a need to know more about our relatives in Malaysia. And it would be good if they can tell me something about Gran and Bette. Aren't you curious?' asked Julie.

'Not enough to go to Malaysia, at present,' said her father. 'But we'll love to hear what you find out. Just keep safe and don't take any risks.'

'Oh, Dad, I'll be fine. Oh, gosh, we're boarding. I'll send you a text message the minute I land. Love you.' She kissed her parents quickly and went through the security gates.

The hotel where Julie was staying had arranged a car to collect her and she was swept away from the tourist throngs at the airport feeling a bit like royalty. It was a long drive to the hotel and she was amazed at the newly built, multi-lane highway, the smooth traffic flow, and the highrises and housing developments they passed on the way.

Kuala Lumpur seemed to be full of new apartment complexes, shopping malls, grand hotels and skyscraper office blocks. Occasionally, she glimpsed colourful old areas of shophouses, markets and food stalls still surviving in between the modern glass and steel. Without these reminders Julie felt she could have been in any modern city in the world.

Early in the evening the hotel desk clerk directed her to a block of restaurants specialising in international cuisine. She chose an Indian one, enticed by its smells and the fact that it was not dissimilar to one close to her home in Brisbane.

The following morning she rang Utopia and spoke to Peter who was charming and polite.

'Welcome. We are looking forward to meeting you. We shall come to Kuala Lumpur tomorrow and pick you up. Does that suit you?'

'Of course. If it's not too much trouble. I'm looking forward to getting out of this big city and seeing something of the country.'

'We will certainly do our best to show you our part of Malaysia. See you at nine tomorrow morning at your hotel.'

Julie set out to explore the area around her hotel and found that she was in a very exclusive and expensive shopping area. Shopping complexes flaunted top international designer names and Julie visited one plush mall that had two floors devoted to nothing but designer watches, each costing thousands of dollars. Liveried doormen, thick carpets, chandeliers, art on the walls, perfumed air, banks of orchids and live music made the expensive atmosphere quite different from what she was used to at her local mall.

Then she discovered the food hall in the basement and took photographs for her mother. There were leather lounges, mirrors, fresh flowers, plump sofas and table settings covered with linen and silver. Smartly dressed staff were ready to bring food and drink orders. Customers could choose from a dimly lit cocktail bar, a replica Japanese tea house with beautiful waitresses in kimonos, an Indian restaurant with a tall Sikh doorman in a red uniform with gold braid, a Swiss chalet and a Chinese garden restaurant.

Julie decided to eat at the Noodle House, which appeared to be comparatively inexpensive. Sitting up to a long bar where she could watch the strolling shoppers and people relaxing and socialising, she felt that she was in a sort of club. Later in the afternoon she took a tourist map and explored other parts of the city until she was too tired to walk another step. She took a taxi back to the hotel feeling on overload from the astounding sights of a city going skywards at an amazing rate.

It occurred to Julie that she had no idea what her cousins looked like but as she stood in the lobby with her bag at her feet she spotted Shane and Peter the minute they came through the revolving door. The two brothers were both slim with dark-brown hair. One had a slight curl, the other's straight hair flopped into his eyes. Both wore white, short-sleeved, open-collared shirts tucked into smart well-cut slacks. Even at a distance Julie could see that their leather shoes and belts were expensive.

Seeing her standing there, they broke into smiles and came to her, hands outstretched. 'Julie?'

She wished she had dressed up a little more and not just worn her white cotton jeans and loose shirt. 'That's me. So who is cousin Shane and who is Peter?'

'I am Shane.' The curly haired, slightly older brother shook her hand. 'And this is Peter. The baby. He's two years younger.'

'I'll ignore that comment,' said Peter. 'We are so happy to meet you. We hardly know our Australian side of the family, so this is wonderful.'

'Is this your bag?' Shane nodded to one of the porters and waved towards the door. 'Our car is here. It is a bit of a drive to Utopia, but you'll find it interesting. And we can catch up on each other's news, yes?'

Julie thought she detected a faint accent more European than English. The cousins seemed, like their email correspondence, to be formal, polite and correct.

When she stepped outside she was a bit stunned to see a sleek new silver Jaguar waiting at the entrance. An Indian driver was putting her bag in the boot, as the hotel concierge held the back car door open for her. Julie got in and sank into the soft, new-smelling, dove leather. Peter sat beside Julie and Shane got in beside the driver.

'This is Ramdin. He's been with the family a long time. His grandfather, Hamid, drove great grandfather Eugene,' said Shane. Ramdin turned and flashed Julie a wide smile.

On the three-hour drive north, the Elliott brothers

told Julie about Utopia, and how they were trying to move it forward into new business practices. They said that they were part of an international group dedicated to raising the standard of plantation operations to make them more sustainable and environmentally safer, at the same time making them more productive and setting sections of natural habitat aside for wildlife protection.

'We have a larger community of workers than they did in my father and grandfather's day,' said Shane. 'And like us, several generations have grown up on the plantation so the trees, the workers and our family are all intertwined.'

'It's probably better if you wait till we show you around before we try to explain how it all works,' said Peter. 'There is quite a lot to Utopia and its subsidiaries. We have taken the company in a slightly new direction, increasing our yield with new research and development, so it's a lot more scientific than in our father's day,' he added.

'I know very little about Uncle Philip, your father,' said Julie. 'I suppose that's because he was brought up here while my mother lived in Australia.'

'Our father spoke a little about his sister in Australia,' said Peter. 'We were told there had been a falling out between our grandparents. I suppose, being a boy, our father was expected to stay here and learn the family business.'

'I believe it was the war,' said Shane. 'It disrupted many lives. Very sad.'

'It would be interesting to know the whole story,' said Julie. 'Do you know anything about our Great Aunt Bette?'

'As we said in the letter, we know only a little. We were surprised when Dr Cooper contacted us. We didn't know about her exploits in Borneo until he told us. But if you want to know more about your grandfather, you could read his war memoirs,' said Peter.

'That sounds interesting,' said Julie.

'I suppose it is, if you're interested in his war exploits,' said Shane.

'And your parents? My mother said there was an accident?'

'Tragically, yes. They were both killed out here in a car accident about fifteen years ago,' said Peter.

'So you both grew up here? Did you go away to school like our grandfather Roland and your father?' asked Julie.

'We were educated in England and in France at the Sorbonne. I did a special horticulture course in Holland,' said Peter. 'Shane spent more time in France – it's where he met his wife, Martine,' he added with a smile.

'And she is living at Utopia?' asked Julie.

'Yes. But at the moment she's in England visiting our children and then she's in France to see her family, but she'll be home fairly soon,' said Shane.

'And you, are you married, Peter?' asked Julie.

'No. But I have a girlfriend in Holland,' he answered. 'I would like her to come here but she finds it a bit . . . far away from Europe. And she has a very good job in marketing and promotions.'

'Really! That's my field,' said Julie.

'Ah ha. Then you know how driven she is and how she works in something of a pressure cooker,' said Peter.

They sped down a broad motorway. Julie was staggered at the endless stretches of neat and regimented acres of palm oil plantations marching from the edge of the freeway across the countryside and into distant hills.

They stopped in a large township which, for the first time, gave Julie a sense of the exotic with its bustling small businesses, restaurants, car repair places, stalls and markets. Ramdin parked the car at the back of a small supermarket and stayed with it, leaning against the driver's door, smoking a cigarette. Shane and Peter took

Julie into a small restaurant. Out the back were clean toilets, including a western toilet, which she was pleased to see. The squat-style hole on a small, raised, tiled platform looked incredibly uncomfortable to her. Julie then joined the brothers and they all sat at an outdoor table where Shane suggested that Julie try the murtabak.

'It's like a stuffed hamburger, very delicious. Pour some curry sauce over the top,' said Shane.

'We were thinking that on the way to Utopia, we'd stop and show you one of the places first built by our great grandfather Eugene,' said Peter.

'Wonderful. What is it?' asked Julie.

'It's a small place on one of the original estates,' said Shane. 'It's not used any more, though we sometimes have informal board meetings up there.'

'It was used during the Emergency by some of the British as a clandestine meeting place,' said Peter.

'Really. I'm afraid I'm a bit vague about Malaysian history,' admitted Julie.

'We'll let things unfold rather than give you a potted history,' said Shane. 'Shall we go? Ramdin has cold bottled water in the car if you need it.'

The car eventually turned off the highway onto a trunk road that wound upwards through thick forest until it turned onto a small local road where palm oil plantations covered the hills as far as the eye could see.

They drove through an entrance marked by two large trees, across a grassy knoll and stopped under tall pine trees. Stretching into the distance was a spectacular view over the plantation, patches of jungle in the distance. At this high point, at the very edge of the knoll, sat a heavy wooden seat facing the stunning vista.

Further back stood a tiny white church, its roof of faded red tiles, a well-tended garden in front, bordering the white gravel path to its door.

'What a sweet little church!' exclaimed Julie. 'Is it still used?'

'Only very occasionally. We were both christened here,' said Peter. 'And Shane and Martine were married here. They were the first to do so.'

'Were your children christened here, too?' asked Julie.

Shane nodded. 'Yes, it's a family tradition. I expect your mother was christened here, too.'

Julie walked slowly down the path to the church door thinking how some places, be it a house or a church, a seat on a knoll or an entire plantation, could connect you to the past. Her grandmother's house in Brisbane linked Julie to her very first memories.

'I wonder why Roland didn't marry Gran here, instead of the church in KL,' said Julie.

'Convenience. Too hard to have all the guests trek out here, I expect,' said Peter.

'Yes, I suppose so. Can I go inside?' asked Julie.

'Of course.' Shane led the way and unlatched the heavy front door.

Julie found the whitewashed interior surprisingly cool. Sunlight shone through the stained glass window above the tiny altar and coloured beams bounced off the old wooden pews. The atmosphere was warm and friendly and not the lonely, remote place she thought the setting might make it feel. Then she noticed the old family photographs set in wallmounts beneath a small carved cross and she recognised her grandmother in one of them.

'We used to keep the family Bible here, but the climate made it deteriorate, so it's in the air-conditioned computer room in the big house,' said Shane.

'Does it have the births, deaths and marriages of the family listed in the front?' asked Julie, with a smile.

'It does indeed. Your mother is in there and so are you and your brother,' said Peter.

146

Julie immediately thought of her brother. Adelaide seemed another universe from this little church and she doubted Adam would have much interest in this side of the family in such a distant place.

Shane locked the church door behind them and Ramdin got out of the car and opened the back door for Julie.

'Julie, a moment. There's one more spot you might like to see,' said Shane.

She followed the two men around the side of the church to where a cluster of trees shaded a small grassed area, which she quickly realised was a small graveyard. In it centre was a grave, surrounded by a small iron fence and a large headstone at one end. The inscription on it read:

In loving memory of Eugene Orson Elliott
Husband of Charlotte, devoted father to Roland
Died 1941
Founder of Utopia, pioneer and philanthropist
RIP

Julie stared at the grave, so quiet and sheltered, so far from where he'd been born. Slowly it dawned on her that the man buried here was her great grandfather. This was a place so far from Australia, and yet she was linked to it. Nearby were two more graves, lying side by side. A single headstone marked their place. On it Julie read:

Philip Elliott and Stephanie Elliott
Loving parents of Peter and Shane
Died 1994
United forever

'I wish we'd known more about the Elliott side of the family,' she said softly. 'Why is it we rarely think about our families, or ask the people connected to us, until it's

147

too late? I keep wishing I'd asked my grandmother more about her life here.'

'The same for us,' agreed Peter. 'Our father hardly ever mentioned anything about his life when he was young, and we were never really curious enough to ask him, and then he was killed suddenly, and it was all too late. And there's Grandfather's grave. It's just over here.'

Julie looked at Roland's grave and realised that she was looking at the resting place of her grandfather, a man she had never known. It all seemed very sad.

'You just get on with day-to-day living and don't think much of the past,' said Shane. 'Anyway I don't believe men, in general, worry too much about family and people far away.'

'Well, I'm here and I'm curious,' said Julie. 'Where is great grandmother Charlotte buried?' she asked as they walked back to the car.

'In England. She spent a lot of time there and as she got older she preferred to be there. Apparently Charlotte hated the heat of Malaya and Eugene loathed the cold weather,' said Shane. 'We have other family over in the UK as well that we don't see much of either.'

Julie shook her head. 'I came to find out about my grandmother and my great aunt, and now I realise there's a whole family tree I've never climbed.'

The entrance to Utopia plantation was impressive. It was not just the massive timber archway, flanked by tall trees, the landscaped gardens and high fence smothered in a solid scarlet wall of spiky bougainvillea that caught Julie's eye, she also saw the chimney and roof of a large factory plant and what looked like office buildings in the plantation grounds. The Indian sentry at the boom gate snapped a smart salute as he waved them through.

'This is the administration block, and over there are the research and development buildings, the seed nursery and staff area. The processing plant, refinery and factory are down that way and what we call the town centre is also over there,' said Shane.

'Town centre?' said Julie. 'This is a whole town?'

'There's a Hindu temple, staff shop, bakery, the school, as well as a medical clinic. There's also the recreation and sports area, including an indoor badminton court. And down by the river we have also built shophouses,' said Peter, adding, 'We have six thousand people working here.'

'We'll show you around tomorrow. We brought you in by the front entrance to give you a sense of the place. Normally we come in over the hill the back way through the jungle reserve, it's quicker,' said Shane.

'The family compound is on the original holding and separate from this, but it's only a fifteen minute drive away,' said Peter.

Julie was silent as they drove past buildings, rows and rows of oil palm divisions, and then through the housing estate of neat white, identical, two-storey terrace homes set in blocks of four.

'They're very neat and modern,' said Julie, quite surprised.

'Yes, things have changed since grandfather and great grandfather's day,' said Shane. 'Providing a stable and supportive community has been a way to get the best from our workers. We have a lot of the women working for us, too, in the laboratory and plant nursery. Others work as cleaners and shop assistants, all kinds of things.'

'They'd hardly need to leave the estate,' said Julie, thinking that while it appeared rather paternalistic, almost colonial, the conditions probably suited the workers as much as the owners. 'I see quite a lot of people own cars,' she commented, seeing small cars under carports in some houses.

149

'Yes, since Malaysia started producing its own car, the Proton, more people can afford to own one. So we've had to add carports to a lot of houses,' said Shane.

'Slim River is close by here and is quite a large market town,' said Peter. 'Utopia's not as isolated as it looks.'

'Times are changing, though. As the younger generation receives a better education and goes to university and that sort of thing, the young don't want to come back here to work. They prefer the towns and cities and the opportunities there. Now most of our field workers come from Indonesia, not India,' said Shane.

Peter continued, 'However, what we would like to do is to provide an opportunity for those with an education to work here, as their parents did, but as staff in the offices, supervisors in the factories, working in R&D, that sort of skilled work. I guess that these changes to the plantation staff and the old family connections are inevitable, just a natural development.'

They finally arrived at the main house, which was set at the end of a narrow red dirt lane. The house was screened by large shrubs and a pretty garden. The car swept under a high portico to the big front door.

'Come inside and have a cool drink, then we'll take you to your guesthouse,' said Shane.

Ramdin smiled at Julie as he held open the car door. 'Enjoy your visit, mem.'

Shane led the way through the house to a screened sunroom that overlooked a garden and a modern swimming pool. Julie's first impression was of high ceilings and fans and rooms full of heavy furniture that looked as though it had been in situ for generations. There were, however, some contemporary touches. The furniture in the sunroom was covered in bold Scandinavian-style prints and the pot plants and flowers were placed in large, bright ceramic Chinese pots. A shy, dark-skinned Malay woman carried in a tray with a jug of fresh lime juice and glasses and placed it on a table. She gave Julie an interested glance.

'This is a lovely room,' said Julie.

'Yes, we screened it properly,' said Shane. 'Martine has done some decorating, but the house is furnished pretty much as Grandfather and his father had it. Come and I'll show you Great Grandfather's pride and joy.'

Julie followed her cousins down the corridor and into what was not only the study but the trophy room. On the walls were the mounted heads of boars, deer and some animal Julie couldn't identify. On the floor was a tiger skin. She looked about her in fascinated horror.

'Not very PC now, is it?' said Shane. 'But different times, different customs. Grandfather was a keen hunter, too. He shot that tiger.' He pointed to the floor. 'I believe it was in Tampin, near Malacca. Anyway, he was rather proud of it.'

'And Peter, where do you live?' asked Julie, thinking that while she loved her grandmother's things around the house in Brisbane, Caroline had somehow made the décor look fresh, airy and modern. Eugene's home, by contrast seemed dark and a little depressing, even without the dead animal's heads on the walls, though she supposed the drawn blinds and curtains kept it cool as well as dark.

'I live in Grandfather Roland's house, where my father was born,' said Peter. 'Our grandmother must have prettied it up somewhat when she married Grandfather, so it's still full of family keepsakes.'

'But Grandfather's war memoirs are here, aren't they?' Julie reminded them.

Peter smiled. 'We haven't forgotten.'

Within a few days Julie had familiarised herself with the layout of Utopia and discovered the joys of the bakery near the general store. Peter told her that a colleague of their

151

grandfather's had come from Holland on a business trip and stayed at the plantation. When Roland had lamented the lack of good bread, Grandfather's colleague had come to an arrangement whereby a Dutch baker came from Amsterdam, complete with a special brick oven, to set up a basic bakery. The baker became enamoured of a pretty Malay girl, loved plantation life and decided to stay. As the years went by, the bakery grew larger and larger, turning out breads, pastries, Indian breads and savoury treats for everybody on the plantation and the nearby villages, and now it also supplied bread to Slim River.

'We've had offers to sell Utopia breads in KL,' said Peter. 'But we can only just meet local demand and we're not really in the bread business. Come and try the best curry puffs in Malaysia and also the coconut cream pies made with our own coconut. Coconut is very healthy for you, you know. In fact, a lot of the baking is done with our coconut oil.'

'Healthy? I thought it clogged your arteries,' said Julie walking into the spotless bakery that smelled of warm bread and spicy cakes.

'Not at all. We are developing some big coconut plantations here. Coconut oil's had bad press, which has been put about by the soya bean companies,' said Peter. 'But that's been proved to be wrong.'

At the weekend Peter and Shane invited several of their friends for lunch and to play tennis and meet Julie.

'Tennis parties are a family tradition. Father loved them, and so did Grandfather,' said Shane.

Julie hadn't brought anything suitable for tennis but Peter spoke to Siti, the housekeeper at the guesthouse where Julie was staying. She took Julie to a room that was filled with boxes, trunks and an overflowing wardrobe and flung back the doors. 'You look, in here, mem. Many sports things.'

'My gosh!' laughed Julie. She lifted out a heavy wooden tennis racquet. 'This could have belonged to my grandmother! Ah, here's something more modern. And shoes, I'm sure I can find a pair to fit me. Look at this! Old swimsuits, paddles, fishing rods, a croquet set!' She found a pair of tennis shoes and a reasonable tennis racquet, and went to her room to change into shorts.

Julie looked around her. She couldn't believe that she was staying in a large, three bedroom bungalow, which she had all to herself. It was a contemporary design and she supposed that it was built for businesspeople and friends who came to stay. The bungalow was fully air-conditioned as well as having ceiling fans. These whirled slowly all day and evening.

Each morning, Siti prepared Julie's breakfast and set it out in the sunroom that looked over an enclosed garden where banks of orchids grew up old trees and where a faded hammock hung on old ropes. On the other side of the house, was a large kitchen garden and a comparatively modern kitchen was separated from a dining room by a swinging door. This domestic area was obviously the domain of the staff, for when Julie had picked up her empty breakfast plate and taken it into the kitchen Siti looked surprised and a little offended.

'No, no, mem. My work. Siti do.' And she hustled Julie from the kitchen. Julie never set foot in there again.

Julie was pleased to find that the tennis party was more social than tennis. The original tennis court was surrounded by a large fence completely smothered in vine that hung with bunches of flowers like pink grapes. It was almost a foot thick, screening the court and sheltering it from any wind. There was a large pavilion at one end of it, housing the change rooms and an entertaining area, where a refrigerator was stocked with cold drinks. One of the houseboys poured the drinks and brought out trays

153

of snacks from the kitchen. An elderly Indian gardener enjoyed himself acting as the ball boy.

Julie found Peter and Shane's friends to be a fun group. They comprised of two English couples, both in their thirties, a German couple, an Australian, the same age as Shane, and two other single men. One was Chinese, the other of Scottish descent, who, like Shane and Peter, had grown up in Asia. All of them were intrigued by Julie's connection to Shane and Peter and Utopia.

'You've waited a long time to visit,' said Cynthia, one of the English women.

'It's a bit of a long story. But I'm planning on making the most of this trip,' said Julie.

'Will you be here when Martine gets back? We'll have to have a big party then,' said the other girl.

'She'll be back any day,' said Shane. 'A party would be wonderful.'

'Is she seeing her family in France?' asked Cynthia.

'Yes, as well as the children in England,' said Shane.

Everyone was friendly and well travelled, and either ran their own business or were connected to the palm oil industry in some way. Christopher Nichols, the Australian, was a good friend of Peter's.

'And are you in the palm oil business, too?' Julie asked him.

Christopher shook his head. 'No, I'm the ring in. I'm in the Royal Australian Air Force, following a family tradition. I'm at Butterworth here in Malaysia.'

When Julie looked blank, he added, 'Butterworth Air Base. Near Penang. It's now run by the Malaysian Air Force, as a training facility there. My father was stationed there in the sixties, and I'm there now.'

'Oh. I see,' said Julie. 'You do have a connection to this country then.'

While most of the group lived some distance from a

major city, they seemed sophisticated and well-to-do. It was stimulating to be around people different from those she mixed with in Brisbane. After they finished playing tennis, they walked over to the big house and settled themselves into cane chairs on the verandah. A drinks trolley was waiting. As the houseboy lowered the chick blinds against the late afternoon sunlight, everyone chatted over some fine French wine, a beer or a gin and tonic.

'Do you get Australian wines here?' asked Julie. 'They're exceptionally good, you know.'

'Yes, I do know that but my wife's family owns vineyards in France,' said Shane. 'So they ship their wines out to us.'

'Maybe we should support our grandmother's country and order some Australian wines,' grinned Peter. 'Stir up your in-laws a bit, eh, Shane?'

On Sunday the boys took Julie by speed boat upriver for a picnic. As they sped past the jungle thickets at the water's edge, Julie had her first hint of the wilderness that surrounded the plantation.

'This is beautiful,' she said, getting out onto a small jetty where a recently mowed lawn swept down to the riverbank. A picnic table and barbecue were set up under a shelter beneath the shady trees. All around them was forest and Julie could see a track leading into it.

'Do we swim in there, where the netting is?' asked Julie, looking at the wire mesh strung between strong poles. 'It looks like a shark net.'

'The crocs here must be as old as the pagar so we thought it was time to replace it with something stronger,' said Shane.

When Julie was dropped back at the guesthouse after their swim and barbecue, Siti handed her a scrap of paper with a phone number on it.

'Message for you, mem.'

'Oh dear, a message? I wonder what's up,' said Julie.
'Is KL number.'

'Really? I don't know anyone in Kuala Lumpur.'

'He say he your friend,' said Siti. 'You take coffee?
Cold drink?'

'Some of that fresh pineapple juice would be lovely.
Can I use the phone?' asked Julie, wondering who would
know this phone number to call her.

'Hi Julie. How are you enjoying Utopia?'

'David? Is that you? Where are you?' said Julie, recognising David Cooper's voice. 'Is everything okay?'

'Absolutely. I'm in KL. Your parents send their love.
Saw them a couple of days ago. So what do you think?'

'About Utopia? My cousins? Malaysia? It's all good,'
she said quickly. 'How are Mum and Dad? Anything new
with the council bypass?'

'Still very quiet. My guess is that the council has
retreated, licking their wounds to reassess. But your
mother and her committee are having war cabinet meetings, just in case.'

'And Dad?'

'Missing you, but otherwise fine.'

'Are you coming here?'

'No, that's not why I rang. You said you wanted to
get out into the jungle to see the orangutans.'

'Oh, yes, I suppose so.'

'Well, I'm heading to Sarawak in a couple of days
and I thought you might like to come and see some
really wild country. I'm travelling with a zoologist and a
photographer.'

'I'll have to talk to my cousins. I am their guest.'

'I'm sure they wouldn't mind. It would be a great
opportunity to see another part of Malaysia.'

'You're right, it would be. I'll talk to them. What are you doing in Sarawak?'

'We're meeting with some Iban to talk about the problems they're having with their land being reclaimed and the enforced government resettlement. The Iban way of life is disappearing fast and I want to record what I can of it, before it all goes. I'm sure your cousins would be happy for you to experience traditional life in the longhouses.'

'You're right, it does sound interesting, and it would be a wonderful opportunity for me. Let me get back to you. How long will you be away in Sarawak?'

'Initially only a week or so but after I return you to Kuching we're planning to move much further inland, and could be gone for some weeks. It'll be pretty casual, but I'll talk to you more about the gear you should bring when you ring me back.'

'You sound very confident I'll go into the wilds of Borneo with you,' said Julie.

'You'd be crazy not to! I'll look after you, Julie, I promise. This will be something special, believe me,' he added sincerely.

'I'll talk to the boys.'

Shane and Peter were immediately enthusiastic.

'It's a marvellous opportunity, Julie!' said Shane.

'This David seems to know all kinds of people. He's an interesting fellow. And you say he has a team with him? You'll be quite safe with them,' said Peter. 'Is he a good friend of yours?'

'Oh, no. Well, what I mean is, he's become a family friend. He's helping my mother with a campaign at home to save our neighbourhood.' Julie was slightly flustered that they thought David might be her boyfriend.

'He knows a bit about Great Aunt Bette. If you find out any more you can share it with us,' said Shane.

'I don't think he knows anything more about her

than the book she wrote. I wonder if he's going anywhere she went.' Julie was suddenly keen to go along on this expedition.

'It will be an adventure. And when you come back Martine will be here with us. I feel badly we are not entertaining you enough. Martine will show you around more. You'll like her,' said Shane.

'You could take Julie to KL with you when you go to get Martine. Then Julie can fly from there to Kuching,' suggested Peter.

'That would be great. I'll call David back and make arrangements. I was wondering what I should take with me,' said Julie.

'We'll get you kitted out. As you've seen, there's everything here. From tennis racquets to tents,' said Peter.

Shane and Peter seemed relaxed and happy about Julie going off with David for a week into Sarawak. She got the feeling they were pleased that she was a guest who could look after herself.

David Cooper met Julie at Kuala Lumpur airport and surprised her by greeting her with a big hug. 'Hey, it's great to see you. And so far from home!' He shook Shane's hand. 'Very nice to see you again. This trip has worked out very well.'

David introduced them all to Matthew the zoologist who was a quiet, thin Englishman in his late thirties with a strange arrangement of hair shaved into a thin, dark line around his chin and upper lip, and Barry who was recording the trip on video. Barry was an Australian, in his forties, living in Bangkok where he worked for a photo agency.

'You been up-country before?' asked Barry.

'No, I'm looking forward to it,' said Julie.

'Hope you've come prepared. We'll be camping in a longhouse for a few nights,' said Matthew.

'Yes, my cousins have given me more than enough gear,' said Julie. She turned to Shane. 'Thanks so much for driving me here. I'll be in touch when I get back from Sarawak.'

'We'll take good care of her,' David assured him, putting an arm around Julie's shoulders.

'Thank you. And Julie, when you get back we'll send Ramdin to pick you up. Have a good time,' said Shane.

The flight to Kuching was brief. As they approached the coast of the large island of Borneo, the South China Sea below was dotted with sampans and the sails of small fishing boats. Behind the mangroves and mudflats was dense jungle that wrapped the contours of the peaks and valleys like a crocheted green blanket. Occasionally a trickle of muddy water was visible making its way to the brown sea. Clinging to the coast were small villages on stilts. Dugout canoes, tied up in front of the houses, were the sole means of reaching the world beyond the rainforest. But in some places, like an unhealed scar, was bare earth, a hole gouged through the green blanket. Matchsticks of piled logs lay on the red earth. Then Julie saw the shining silver of tin roofs, a road with dots of vehicles, and then thatch and red tiles indicating a little town. Shortly afterwards, the plane began to circle the small city of Kuching.

As they drove from the airport, Julie saw that the broad river that dissected the city, was bordered by a landscaped esplanade, and ships and long flat freighters crowded the main wharf. Several streets were lined with highrise buildings, shops and hotels, but a glimpse of old shophouses and a few white colonial buildings hinted at the past, while an urban sprawl fanned away from the city centre. The city was small but scenic with the jungle at its back door. Julie immediately fell in love with it.

'It looks beautiful. Very clean, too,' said Julie to David.

'One of my favourite places,' he agreed. 'The White Rajahs, the Brooke family, ruled it as their personal kingdom for a hundred years, until the Japanese invaded. The first rajah, Sir James Brooke, was ceded Sarawak and his family ruled it as absolute monarchs. They had their own money, stamps and flag and even the power of life and death over their subjects. After the war, the third rajah, Charles Vyner Brooke, gave Sarawak to the British and after independence it became part of Malaysia. Many of the imposing colonial buildings were built by the second rajah, Sir Charles Brooke.'

Julie couldn't wait to explore the quaint city as they drove past the imposing white courthouse, where the white arched colonnade shaded a mosaic tiled footpath. Interesting shops, the smell of spices and the waterfront promenade were all utterly enticing.

'Oh, look at the cats!' she exclaimed as their taxi rounded the spectacular statue and fountain.

'Kuching means cat in Malay,' said Matthew. 'Every souvenir in this place is either a picture or a toy of a cat or an orangutan.'

'Back in Brisbane, you said that you could arrange for me to see some orangutans, David. Are they still out there in the jungle?' asked Julie.

'You saw the logging as we flew in,' said Matthew. 'And oil palm plantations over the border in Indonesian Kalimantan are also gobbling up their space. Orangutans are vegetarians and need a lot of ripe fruit, seeds, nuts and bark. In other words, they need to have a lot of trees to survive, and the forests they live in are being destroyed, fast. Poachers and illegal logging don't help, either.'

'But they're still around,' said Julie. She hadn't expected to see the great apes on this trip, but now the opportunity seemed to present itself and she couldn't wait.

'Thanks to the breeding programs and sanctuaries and rehabilitation sites that were started in the 1980s. Now orangutans are a big tourist attraction in both Borneo and Sumatra.'

'There's a good sanctuary not far from here. I've filmed there,' said Barry. 'You could go there,' he said to Julie.

Julie shook her head. 'It's incredible. I just love Kuching. I suppose my Great Aunt Bette must have come here?'

'She must have. It's the gateway to Iban country – up in the hill country,' said Matthew.

'How do we get to the Iban?'

'I'm arranging a boat and a friend to take us upriver,' said David. 'But we'll enjoy a day or so here first. Kuching is very pleasant.'

That evening the four of them headed out to where it was lively. Families were walking, children played on the public lawns and people were eating in the cafés and restaurants that faced the water. They ate in a small, smart bistro decorated with pictures from the era of the White Rajahs. The rattan furniture was covered in batik, fans and a Dayak headdress were hung on the walls and the menu was a mixture of local cuisine and colonial excess. While it was humid, the weather was bearable and later, they enjoyed strolling along the esplanade. The lights which were strung along its length twinkled in the Sarawak River. Food stalls were busy and couples and a few tourists sat on the benches, enjoying the views of the modern legislative assembly building, the rajah's palace, and the old fort.

'Rajah Sir Charles Brooke called most of the forts in Sarawak after female members of his family. That one over there is Fort Margherita. Then there's Fort Alice and Fort Sylvia and I can't remember the others,' David said with a smile.

The little shops and markets of the old town opposite the esplanade were busy and while the three men ordered a beer at a café in the park, Julie meandered through some of the shops, instantly finding examples of the tourist culture. Most shops had, laid out in front of them, tables covered with T-shirts with pictures of headhunters and orangutans. There were also toy orangutans of every description, fake blowpipes, sarongs, imitation lengths of the fine woven fabric made by Iban women, paintings of longhouses, and picture books on the jungles of Sarawak and the "Wild Men of Borneo". It was sensory overload.

The following day Julie decided to go to the museum while the others were finalising the details of their trip upriver. The gracious colonial museum was set back amongst lawns on a slight rise, and was another building constructed by Sir Charles, the second of the White Rajahs. The moment Julie walked inside and saw the cluttered rooms and the sweeping wooden staircase to the upper floor, lit by glass domes, she wished she had days to explore.

A friendly staff member explained to her that the ground floor held the natural history collection of local fauna, while upstairs were exhibits of ethnographic items such as models of longhouses of the various ethnic groups of Sarawak, musical instruments, fish and animal traps, handicrafts, models of boats, and ceremonial clothing and artifacts. Clearly, it was too much to take in for one visit.

Julie sat inside the model of a longhouse, or a rumah panjai, on a woven mat, looking at a set of photographs that showed how the interior was arranged. Essentially one long wall ran along the length of the building and served as a sort of corridor and communal verandah. Partitioned sections served as spaces for family units. Cooking fires were either in the corridor or in an adjoining area at the end of a suspended walkway. The photos gave only a sketchy sense of what a longhouse might be like, but now Julie's interest in the life of tribes like the Iban was really piqued.

Had her great aunt sat in a smoky longhouse somewhere in Sarawak, talking with these people who were once known as sea Dayaks and had been pirates and headhunters? Julie wished she'd had the time to retrieve Bette's book from her mother and read it before she came away.

Finally she found her way to the museum bookshop. This too, was a treasure trove of information, history and art. The woman behind the counter, who looked to be in her late forties, was a mixture of Malay and possibly Iban, judging by her deep olive skin, dark button eyes, small flat nose and straight dark hair. She was keenly attentive, which was not surprising as Julie was the only customer browsing among the bookshelves, carvings, artifacts and souvenirs.

'Are you looking for anything special?' asked the woman.

Julie shook her head. 'Not really. Everything is so interesting.'

'Your first time in Sarawak? Are you staying long? Where are you going?'

'I'm with friends who are taking me upriver to meet some Iban. I was hoping to learn a little bit about them before I went,' said Julie.

'You are a tourist? An academic or business person?'

'Tourist, I suppose. Except my family spent a lot of time in Malaya in the old days so I'm sort of retracing a bit of family history.'

'Your grandfather was in the war? You are Australian. I know the accent.'

'My grandfather was English. He ran a plantation at Slim River and I'm visiting here for the first time,' said Julie.

'Tracing family roots, eh? We have quite a lot of family histories recorded here. I run the library as well,' said the woman.

'This is a brilliant museum. I mean, really impressive when you consider the collections,' said Julie.

'We had a very wonderful curator after the war until the sixties. A true eccentric Englishman, a most interesting character. I am Mrs Ping. If I can be of any assistance . . .'

'Thank you. Actually, I wonder if you might know about my great aunt. She wrote a book about her time here in the early '70's . . .'

'As so many did, mostly the men, as they undertook more adventurous exploits. What was your auntie's name?'

'Bette Oldham. She wrote about spending some time with the Iban people.'

'Yes, of course, I know it. We had a copy here some months back. Quite a rare publication. I believe we sold it. She was interested in the orangutans, too, was she not?'

'I'm afraid I don't know. I only know about her book about visiting Borneo and her time staying with the Iban. Did she write about orangutans?'

Mrs Ping squeezed her eyes shut and rubbed the bridge of her nose. 'I'm trying to think. I'm fairly sure she wrote a pamphlet of some kind. It was early days then. Logging wasn't at the level it is now, which has caused such problems for the animals. The 1970s was the start of what is happening. Perhaps your relative saw the problem before anyone else.'

'I do wish I could have met her or known more about her,' said Julie.

'There could well be people still alive who knew her,' suggested Mrs Ping.

'Really, do you think anyone might remember her? My aunt would have been in her late eighties now, if she were still alive.' The thought that she might be able to meet someone who had known Bette thrilled Julie.

'I'll make it my personal challenge to find out something for you. Where are you staying? Do you have a mobile phone number?'

'Yes. This is so kind of you. We're going upriver in a day or so, where I doubt there's any reception. I'll check in with you when we get back.'

'If you have some time before you go, perhaps you'd like to go out to the wildlife sanctuary. I'd be happy to take you. I work there as a volunteer. Here's my number. Give me a call if you find that you have time,' said Mrs Ping.

'You mean to take me to where the orangutans are? That'd be fantastic. I'll have to check with my friend arranging my trip to see the Iban. He's an anthropologist and he has a small team with him. I'm tagging along.'

'Lucky you. What's your name, by the way?'

'I'm sorry. I'm Julie. Julie Reagan.'

'I'm Angie Ping. We shall see each other again, soon.'

When Julie told David of her meeting with Angie Ping at the museum bookshop, he was pleased for her.

'There you go! See, I knew you'd enjoy it here. There's so much to see.' He hugged her. 'We're going to have an amazing time.'

Julie found herself, unusually for her, taking a step backwards. David's enthusiasm was a bit smothering and, while she found his company enjoyable and his help invaluable, she thought he could be a bit over the top at times.

'How are Matthew and Barry going with the preparations?' she asked.

David frowned and sighed. 'The usual hold ups and delays. The men bringing the boat downriver on the last jungle leg of the trip had to attend some ceremony. A burial, I think. So they've gone to the Ruming longhouse, which will delay us a few days. But transport from Kuching to the first-stage landing is all on schedule. Unfortunately, I have to catch up on paperwork. Getting expeditions up into the backblocks requires a lot of form filling and discussions with the authorities. Just when you think you've given them everything they want, they think of something else.'

'I see. That sounds frustrating,' said Julie.

'It is, but it will all work out. I'm sorry for the delay. I'll try and keep you entertained while we're stuck in Kuching,' said David.

'Please, you have enough to do. Actually, this delay is great as I've had an invitation to go out to the wildlife sanctuary with Angie from the museum, and I'd like to do that.'

He gave her a quizzical look. 'You move fast! A stroll in the jungle with the men of the forest . . . go for it. I had hoped to take you myself, but I don't want to leave Kuching in case the authorities think of something else they want me to do. You can tell me all about it over dinner tomorrow night.'

Julie was tempted to say she might have other arrangements. She'd been thinking of having dinner with Angie Ping, she seemed such a nice woman, but Julie didn't want to offend David – he had arranged the trip and was looking after her. Instead she said, 'Sounds good. I'll be in touch. Now this afternoon I'm off to see the rest of the city. Kuching is really delightful.'

6

ANGIE WAS DRIVING JULIE out of Kuching on a good road but within minutes the jungle asserted itself. A deep green presence on the periphery of towns and villages, it was a living wall between those who lived on its edge and those creatures who lived within its heart.

'This is so kind of you to take me to see the orangutan sanctuary. I'm really looking forward to it,' said Julie.

'It's my pleasure. I just love going there and seeing my friends,' replied Angie.

'You mean the people working there?'

'Well, yes. But the orangutans are also my friends. Wait until you see them, then you'll know what I mean. Most times several of them show up at feeding time.'

'What kind of animals are out there?' said Julie, pointing into the jungle.

Angie glanced at her quickly before returning her attention to the road ahead. 'Sun bears, monkeys, small nocturnal creatures, the slow loris and birds, not to mention insects, bats and reptiles. But, you know, the numbers are declining because of the loss of trees due mainly to logging, and poachers have always been a problem, too. The illegal trade in wildlife is appalling.'

'That's terrible. Are the sanctuaries helping?' asked Julie.

'Certainly. Some orangutans can't look after themselves in the wild, and some mothers haven't learned how to rear their babies, so many of them rely on the feeding stations in the sanctuaries to survive. These, of course, attract tourists because this is where they can watch the apes up close. But, if it's a good season, the orangutans stay in the jungle to feed and, because they forage over a vast area, visitors to the sanctuary might not see them. It can be a bit of pot luck.'

'And you've been coming out here for a while? You must know the animals pretty well.'

Angie smiled. 'Yes, I have my favourites and I like to think I've established a bond with several of them. I'm looking forward to introducing you.'

Julie nodded.

Upon arrival Julie thought that the sanctuary looked rather touristy with its fancy entrance, administrative buildings, small cafeteria, information centre and souvenir shop. Painted signs and paths led through the grounds from the parking area, but once she lifted her gaze, Julie saw that they were surrounded by a solid wall of forest. She found it was hard to believe that a short distance from her modern world was a world older than humankind.

A small coach had disgorged a tour group. The tourists were now filing after their leader to a fenced area, where there was a wooden platform several metres from the ground, encircling a tree. Ropes and cables looped between the platform and the tree, and as Julie looked around she saw that there was more of the same maze of wires strung between the trees in the deeper parts of the forest. A game-keeper in a smart khaki uniform brought a bucket filled with pieces of jackfruit, pineapple and banana and spread them on the platform. The tourists crowded at the fence, jockeying for good positions, cameras ready.

'Don't worry about this. Come with me,' said Angie, leading Julie past a small building, through a short tunnel and across a bridge. Suddenly they were on a narrow track leading into the thick forest. The trees towered above them, tangled vines seemed to lash the trees together, and the dense canopy above them blocked patches of the sky. They'd stepped into a different world.

All was quiet. It was very humid in here and Julie felt perspiration begin to run down her face and between her breasts, soaking her shirt. The sudden shriek of a bird made her jump. Angie walked slowly, silently pointing out the roots jutting across the path so that Julie wouldn't trip. Julie paused every few steps to look around. The jungle was overwhelming. Then Angie stopped and pointed up. A large bird flew from a tree, the branches of which began to quiver.

'They're coming,' she whispered.

The women stood, peering upwards. The trees shook, a few small branches fell. Then suddenly a dark shape was discernible through the leaves, and Julie was amazed to see an orangutan become visible in the tree above them, swinging from one tree branch to the next, using its feet, arms and tail.

'That's Carla. She's a young female, about three years old,' said Angie softly. 'So her mother should be close by, too. The young stay near their mothers for the first four or five years.'

'There she is,' said Julie feeling excited. She could hardly believe she was seeing these great shaggy, ginger primates in the wild. She watched the mother move easily, a bright-eyed baby clinging to her side. The apes stopped and began pulling seeds from the branch above them. Suddenly there was a high-pitched shriek and another, slightly bigger, orangutan came closer, flinging itself from branch to branch. Then it stopped and began to break off leaves.

Julie reached for her camera, zooming in on the orangutans who were now busy eating, preening and ignoring their audience. She had no idea how long the two of them stood and watched. Julie was so fascinated that she stopped taking photos until Angie offered to take one of her with the orangutans in the background. Before she had a chance to do so, the two of them were interrupted by jarringly loud voices as a small group of tourists, red-faced with the heat and exertion, hurried towards them along the track, stopping when they saw Julie and Angie.

Quickly the apes in the trees above them were spotted, and there was much talk, exclamations and activity with video cameras. Julie was annoyed at the intrusive banter and what she considered to be banal remarks.

'We saw them eating at the feeding platform. Much closer than this,' said one man.

'But this is how they do it in the wild,' replied a woman.

'Get the baby to turn around so we can see its face. Do something, George.'

George clicked his tongue, hissed and made kissing noises before clapping his hands, with a commanding, 'Hey!'

A Japanese tourist, who hadn't taken his eye away from his camera screen, spoke rapidly to his wife and it was apparent he didn't approve of George's antics either. Nor, apparently, did the orangutans, and they rapidly swung away from sight.

170

George looked around and addressed the tour guide. 'Is that it? They coming back or what? Where are the rest of them? We were told there must be thirty or forty in here.'

'If the trees are in fruit, they'll be high up, looking for it. Look, there's a macaque,' said the guide, relieved to be able to point out the quick, pretty-faced grey monkey.

The tour group stood around, mopping dripping brows, then, as several people began to head back along the path towards the headquarters, a new female appeared. Like a trapeze artist she swiftly launched herself from highwire to tree branch, as if deliberately showing off. The tourists were delighted.

'That's Amber,' said the guide.

Angie, looking elsewhere, nudged Julie and then said something in Malay to the tour guide.

There was new movement in the treetops. Amber gave a shriek, and, swinging into a tree opposite the group, gave them all an excellent view.

'Ritchie is coming,' said Angie.

'Who's that? One of the males?' said Julie in a low voice.

'He's the oldest dominant male,' said Angie. 'He's chasing Amber to try and mate with her. But I don't think she's interested.'

The group had fallen silent, surprised by the apparent strength of the approaching male. Then there was a collective gasp as the huge male lazily heaved himself onto a nearby branch and sat, staring at the tourists. Everyone shrank back slightly as the orangutan contemplated them with keen and intelligent eyes.

'Looks like my mother's shag carpet,' joked George. 'Or Marge Simpson on a bad hair day.'

Amber was not amused, and she took flight, scurrying along tree branches and then suddenly landing directly above the group.

The tour guide signalled everyone to move back. 'Go slowly, just keep away. Ritchie will be coming after her.'

And sure enough the massive male reached for a branch that didn't look capable of carrying his weight, and then lumbered to the ground. He was close to the size of a very large man.

There were squeals and the crowd stumbled over each other as they retreated.

'Don't panic. He's only interested in the female. Remember you are in his territory. This isn't a zoo, it's the jungle,' said the guide.

Angie took Julie's hand and pulled her forward, pointing at a tree stump. 'Sit there. Just be still. He's not interested in us.' Angie stood beside her as Julie sat on the stump, her eyes glued to Ritchie. He was standing, gazing up at the female orangutan who was also sitting still, but looking around, obviously plotting her next move. In an instant, Ritchie moved, so quickly that Julie was amazed and the rest of the tourists hurried even further away.

Despite his great size, the male orangutan leapt into a tree and seemed to walk swiftly and easily from branch to branch until he was just below the female. She shrieked and scrambled further upwards into the flimsy branches, scattering leaves and twigs as she went.

Ritchie squatted on an impossibly slim branch and looked annoyed. He waited, and then Amber made her move. Leaping through the air, arms, legs and tail spread wide, clutching at tree branches, Amber was away and out of sight in seconds.

'What's he going to do now?' asked Julie.

'Eat, probably,' said Angie. 'There's fruit over there.'

They all watched Ritchie unhurriedly lumber away, then stop and daintily pick up a small fruit. Turning his back to them he ate it nonchalantly. The tourist guide rounded up his charges and moved them all towards the carpark.

Angie stood up. 'Come on, Julie, I'll show you a little more of the sanctuary.'

'Angie, that was just extraordinary. I can't thank you enough,' said Julie, glancing back at the great orange hulk sitting and eating quietly. 'I'm so glad everyone else left. I feel like I'm on safari and way out in the wilds. I mean, could anything go wrong? Would big Ritchie attack anyone?'

'Well, not so far. Orangutans are not known to be aggressive but as you saw today some tourists can be rather silly. People forget we are in their domain. And Ritchie is well over one hundred kilos, so it's wise to be cautious.'

They wandered back to the information centre and Angie showed Julie the photographs and histories of all the orangutans that had been released into the sanctuary.

'Can you believe this pathetic little thing was Ritchie?' asked Angie, showing Julie a story and photo from a local newspaper about a baby orangutan who'd been kept in a cage by poachers.

Julie looked at the photo. 'Oh, the poor thing! This was twenty years ago. He was rescued by a reporter?'

'Yes, the reporter was James Ritchie. He was onto the story of some illegal wildlife poachers and he caught up with them at Nanga Sumpa Iban longhouse. Nanga means estuary in Iban. James wanted to make a citizen's arrest but he was in the middle of nowhere and there were no police around. So he bought the poor thing for fifty ringgit, and took it back to his place. He was only about six months old. James had him dewormed and the next day the forestry officials came and brought him here. The state secretary though it would be nice to name the little orangutan after big Ritchie, so that's how he got his name.'

'Wow. What a great story.'

'Come with me and we'll see if we can find my favourite old grandmother.'

Angie led Julie away from the buildings to a separate dwelling which Julie realised was the infirmary and health clinic for the orangutans. Angie told her that any new arrivals were kept here in care till they were strong enough to be released.

'There's a quiet area at the back, and that's where the grandmother is.' Angie collected several bananas and went to a small clearing and, looking into the trees, began to call out and whistle.

'Naaaana, naana. Come, come.' Angie paused, listened and repeated her call.

'What's that? Up there, look!' exclaimed Julie as she sighted the shiver of a tree and, there on a limb, was an orangutan holding a very small baby.

Angie went closer, holding out the banana. Julie stayed still, watching,

'This is Booma. She's old, a grandmother many times over. And this is her baby. Her last baby. Chick, chick, come on,' called Angie quietly.

Julie could well imagine that the old female was a grandmother. Her fur wasn't lustrous but looked straggly and patchy. Her expression was tired, not the bright darting eyes of the other orangutans she'd seen earlier in the forest.

'Poor old girl,' said Julie. 'Her baby is very young. So tiny.'

'I looked after this old girl once when she was sick. She's back in the forest now, but she keeps coming back for her banana treat. So she knows that when I call, I'll have something nice for her.'

Slowly, not with caution but at her own pace, the old orangutan climbed down from the tree, hitching her infant up onto her back where it clung, just peeping over her mother's shoulder. Angie squatted on her haunches and held out the banana.

'Come and crouch beside me. She won't mind.'

Hardly daring to breathe, Julie moved slowly beside Angie. The elderly mother waddled forward, grasped the banana and carefully peeled it before eating it.

Angie handed Julie some peanuts she'd been carrying in her pocket. 'Hold them out in the palm of your hand.'

Julie did so, and to her delight, a wrinkled leathery hand flashed out and picked up several of the nuts. Booma chewed them, spat them into her hand and held the mushy nuts over her shoulder for the baby to eat. It was a leisurely procedure and when the nuts were gone the baby climbed around to the front of its mother and stared expectantly at Julie.

'I'd love to stroke her,' whispered Julie.

'Sometimes she'll let me touch her. But Booma's protective of her babies when they are so little.'

Slowly Angie reached forward, holding open her hand. The old mother took no notice, but the little one, obviously hoping that there might be nuts on offer, grabbed her fingers and as Angie lifted her hand the baby clung on, its small tail wrapping around her arm.

As Angie held the baby under the watchful eye of its mother, Julie tenderly stroked its back and head. The baby looked at her with large round eyes and for an instant Julie felt she was looking at a human baby with its trusting eyes, clinging touch and pursed lips.

But, quickly, Booma leaned forward and retrieved her infant, holding it possessively to her chest. Then, to Julie's joy, the old mother leaned down and tenderly kissed the top of her baby's head, a gesture that seemed so familiar. And with that, Booma ran rapidly in a loping gait across the clearing, one arm dangling, the other holding her baby and was swiftly up a tree and gone from sight.

'I can't believe that just happened,' said Julie, awestruck.

Angie straightened up. 'I never cease to wonder at these creatures. They, and chimps, are our closest biological relatives and they have their own personalities, habits and idiosyncrasies.'

The two women headed back to the parking lot.

'Thank you, Angie. When you actually meet orangutans, you can understand why people are so passionate about protecting them. They are the most beautiful animals. You do feel a kindred attachment to them.'

'I'm glad it all worked out. It doesn't always. Let me know when you're back from your trip upriver,' said Angie. 'Come on, I'll drive you into town.'

The river was wide and broad, fast flowing. The dugout canoe, a hollowed log with a few planks nailed along the sides, had a powerful outboard motor attached to its stern, propelling it through the thick water. Because the dugout was so narrow, they sat one behind the other with barely a hand span free on either side of their seats. The group had driven from Kuching at dawn, stopping in a small village where one of Rajah Brooke's forts, now converted into the village post office, still stood above the river. They'd been met by the two boatmen, father and son, who led them down to the river where the dugout waited.

Now one of the boatmen, perched in the bow, kept a watch for floating debris, rocks and shallow channels. Ngali was a young Iban who took his role very seriously. Occasionally he flicked an arm left or right to indicate that the ripples on the surface meant shallows or rocks ahead. Ayum, the old man at the tiller in the stern, took the appropriate evasive action.

Lined up, single file, behind the bowman, sat Barry with his camera ready, then Matthew, then David and behind him their Iban interpreter, and then Julie. The Iban boatmen were from a longhouse that Matthew and David had visited before and its headman had agreed to let them return.

Julie had been surprised when she met Matthew and David's interpreter. Chitra was a tall, elegantly beautiful Malaysian Indian in her twenties. Dressed in jeans and a pale-blue shirt, a designer belt showing off her narrow waist, a Nike cap perched over her thick dark hair, which fell in a braid over one shoulder, she looked like a Bollywood star on safari. Her brown eyes were huge, although frequently hidden by dark glasses, and her silky dark-skinned arms were ringed with several elaborate gold bracelets and bangles. On her feet she wore expensive soft leather hiking boots.

'Chitra works at the Swinburne University campus in Kuching. She studied at Swinburne in Melbourne and then moved back when the university expanded here in Sarawak,' said David as he introduced her to Julie.

'Lovely to meet you, Julie,' said Chitra. 'Are you looking forward to your first visit to a longhouse?'

'Yes, I am. You've been upriver many times before I assume?'

'Yes. I've been studying traditional culture for some time. I speak several dialects but I am most comfortable with Iban,' said Chitra.

'We met Chitra in Melbourne when she was studying there, so we've kept in touch,' added Matthew. 'Okay, let's load up.'

In the busyness of balancing their backpacks and gear in the narrow boat, Julie hadn't had much of a chance to ask Chitra any more questions. Chitra looked graceful and languid, and totally at home in the rough-hewn dugout. Julie, however, initially clung to its sides, afraid they could all easily tip into the river. But once they were underway, the breeze in her face, the last of the river villages no longer visible and no more river traffic, she felt she was at last experiencing the real and unspoiled jungle scenery she'd previously imagined, and she began to enjoy the trip.

The jungle came straight down to both sides of the river, impossibly thick, not an inch to place a foot or even a toe.

'Are there crocodiles in here?' she shouted above the engine to Matthew.

'And worse,' he called back.

But conversation was too difficult, so Julie sat and watched Barry film the scenery. They were going too fast to see any wildlife, though birds rose from the treetops as they passed and, at one point, the old man stopped the engine and as everyone turned back to look at him in alarm, he pointed and Barry raised his camera to his eye.

Swooping above them flew a pair of hornbills, unmistakable with their bright red casques on their long, curved beaks. Two dark silhouettes trailing long tail feathers, they hooted as they dipped and soared, suddenly breaking into what Julie thought to be wild, hysterical laughter, a dominating and arrogant sound.

She looked back at the boatman who was gesturing to the boy at the front. He waved his fingers above his head. Julie looked puzzled and she glanced at Matthew and David, but it was Chitra who explained.

'They used to hunt hornbills for the tail feathers to put in their headdresses. One species was hunted for the casque on their beak, which was hard and a golden colour. Years ago it was carved into objects and known as gold ivory. Very highly prized as a lucky omen by the Chinese. Even more so than precious jade,' she added.

'You know a lot. How come you studied the Iban?' asked Julie as the engine started up again.

'I grew up in Sarawak. My father worked in the Civil

178

Service. My mother trained in India as a doctor but nursed in Melbourne, and met my father there, and came back here to live. She started working as a medical officer and helped establish clinics up-country for the village people. My father still works in the state administration.'

'And you work at the uni?' asked Julie.

'Yes, I'm a teacher. Translating is a sideline,' said Chitra. 'I enjoy the opportunity to get out into the remote parts of the country.'

The engine spluttered and restarted, and they turned their attention back to the river. By now the water was flowing faster, but it was clear and the river was narrower. Soon the water seemed to boil and boulders jutted at its surface, making sharp stepping stones across the river. At one point the bottom of the dugout crunched over rocks. Ayum cut the motor and tipped the propeller up out of the water as Ngali pulled out a long stout pole from under the seats and began poling them forward.

David and Matthew also reached down for two more poles and they stood to punt the heavy dugout forward, while Barry filmed the exercise. When the boat flopped into a deep pool, Ayum revved the engine to life and they darted forward, just passing over the rocks, which now foamed with white-tailed froth.

Two more punting attempts finally found them jammed between two rocks, unable to move. Chitra, translating Ayum's commands, had them all step out of the dugout, and, stumbling and sliding, they pushed it over the slimy rocks and through the rapids. When there was smooth, deep water ahead of them, they scrambled back into their craft and surged forward once again.

'There's no way ahead!' exclaimed Julie some time later as the engine stopped below a small waterfall tumbling over the rocks. 'What now?'

'Portage,' sighed Matthew.

'We carry everything around the waterfall,' said David, hoisting his backpack.

'And then what?' wondered Julie.

'There's another dugout waiting for us to go upstream,' said Chitra, stepping daintily into knee-deep water, mindless of her expensive boots.

'Okay.' Julie stepped gingerly out, too, turning back to pick up her backpack. But the old man stopped her and as Ngali dragged the bow of the dugout towards the bank, he took Julie's arm to steady her and they inched together over the slippery stones to a large dry rock. Silently he handed her the backpack and returned to help his son manoeuvre the dugout closer to the bank.

All the gear was piled onto the large flat rock and, with Ngali leading, everyone carried their bags and the extra equipment and headed along a small track over the rise. The path was merely a foot wide, it led around a bend and back down to the river again. The sun was now beating down and Julie felt hot and sweaty. In front of her, Chitra walked easily, looking cool and comfortable, despite her waterlogged boots. As they waited at the river, the two boatmen made a return trip to the dugout and came back carrying the motor and petrol jerry can.

'Where's the taxi?' joked David.

Chitra spoke to the boatmen, who nodded their heads and sat down on the grass to smoke.

'Someone will be here soon,' she said. 'That could mean minutes or hours.'

Everyone opened their water bottles and shared a packet of biscuits.

'The water looks calm, could we swim?' asked Julie.

Matthew shook his head. 'I wouldn't. You never know what might be in there.'

Ayum cocked his head. 'Coming.'

'A boat is coming? Yes, I hear it,' said Julie.

They waited as the engine noise grew louder and, around a bend in the river, came another canoe manned by an Iban who looked older than Ayum. Even at some distance Julie saw that it was smaller than their original dugout and lower in the water, giving her the impression that it could be leaky.

She was right, and by the time everything had been loaded and they were all seated, the gunwale was only inches from the water. Julie held on tight, her fingertips trailing in the river.

'No more changes,' said David cheerfully.

'Have you noticed how the boats get leakier each time we change over?' said Matthew.

'Oh, no,' sighed Julie.

'The river is very low at this time of year, so boats can't get all the way up. In the monsoon season you don't have to stop at all,' said Chitra.

'Bit of a pain to go to the shop for bread,' commented Barry.

'Well, you asked for remote, traditional, picturesque,' David reminded him.

The dugout was now travelling close to the bank when, suddenly, there was a shriek, and a group of monkeys swung through the trees, chattering and calling. Then, for the first time, Julie saw human activity as they passed two Iban men tending their fishing nets, and, around the next corner of the river, she saw her first longhouse tucked among the trees. It was a long, intricate wooden and thatched building. Julie was surprised by its length. Dugouts and small praus were pulled up on the bank beneath it.

'There's a white flag. What does that mean?'

'No visitors. Hospitality along the river is a given, once you observe the protocol and are formally invited by the headman. But a white flag means there is something wrong, an illness, a death or that there is some ceremony taking place,' said Chitra. 'Just as well this is not where we're staying.'

Julie gazed at the shadowy, intricate structure up on its high stilts. 'Exciting. It's such a different existence, isn't it?' she said to Chitra.

Chitra glanced at her over her shoulder. 'It is. And it's disappearing. Changing. This is why it's important that the existing family structures and customs are documented, while we still can. I think it's a shame what's happening in some areas. You'll see.'

Julie sat back marvelling at the peaceful scene as they chugged along the narrow river. Thick jungle on either side looked as though a green curtain had parted and they were entering a sparkling stage, where butterflies darted. For the first time since she'd been in Malaysia, Julie realised that the sky she could see was blue.

'Blue sky. How clear and blue it is. I was getting used to seeing a yellow haze every day,' she said.

David threw her a look. 'You're not wrong there.'

'It's worse than the smog on a bad day in LA,' added Chitra.

'Ask anyone in Malaysia why it's so hazy and they'll say it's due to Indonesians burning the jungle in their country,' said David.

'But that's only partly true. It's caused by the expansion of palm oil plantations in both countries in areas of peat land,' added Matthew.

'Why? What's the connection?' asked Julie.

'Well,' explained Chitra, 'there is a great demand for palm oil, especially in Europe, because the canola crops there, which used to supply the food industry, are now used for biofuels, so food and cosmetic interests have switched to palm oil. As a result, the Malaysian and Indonesian governments have released hundreds of thousands of hectares in Sarawak and Kalimantan to grow it.'

'And when they clear the forests by burning them to create these palm oil plantations, it causes the air pollution,' said Julie.

'Sort of,' said David. 'Fires are set to clear the land, but the land is actually vast areas of peat, you know, carbon that was laid down thousands of years ago. When the destructive fires get out of control, the peat is set alight, too, and it just keeps burning because there is so much of it.'

'You mean the peat stays burning?' asked Julie. 'That won't do much for levels of carbon in the atmosphere, will it?'

'No, you're right, you should look at the satellite pictures. If the peat fires continue as they have been, they will certainly be responsible for helping to raise the earth's temperature. It's pretty scary,' said Chitra.

Barry switched off his camera and held out his hand, rubbing his fingers together. 'Money. There'll be someone making money from all this. Big companies, rich men. They blame the indigenous people for their slash-and-burn agriculture methods. That's rubbish.'

Chitra spoke to Ngali who answered vehemently and she translated, 'He says the Iban system of moving on to clear a new patch of jungle to grow food every few years has been happening for thousands of years and there are strict rules they've always observed. They are not responsible for the wholesale land clearances.'

Julie was silent. This rampant destruction seemed such a contrast to the ordered, well-run, responsible approach at Utopia, where the workers were cared for, sustainable practices were advocated, science and technology were used to develop better methods of harvesting, chemical spraying was avoided, and palm oil was marketed as a sustainably produced food ingredient. But she kept quiet.

Suddenly there was a lot more activity as Ayum nosed

the dugout into the small landing between a channel of rocks, formed into a rough semicircle.

'That's one of the bathing and washing spaces for the villagers,' said Chitra.

Through the jungle trees and cultivated bananas and fruit trees, Julie saw the longhouse. Then she saw the access to it from the river: a long, narrow log ladder with notches in it, barely enough for a toehold, was followed by a woven, swinging pathway bridge and then, finally, a goat track.

'I'll never get up there. Even without gear,' she said to David as they pulled their belongings out of the dugout.

'Yes, you will. Come on, we'll help you.'

Children came scampering down to meet them, bare feet barely touching the fragile looking steps and swaying bridge. They stared shyly at the Europeans but once Chitra spoke to them, they clustered around her bursting with questions.

'Here comes Tuai Rumah, the chief. He's the headman of the longhouse, and he will issue our formal invitation,' said David. 'He's also known as James and he speaks some English. His son, Charles, is quite well educated, but I don't know if he's here. There'll be a bedara, a welcome ceremony, later.'

Julie tried to absorb everything. She followed Chitra, carrying her backpack but when she came to the narrow ladder, she stopped.

'Barefoot is easiest. Turn your feet sideways and go up like a crab. Hold onto the bamboo railings. Someone will bring your gear,' Chitra told Julie.

Cautiously, Julie managed to scramble up the long ladder. She was followed by two little girls who just walked up it without hanging on, carrying Julie's backpack between them.

Two bare-breasted women in sarongs waiting at the

woven cane bridge were full of welcoming smiles and giggles. The older woman with her dry breasts like deflated balloons, long looped earlobes and missing teeth had bright black button eyes that were full of mischief and fun. The other woman, a baby tied to her back by a length of red cloth, was sweet faced and took Julie's hand as she stepped onto the swinging bridge.

The longhouse was surrounded by bananas, jack fruit and durian trees, and a garden plot. A rice field could be seen further up a hill. Under and around the raised longhouse were dogs, chickens and pigs. Several notched logs led up onto the long open verandah, or tanju as Chitra called it. Here washing hung, large looms with half-completed woven rattan mats leaned against the wall, a bitch lay feeding a litter of puppies and children played while families gathered to watch the visitors.

Stepping onto the tanju, Julie felt the slatted wooden floor creak and move with her weight. Shoes were removed, and they moved into the gloomy shade of a parallel long corridor that was the communal living area. Baskets, tools and storage bins were suspended from a loft and outboard motors, plastic tubs, a pile of gourds used to carry water, lengths of rattan and several large woven conical hats were piled against the walls.

'This is the ruai, the main indoor verandah, and those are the bilek, individual living quarters for each family,' said Chitra indicating the row of doors partitioning off each small apartment.

David took Julie's arm. 'Here we are. Because of the number of families in residence we might have to share rooms.'

'I don't mind sharing with Chitra,' said Julie quietly.

'Ah, she'll be sharing with Matthew.' David gave her a big smile and wink. 'They're old friends.'

'Oh.' Before she could ask where she would be sleeping,

the headman came to them and introduced his wife. She smiled, picked up Julie's bag and led Julie to the centre bilek and ushered her inside. The room was big, but cluttered. Two large mats had a traditional woven blanket on each while an intricately designed, half-completed blanket hung from a long loom leaning against the wall. The old leather suitcases and a basket in one corner probably held clothing, Julie thought, while sarongs, shirts and some bead necklaces were displayed along the bamboo frame of one wall. Large pots, including a Chinese ceramic one, water carriers, a brass gong and other metal ornaments, and a beautiful feather headdress were scattered about the room.

There was a roof flap, which was opened by a pole, letting in fresh air, and a bamboo door was propped open, showing a walkway that crossed to another small room. It was built with bits of corrugated iron and was obviously a detached kitchen. It occurred to Julie that fire must be a dreadful hazard in longhouses, even when the cooking fires were separated from the main dwelling. She recalled now seeing a small fireplace in the ruai, but this must be for warmth and not for cooking.

As she glanced around she realised that this room was the Tuai Rumah's bilek, which he shared with his wife. Julie hoped she wasn't being asked to share with them. But the chief's wife handed her a rolled mat and one of the beautiful blankets and beckoned her to follow. Julie was led to a smaller bilek next door, which was more simply decorated with fewer possessions. The woman took Julie's blanket, spread it on a floor mat, and dropped Julie's bag onto it. This room was to be her lodgings, but who her roommates were she had yet to discover.

When Julie returned to the ruai, it seemed that the bedara, the welcome ceremony, had already begun. Everyone was seated in a circle. The women and children were on the outer circle, the men and the visitors at the front.

Seated beside the headman was a very old man, his sculptured face cast in relief in the dim coolness. He wore his grey hair cropped in a short pudding-basin style with a fringe clipped in a straight line across his forehead. His ear lobes were splayed and hung heavily, almost to his shoulders, and he wore only a cawat, the local-style loincloth, folded in the front from the waist. He was heavily tattooed, even on the backs of his hands. Everyone showed him great respect.

'This is Tuai Rumah Jimbun. He is the father of Tuai James. He's eighty years old and used to work in the Sarawak Rangers in colonial times. He is greatly respected, not just because of his age, but because he has won a George Cross and, as you know, that is a very great honour,' said Chitra.

The old man made a short speech and the wife of Tuai James placed a jug in the centre of the circle and glasses and plastic mugs were handed around.

'It's tuak, which is fermented rice wine. But you can't refuse to drink,' David whispered to Julie. 'That causes offence.'

There was much laughter, explosive declarations, teasing and cajoling as the glasses were filled and passed. Julie took a sip of the tuak and found it to be extremely strong, but when she went to pass the glass on to Chitra there were howls of objection from everyone. Julie had no choice but to empty her glass. However, after three glasses, Julie felt quite dizzy, and looked at Chitra for help.

Chitra spoke to James's wife and then said to Julie. 'Nenek, grandmother, will take you outside. To the toilet space. It's rather rustic, I'm afraid.' She smiled apologetically.

Chitra was right about the toilet but as Julie made her way back to the ruai, she met a group of children playing outside. Some of the boys were scampering up a tall jackfruit tree to collect the heavy, spiked fruit. Two little girls, overcoming their shyness, tugged at Julie's hand and led her under one end of the longhouse where there was a chicken coop containing some recently hatched chickens. One of the girls reached in and brought out a chicken for Julie to stroke. In a large bamboo cage nearby perched a sleek cockerel, which Julie assumed was a fighting cock.

By now it was late afternoon and the evening bathing ritual began. Julie was wearing a swimsuit under her shorts and shirt, but Chitra emerged from the longhouse in a sarong and the two of them followed the other sarong-clad Iban women upriver while the men headed in the opposite direction.

In the river all the women chattered as they washed their long glossy hair, dunking themselves into the cool water. Chitra let her own dark hair swing loose, and to Julie she appeared to be at home in the water, like a sleek seal, her large, dark eyes shining. Julie floated and drifted away from the women until a voice called to her and she stood up, looking around.

A man was standing on the bank and while he was an Iban with the traditional long hair tied back in a smooth, knotted ponytail, his skin a deep honey colour, his features finely drawn, he looked out of place here because he was wearing aviator sunglasses, a stylish watch, and a pale-blue safari-style shirt tucked into well-cut shorts.

'Be careful, there are sharp rocks a little further along, near the men's pool,' he said.

'Thank you.' Julie scrambled to her feet, the water swirling above her knees. 'It's just so refreshing.'

He nodded and turned, heading towards the longhouse.

As the Iban women walked back along the path carrying babies and watching their children frolicking, Julie asked Chitra about the man she'd seen.

'A boat just came up. That'll be Charles, Tuai James's

son. The old chief's grandson. He works in Kuching in the police force.'

By now the visitors were becoming less of a novelty, and life in the longhouse proceeded as normal with the preparation of the evening meals and children to be fed and soothed, although it seemed to Julie the children were allowed to do as they wished and were not scolded. They clambered over the old people, played with the dogs and ran along the tanju squealing with joy. But Julie soon learned that the older children had tasks to do, carrying water, winnowing rice and picking out any fragments of husk, chopping wood, feeding the animals, and learning to repair the fishing nets.

'Don't they go to school?' Julie asked Chitra.

She shrugged. 'They are not forced to go. Travel is difficult and if they stay at a school in a town, the children don't like to be away from their families. The old chief Jimbun is trying to keep the old ways going and because these people are so far away from any of the towns, it's possible. But his son James is more inclined to value education, which is why his son Charles has such a good job.'

'No TV, no radio, no internet, I suppose that helps this to stay a backwater,' said Julie. 'I feel really privileged to experience it, while I can.'

David came and sat beside them. 'Yes, enjoy this while it's still here. It's a disappearing lifestyle. The cash economy is encroaching. The Iban grow rubber and pepper and sell woven cloth, blowpipes and carvings to traders but self-sufficiency is becoming harder. And the Iban also like modern things, like outboard motors and kerosene lamps.'

The meal, served on the woven floor mats, was made up of bowls of rice, dried fish, pieces of chicken and some root vegetables with fresh fruit. A bowl of water was passed to wash hands and then the food was shared. As darkness fell, oil lamps were lit. Some of the young girls, wearing glass bead necklaces, knelt in their short wrap skirts to play music on a set of small gongs.

As children fell asleep and the women sat in the background quietly talking, the tuak was brought out again and David, sitting close to Julie, said, 'Take a sip and pass the rest to me. Just be glad it's not a festival. These people know how to party. And dance!'

Charles had now changed out of his western clothes and into a checked sarong. He sat between his father and grandfather. Matthew and David began to ask James questions.

Julie listened, but also watched an old lady teaching a younger woman how to make the pua weavings with the intricate designs that had been handed down for generations. Matthew had told her that in the old days every man took a human head as a fertility rite, while every woman wove an heirloom blanket. Happily, he added, the men no longer take heads, but the weaving continues.

But tonight the talk was of tomorrow. And the tomorrows to come.

'The government has moved some Iban longhouse communities,' said David. 'And apparently some of these people like the new settlements and the new-style modern longhouses.'

Tuai James shook his head. 'That is true, but they no longer own their land, and they cannot practise the old ways of farming. The younger people go away to school and when they come back they do not always respect our customs. They are clumsy in the prau and have little knowledge of adat, the law.'

'Four thousand people have been moved out,' said David. 'Surely your time will come too.'

Matthew looked at Charles. 'The dams? That's the biggest threat isn't it?'

Julie turned to Chitra. 'What dams?' she asked.

But before Chitra could reply, old Tuai Rumah Jimbun began thumping the floor and shouting in poor, but very understandable, English, 'We will not move! Come what may! We will fight, as some of the Penans fought.'

'But they still lost their land, their forests are logged, highways eat into the jungle and their way of life is gone. The animals are gone. The politicians, the men in the suits in the cities and their friends get rich,' snapped his son Tuai James.

Charles put a calming hand on his father's arm on one side and his grandfather's on the other. He also spoke. 'It is true. The dams will change Sarawak. Hydro-electric schemes and underwater cables to take their power to the rest of Malaysia, smelters and mines are planned. Longhouses like ours may also be flooded for more dams.' He shrugged. 'The old people do not want change.'

'Is there anything that your grandfather can do?' asked David.

'He is keeping his fingers crossed. He hopes that the petara, the demi-gods will protect his family. He will ask the manang, the shaman, to call out to the dieties, Prince Kelieng and Princess Kumang in a special Gawai ceremony. They will kill a fat pig and smear the blood over his longhouse and family members to enable the gods to protect them!' He paused. 'This is my grandfather's wish. But there are those who think that this is not enough and would like to take more action to fight the dams. But to fight the corruption, the political plans, the big business, the outside influence and investments is beyond simple people like us.' He turned to Barry. 'But it is a story I hope you will tell people. Show them what is being lost.' And with that Charles rose and walked into the darkness.

The tuak was passed and the old women also began talking and it was obvious to Julie that everyone was talking about what the old headman had said.

191

Soon the music and singing began. The old songs, which told the stories of their past, the legends and the battles, echoed through the wooden longhouse. Children fell asleep where they were and the dipper went into the rice wine barrel to refill the jugs.

Julie was feeling lightheaded even from a few sips of tuak. David, who had had Julie's share of the rice wine as well as his own, was certainly starting to enjoy himself. Julie decided that she needed to step out onto the tanju for some fresh air, so she shuffled to the rear of the circle and, picking up her torch, quietly left the party.

She stood at the railing, gazing at the outline of the jungle across the darkened river. What animals were about, she wondered? Would she ever be brave enough to sit out there, sleep in the jungle at night as her Great Aunt Bette could have done? Suddenly the jungle seemed too close and too confronting. But the laughter and singing behind her, the glow from the oil lamps, were comforting. She walked to the end of the open verandah and looked up at the mountains etched against the dark night sky. It was the first time she'd seen the stars clearly since being in Malaysia.

She felt the bamboo slats beneath her feet shudder with silent footsteps and she was about to turn around when a monkey, quite close to her, let out a screech followed by squeals. Julie shakily turned on her torch and swung it around but she could see nothing out there in the night. As the beam of light swung back onto the tanju she let out a small scream and jumped.

In the beam of the yellow torchlight faces leered and gaped at her. Empty eye sockets, grinning mouths, open in silent screams, a row of heads strung along a beam of light glared back at her.

'Do not be afraid. They are old and harmless.' Charles stepped forward. 'They are trophies my forebears took in battle.'

'Tuai Jimbun? Your grandfather?'

There was a flash of white teeth in the gloom as Charles smiled at her. 'Yes. He was one who took heads. Did you notice that the backs of his hands are tattooed? It is the sign that he has taken a head. It was a ritual to set one apart from other men. The White Rajahs tried to stamp out the custom. Like many things, it took some time, but the heads that were taken long ago are still highly prized and respected.'

'What you said in there, about the future with the flooding from the dams, the development, the changes that will come, does that make you sad?' asked Julie. 'My family's home is threatened by development, too, which makes my mother and me sad. But we are fighting to stop it.'

'Sadly, it seems too late for us, the power of money is too strong. And many people think the change for the modern world sounds good. An easier life. I feel sad at the loss of the jungle – for the creatures. And for us. It holds many secrets we are yet to learn.'

'Like medicines?'

'For one, yes.' Charles began to walk back along the verandah in the darkness.

Julie walked beside him. 'And what about your grandfather's faith in the spirits and gods? Will that be any help?'

'Who knows? We believe in summum bonum – good fortune, a sign of favour from the gods. Tuai Rumah Jimbun hopes we will be blessed with luck and I hope for as long as he lives he has that hope. For me, I know that the Iban will have to adjust to changing times.' He paused. 'But we try to keep the traditions alive, no matter where our longhouse may be.'

'That's good,' said Julie softly.

She was thoughtful. 'I had an aunt, my grandmother's

sister, who lived in Malaysia after the war. She was married to a Chinese man, which is why she was ostracised by the rest of the family. But she spent time among Iban people, I'm not sure where abouts in Sarawak, and she wrote a book about it. That's the reason I came here.'

'What did she tell you?' Charles was interested.

'I never met her. David found the book she wrote during his research. It was the first our family knew about my great aunt's adventure.'

'A lady adventurer! There have been many white ladies coming to Borneo to do extraordinary things. Sometimes for themselves as much as for the people and the jungle animals,' said Charles. 'Maybe my father or grandfather has heard of your relative.'

'She wrote the book in the early seventies,' said Julie. 'Do you think Tuai James, your father, might know anything?'

'I shall ask him in the morning. For now the dancing is starting. Come and see how the hornbill comes to life,' said Charles cheerfully as they went back into the ruai.

Julie was taken aback by the escalation in the festivities. Two of the men had donned elaborate feather headdresses and were dancing to the beat of drums and gongs, their arms mimicking the horned beak and the swaying of a large bird. Julie was instantly reminded of seeing films of Aboriginal corroborees where the dancers perfectly mimicked the kangaroo or emu.

Some of the girls were pulling the visitors up to dance, and Matthew and David, both very merry now, staggered about in an attempt to follow the lithe male dancers. Barry refused to join them, but lifted his camera to capture the action. Julie just felt exhausted from the very long day and wanted to go to sleep.

Charles sat back down by his elders but was swiftly pulled to his feet by one of the pretty young women. The

194

women didn't dance but clapped their hands, laughed and cajoled the men to get into the spirit of things.

While David and Matthew were making what Julie thought was something of a spectacle of themselves as they stumbled and swayed about, everyone seemed happy and they were enjoying themselves.

Chitra tapped her on the shoulder. 'If you want to go to sleep that'll be okay. Where did Indai Tuai, the old lady, put your things?'

'She put me over there. I'll just sneak away. See you in the morning.'

By her torchlight Julie saw that there were two teenage girls sound asleep on mats on the floor and her bag was sitting in a corner near a mat that was covered with a blanket. In the darkness she undressed, wrapped herself in a sarong and lay down, pulling up the blanket as the night was surprisingly cool.

The music continued, but the shaking and movement of the floor subsided as the dancing tapered off and a chanting, sing-song began in its place.

Julie wasn't sure if she'd slept or not but she was aware of shuffling as someone else came into the bilek. She rolled on her side and stifled a gasp as a hand touched her shoulder.

'Hey Julie . . . You awake? Come on, you wanna dance?'

'David, no. Go away,' said Julie firmly, tightening the blanket around her.

'C'mon, then let me get warm.' He started to lie down beside her, stretching out and dropping an arm over her shoulders. 'Did ya like the dancing? Hornbill, it was.' He started to stifle giggles.

'David, you're pissed. Get out. Go away,' snapped Julie.

'I did you a favour, drank your tuak.' He leaned over trying to kiss her.

'Well, you shouldn't have. C'mon, stop it. This is disgusting.' Julie sat up. And as he started to talk, somewhat incoherently, she pushed him away from her. 'I don't want you in here.'

'S'orright. Iban very relaxed 'bout sex. Very healthy, very natural,' he slurred.

'Maybe, but I'm not. I'm choosey.' She pushed him hard and yanked her blanket away, leaving him lying on the floor. She grabbed her torch and, wrapping herself in her blanket, debated about sleeping in the far corner of the room, next to the girls or curling up outside in the ruai. She stepped outside and closed the loose-woven apartment door behind her. A few figures were moving about at the far end of the ruai, and the coal embers of a small fire burned in a metal ring. The bitch and her litter were stretched out beside it. Julie curled up in her blanket by the soft warmth of the dying fire and promptly went to sleep.

She slept very soundly, and when she stirred just before dawn she wondered if she'd dreamed that a figure had stooped over her in the night then continued past her. Her sleep had been heavy and she felt quite stiff. Several women were moving around. Another woman sat breastfeeding her baby. Two of the women picked up some water gourds and a plastic bucket and headed outside to fetch water. Julie followed them to freshen up and find some privacy.

The morning was coolly crisp, mist swirling away over the jungle, and the sun not yet up. The world was utterly peaceful.

Julie joined the women in the river, and they giggled as she shivered in the cold water. One handed her a spare sarong to dry herself and when she hurried back to the longhouse the smell of the wood fire and the blue curl of smoke coming from the kitchen was a welcome sign that breakfast was underway.

David looked bleary eyed as he sat cross-legged in the ruai, a blanket around his shoulders, poking at the remains of the small fire in an attempt to get a blaze going.

'Good morning, David,' said Julie coolly.

He grunted. 'Bloody tuak. Gets you every time.'

'Not me,' said Julie as she went to dress, thinking how annoyed she was with him. While she could dismiss his drunken pass at her as the result of too much rice wine, he had, nevertheless, sunk in her estimation and she found she actually didn't like him very much at all. She appreciated his help with her mother's bypass fight and the fact that he'd opened a door to her family's past, but these actions didn't give him any rights of possession, which he'd been suggesting, not just last night, but for the last few days. Now she wondered how she was going to put up with him for the rest of the week.

Nevertheless the day passed quickly and was full of interest. Tuai James, acting as tour guide, took them into the jungle, showing the area that had been cleared for their rice fields and other crops. He gave them a demonstration of hunting with the blowpipe, though he said that it was seldom used these days. By the river they watched the Iban catch fish by herding them into the big woven nets and traps and, finally, a group of men showed them how they cleared the jungle with the large and lethal parangs.

They came to a beautiful, clear stream in a magical setting and waded upstream while Tuai James pointed out plants, monkeys and the paw print of a large animal. Barry filmed it all, including the time spent just sitting and smoking. By the time they trudged back to the long-house it was sunset and Julie found that bathing in the river with the women and children that evening was a cool and welcome relief.

There was no singing and dancing that night. After

the meal Tuai Jimbun lay back with his cigarette and everyone settled comfortably, looking expectantly at him.

'Grandfather is telling a story,' Chitra told Julie and she translated as the old man's voice droned on, reciting one of the crowd's favourites.

Later, as Julie walked down the ruai to her bilek to go to sleep, Charles stopped her.

'In case you're interested, I am going downriver tomorrow. I have to return to Kuching. If you wish to come with me, you're welcome. I understand the team has a lot more field work to do. Perhaps you are not all that interested in scientific work.'

Julie leapt at the opportunity. 'Yes, I'd like to. That would be great. Very kind of you. I'll tell the others in the morning.'

Charles nodded. 'In that case we can talk on the journey.'

Julie thought it an odd comment, the way he put it, but when she joined the girls on the mats in the bilek she had no trouble sleeping.

David was surprised by her decision to leave suddenly. He said that he was concerned for her welfare and wellbeing, and was worried about her going back to Kuching with Charles. But Julie thought that he was just miffed that she was taking off.

'Charles seems very competent and Ngali is taking us. I'm keen to get back and spend more time in Kuching. I'd like to meet up with Angie again. This has been a wonderful experience and I can't thank you enough for bringing me along, but you have your work to do and I don't want to get in the way. We'll catch up again,' she said vaguely.

'I feel responsible for you, that's all,' he said. 'I promised your mother . . .'

'David! I'm a grown woman and while I mightn't be as knowledgeable about the jungle as you, I'm perfectly safe with Charles. Now I'll just say goodbye to the others.'

Chitra explained the order of farewells and the appropriate expressions of thanks that Julie should say to the Iban, and by the time she had completed them all, the others had left on their field work. A small posse of children and some of the women followed her to the boat where Charles and Ngali were waiting for her.

With fewer people and little gear in the boat, the trip downriver was easier and smoother.

Apart from pointing out a few things of interest as the boat nosed through the cocoa-coloured water, Charles had little to say. But the return journey was as relaxing and as interesting as the trip upriver had been.

It wasn't until they'd got to the village near the old fort, thrown their belongings into Charles's old car, which was 'fully air-conditioned' when all the windows were wound down, and had a sweet kopi susu, the local coffee, at a little shop, that Charles took off his dark glasses and seemed to relax.

'So have you found this little adventure useful?' he asked.

'Interesting but for me it's not like I'm researching, filming or writing anything. I was just trying to get a sense of how things used to be. I feel very privileged.'

'How things were when your aunt visited the Iban?' he said.

'I suppose so. I don't imagine a lot has changed since then.'

'I spoke to my father and he thinks he knows about your aunt. She was married to a rich Chinese trader and came with him to Sarawak. Later she came by herself and stayed with some local people. I asked my father many questions but she didn't stay at our longhouse so he doesn't know very much. She stayed closer to the Kalimantan border. I gather she was also interested in the orangutans.'

'That's amazing,' said Julie. 'I wish I could ask Tuai James and Tuai Jimbun more questions.'

'I don't think they know any more. Have you been to the museum in Kuching?'

'Yes, the lady there was very helpful.'

'Mrs Ping,' said Charles.

'That's right.'

'If anyone can find out anything more, she will. Summum bonum. Hang on to the idea of good luck falling on you.'

'It seems to be,' said Julie.

Charles rose. 'We must go.'

When Julie walked into the Sarawak museum, Angie Ping looked up and smiled at her.

'The traveller returns from the jungle. Was it all right? I thought you'd be away longer.'

'I didn't want to hold up the team, they had work to do. So when there was a chance of a lift back with Charles, the grandson of the old headman, I grabbed it,' said Julie.

'Ah Charles, Tuai James's son, and Tuai Rumah Jimbun's grandson.'

'He did give me some exciting news on our way back. His father and grandfather remember my Great Aunt Bette.'

'That is exciting for you,' said Angie. She shuffled some books and papers on the counter. 'Here, I found this.' She handed Julie a small bound booklet with a faded photograph of an orangutan on the cover. Above it was the title, *In Peril – the Lost World of the Orangutans*, Bette Oldham.' Angie smiled. 'I've photocopied it for you. She sounds quite a woman, your aunt.'

Julie took the stapled, photocopied copy of her great aunt's booklet. 'This is amazing. I'll read it as soon as I can, and thank you so much for finding it.'

'I'm so glad I could help. Come along, I'll take you to my favourite place on the river for a coffee. It's called the Rajah Brooke's Café. More history,' laughed Angie as she closed the museum shop and hung a sign, 'Back in 15 mins' on the door.

7

CURLED IN A DEEP rattan chair after a swim in the pool, the chick blinds lowered against the late afternoon sunlight, a gin and tonic in her hand, Julie felt relaxed and very at home. Shane, Peter and Martine, Shane's beautiful wife, were eager to hear about her trip upriver in Sarawak.

'I haven't been to a longhouse and when we went to see the orangutans, there weren't any,' said Martine in her musical French accent. 'I must try again. What do you think, Shane?'

'It was fascinating,' said Julie. 'I fell in love with the orangutans. They have the most wonderful personalities. And the Iban are lovely people. They might have been headhunters once, but they have a very polite and caring society. I can see why Great Aunt Bette was so intrigued with their culture.'

'We didn't expect you back so soon,' said Peter. 'We thought you'd be gone for at least a week with the research team.'

Julie shifted in her chair. 'Oh, well, they had work to do and the living conditions were very primitive.'

Martine smiled at her. 'And? I sense there is something else?'

Julie returned her smile. 'Trust a woman! Actually I was a bit uncomfortable, no, annoyed, actually, with David Cooper. He overdid the tuak, the rice wine, and made a pass at me . . .'

'That stuff's lethal. But you can't really hold that against him, can you?' said Peter.

'That's such a male thing to say,' said Martine. 'You can't use tuak as an excuse, especially if one doesn't reciprocate the feelings.'

'Exactly,' said Julie. 'He's one of those men who's always touching you and being overattentive. If you like the guy – fine. But he's just not my type, not that it registered with him. I certainly didn't want him looking after me. It became unpleasant, so I came back under my own steam, and here I am.'

'Well, you timed your return well. We were planning a quick trip and thought you might like to come along and now with your early return from Sarawak, the timing is perfect,' said Shane.

'Where were you planning to go?' asked Julie.

'Langkawi Island. Friends of ours run a resort there, which is rather fun. There'll be several of us going. Do you think you'd like to join us?'

'I'd love to, if it's not wildly expensive. What's at Langkawi?' asked Julie. She thought that an island resort would be a nice change from the jungle setting she'd just experienced.

'There is a series of islands north of Penang, bordering

Thailand. The main island is Langkawi and it has rainforest, resorts and some nice eateries.'

'And very lovely spas,' added Martine.

'We're planning to share a house for a few days at a resort which is made up of old traditional Malay houses . . . but they are done up with comfortable furnishings,' said Shane.

'So maybe there'll be seven or eight of us. I wish my girlfriend was here,' said Peter. 'Do you like fishing, Julie? We can hire a boat. Chris is coming. You met him here. The RAAF chap. He's mad for fishing. And we can always climb up to the lake, if you're feeling energetic.'

'I love the spa and relaxing by the pool,' said Martine. 'It's a very stylish place.'

'That sounds good to me, too,' said Julie. 'I like fishing but I'd like to explore too, as I might never get back there again.'

After dinner that evening, Shane took Julie into their great grandfather's library. She tried to ignore the glassy-eyed mounted animal heads and watched as Shane opened a drawer in the large, elaborate old desk in the corner. He pulled out a bound notebook and handed it to her.

'Roland's memoir. It's the original. I thought you might prefer to read it in his hand.'

'How wonderful.' She fingered the old notebook. 'I don't think that I've ever held anything that belonged to him before. Can I read it here?'

'Yes. It's not a diary, it's really a short account of his war years. It wasn't meant for publication or anything like that. I don't even think that it was for the family. I know that many men who served wrote some account of their time in the war,' said Shane. 'It may have been the highlight of their lives. In our grandfather's case, his whole life was quite eventful, but when you read this, you realise that he revelled in his years fighting in special operations behind the lines.'

'I'll look forward to reading it.' She glanced at the handwritten title neatly underlined in red ink and when Shane left her, she began to read.

Behind the Green Curtain. A Memoir. By Roland Elliott.

On reflection, one wonders how more people didn't see it coming. The war. The invasion. The rise of communism. I suppose hindsight is a wonderful thing. We thought that we were important to England, but found that we weren't. White-hall had more important priorities in Europe and we were betrayed. Even after the Japanese war was over, the times have changed and the mood is no longer complacent in our neck of the woods. Life on our plantation appears to have returned to normal, but the scars run deep. Even now, I realise that the halcyon prewar days will never return and I am doubtful that Malaya can become united. Too many races, cultures, creeds, too much betrayal. But, as my dear father was wont to say, 'twas ever thus.

But that is now. The days before the war were carefree. The word of the white man was obeyed without question and we had the best of times, the best of whatever was available from here and from abroad, and, along with the sense of privi-lege, we also had the freedom to do as we wished. We were treated as honoured guests in the villages, given a meal that could have cost a family a day or more of hard toil. And we took it as our due. And when the war came, when we were reduced to being no better than coolies in the eyes of the invad-ers, when the loyalties of those we'd looked down upon came to save us, to help us shelter or escape, and inevitably, at the end, we let them down.

Of course, many never expected the war with the Japanese

to come anywhere near us in Malaya or Borneo. Life went on at its indulgent pace with parties, dances, hunting and tennis, love matches, courtships, and the business of making money. If you were rich, influential, educated, no matter what your skin colour, you mixed with us. My father occasionally commented that Malaya was run by the British for the benefit of the Chinese or, depending on your viewpoint, Malaya was a country run by the Chinese to benefit the British. The Malay elite had a sense of entitlement, which perhaps is not surprising. It was their country, the other races were immigrants. But, of course, if you have money, position, power, you can enter any of the worlds of Malaya. But the poor, the Chinese coolies, the Indian plantation workers and the native Malays, with neither wealth nor influence, were overlooked or dismissed by the ruling powers. This was the Malaya I lived in before the war, which changed it all.

Although war had erupted in Europe in 1939, it was thought, especially in England, that the European war would never touch the Pacific. Indeed Whitehall thought that the strategic defences of Malaya could be kept minimal. The belief was always that 'Singapore will be held', an invincible island fortress, we were told. And who would attack us? The Japanese had already invaded Manchuria and then China and it was well known that they wanted to control the oil fields of the Dutch East Indies, but Father thought that was all very unlikely. So life went on, keeping up appearances, a stiff upper lip, and worrying about family back in the old country. My mother was living there with her elderly parents and my father was concerned for her safety.

But some of us, myself included, were worried about the Japanese. We knew that the Jap community had been busy for years, poking about in the jungle around the estates. They also had holdings at important rail and road junctures, in mining areas. One could hardly avoid noting the ore that was being shipped to Japan those past years, undoubtedly to be put to use in making armaments. Later we found out that their business organisations were not only sharing important information with their government, but were a cover for spying and intelligence gathering and other political activities. Small businesses were established at convenient locations where they could observe the activities – or lack thereof – happening at the aerodromes, ports, around the bays and coastline, in the jungles and the swamps. We had been carefully observed, measured and our metier taken since the 1930s. Too late we learned of secret caches of arms and bunkers hidden in rubber estates owned by the Japs. We had been complacent to our cost.

Blame for this ignorance can be placed at many feet, for when information was being collected by natives, telling planters of Japanese activity in the jungles and the remote coast and islands, along with the observations by fishermen, rangers and miners, and sent to the authorities in Singapore, it was, sadly, ignored. Even when I raised the subject with other planters about the rumours swirling around Malaya, my views were considered to be alarmist.

But little did we know that the defence of Malaya had been scaled down by the heads in Whitehall. The war in Europe was considered far too serious to give any thought as to what might happen in their far-flung eastern empire. However, we, in Malaya, pressed on, doing our bit with petrol rationing, rising prices and the inconvenience of routine blackout trials. Even when the Japs moved into Indo-China, the administration did not feel unduly threatened. The feeling was that, 'They wouldn't dare! And if the Nips made any move, we would be ready for them.'

Why did they say that? We had so few defences which, we later learned, were in all the least strategic positions. But anyone who dared to question was pooh-poohed. Everyone with any authority, any connection with the military, became so puffed up with their own importance, so petty minded, bureaucratic and downright insufferable, that the tokenism of our war efforts were laughable. Sometimes I really did indeed think that our society was becoming rather like something from a Noel Coward play or from the pages of a novel by that dreadful Somerset Maugham. Nonetheless I felt I had to do something constructive and I joined the Perak Volunteers. My father wanted to do his bit, but I talked him round. Staying put, I thought, was the best thing for him to do.

Then on December 8th 1941, we were stunned to hear that not only had the American fleet been destroyed at Pearl Harbour, but that the Japs had landed at Kota Bharu in northern Malaya. They were also bombing the main airfields in the north-west of the country, destroying half of the Allied aircraft stationed there. Three days later we heard news that was considerably worse. The battleship *Prince of Wales* and the cruiser *Repulse*, which had been sent to reinforce the British defences only days before, had been sunk with a huge loss of life. Morale dropped.

The consequences of these Japanese actions were catastrophic. As the disaster continued to unfold, my father and I sat in the evening peacefulness at the end of another balmy day, enjoying a stengah on the verandah as flowers fell lightly to the grass in front of us. My wife and her visiting sister gossiped quietly while they sat and knitted for the war effort, which had once seemed so far removed from us and yet unmistakably was coming closer.

Then events moved more quickly.

The inevitability of the war was brought home to us a couple of days later, when the Winchesters, friends of ours from Penang, arrived at Utopia with just a couple of suitcases. Penang had been savagely bombed and they were fleeing the town, leaving almost everything behind.

'My dear,' said the distraught Mrs Winchester, 'we've had to leave everything. I just want to get to Singapore, where we'll be safe. Hopefully we might be able to get a ship from there to

South Africa. I can't believe what is happening. The planes just came over Penang without any warning and bombed the place. There must be thousands killed. We were lucky, as we live on the hill and the Japs only seemed to be interested in destroying the town and the harbour, so we were able to get away, but still, it's all such a disaster.'

(They were never to return. They lost their home and all their possessions in subsequent fighting.)

My wife Margaret and her sister Bette comforted Mrs Winchester, but the news that these people were running ahead of the Japanese forces unnerved Margaret.

'Heavens, Roland,' she said. 'We just can't sit here and wait for the Japs to get to Utopia. We have to do something.'

So I decided then and there that my wife, my son Philip, a mere three years old, and my sister-in-law must also try to get out of Malaya and return to their family home in Australia.

'Margaret, you're right. You have to try and get a ship back to Australia. I'm sure that the authorities will be organising some sort of evacuation from Singapore, which I suppose is safe enough. I'm going to have to join my unit straight away, so you'll have to take Bette, Philip and Father and get to Singapore. But you'll be fine. Hamid will drive you as far as KL and you can get the train from there.'

My wife stared at me. 'You can't be serious. You can't just abandon us to take our chances.'

'What choice do I have?' I tried to explain. 'I have to stay and fight the Japs.'

'Margaret, we'll be fine,' Bette, her sister, assured her. 'We'll have Eugene with us and he knows the country better than anyone, and Gilbert's in Singapore, trying to ship out rubber for his company. He'll organise things for us when we get there.'

But my father had other ideas.

'I'm not leaving the plantation,' he said. 'I have built this place from the ground up. It's been my life's work. Besides I

209

will not leave my people. They have been faithful and I must remain loyal to them. These people trust me, so what would they think if the tuan besar fled and left them to the Japs. No, it's simply not on.'

The decision that neither my father Eugene, or myself would be travelling south threw Margaret into a frenzy of organisation and packing. I tried to persuade her to travel as lightly as possible since time was of the essence and petrol could be difficult to get, but she wanted to take everything. Her sister Bette, a more practical young woman, persuaded Margaret to pack a trunk of her valuables and sentimental possessions, and I quietly buried it in the garden, where I hoped it would remain safe from whatever was to occur.

Before they could leave with Hamid we had two other late-night visitors, also fleeing south from Penang. They told us more about the bombing and the evacuation.

'It has all been such a shambles,' said Ethel Bourke, an old friend. 'We were told that we had to leave secretly. No thought was given to our Asian staff, who were just left to face the Japs. I feel so ashamed that we did that. Surely there must have been some way to help them. Anyway, we came over to the mainland on an old Straits Steamship ferry and then we were supposed to be packed into a train heading south. It was impossibly crowded and I was worried all the time about the train being strafed, but it so happened that my friend Mildred here knew where there was a company car, so we left the train and drove down under our own steam.'

Their story made me reassess my original plan and, taking Hamid to one side, I told him that he would be driving the women and my son all the way to Singapore. My father briefly laid his hand on Hamid's shoulder, telling him that since he had been a faithful driver for many years, he could be entrusted with the lives of the mems and the tuan kechil.

Philip did not want to leave, and he clung to me when I carried him to the car. I told him he was to be brave, to listen and do what his mother and aunt told him. I said that he had to be a big boy until we were all home again at Utopia, when the war was over. My wife flung her arms around my neck.

'You will be careful, Roland. I don't know how I would manage if anything happened to you.'

I had decided that Hamid should drive by night, pulling into rubber trees should there be any danger. Hamid said he had friends who would help them and once the women had safely arrived in Singapore he would make his way back to Utopia. I believed him and felt comforted that he would be here for my father.

I was relieved the next morning that the women were on their way to safety. I said goodbye to my father when I was collected by another volunteer, Bill Dickson, and we drove to meet up with the rest of the unit. Bill, who was some years younger than me, was a fine young man and a cadet in the Malayan Civil Service. I liked him enormously.

The drive was certainly eventful. We took it in turns behind the wheel. Driving hard, fast and incautiously was perhaps not wise. Although it was a road we traversed often, we were generally in the hands of our syce, and our drivers knew every inch of these roads, whereas Bill and I were often caught unawares. Suddenly we saw the dirt on the road ahead of us exploding. Coming very low towards us over the top of the road zoomed a Jap plane. Instantly, Bill slid off the road into the edge of a plantation and we rolled out of the car, trying to make for shelter in the undergrowth. As we crawled in between the rubber trees, we heard our car being strafed. Seconds later, the plane had gone. We waited, hoping there were no more planes, and were astounded that the vehicle had not burst into flames.

'That was a close call,' remarked Bill, in a tone of voice that suggested he was used to these sorts of encounters. 'How are we going to get the car out of here?' The task of pushing the car back onto the road was indeed going to be difficult, for although it seemed relatively undamaged, one wheel refused to move as the mudguard was flattened against it.

While we were trying to straighten out the mudguard, a frightened whisper came from further in the plantation. Shyly, an Indian girl, holding an infant, came towards us. In a mixture of Malay, Tamil and English she told us everyone in their village had left because a Jap plane had machine-gunned it and they were too frightened to come back. She had been hiding in a rice paddy, but she was now alone, so we offered to drop her and her child off at the next village once we got the car going. As we banged at the jammed mudguard the woman went back into the plantation and returned with a tapper's knife and small axe. With these we were able to free the mudguard.

She shook and wept in the back seat, the child at her breast until we left her at a nearby kampong.

We were near to our destination when I remarked, 'If we can drive through the back roads and the plantation roads, what's to stop the Japanese doing the same? Why would they just stick to the main road? They'll come around, behind our troops.'

I already knew Bill's reply. 'I suppose that's their plan.'

We joined our unit, fired with enthusiasm to prevent the Japanese advance. But, to our frustration, annoyance and disappointment, our observations and suggestions were ignored by the officers of the regular troops. The Perak Volunteers were treated as ill-informed amateurs.

'Those regular troops are damned silly,' said Bill. 'With our local knowledge of the topography and back roads and our contacts we could set up a great intelligence network. We know which are the best places to take on the Japs.'

'I think that although the regular soldiers are pretty good fighters, their commanders don't really know what they're doing. I wonder about their competence,' I replied.

'I would never accuse our British troops of being lily-livered,' said Bill. 'But, it seems to me, that as soon as any troops get within range of the Japs, they are ordered to make a strategic retreat.'

I had to agree. 'The trouble is that there is no full backup either. There's no air cover and no big guns. And it seems to me that we're losing a lot of ground without putting up much of a show.'

'You know, there's another problem. It's as though the Japs and us are fighting different wars,' said Bill. 'Our men are weighed down with gear and heavy equipment, while those Japs paint themselves green, stick leaves on themselves and stalk us in rubber-soled shoes with small-calibre guns. It's just not cricket.'

We both agreed that another of the great oversights by authorities was their refusal to make use of the loyal Chinese.

'There must be a quarter of a million Chinese of all classes and cultures in Malaya who are united in their dislike of Japan especially after the Japs invaded China. I bet they would love to have a crack at that enemy,' I added.

'I'm afraid the pooh-bahs turn up their noses, just because they're Chinese and therefore aren't thought trustworthy enough to defend the British empire,' said Bill.

'I suspect that there is another reason. Some of the Chinese workers here are tainted with the whiff of communism. They say that they are working towards an independent Malaya. Won't happen, of course, but it makes the authorities nervous. That's another reason why they won't work with them.'

'Yes, that's true,' said Bill. 'But what the British authorities forget is that the Chinese hate the Japanese more than they hate us, especially after the terrible Rape of Nanking.'

Having aired our grievances we decided that, as we were volunteers, we had a choice in the matter of how we fought. And after several more days of endless retreats, we thought that the whole Malayan peninsula was going to fall, so we had to make a decision about what we were going to do.

'I say it's pointless waffling around with the tommies. Their damned officers still don't know what they're doing,' said Bill.

'I think that if we don't decide to get away quickly, we're going to be caught by the Japs and then what good would we be?'

Bill jumped at this idea. 'Listen, I've still got that small sailboat down on the coast. What if we find it and try to get away and head for Colombo?'

So we decided to strike out for the coast, get Bill's boat and sail to Ceylon. Luck was with us and we made the twenty or so miles to where Bill's boat was on the coast with hardly any problems. We camouflaged it to look like a fishing craft and we travelled at night, until we made the open seas of the Indian Ocean. We made landfall at the Nicobar Islands and, as luck would have it, a small freighter was able to take us on to Colombo. We realised just how lucky we had been when the Nicobar Islands were taken by the Japanese only a couple of weeks later.

In Colombo, where we fell in with compatriots, we learned that Malaya had by now succumbed to the Japanese. Days later we heard that Singapore had also fallen, and that thousands of allied troops were now guests of the Emperor. We both felt very glad that we had been able to get away. Although I had heard nothing at this stage about my wife, or the rest of my family, I was sure that they would have had time to be evacuated and I prayed mightily that they were safe. I was also concerned about the welfare of my parents and hoped that they were both safe as well.

At first our time in Colombo was frustrating as we felt we weren't doing enough to help towards the war effort. We were too far from all the action, although the Japanese were beginning to get closer to India. We both managed to find desk jobs with the army, organising supplies for the troops and other mundane, but necessary, tasks and we were eventually moved after many months to New Delhi, to take up positions at South East Asia HQ.

We knew there was a lot of intelligence gathering from

behind enemy lines, and, when we heard about Force 136, both Bill and I latched onto the idea of joining it as a way of being more useful.

'Force 136 is training and sending men into Japanese-occupied territory. What they need are local people like us who know the country, the jungle, the interior, and have local contacts,' I told Bill.

'Sounds like a good thing to do,' said Bill. 'No one else has valued our local knowledge.'

So we decided to make pests of ourselves until we were eventually asked to join the special intelligence unit and we were flattered by our reception.

'You're just the sort of chaps this unit needs,' said the CO. 'You know the people, speak the language and understand the natives.'

Bill and I felt greatly pleased that our local knowledge was to be put to use.

'What do you need us to do?' I asked.

'As you two would know,' explained the CO, 'prior to the outbreak of war there were several communist cells in Malaya formed for the express purpose of getting rid of the British. Well, things have changed. Most of the commies are Chinese and many of them have decided that the Japanese are worse enemies than the British, so they have proposed a truce.'

'I'm not surprised by that change of heart, sir,' I responded. 'How are you able to use it to your advantage?'

'As a fifth column. They can get about the country behind enemy lines. They are saboteurs, but this is not their main function because we know that the Japs retaliate to that sort of thing with dreadful reprisals, so we primarily use the communists as intelligence gatherers in preparation for an Allied invasion.'

'What do you want us to do? Act as go betweens?' asked Bill.

'More or less. We've got several chaps working with communist units, but we want you to try and make contact with one of our chaps in particular. He's been working in the central mountains, staying with the Orang Asli, in one of their villages, but we haven't heard from him for quite some time. The communist unit he was working with was extremely effective, and we would like to make contact with it again as well as finding out what happened to our man, Roger Burrows.'

'How do we find this village and the communist unit, and what makes you think they will trust us?' I asked.

'I don't think trust will be a problem. Here, I'll show you on a map where Roger's village is.'

When the CO pointed out the place, Bill shouted, 'I know that place. I've even been there a couple of times, doing some research for the DO, counting heads, that sort of thing. I can even talk a bit of their lingo.'

'Excellent. We'll try and get you in there as soon as we can.'

Our training was brief and before we knew it we were dropped behind enemy lines, with limited rations and a radio, into what was once our own country. Unfortunately for us, we were dropped near the coast rather than in the mountains. The weather had unexpectedly closed in, making things very difficult for the pilot, but good for us, as the low clouds and the dark night protected us as we landed.

It was strange to be on the run, crawling on hands and knees through the undergrowth, slashing our way through mangroves, sinking in mud, skirting kampongs and slinking through plantations where once we had walked as tuan besars. We knew we were never far from the enemy.

'Even when we can't see them,' said Bill.

At one stage, stopping in a small clearing, we ate some of our rations. We could see a Japanese watchtower in the distance, built of bamboo and giving a good view of the trunk road. But we managed to skirt it easily by keeping to the trees. The night was chilly and damp and, with no fire, very uncomfortable.

'What is hard to swallow is that we can no longer trust the local people,' said Bill. 'An Indian riding his bicycle along the road, a woman carrying water, a coolie collecting firewood, they could all turn us in.'

And, because we were carrying a radio, we knew the Japs would have no mercy and not bother with taking us prisoner. We'd be shot at once.

'It's a long walk into those mountains,' said Bill. 'And I wonder if our luck will hold.'

'We're pretty near Teluk Anson,' I replied. 'And that gives me an idea. There's a Sinhalese gentleman there who's an old friend of my father's. I think that he would help us, if we can get in touch with him.'

Bill agreed that trying to contact Father's friend could be risky, but so was wandering around the Japanese-held coast. 'We'll give it a go, then.'

So a couple of tiring days later, living on pineapples, bananas and our army rations, and continually skirting kampongs and any other habitation, we arrived on the outskirts of Telok Anson, a small town near Slim River, to find the Japanese flag flying and soldiers everywhere.

'Going to be difficult getting into this part of town without being spotted,' said Bill.

'Impossible, I'd say. Let's just stay hidden outside the town and see what happens,' I replied.

The local citizens seemed to be going about their business as usual, but we thought we would be relatively safe if we stayed in the swamps near the ghats of a dhobi wallah. We watched the dhobi wallah for a while, and it seemed that he and his family were doing the washing of the Japanese. Because these washermen were Indian, I felt sure they would know of my father's Sinhalese friend, Mr Gupta, who was well known as an engineer as well as being quite a philanthropist. I just hoped he hadn't been arrested or killed by the Japs.

That evening as one of the dhobis approached the old

sunken cement tank that was being used to soak the dirty linen, we decided to take our chances and approach him. He jumped in fright as two white faces suddenly rose up before him, fingers to lips.

Bill spoke quietly to the man in Tamil, who swiftly understood our predicament. However, the dhobi wallah was clearly afraid, he began to shake with fear.

Bill told him that we needed his help, and that we wanted him to get a message to Mr Gupta. He agreed to do so as Mr Gupta had helped his son once. He suggested that we stay well hidden in the tank because if the Japs found us, they'd not just shoot us, but him and his family as well.

'Ask him if we can buy some rice and sambal from him, now,' I said.

A short time later a woman came to the ghat with a load of washing. From beneath the linens she produced a tiffin carrier filled with rice, pickles and a little chicken. Everything was lowered into the tank where we crouched. We thanked her, passed her some money and feasted before sleeping on top of the dirty linen she had left behind.

At daylight, a young boy appeared and handed us long Indian shirts, baggy trousers and a couple of turbans which we wound tightly over our heads, and he led us from the ghat. A close examination would reveal that we were not Sikhs, but we prayed that from a distance we would pass muster.

Keeping our heads low, we skirted the main part of town until we reached the wealthy residential section of the city. The boy took us down a side alley by a large compound and through the back entrance of a substantial house. Once inside, we were taken to meet its owner.

A tall, solidly built Sinhalese man came to greet us and was very surprised when I introduced myself. 'Mr Elliott! This is a surprise, we meet under difficult circumstances,' said Mr Gupta. 'How is your dear father and how may I help you?'

I told him that I had heard nothing from my father for

218

almost eighteen months and then I told him of our predicament. He listened, and swiftly agreed to help us.

'I may be able to drive you into the Cameron Highlands, and you can walk into the jungle village from there.'

'May I enquire as to how you can do that?' I asked, rather surprised.

'When the British retreated from here, they destroyed the filtration system of the town's water supply. This was not only an inconvenience for the town, but dangerous because the water became too hazardous to drink. I persuaded the Japanese that I could mend the system, which not only saved the town's people from getting ill, but also the Japanese. As a result, I was not only allowed to stay in my house, but I was able to keep my car.'

'We appreciate your helping us, but we don't want to jeopardise your life,' said Bill.

'Please, it is fellows like you who will help get rid of the Japanese, so I will see to it that I get you to the mountains. In the meantime, please use the amenities of my home. There is now clean hot water and my wife will prepare you a meal. It is best the servants do not know of your presence. Many Indians wait for the days when the British will return, but others believe the Japanese when they say that the days of the British are over. This, myself, I do not believe, but others may be gullible and they will aid the Japanese by betraying you.'

The next day, still disguised as Sikhs, we left Gupta's house to drive to the highlands.

'Listen, Gupta,' Bill had said earlier that morning. 'Our disguises aren't very good. We don't have beards, our skin is too light and my eyes are blue. If the Japs stop us and have a close look, they'll see we're not Indian.'

'You are not to worry,' replied Gupta. 'I will make you my driver, and you can wear some old sunglasses of mine. I doubt, however, that they will look at you. Servants do not rate much

219

attention. Mr Elliott will be a coolie, sitting in the front of the car beside you. I will tell the Japanese that I am concerned that if I do not check the water sources for the town carefully, they may be exposed to cholera. They are very frightened of cholera, so they will let me pass.'

Events happened much as Gupta said they would. The Japanese did stop his car, but Gupta was magnificent and the possible threat of cholera was enough for us to be waved on. There was little traffic on the road to the Cameron Highlands and we made good time. When we had driven as far as the road would allow, Gupta let us out, handing us some food for our travels and bidding us good luck. He turned the car around and headed straight back down, leaving us on the side of the road with the knowledge that we had a lot of jungle to tackle before we reached our destination.

The jungle was dense and unforgiving, but Bill had been in this region before and was able to follow the narrow paths with seeming ease, so that within a few days we arrived in the village where we hoped to make contact with Roger Burrows, as well as the local communist leader.

'What do we do now?' asked Bill as we gazed through the trees at the little kampong with its attap-roofed huts. 'Do we just walk in and hope for the best?'

'We might as well. I'm sure that the villagers are aware of our presence by now, anyway. You did say that you knew enough to be able to converse with these Orang Asli, didn't you?'

As we strode into the village, trying to look as masterful as possible, we were met by the headman, whom Bill greeted politely. The old man looked at him for a while, and then broke into a toothless grin and greeted Bill in return.

'He remembers me from my visit here about five or so years ago. We got on famously, so I know we'll be all right here.'

'Ask him about Roger,' I said.

Bill spoke again to the old man, who nodded and signalled

us to follow. We entered a hut and there we could see a man lying on the floor matting.

'Roger?' I asked.

''Fraid so, old chap. Who the hell are you?'

I introduced Bill and myself and told him that HQ has sent us in to try and find him.

'Well, here I am. The radio broke down about nine or more months ago and I haven't been able to get the right parts to mend it, so I couldn't let anyone know what was going on in this part of the world.'

'And you, how are you?' Bill said.

'Not too bad. I've got a touch of malaria at present, so I like to stay in here where it's dark. The light hurts my eyes, but apart from that I'm in good condition, considering the circumstances. The communist leader I've been working with is bloody brilliant. Gets me medicines when he can and tells me what the Japs are doing. But of course that's no use without a radio to relay the info.'

When we told him that we'd been able to bring a radio in with us, he was delighted.

'How soon do you think that you can set it up? I've got so much that I want to tell HQ. But before any of that, tell me, how's the war going?'

Over some tea, which we had carried in with our rations, we told Roger of the war's progress and in particular the Burma campaign, as that was most important to this region. We had to confess that for quite some time it had not gone well, and that Japanese troops had actually come right up to the Indian border.

'Since General Slim has been in command, things have changed,' said Bill. 'He's gradually pushing the Japs back, but I don't expect that Malaya will be liberated any time soon.'

As we talked, sitting on mats in the hut, a figure appeared in the doorway.

'Ah, it's my young communist leader. I'm glad you can meet him so soon, he's just been a tower of strength and a wonderful guerilla. If we had more like him, the Japs would have all left Malaya by now,' said Roger.

As the young Chinese man made his way in to join us, I could hardly believe who I was seeing.

'Ah Kit, I'd like you to meet Captain Elliott and Lieutenant Dickson. They've been sent to find me and they have a radio.'

'Good evening, Captain Elliott,' said my former number one houseboy.

'Ah Kit, this is quite a surprise. No wonder HQ said that I would have no trouble working with the communist leader here. Bill, Ah Kit was my houseboy at Utopia.'

Bill shook Ah Kit's hand. 'Roger tells us great things about what you've been doing. It will be a pleasure to work with you.'

'Thank you, Lieutenant.'

'Tell me, Ah Kit, have you heard any news from Utopia or from my father?'

Ah Kit joined us on the floor and slowly began to speak. 'Captain, things are very bad. Utopia is now the headquarters for the Japanese in the area around Slim River. They have moved into the big house and live in it.'

'My father . . . Where is he, Ah Kit? Is he a prisoner?'

Ah Kit looked at the floor and shook his head and took a moment to answer. 'Captain, it is bad. Tuan besar, tuan Elliott . . . He is gone, sir.'

I tried to digest this remark. 'Gone? Where? Where is my father, Ah Kit?' I knew my voice was rising.

He lowered his head, not looking at me. 'Dead, Captain. They killed him.'

'No, no. How did this happen?' I asked, scarcely believing what I was hearing, but realising the truth of the matter.

'Tuan Elliott would not leave the estate. He sent us all away. But many of his people would not leave. It was their home, too. Several days after you and the mems left, the

Japanese soldiers arrived. Tuan Elliott met them on the steps of the big house and told them that they were not to hurt the plantation workers, who were not at war with Japan. But the Japanese soldiers laughed and one of them shot him. They tied the tuan's body to a tree in the yard and told us that if anyone touched it they would be shot, too. Then the soldiers went to the kampong and raped many of the women and killed some of the tappers who live there. Ho and I were too frightened to cut down the tuan's body, but after two or three nights, we decided to try. The Japanese soldiers had found the alcohol that tuan always kept in the house and many of them were drunk, so we quietly moved into the garden and cut down the tuan's body from the tree and buried it in the kampong, where no one will find it. The Japanese soldiers said nothing the next day because I do not think that they wanted their officers to know that they had been drinking.'

I tried to straighten up. I wanted to leap to my feet but I knew my legs would not hold me. 'So these soldiers are still in my home?'

'Yes, Captain.'

'The workers?'

'All gone away.'

'The plantation? The trees?'

'I do not know. I left too.'

'There's no one to look after anything. Ah, Bill, this is terrible news.'

'I am sorry, Roland. Your father was a very good man.'

'How long have you been a communist?' I asked Ah Kit.

'A long time, Captain. On Utopia I know that tuan Elliott was a good man. He was concerned for his workers and yet we were not treated as equals, only as cheap labour. We work many hours for little pay so that your family can be rich. I do not think that is fair. I think that the British exploit us. I think that the British should leave Malaya.'

I had known this man all my life and yet I found that

I really knew nothing about him. I had seen Ah Kit playing around the Kampong when we were young but later I knew him only as a servant. Now I learned that he not only had political views very different from my own, but that he was a brave soldier.

'Ah Kit,' I said, 'first you must help us get rid of the Japanese.'

As soon as we could, we got the radio working and let Delhi know that Roger was alive and well. We were ordered to stay in the jungle and continue the reconnaissance work. And so began many months working in the jungle with Bill, Roger and Ah Kit. Sometimes we worked separately other times we worked together.

Ah Kit introduced us to more men from the Orang Asli, people who seemed willing to work with us. These natives were clever at being able to locate Japanese patrols and enjoyed terrorising them by quietly seizing the last man and silently killing him. This meant that the Japanese were terrified to go into the jungle and so, if we kept our heads down, we were pretty safe in our kampong. The Chinese communists brought us intelligence about ammunition dumps and watchtowers and the deployment of the Japanese soldiers and we would radio this information back to HQ.

Since we had this network of Chinese communists, and we thought that we could trust the villagers, we began to move about the jungle and into other areas. This decision led to one or two close calls when we were betrayed by a loose tongue or a villager who wanted a Japanese reward.

Probably the worst of these events occurred one night when I was alone and came across a Japanese encampment comprising of eight soldiers. Before I got close to them, I made a fatal error. Believing that I could get a better view of their camp, I decided to leave my jungle cover and try to cross the small river that lay between me and the Japs.

I was lucky that it was only one guard and not the entire

224

patrol who saw me. I was hit in the shoulder, a sharp burn, the force pitching me forward. I rolled into the shallows of the river and pulled myself beneath the surface, holding my breath, and tried to move downstream with the current. The jungle came down to the water and when I couldn't hold my breath any longer I raised my head and found I was in the long grasses, roots and weeds fringing the bank. I lay there holding on, beginning to feel weak, knowing I was losing blood.

No more shots were fired. I suppose that the Jap thought I was a native, for I was dressed in a sarong, and as I was in an impenetrable section of the river, he had decided not to follow me.

I considered my options and thought that all I could do was pull myself out of the water and try to get some sort of foothold on the bank and hope that I'd be found, though I had no idea if I'd last until then. There was a tree with low over-hanging branches and a thick trunk. I finally reached it and managed to secure myself to a stout branch with my sarong. If I passed out, I would not slide back into the river.

The last thing I recall was the screeching of monkeys.

I'm told I lost a lot of blood and nearly forty-eight hours passed before I was found by Ah Kit and one of the native trackers who'd been searching the river for me. They carried me for several days, back into the jungle and towards one of the safe villages. All the time I drifted in and out of consciousness. I have no idea how they managed to carry me on a very rough stretcher. We were still quite some way from safety when we nearly stumbled into another Japanese patrol. The native, poor soul, realising at once that if they were caught with me they would be executed, fled. But Ah Kit told me to be very quiet and hid me under some leaves and jungle detritus. We remained safe. Ah Kit told me to stay there and he would get help. I completely lost track of time but when I opened my eyes, I found that I was looking at Bill.

I took quite a while getting over that adventure. Ah Kit

managed to find some bandages and some Condy's crystals and, amazingly, the wound did not become infected. There was no doubt that Ah Kit saved my life. But when I tried to thank him, he only replied that he needed me alive to help him fight the Japanese.

During the time we spent in the villages of the Orang Asli, I came to learn that Ah Kit was looked upon with great respect by the other communists and even the Orang Asli. I enjoyed sitting and talking with him when we had the chance, although it was obvious that apart from our intense dislike of the Japanese, we now had very little in common.

'When this war is over, old boy, you'll have to do something for Ah Kit,' said Bill.

'I certainly will. He can hardly go back to being my houseboy for, as much as I would like that, I don't expect he would.'

We continued our work for several more months, but Roger's malaria attacks were becoming more and more frequent and severe, and Ah Kit was finding it harder to supply him with quinine. Then the radio started to falter. The high humidity was certainly playing havoc with it. Ah Kit managed to get some spare parts smuggled in to us, but, often, by the time he did and we repaired the thing, all the passwords at HQ had changed and we had difficulty persuading our contact that we were legitimate and not being held by the enemy.

Eventually, HQ decided that it was time to get us all out. The plan was that we would travel over the mountains and through the jungle to the west coast, to meet up with a submarine, which would be waiting for us off one of the coastal islands. By this time, none of us was feeling all that fit. All of us had been ill with various tropical diseases. Bill had had a particularly nasty bout of blackwater fever, as well as the ever-present malaria. The long trek down to the coast was daunting.

When we looked at our map, Bill said, 'If we were to walk due west from here, we would get out of the mountains much faster that if we go north-west.'

Roger nodded in agreement. 'It certainly would be easier, but then we are exposed to quite a long hike along the coast and the Japs are very likely to spot us.

'Not if we were disguised. We were Sikhs to get here, couldn't we do the same thing again?' I suggested.

'You and I don't know the lingo, old chap. We'd be caught as soon as we opened our mouths,' replied Roger.

Ah Kit had been sitting very quietly. 'Plenty of Chinese coolies on the west coast. Maybe you should be Chinese.'

'But the problem still remains. As soon as we have to speak, the Japs will know we're English,' I said.

'I will come with you and I will do all the speaking,' said Ah Kit.

Ah Kit seemed to have little trouble procuring clothes for us, and a few weeks later, after we thanked the villagers for their help, we made our way to the coast and the rendezvous spot dressed as coolies, carrying large, although not very heavy, loads on our backs.

Once we reached the coast, we were amazed by the numbers of Japs that we saw. They seemed to be everywhere. Ah Kit did all the talking and we kept to the edges of the road and inside any plantations as much as we could.

One evening, after we had been walking all day in the tropical heat and wearing very uncomfortable sandals, we camped under some rubber trees for the night. Ah Kit went off for a while and returned, bringing us some coconuts, which cheered us up because the coconut milk was very refreshing.

'It is a pity, Captain Elliott, that we did not have coconuts when you were wounded. The milk is very clean and many people use it to wash wounds,' said Ah Kit.

'Yes,' I replied. 'And the taste is wonderful. A lot nicer than Condy's crystals.'

Our luck held. Ah Kit managed the Japanese very well. Although they shouted at us and questioned us about where we were going, Ah Kit was able to answer them in such a way that none of them came close enough to our party to discern that we were not Chinese. And I must say that we looked so ragged and unhealthy that they were probably quite pleased to give us a wide berth.

Our meeting with the submarine was to be off one of the coastal islands, and so we had to hire a boat to get there. This was the most dangerous part of the journey, for there would be no way a boatman would not notice that we were not Chinese, but Ah Kit assured us that this problem could be solved.

'I have been told by Chinese friends which of the Malay boatmen on the coast can be most easily bribed. And my friends have given me enough money to be sure that no questions will be asked and that the man they have named will take you safely.'

'You're not coming?' I asked.

'No, Captain Elliott, there is no further need for me.'

'I don't know how we can thank you,' I replied. 'I owe you my life. In fact, one way or another, we all do.'

Ah Kit smiled. 'I hope that after the war is over and we both want different things for Malaya, you will remember that.'

Roger and Bill both shook Ah Kit's hand and also thanked him.

'Great chap,' said Roger, when Ah Kit had gone. 'Wonder what he'll do after the war. I don't suppose he'll settle down to being a houseservant, again. Good men, those Chinese commies, good fighters, but I think they might cause the British problems when the war finishes.'

That evening there was no moon and the boatman sailed us to the island. While we were sailing across, we made radio contact with HQ and we were told that the submarine would be able to collect us the next night. So we met it and sailed back to Ceylon and from there we made our way to New Delhi and some very mundane war work, since we were judged not fit enough for anything more exciting.

'Disappointing, but I think we did our bit,' said Bill.

We were still in New Delhi, when the atomic bombs were dropped on Japan and the war ended.

When I finally returned to Malaya and Utopia, nothing could prepare me for the devastation of the plantation. The trees had been destroyed and the kampong and the workers' huts were burned. The big house was in surprisingly good condition because the Japanese had used it as an administration centre, but Margaret's and my house had not been so well cared for. The furniture had been badly damaged and the garden destroyed.

Several months later I was joined by my wife who had seen out the war in Australia and I was reunited with my son, Philip, who had spent the war in a Japanese internment camp in Sarawak with my sister-in-law, Bette.

Gradually the estate workers and their families came back and I was able to replant the rubber trees. Ho, who had survived the war, showed me where he and Ah Kit had buried my father and I reburied him at our little family churchyard.

'It will never be the same,' said Margaret one night, not long after we came home. 'The parties, the friends, the servants, the lifestyle, the luxuries we enjoyed. That life won't come back.'

'Perhaps not. But while it might be different, it could be better. One day it will be,' I replied.

There the memoir ended. Julie closed her grandfather's small book and put it to one side. She sat there, quite stunned. She wanted to call her mother immediately and say, 'Oh my God! Great Aunt Bette and your brother Philip were in a Japanese POW camp during the war and we didn't know. How could Gran not have mentioned this?' It seemed inconceivable.

She found her two cousins still up, sitting with brandys, watching a football game on the satellite TV.

'Hey, we thought you'd gone to bed,' said Shane.

'Is something wrong?' said Peter. 'Would you like a drink?'

'Absolutely. Thank you. I've read Grandfather's memoir and I'm in shock.'

'Turn the sound down, please, Shane,' said Peter, rising to get Julie a G & T.

'What's upset you?' asked Shane.

'I finished reading our grandfather's memoirs and at the end I discovered that your father and Great Aunt Bette were in a POW camp. My mother and I had no idea. How on earth? What happened? I mean, I can't believe my grandmother never ever mentioned this? Why?'

The two boys stared at her, realising that this disclosure was a huge revelation for their cousin.

'Do you really mean that you had no idea of what had happened to them? Dad mentioned it to us but all he said was that he was very young, a small boy at the time and that he didn't recall much,' said Shane.

'Actually, he didn't want to talk about it at all,' added Peter.

'But he was there with his aunt and not his mother. Why was that? I mean, it seems incredible to me. And for how long? It must have been years. Our grandmother said she sat out the war in Brisbane . . . And all the while her son and her sister were interned!' Julie shook her head. 'Do you know, I don't think that my mother knows about this either. Why? Why would our grandmother have kept it quiet all this time?'

'I suppose things happened during wartime. Grandfather talked about hiding in the jungle, about how crazy the war years were with the Japanese occupation,' said Shane. 'No, when I think about it, he really didn't say much about the war. Most of what we know came from that memoir.'

'Grandfather was rather self deprecating, very modest,' said Peter.

'When we did ask him what he did in the war, he talked about the lighter side of things,' said Shane.

'Such as how he and his friend Bill dressed up as coolies, that sort of thing. In retrospect he made it all sound a bit of a Boy's Own Adventure. We were adults before we realised how courageous he was,' added Peter.

'After Grandfather died, so many people came forward with stories about how brave he'd been. But he always downplayed all he'd done,' said Shane. 'It was Bill who spoke at his funeral and said that Roland should have been given a lot more recognition for his actions behind the lines.'

'Because they were an intelligence unit, a lot of what they did was kept secret and didn't come out for years,' said Peter. 'Then we realised the little we knew was from his memoir. Grandfather was very reserved and rather formal. As far as he was concerned, it wasn't done to blow one's own trumpet, y'know.'

'We both admired Grandfather but we were a bit in awe of him and maybe we thought him a bit stuffy, in an old-world kind of way,' said Shane.

'I wish I'd known him,' said Julie. 'My, our, grandmother, Margaret, never talked about him in personal terms. And she never talked about why they split up. It's all such a mystery.'

'Well, perhaps it was the era,' said Peter. 'Perhaps Grandmother Margaret was also not one for airing one's true feelings, like our grandfather.'

'And Grandfather doesn't say why or how our father got captured in that memoir,' said Peter. 'I read it long ago, but I don't think that he explained how Philip was separated from his mother. And, I must confess, it wasn't the part of the story that intrigued me so much. Our father was little and always said he didn't remember much and would only say we should appreciate what Grandfather and those like him did to help save us from the Japanese.'

'Maybe. But I'm still very curious. Are there any other notes, diaries? Anything of our grandmother's here?' asked Julie.

'No, nothing at all,' said Shane.

'I suppose it must have been a traumatic time for a small boy, which is why he didn't talk about it,' said Julie. 'He was how old?'

'About three or so. But really, I think he took a note from Grandfather and didn't want to talk about the war. But he was very young,' said Peter, looking at Shane as they tried to recall what their father had told them.

'That's right. But he had a playmate, Marjorie . . .'

'Mrs Carter! They were in the camp together. He used to say she was like his big sister who looked after him, his war amah,' said Shane.

'She was in the camp with him?' exclaimed Julie. 'Did you know her?'

'She was Marjorie Potts then. Her family were Civil Service people, I believe,' said Shane.

'Is she still alive?'

'Oh, yes,' said Peter. 'She's as fit as a fiddle and great company.'

'Could I find her?' Julie jumped up, elated.

'Hey, it's the middle of the night,' laughed Peter.

'So tell me all about Miss Potts or Mrs Carter, as you call her,' said Julie.

'Well, as we said, she and my father were playmates in the camp, although I think she was about ten years older than Dad,' said Shane. 'After the war, she and father kept in touch, even when she returned to the UK.'

'Didn't Dad stay with her on school holidays sometimes?' interrupted Peter.

'Yes, I think so. Later, when she was living in Scotland, she used to come out to Malaysia every winter and stay on Langkawi Island at a holiday house Dad owned there.

We sold it a few years back, but she still went to the island for holidays. Then she bought an apartment on the hill in Penang. We had lunch with her at the E&O not long ago. We'd have her phone number somewhere. She's a great old stick even though she'd be about eighty now,' said Shane.

'I'd love to speak to her. If she was friends with Uncle Philip she'd remember Great Aunt Bette as well. Oh, this is so amazing,' said Julie.

'Yes, perhaps we could do something about it in the morning,' said Shane. 'Er, could we put the sound of the game back on?'

Julie laughed. 'I know this doesn't mean as much to you as it does to me, so, please, go ahead and finish watching the football. I'm going to re-read parts of Grandfather's book. Thank you so much for showing it to me.'

The next day, as soon as she knew her mother would be at home, Julie rang.

'Darling, lovely to hear your voice,' said Caroline. 'Is everything all right? Why are you calling?'

'I've found out something amazing about Bette, and your brother. It's stunning. You weren't all that close to your brother, were you? I mean did Uncle Philip ever talk to you about the war?'

'No, not at all. Why should he?' Caroline paused, trying to remember. 'As I've already told you, I was ten years younger than Philip, and he was sent to boarding school in the UK. Then Mother and I came back to Australia to live and I really never got to know him. No. I never talked to him about the war. But what was there to talk about?'

'And Bette? Where was she during the war?'

'Back here, too, I assume. Why? What have you found out? This is all very intriguing. Are you having fun? Are the boys nice?'

233

'Lovely. I'm enjoying myself immensely. Wait till I tell you about the orangutans and the Iban. It's all been such an adventure. But that's not why I rang. I've just read a small memoir that Grandfather Roland wrote and, in his version of events, the family and the war in Malaya is quite different from what we have always assumed.'

'Goodness, whatever do you mean? I'm not sure that we assumed anything about the war in Malaya, because my mother never talked about it. Kept her own counsel. If she talked about Malaya, she only wanted to talk about the fun days before the Japanese.'

'Hmm. I know why.' Julie drew a breath. 'Great Aunt Bette and Philip didn't escape on the ship out of Singapore. I don't know what happened, but Gran made the ship and Bette and Philip didn't.'

'What do you mean? How did they get out of Malaya, then?'

'Mum, they didn't. They were sent to a POW camp in Sarawak.'

There was an intake of breath from Caroline. 'What? You are joking. No, you're not. So Mother lived here in Brisbane while her sister was with Philip in a prisoner of war camp. How dreadful for them. How awful for Mother.'

'Yes. Obviously it couldn't have been deliberate, but why didn't Gran ever talk about it?'

'I don't know. Maybe she felt guilty and thought that she had failed her son. It would certainly explain why she only wanted to talk about the times before the war. Oh, if only I'd known and could have asked her the right questions. Poor Mother, poor Bette and Philip. How terrible.' Caroline sighed. 'Do the boys have any more information?'

'No, but there was a girl in the camp with Bette and Philip, and, although she was older than Philip, she was his friend and they kept in touch.'

'Oh, how nice. I suppose that when Philip was killed, that changed,' said Caroline.

'Apparently not. Shane and Peter regard her as an old family friend as she comes out to Malaysia regularly from Scotland. She doesn't like cold winters. Peter and Shane think that I should call her.'

'Well, it would certainly be interesting to find out more,' agreed her mother.

'I'll let you know what happens. I'm going over to Langkawi Island with the boys and Martine and some of their friends.'

'Lovely. Is David going too?'

'No. He's working, Mum. Doing his research and stuff. I'm sure he'll be in touch with you when he gets back to Australia. How're things there?'

'Good. A moratorium's been called with the council. Don't you worry, darling, the house will still be here when you get back.'

'That's good.'

'This call must be costing a fortune. It's all very exciting. Send me an email when you know more.'

'I just wanted to call and tell you. I was pretty gob-smacked,' said Julie.

'Me too. I'll sit down with your father and digest it all. Take care, Julie.'

'Love you, Mum.'

'I love you too. I'm really glad you've made this trip.'

'Me too.'

Julie put the receiver down. She realised that there were still a lot more places to see and, she felt sure, more of her family's story to unfold.

8

ON THE SHORT FLIGHT from Kuala Lumpur to Langkawi
Island Julie found she was laughing more than she could
remember in years, as did everyone else. There was Martine, Shane and Peter, Tina and Carl, who lived in the
Cameron Highlands and had a tea plantation, Christopher
Nichols, the Australian RAAF officer from Butterworth,
and the Stevensons, a couple in their late forties who were
staying on the other side of the island in their apartment
at the marina on Telaga Harbour.

'You must come over for lunch,' said Ursula Stevenson. 'We could take our boat out. There are some amazing
things to see on the island.'

'They are in the shipping business in Europe,' Martine whispered later to Julie. 'Very rich. They come here
every year.'

'Langkawi seems to be a popular place. I see why Marjorie Carter must have enjoyed it here,' said Julie as they flew over the blue Andaman Sea dotted with lush green islands that lay west of the Malaysian and Thai coasts.

'Oh, yes indeed. She was tempted to buy here too, when she saw Ursula's place, but she changed her mind and bought a penthouse in Penang instead.'

'Does she go there often?' asked Julie.

'When it's cold and draughty in her daughter's house in Scotland, where she usually lives. She comes out here for the warmth and sun. I'll get her phone number out of my mobile, I know how anxious you are to talk with her.'

'Yes, I am. I'm so curious about Great Aunt Bette and Philip, too. I suppose the boys grew up knowing the story of what happened to their father during the war, so this is not as exciting for them as it is for me because I know nothing.'

'I'm sure Marjorie will be able to tell you something. Shane said she was only about twelve when she was in the camp. She was like a big sister to their father, which is why they kept in touch. And when Philip and Stephanie were killed, Marjorie still kept in contact with the boys. We're landing. I hope you like it here. We're staying at a cute place. Wait till you see it,' said Martine.

'I'm sure I'll love it,' said Julie. 'Is there lots to do? Peter talked about the fishing.'

'There are wonderful things to do or, if you like, you can do nothing. That's what appeals to me,' said Martine. 'When we had our own house here there always seemed to be too much work maintaining it, even with the girls to help. This is much easier.'

After collecting their bags they divided themselves between rental cars and a taxi. Julie sat with Christopher in the taxi as they followed Shane and Peter.

'So you know the island pretty well?' asked Julie.

'Yes, I've been here a few times. It's not the place to come if you're in to nightlife, movies, shows, and that sort of thing. But the nature and wildlife are spectacular.'

'And the fishing?'

'Iffy. I just like the idea of hanging out on a boat. Any fish I catch is a bonus. If I'm really in to serious fishing, I go to the Barrier Reef or the Top End. And don't expect too much from the beaches. They're not what we're used to. We Australians are so spoiled when it comes to beaches, it makes the ones here a bit disappointing,' he said.

'I like the idea of exploring the local nature. I loved seeing the orangutans in Sarawak.'

'There's some wonderful birdlife here. There are plenty of monkeys, and, if you like, we could go on a hike. You'll have to meet our pal Aidi. He's a local naturalist who's just the best. Every time I see him, I learn amazing things. I'll arrange for him to take us on an expedition.'

'Sounds good. So explain about the place where we are staying?'

'It's run by two Australian women. Nerida started it, gosh, maybe eighteen years ago. The hotel has just grown . . . but in a nice way. It used to be closer to the sea but land was reclaimed so now the compound is on the edge of some lovely rice fields. Nerida started collecting traditional Malay houses that were going to be pulled down and had them moved to her place, which was once a coconut plantation, and saved them from demolition.'

'What a great thing to do!'

'Yep, she's shipped them in from every Malaysian state, so the houses she's got are all different architectural styles. She's made them very classy and comfortable. All are set in the lovely hotel grounds and come complete with lap pools,' explained Christopher.

'It sounds amazing and different.'

As they drove the short distance to the resort, Julie was enchanted by Langkawi. She could see the blue sea through the waving palm trees, glimpses of casual streets lined with thatched-roofed bars and outdoor restaurants, and a few holiday shops selling sarongs and souvenirs. They passed lush emerald rice fields, where lazy water buffaloes wallowed, watched by a solitary farmer in a peaked straw hat.

'Very picture postcard, isn't it?' she said to Christopher.

'There's a rice museum on Langkawi, where you can learn all about this staple of Asia. Now, here's the turn off into our resort.'

'Oh, it's so tropical. I love all the coconut palms. I feel like I've come into some magic village,' exclaimed Julie as the cars drove down a small lane and stopped outside a wonderful Chinese house.

'I wonder what state they've put us in,' said Christopher.

Julie was mystified by this remark until she began to look around and saw all the restored buildings that had been rescued from various parts of Malaysia. Chinese, Malay and Indian houses, plantation workers' cottages, as well as a colonial mansion were cleverly spaced around the secluded gardens, all representing the architecture of the various Malay states.

Julie was accommodated in an old Malay house, which had originally been a fisherman's hut but had now been transformed into a summery, colourful house. There was a balcony at the front and at the back was a secluded open-air bathroom and sun deck, holding a big old wooden bathtub. Inside, the bed was swathed in a mosquito net. There was a ceiling fan, turning slowly, but Julie noticed that there was also an air conditioner. The windows had intricately carved shutters and an inviting daybed on the sundeck was covered in colourful silk cushions. The whole house was simple and stylish, and, despite its old world charm, she was glad to find all the modern amenities she might need, including a cat.

As she started to unpack, a large black and white cat with a short tail with a kink in it strolled up the front steps and made itself at home. When she explored the gardens later, she found cats lurking around the red altar in the temple yard. The animals sat by the long lap pool or lazed on top of an old stone wall, which surrounded the large two-storey Chinese villa where Martine, Shane and Peter were staying.

'Come on in, Julie, we've opened the bar,' called out Peter from its upstairs balcony.

Seated on the wide verandah in comfortable planters' chairs and surrounded by antiques, Julie sipped a cold drink. As the fan above her slowly whirred, Julie could imagine that she'd stepped back a hundred years in time. They were soon joined by Christopher, Carl and Tina and the owner of the resort, Nerida, whose dream this place had been. The hotel staff were young and friendly but unobtrusive, quietly delivering a tray of delicious hors d'oeuvres and a platter of fruit to the new arrivals.

'You can see why our kids love it here,' said Shane. 'There are all those grounds out there to explore, and the house has a film and video room, a table tennis table and even a mah jong set.'

'Two big families can stay here and not have to meet unless they want to,' added Martine. 'We've had some fun family holidays here. Carl and Tina bring their kids, too.'

'What's with all the cats?' Julie asked Nerida. 'I saw lots of cats in Kuching, too. Where did yours come from?'

'I've lived on Langkawi for nearly twenty years, although I go home to Australia to see my family every year,' said Nerida. 'And years ago I started taking in stray animals, trying to help the neglected dogs and cats. There

240

were a lot of them, so I started an animal shelter and sanctuary to care for abused and needy animals. Now we also run an animal clinic, a charity project aimed at the sterilisation of the stray cat population. Both of these projects are non-profit making ventures, staffed by volunteers and aimed at improving the lives of unwanted animals. I've adopted a lot of cats, as you can see,' she explained with passion.

'And the crooked tails?' asked Christopher.

'It seems to be a genetic trait,' said Nerida. 'Ah, there's Aidi. You'll enjoy his company,' she said to Julie. 'He's the island's top naturalist and guide, and a good friend to me.'

Aidi wandered over to the house and Nerida introduced him to Julie. He seemed to know everyone else. Aidi was dressed in khaki shorts and shirt. His round, affable face, a mixture of Malay and Chinese, seemed to be constantly wreathed in smiles and Julie liked him immediately. He joked and laughed a lot, but she quickly found that a fascinating torrent of information poured out of him.

'Aidi knows the island intimately and if he takes you on one of his tours, you'll get a look at another world,' said Nerida.

'So Christopher mentioned,' said Julie.

'Could I come along with you?' asked Christopher. 'I haven't been out with Aidi for ages.'

'You're always too busy fishing or lazing by the pool,' said Peter.

'I'd better get back to work and relieve Alice, she's my business partner,' said Nerida. 'We're opening some other residences in Penang, so we're back and forth all the time. She's heading over there tomorrow to see how the renovations of our old Chinese shophouses are going.' Martine and Nerida walked to the entrance talking in low voices.

Aidi turned to Christopher and Julie. 'You two want

to meet me at six o'clock tomorrow morning? Spend a few hours discovering the secret parts of the island? Bring sunscreen, hats, cameras. I'll bring cool drinks.'

'Sounds good,' said Christopher. 'You okay with that?' he asked Julie.

The start seemed very early to Julie, but she knew that they would have to head out before the sun got too hot. 'Can't wait.'

'You could meet us for dinner tomorrow night, Aidi,' suggested Christopher. 'Bring your family along.'

'How about you all come down to my neck of the woods? There's a great local seafood place,' Aidi replied.

'Now don't do too much planning,' said Martine coming back into the room. 'This is a place to relax.'

After enjoying a leisurely lunch, everyone did their own thing – reading, sleeping, swimming or taking a short walk. These people are so easy to be with, thought Julie. There seemed to be no pressure as there had been with David constantly at her elbow, though, to be fair, being in a longhouse in the jungle was a bit different from staying at a lovely resort like this.

At sunset they took two cars down into Telaga Harbour. This gave Julie a totally different view of the laidback island. Here, at the harbour, she felt as though she'd been dropped into Monte Carlo, or some other European coastal hotspot. The glamorous new marina was filled with millions of dollars worth of shiny white motor cruisers, sleek yachts and massive ships equipped for weeks at sea, fishing and adventuring. Reflections of the coloured lights that were strung along the promenade danced across the water. All along the waterfront was every kind of restaurant, cheek by jowl, interspersed with a few smart providores, catering to the boating fraternity.

Restaurant tables, covered with snowy tablecloths, were being set, candles lit, flowers arranged. There was a small square with a fountain, looking like a smaller version of the Spanish Steps, which led to an upper level of buildings and apartments, while further across the water gleamed brand new, but incomplete, hotels and office buildings.

Julie was stunned. 'What a contrast to being up-country with the Iban!'

'This looks a bit like Disneyland, a kind of Lego world,' commented Christopher. 'But I guess the dollars here are real.'

'There's a zillion dollars been spent on all this. For tourists?'

'There are a lot of wealthy Malaysians, as well as foreigners, who are making a heap of money out of this country, one way or another,' said Christopher.

'But it doesn't seem to be exactly spread around evenly,' said Julie. 'There are people like the Iban, fighting for their land – which has always been theirs, and with very little material wealth, but then, if you have the bucks you can come and live in a place like this, where it's conspicuous wealth overload. I don't think it's fair.'

'Well, there are always rich and poor in every society, but you're right, it's accentuated in places like this.'

'I wouldn't want to live here anyway. It's fun for an evening but I prefer our side of the island and the more traditional architecture and it's a lot more peaceful,' said Julie looking at the pink and peach, ochre and cream buildings.

They had drinks at Werner and Ursula Stevenson's luxurious apartment overlooking the harbour and afterwards they all wandered down to the waterfront, looking for a place to eat.

'This is where the action is,' said Christopher quietly to Julie.

She glanced around, not sure if he was serious, then

giggled as she realised that there were hardly any other tourists around, only a few locals.

'It's probably too early for everyone else,' she said. 'Though it's a shame they'll miss the sunset.'

They strolled along the waterfront, reading the blackboards and menus displayed outside each venue.

'There's even a Russian place,' said Julie. 'But I don't think I fancy heavy Russian food. A nice fish or pasta will do me.'

'That Russian place gets pretty boisterous as the evenings wear on,' said Shane. 'The customers like to sing, as well as drink.'

Eventually, they all decided on Mediterranean food and Werner ordered Italian wines. Julie looked at the prices on the menu and mentally compared them with prices in Brisbane. It seemed to be very expensive, even the ordinary Australian wines weren't cheap.

'I'll stick to the local beer,' said Julie.

Christopher leaned over and murmured. 'My shout tonight. You can do the honours tomorrow night at Aidi's joint.'

She smiled at him. 'It's a deal.'

The sky was rosy as the sun began to rise. Clouds fluffed along the horizon. Aidi led Julie and Christopher across the beach to where his boat, with its bright blue plastic roof, was pulled up to the edge of the water. As Julie and Christopher clambered into it, they were introduced to Jan, the skipper.

'He's a local and speaks a little English, but he really knows these waters,' said Aidi.

The boat sped off, bumping across the water, rounding a peninsula, and heading out to sea. Over the noise of the wind and the hull slapping on the water, Julie asked Aidi how he came to be doing this job.

'I grew up in KL. My father was a schoolteacher and historian. I asked for a book as a birthday present and received a Life Nature Library book called *The Sea*. This got me keen on nature but at that time studying nature was not quite as acceptable as it is now. I became a flying instructor and kept my interest alive by reading and doing aerial surveys for nature-based organisations.'

'Christopher is a pilot, too,' said Julie.

'He flies jets though,' said Aidi. 'My experience was more modest. Anyway, while I was managing a crop-dusting operation, I noticed that the chemicals were indirectly affecting the waters offshore. I decided then to leave aviation and I studied and looked for work as an environmentalist. I came to Langkawi and fell in love with it, and I got a job as a naturalist at a resort, so I was doing what I always wanted. Later I met the manager of a new five star resort, which was being built very close to a man-grove forest. So I spoke to him at length about the potential side effects of a large development so near mangroves. The result of this conversation was that I was offered a job as the naturalist for that resort and I worked closely with the developers while they built it. Now that it's finished, I try to educate as well as entertain guests who stay there.' He smiled. 'My life story, in a nutshell.'

From the boat, he pointed to some discreetly screened buildings buried among trees and set back from a sandy beach. 'That's my resort there. It's very well designed, and the owners care about the local environment.'

A little further along, the boat turned into a man-grove forest which fringed the shore and for the next hour they weaved through the narrow tidal channels. Every so often Jan would stop the boat and Aidi would explain the importance of mangroves, not only to the ecosystem around them but also globally.

'This is the bridge, the forest, that not only links sea

and land, they intertwine,' he said. 'Mangroves, perhaps even more than rainforests, cleanse the planet.'

'How is that?' asked Julie.

'One hectare of natural mangrove will take one hundred kilos of carbon out of the air. The living mangroves also filter the water. If mangrove forests are destroyed, rivers will be salty much further upstream. The mangrove forests sustain and nurture fish and crustaceans and also shelter birds and monkeys and other wildlife. If mangroves are removed, the coast will be quickly eroded because the mangroves protect the land from wave and storm damage. For centuries they have also provided all manner of important uses for local communities, but now . . .' he lifted his shoulders in a despairing gesture.

'And now this habitat is threatened,' said Julie. 'I can't say that I'm surprised after the damage to the environment that I saw when I was in Sarawak.'

'Yes,' said Aidi. 'Unfortunately it's taken too long for people to recognise the value of mangroves. They're not just useless wastelands. They are an essential part of the ecosystem, just like rainforests.'

'It's true, but they're looked on as ugly swamps that have to be removed,' said Christopher.

'But in here, among the mangrove trees, it is utterly beautiful,' said Julie. 'I've never seen anything like it. From the sea you just see a tangle of roots holding up a green canopy and it looks sinister, and the grey mud is smelly. But when you get in here, into these little channels, you're in a magic kingdom! Don't you think so, Christopher?'

'I have to agree. I went mud crabbing in mangroves with some mates in Queensland but I had no idea what was beyond the perimeter of the mudflats until I went in and looked and realised how fascinating they are.'

Aidi smiled as the boat putted quietly on. Jan crouched

at the tiller, appearing to be familiar with every inch of this backwater.

'Y'know, there are some very plush golf courses on Langkawi, but when they use fertilisers, the chemicals get washed into the sea and the toxins cause what is called a red tide. Then you can't eat the fish or crustaceans. But this never happens around the mangroves because they have such a brilliant filtration system, they get rid of salts through their aerial roots and salt-filtering leaves. They are like desert plants, and can store water in their leaves. In case you're ever stranded and need fresh water, try mangrove leaves.' Aidi laughed.

'If it doesn't make sense to get rid of mangroves,' said Julie, 'why is it done?'

'The land is often reclaimed for oil palms and shrimp farms. Aquatic farming is a big deal, but shrimp farms have been a disaster. Very few are run cleanly and properly. When there are problems people just fill them in and a new one is made straight away, rather than giving nature a chance to recover. It is so silly economically, too, because while one shrimp farm is employing a few people, it is ruining the fishing for several hundred families.'

'It's such a shame that the value of places like this is not widely understood,' said Julie. 'These mangroves are like living sculptures. The patterns, the interweaving roots, the whole incredible maze is extraordinary.'

'Everything you see is designed for a purpose; the way a leaf grows vertically to avoid the midday sun, the porous roots, snorkel roots, the way they've evolved to survive, that's its beauty to me,' said Aidi.

Jan stopped the boat as they reached a mudflat and they leaned over the side of the hull, to watch the strange mudskippers slither and slide through the silky grey mud.

'Look at those crabs with the bright red, blue and white claws. The way they are waving them about makes them look as though they are bopping to some music we can't hear,' said Christopher, and laughed.

'I wish I knew where they get their energy, I want some,' agreed Aidi.

'It must be all the extra oxygen in here,' said Christopher. 'Good place to come if you have a hangover!'

Julie couldn't believe that they'd spent two hours in the mangrove forest. 'Did you ever think you'd enjoy hanging over the side of a boat for ages, watching fascinating creatures run around in the mud?' she said to Christopher.

Aidi laughed. 'The resort didn't believe people would pay money to come and do this either! But they do. Now I'll take you round to the limestone karsts, through the caves and then out to the sea eagles.'

In the quiet bay, surrounded by dark distant hills, they bobbed quietly. A small boat filled with other tourists came alongside them, revving its engine. Then, after the engine cut out, several large birds suddenly swooped above them.

Aidi pointed. 'Those birds are Brahminy kites. Look over there, here come the white-bellied sea eagles.'

It was a magnificent sight. Everyone sat enraptured as the graceful, powerful birds plunged above and around them, scooping up the scraps of chicken that were being thrown overboard from the tour boat.

'This is so great,' said Julie. 'How did this feeding frenzy start?'

'Ah, that's a story,' said Aidi. 'Some years ago, there was a charcoal factory that was harvesting mangrove trees. They cut down so many trees to make charcoal that the mud islands became unstable. The water got very muddy as a result, and this reduced the fish stocks, so the birds had to find lunch somewhere else. They moved to the airport because the grass was mowed regularly and that exposed ground creatures, which the birds loved. Now birds and planes in a limited space is a sure-fire recipe for disaster. We lost about eighty per cent of the bird population and three aircraft engines. So the charcoal factory was closed and a bird-feeding program was started to attract the birds away from the airport. As you saw, the program has been very successful and now we're almost back to the original numbers of birds.'

'We should just leave mother nature alone to sort things out,' said Julie.

'Humans can't help but interfere,' said Christopher. 'Aidi, is tourism going to destroy this area?'

'Unbridled tourism will, but well managed tourism will help the region, not destroy it. You have to give people an alternative source of income by conserving what's here, not destroying it,' he answered.

'I hope you're right,' said Christopher.

They returned to the beach, and Julie and Christopher thanked Aidi and Jan and made arrangements to meet Aidi later for dinner.

It was a lazy afternoon back at the resort. Julie had a swim and dipped into a book, but found she was putting it aside and stroking the cat that had curled up on the daybed beside her, while she thought about Grandfather Roland's diary.

Although they all gathered for a sunset drink, everyone had different plans for the evening. Martine, Shane, Carl, Tina and Peter were having drinks with friends of the Stevensons on a huge cruiser at the marina at Telaga Harbour.

'You two are welcome to come along,' said Shane.

'We're having dinner with Aidi and his family,' said Christopher. 'Maybe we can hook up later somewhere, it won't be a late night. What do you think, Julie?'

'I don't mind.'

'Well, Julie, don't make any plans for tomorrow evening,' said Martine mysteriously.

Julie and Christopher caught a taxi downtown to a sprawling but simple restaurant called Wonderland, which was situated beside a small tidal inlet. When they told the owner that they were meeting Aidi, he beamed.

'Ah, yes, I am Tun, please come this way. We have a nice table for you, outside here.'

Christopher ordered two Tiger beers and they studied the menu.

'Everything that's cooking on that charcoal brazier over there smells terrific,' said Julie. 'And don't forget, it's my turn to shout.'

When Aidi arrived with his pretty wife, and young son and daughter, he ordered food for everyone. 'This is Malaysian Chinese-style seafood and you must try the fresh prawns,' he said.

Julie and Christopher burst out laughing at the sight of the platter of prawns. Each prawn was almost the length of their forearms. The prawns had been split in half and grilled over an open fire, and were served with a spicy dipping sauce. Smaller prawns, calamari, chilli crab and fish also appeared accompanied by fresh, crunchy vegetables.

'What's this vegetable?' asked Julie picking up a long green soft vegetable with her chopsticks.

'Kang kong, water spinach, but we add belacan, the shrimp paste, which gives it a strong flavour,' said Aidi.

'I like the ikan bahar, the spicy fish,' said Christopher to Julie.

'I like everything,' laughed Julie.

Julie and Christopher hugged Aidi and his family goodbye and wandered back towards the harbour, agreeing that it had been a lovely evening.

'I think that I got out of tonight's dinner very cheaply,' said Julie. 'All that delicious food and it hardly cost a thing.'

'Yes,' agreed Christopher. 'I think that eating foreign

cuisine in a place like this is a bit silly, when the local food is so good.'

They strolled along the main street and decided not to go into any of the small bars but bought ice creams instead, before heading back to their hotel.

'Have you got company in your bed?' asked Christopher. 'I mean, the cats.'

'Oh, yes. I made the mistake of putting down a bowl of milk that was left over from breakfast and I soon had three of them in residence. I rather like it. They seem quite clean and they are very friendly.'

'Sleep well. I'm off fishing tomorrow, at dawn. So I might bring back dinner for Nerida's chef.'

'Good luck. And thanks for coming out with me today. It was fantastic.'

'I enjoyed it too. Selamat malam.'

Julie went for an early morning walk, accompanied by two cats who followed her faithfully around the gardens, the pool area, the rice fields and along a dusty road, before she swung back to the resort and went into the resort's open-sided restaurant as the early morning rays from the sun glinted on the nearby lagoon.

She ordered breakfast and sat in a dreamy state indulging in the peacefulness of the morning and enjoying not having to worry about work, or make any momentous decisions.

Alice, Nerida's business partner, placed a coffee pot and a platter of fresh fruit in front of her. 'Feel like eggs? Pancakes?'

'Good morning, Alice. Pancakes sound delicious. Thank you. Did you go to Penang?'

'Yes, but everything there was well in hand, so I didn't stay. What are your plans for today?'

Julie poured her coffee. 'I'm not making any. Just

see how the day unfolds, though Martine seems to have something in mind.'

'Enjoy the day. I'll tell chef to start on your pancakes.'

'Thanks, Alice.'

She finished breakfast, changed from her walking shorts and joined the others in the big villa.

'I wish I'd thought to ask Chris if I could go fishing with him,' she said to Shane.

'Oh, another time, perhaps. Those friends of Ursula and Werner sometimes take their boat out. The tender on it, I mean.'

'A big mother ship with a crew of eight isn't what I call fishing,' said Julie. 'I'm more into a small open boat and a couple of rods.'

Martine, dressed immaculately in crisp white linen shorts and a striped French T-shirt, came in and helped herself to lemon and ginger tea.

'Are you making plans, Julie? We've got something arranged for lunch and for dinner.'

'Oh, I don't want to impose,' said Julie quickly. 'I'm very happy just hanging around here. I'm hoping Christopher might bring back fish for dinner.'

'Dinner is arranged,' said Martine, sitting down beside Julie. 'We have a surprise planned.'

'For Christopher?'

'No, cherie. For you. We're going to the big beach resort for dinner . . .'

'Lovely! I hear it's gorgeous.'

'It is. We're having dinner with a guest who's staying there, an old friend of the boys, Marjorie Carter.'

'Oh!' Julie was speechless for a moment.

'I hope you're pleased,' said Shane, smiling at her. 'We're all in on Martine's plan.'

'I can't believe it. How did this happen? How lucky we're here at this time!' said Julie feeling quite overcome.

'Thank Martine,' said Peter. 'She persuaded Marjorie to fly over from Penang and have a little holiday to catch up with us – and to meet you.'

'I don't know what to say,' said Julie, putting down her cup of tea. Her face was jubilant.

'We thought we could all have a little social get together tonight, and then you and Marjorie can spend some time together tomorrow perhaps,' said Martine, pleased at making Julie happy.

'I can't thank you enough. Is Marjorie happy to share her memories?'

The idea of sitting down and talking with someone who had known Great Aunt Bette and Uncle Philip, and the extraordinary time they must have shared, was wonderful. How she wished that her mother was there with her so that she could meet Marjorie as well.

'It must have been a difficult time for her, too, as a prisoner in a Japanese POW camp. Did she have any family with her?'

'You can ask her the details, but I know that she was there with her mother, isn't that right, Shane?'

'Her father, Lionel Potts, was a district officer in Sarawak. I don't think that our family knew them before that.'

'So her father wasn't in the camp with them?' asked Julie.

'Let Marjorie tell you what she knows,' said Shane gently.

When Christopher returned from his fishing trip, he came over to Julie's house where she was sitting on the balcony.

'Knock, knock. How's your day been?'

'Quiet. Restful. Nice. I'm looking forward to tonight. How was the fishing?'

'Great, no, not really. All the big ones got away. There's really no big-time fishing here, but it's an excuse to hang out on a boat, have a few beers, trawl around the island. But I won't be barbecuing a monster tonight.'

'Never mind,' she said. 'There are other plans.' Julie explained to him about Marjorie Carter and how Martine had arranged for them all to have dinner at the exclusive, upmarket resort.

'Intriguing stuff. From what you tell me, she's an important link. It should be an interesting night.'

'Are you coming along?'

'I hadn't planned to, it seems more of a family night out.'

'Come on, Christopher. It's just Peter, Shane, Martine and me, and I know that all the others have also made plans. You can't stay on your own. Wouldn't you like to meet Marjorie? She sounds like a legend.'

Christopher smiled. 'I would like to come. I was going to say, do you want to meet for a swim and maybe a cold beer now?'

'Sounds good. I haven't done a thing all day. Just been sitting here thinking about Grandfather's memoir that I read when I was at Utopia. Do you know that when he got back to the plantation it was a shambles, his father was dead, and his son had been separated from my grandmother and wasn't back in Australia as he had assumed?'

Small electric buggies, driven by charming staff in smart uniforms, zipped them through the floodlit tropical gardens of the exclusive beach resort, stopping outside the entrance to the elegant seafood restaurant.

'You might get your fish dinner, after all,' said Julie as Christopher helped her from the buggy. They walked past flaming torches and into the restaurant and were taken to a table in a private section, separate from the airy, open dining area with its polished wood and rattan furniture.

Marjorie was already seated at the table, leaning back among silk cushions. Her hair was coiled on top of her head and she wore a dramatic scarlet and green print top, which was matched with sparkling green earrings. Her nails were manicured and painted scarlet, and she wore several gold bangles on her wrist. She smiled warmly at Peter and Shane, who leaned over and greeted her with a kiss.

'Forgive me not standing up to hug you all. Martine, dear, how elegant you look, as always. And you must be Julie. Come, sit next to me.'

'I'm Christopher, a friend of the family,' said Christopher shaking her hand.

'You're Australian, too?' Marjorie spoke with a soft, well-bred accent.

'I can't thank you enough for coming over here,' said Julie shyly. 'To see me, I mean.'

'Dear girl, this place is no hardship.' Marjorie waved her hand towards the restaurant, to the gardens and the strip of illuminated sand in front of the hotel. 'I love staying here. I feel very elegant and very spoiled. But I do hope you will visit me in Penang. It's such an interesting city. Do you know it, Christopher?'

'I do. I'm working at Butterworth,' he smiled.

'Then you're very close. You must pop in and see me, young man. Now, Julie, tell me all about yourself.'

As the champagne was poured, and the others started looking at the seafood menu, Julie briefly told Marjorie about herself, how she and her mother had not known until now, that Margaret and Philip had been separated during the war, that Philip had spent the war years in a Japanese POW camp with Bette.

Marjorie nodded, studying Julie. 'So all this, for you, was a family secret. We all have them, I suppose.'

255

'We didn't even know we had a family secret!' exclaimed Julie.

'One sometimes hears stories that sound too fantastic to be true, but they are. Often one simply didn't want to make public what happened behind closed doors. Everyone might know that things went on but saved face by keeping matters private. It's how it was. Children born out of wedlock, children handed over to be raised by other members of the family or even non-relatives. Sex, love, money, religion, politics, the drivers of extraordinary actions, wouldn't you say?' Marjorie raised her glass of champagne. 'Here's to you, my dear. I hope I can help you in some small way.'

'What would you prefer, Marjorie, the old ways of hushing up family secrets, keeping the skeletons in the closet, or letting it all hang out in public as it is today?' asked Peter.

Marjorie wrinkled her nose. 'I do so hate the way people bare their private lives on TV and so on. But I have to say, honesty is the best policy at the end of the day. Secrets always have a way of coming out, eventually. But Julie, if you would like to know more about my experiences during the war, I could tell you, perhaps tomorrow? Now, what are we ordering to eat? The food is so lovely here.'

In the buggy after dinner Julie and Christopher agreed it was one the most enjoyable evenings they'd had in a long time. Marjorie was a delightful soul who'd made them laugh, and made them think, and made everyone hope they could be as warm, friendly, funny and bright when they reached eighty.

'I'm certainly going to keep in touch with her and pop in and see her in Penang when I get the chance,' said Christopher.

'She'd love to have a handsome young gentleman caller, I'm sure,' said Julie. 'She must have had a hard time during the war and yet she isn't bitter, in fact, she is a very generous spirit.'

'She was young, I suppose that helped. Shane and Peter told me their grandfather was a bit taciturn and didn't like talking about the war years,' said Christopher. 'Maybe that's a male thing. Men never talk about things that have affected them deeply. Or so my mother tells me.'

'Does that apply today? I thought you guys had worked through the snag era and we're all equal when it comes to emotional maturity,' said Julie.

'I'm not sure. I guess what Marjorie said about being honest is the safest way to go. Here are the others.' Christopher jumped out of the buggy as it pulled up at the valet parking reception where Shane's car was waiting.

Julie had arranged to meet Marjorie at her resort for morning tea, so she bought some flowers, popped a notebook into her handbag and called a taxi. Marjorie was in her villa facing the beach and greeted Julie warmly. Julie thought that she looked a little older in the bright light, compared to the candlelight of the evening before, but she was just as charming.

The villa was surrounded by an oasis of lush greenery, which screened Marjorie from the neighbouring villas. In front of it, on the beach, was a gauzy tent, under which sat tables and chairs. The sand had been swept clean in a raked pattern, and flame torches were stuck in it, ready for the evening.

'Wow, is that where you eat?' asked Julie as Marjorie took her out onto the shady deck where'd she'd been relaxing on the daybed.

'That setting is for romantic dinners for two. I'm

happy to get the buggy to the beach café. You can reach it by walking along the sand, but that's a bit difficult for me with my legs, these days. Now, let's sit at the table. I have tea, coffee or cool drinks.'

'A fresh lime juice, if you have it, would be lovely. Thanks, Marjorie,' said Julie. 'Do you stay over here on the island regularly?'

'I do. I loved being invited to the Elliotts' beach house. The boys sold it after Philip and Stephanie were killed, such a tragedy. But the boys have done very well for themselves since then. I hope Peter marries his girl soon, but she doesn't seem keen on the idea of life in Asia. She hasn't been here enough, that's the trouble.'

'It's a beautiful place to visit, but perhaps the thought of life on a plantation doesn't appeal to a young career girl,' said Julie.

'What about you? Could you live here?' asked Marjorie with a quizzical smile. 'After all, your family lived here in the old days.'

'Yes, they did,' said Julie. 'But I didn't know anything about this life till recently, and I'm not sure that I'd be all that keen to leave a career and my way of living to move here, unless I was really in love. What about you? Did you grow up here?' Julie had thought that she would be anxious to plunge in and ask about her great aunt and her uncle, but now she felt she wanted to know more about Marjorie first. 'I found out last night that you lived in Sarawak. I've just been there – it was wonderful. So very beautiful and so interesting. I bet that it's changed since you were young.'

'It certainly has. I've been back to Kuching a few times, and I find it almost impossible to reconcile it with the place where I was born. My parents were Scots. My father was with the Civil Service under the last of the White Rajahs, Charles Vyner Brooke. He was a district officer, up-country. My two older brothers were at boarding school in England, and I had my parents' undivided attention, so I was the spoiled baby of the family. I had a very indulged childhood.' Marjorie smiled.

'Servants? Being the only child?' asked Julie.

'Yes. Though my parents were just ordinary people back home, in Sarawak, I had an amah and there was a lot of staff. My goodness, the life in Sarawak in the thirties was great fun. I remember trips on the river with the Iban, hauling the boat over the rapids, punting in the Sarawak River, hiking through the jungle to a waterfall, being spoiled, a Chinese cobbler who drew around my foot and made pretty embroidered shoes for me. My parents went to wonderful parties at the palace, my father often went on hunting trips. I had some very odd pets and played with the children from the kampong.

'Mother taught me at home. There was a school at the palace, for privileged children like myself, but Mother knew that I would have to go back to England eventually, so she wanted to keep me with her as long as she could. There were only about thirty European women living in Kuching at this time, and she certainly was the only white woman where we lived, so I suspect that she just didn't want me to leave her, as it would have made her life very lonely. But before I was sent away to school, the war broke out . . .' She paused and added, 'And life was never the same again.'

'The Brookes, the White Rajahs, they seem such an amazing family. Do you remember them? I've seen the places they built in Kuching. Their rule in Sarawak seems to be like something out of a novel,' said Julie.

'I'm glad you've been to Sarawak. While it's a very different place from when I grew up there, it's still very lovely. Yes, I remember Sir Charles Vyner Brooke very clearly. He was a lovely old gentleman, very proper and charming.

When my parents and I came into Kuching, which was a few times a year, he would always meet us. He always knew my name and asked after my brothers. Occasionally we would be asked to the palace for dinner. He never seemed to mind when my parents brought me along.

'He always said that all the Europeans working for him had to be accessible to everyone. The locals had to be able to speak to them directly, and that included the rajah. So every evening the Dayaks, Malays and Chinese used to go to the palace and talk to him and tell him what their problems were. He even invited the Dayaks to drink with him, but at eight a gun was fired and that signalled the time for the rajah's dinner and everyone had to leave. Then we would go across to the palace and join him for dinner. It's impossible to forget memories like that.'

'And after the war, you went back to the UK? I know from Peter and Shane that you have a family. Can I ask about it? Do you have grandchildren?' asked Julie.

'Oh, yes, tribes of them back in Scotland. Some of them have been out here for holidays with me because I loathe the cold winters in Scotland, but of course they don't have the same affection for this place as I do.'

The two women had settled themselves at the table under a fan, their backs to the glaring white sand and the stretch of blue water.

'When you look at this peaceful setting, the war must be a distant memory. Or do those years come back to haunt?' asked Julie tentatively.

'Haunt isn't the right word. I didn't talk about it much for many years. But now, what does it matter? Oddly enough, I don't remember when the war actually started, but I know that my parents thought that we would be able to sit it out on the river where we lived because it was so remote. Then they realised that by staying up-country, they were putting the lives of the Dayaks, whom they loved, at risk. If the Japanese found out that they were sheltering us, they would have been severely punished. So my father made the decision to turn ourselves in. We made our way to Kuching and my father was taken to one camp and Mother and I went to another.'

'How terrible it must have been for you,' said Julie, wondering how she would have felt if, as a twelve year old, she had been separated from her father in such a brutal way.

'I believe that I was very fortunate to survive and so I've put it behind me but, occasionally, some small thing will trigger a memory. And what I remember most is not the Japanese soldiers who guarded us, although it is impossible to forget them, but the women who were strong, resourceful, trying their best to be positive. Women like my mother, keeping the little ones fed, occupied and hopeful. It couldn't have been easy. They went without, they stood up to the Japanese, and they continually fought so hard just to keep us all alive.'

'And my Great Aunt Bette? Was she one of these women?'

Marjorie smiled. 'She was one of the best. She was a leader, in spite of her age, she was only about twenty-one. She took some terrible risks. She was a fierce little tiger, always protecting Philip. Amazing, actually, when I think back. I mean Philip was her nephew, not her own child, and yet I know that she could not have done more for him.'

'I'd love to know more about her and Philip,' said Julie.

'I understand that. When Martine and Shane rang me to suggest that I might like to meet you, I was very happy to do so, and the flight from Penang is very short, but before I tell you about Bette and Philip, there's something that I'd like to show you.'

261

Marjorie leaned across and picked up a small flat box from the coffee table. 'I thought you might like to see this,' she said, handing it to Julie.

Julie opened the little box. Inside was some tissue paper, which she carefully unwrapped, around a yellowed piece of paper. On it was a drawing of two young people, one a little boy, the other a young girl. They were sitting on some steps, eating bowls of rice with chopsticks. They both looked thin, their clothes were threadbare and they wore no shoes. And yet between the two was clearly a bond, almost an intimacy, as they watched each other eating. Written on top of the card were the words 'Happy Birthday, Marjorie'.

'Bette made me this birthday card. The drawing is of Philip and me. I don't know how she got the paper. That sort of thing was impossible to get. In a way, it was a dangerous sort of present too, because the Japanese didn't like the prisoners keeping any sort of record of camp life. People couldn't have diaries or make drawings or any anything like that. After Bette gave me the card, it was sewn into a little pillow that I had, to keep it safe. The Japanese never found it, so here it is.'

Julie looked at the card. She looked at the drawing and although she realised that the children were thin, she also saw that they were both full of vitality.

'It's hard to believe that I'm holding something drawn by my great aunt and that the picture is of my uncle. It was all such a long time ago. Have you any idea why they ended up in the camp in Sarawak?'

'No, I never heard the reason. Bette seemed so much older than me, even though she was only nine years older, so I didn't talk to her as an intimate. Anyway, people didn't often talk about their lives before the camp, it was usually too painful.'

'I'm sorry to bring back bad memories,' said Julie quickly.

'That's all right. It's just a part of my life I've put behind me and rarely think about. But occasionally, when I think about those days as a POW, I try to think about the good things, and the good people. Those women were quite amazing, how they held us all together, how we helped each other, shared what little we had. Of course, there were occasions when someone had something they just didn't want to share and it was often Bette who came to the rescue with some suggestion to solve matters.'

'You were a young girl growing up in a POW camp, that must have been hard,' said Julie.

'It was,' sighed Marjorie. 'And your aunt helped me there too. She was very clever. Quick witted. It's a shame we didn't keep in touch after the war. But we were all anxious to get back to our lives, catch up on what we had missed. I kept in contact with Philip and he came to stay with my family in the UK when he was at school, but by the time I finally made it back to Malaysia to stay with Philip and Stephanie at their place on Langkawi, Bette was long gone. I enjoyed myself on Langkawi so much, that I kept coming back to Malaysia regularly and I eventually bought my own place in Penang after Philip and Stephanie were killed. I've always felt a bond with their boys and when I stay out here they take me under their wing.'

'So other than Philip you've had no contact with anyone else from the camp?'

Marjorie paused. 'I know it must seem strange to you, especially after we went through so much. But I was a teenager and I wanted to be reunited with my family and pick up my life back home and my mother felt the same way. We just wanted to start over.'

'No, it doesn't seem odd. My grandmother, Philip's mother, did much the same thing. She never told my mother or me anything about this whole episode. The rift between my great aunt and my grandmother must have been very deep.'

Marjorie nodded. 'Sad when sisters fall out. Everyone around them suffers too. I just hope Bette had a happy life.'

'I wish I'd known her,' said Julie sadly.

'Yes, a very special person.' Marjorie paused as if deciding something, then said, 'Would you like to know more about life in the camp? What it was like for us all and how Bette had to fight so ferociously for Philip?'

'I would like that, very much,' said Julie softly.

'For years I thought that one shouldn't talk about what was past. Move on, get on with your life was my motto. But now, as I am getting older, I don't want the actions of these women, or those of the Japanese, forgotten either. I think that their story should be told.'

Marjorie settled back into her chair and passed her coffee cup to Julie. 'Top us both up, and I'll start from when I first met Bette and Philip.'

9

Sarawak, 1942

MARJORIE AND HER MOTHER, Evelyn, were silent as they followed the other women who shuffled, single file, towards the camp, knowing their world was to shrink to this wire-enclosed hot and dusty prison.

'Looks like a damned chicken coop. All that wire,' commented one of the women in a low voice.

'I just want to sit down, my feet are raw,' said another.

'It's barbed wire! Look at the guards up there.'

The group of women suddenly saw the tower where an armed soldier stood watching them approaching the main gates, where other soldiers waited. The women fell silent again as their internment became a reality. What shocked some of them were the pained and sad faces of the women already inside the camp, who had come to the fence to watch them.

One of them pointed at the new arrivals. 'Bags! They have suitcases. Belongings. Have you got any food?' she called out.

'And medicine?' cried another.

'Oh my Lord. What's going to happen? I haven't got enough to share around. My baby needs it,' said one of the new arrivals fearfully, clutching her bag, which was weighed down by precious tins of powdered milk.

In the new group, Evelyn walked slowly, bent over with pain and fever. Behind her, Marjorie, gangly legs and arms, her hair in a long plait, dragged her mother's suitcase as well as her own bag behind her. Across her chest was slung a cotton bag. She looked bewildered. Her mother had tried to explain what might happen to them, but Marjorie really couldn't imagine what being locked away might be like.

'But why, Mummy? What did we do wrong? Where's Daddy going?'

'We haven't done anything wrong, Marjorie. Don't you forget that. I'm sure your father will be all right. It's hard when grownups fight each other, when people make war on others because they want their country, innocent people get in the way. I'm afraid that's us. We've got in the way of Japanese ambition. But we won't be forgotten. We will be rescued and then life will go on as it always has. You'll just have to be brave until we get out of here,' said her mother in a tired voice.

As she stood in front of the gates, Marjorie looked at the strange fenced-off area. It didn't look like the prison she'd imagined. There were no big cement buildings or high solid walls. 'How long will we have to wait?' she asked as the line of women came to a stop.

Three armed soldiers came towards them. There were raised voices, but Marjorie's attention was diverted. It was as though everything around her had dissipated into soft focus while a bright spotlight shone on the scene further along the fence. A young boy, about three, was at the wire on his knees, trying to retrieve a soft toy he'd poked through the fence. Marjorie put down her bag and went over to him. She picked up the toy, which was a small blue elephant, and pushed it back through the wire. The little boy grabbed it from her and clutched it, regarding Marjorie with solemn blue eyes.

'How did your elephant get out here?' she asked him.

'Run away,' he said and then turned away as a woman called to him.

'Philip! Come over here, please.'

One of the Japanese soldiers ran towards Marjorie and shouted at her. Frightened by this violent reaction, she returned to the other women who were being pushed through the gates. Marjorie picked up the two bags. She could see that Evelyn was at the end of her tether.

In the central dusty yard the women, several babies and children of various ages, were being marshalled into straggling lines by the shouting Japanese soldiers. They had been told to put their bags to one side, but now a soldier had begun to tear them open, scattering their contents. Some of the women began to weep, and when one of them raised an objection she was hit with the butt of a rifle. The woman slumped to the ground, clutching her bleeding head. As other women near her leaned down to help, they were swiftly stopped by angry soldiers.

The women stood paralysed, shocked at this treatment. They watched as their few possessions were examined. Some soldiers picked up food items and other things they considered valuable, they kicked the rest of the luggage around in the dust.

'Damn them, what bastards,' muttered one women. 'They said we'd be well treated.'

Marjorie looked around her. The perimeter of this

main square consisted of small huts roofed with attap and bamboo walls. They looked flimsy and obviously had few amenities. There were women and children inside them, watching through the holes cut in the walls. A Japanese soldier began shouting at them furiously.

'What's he saying?' whispered the woman next to Marjorie, who only managed to shake her head in reply.

Then, as if in exasperation at their stupidity for not understanding him, the soldier suddenly began to shout at them in English, as if to small children.

'You are now prisoners of Emperor of Japan. Emperor look after women and children. You obey rules, and you not get into trouble. You not obey, you will be punished.' He began shouting a list of instructions and rules that were barely understood by the exhausted and frightened women. A few small children whimpered. A baby cried in hunger. After what seemed an age, standing in the hot sun, they were finally dismissed and the women began to scoop up their belongings. Marjorie knelt down and stuffed her mother's clothes into her suitcase, tugging back a dress that another woman was trying to pick up.

'That's my mother's.'

But the other woman was too distraught to notice or care.

An older woman appeared from one of the huts and introduced herself to the group. 'I'm June Humphries. I've been elected as the camp representative. I act as the go-between with the Japs and the prisoners. Welcome to you all.' She began to explain the camp routine as she assigned the women to the various huts.

Marjorie and her mother, clutching their belongings, walked to one of them and blinked in the dimness of its two dormitory rooms. The woman with the little boy that Marjorie had seen at the fence came forward.

'Welcome to what we have, although it's not much.'

'My mother is sick. Can she lie down?' said Marjorie.

'We were told that more women were coming. We'll have to sort out some better sleeping arrangements, but for now your mother can sleep on my bed. I see that you were able to bring a few things. Do you have any medicines?' she asked.

'I have some quinine and aspirin in my cotton bag. The guards took so many of our things,' said Marjorie. 'That's not right.'

'No, it's not. There are many things not right here so we have to make the best of it. When Philip and I arrived, we had very little, except of course Philip's elephant. By the way, I'm Bette Oldham. What's your name?'

'Marjorie Potts.'

'And I'm Evelyn Potts. I'm so sorry to be a nuisance to you,' said Marjorie's mother, faintly from the direction of the bed.

Bette brushed the apology aside. 'I understand, this must be a terrible shock for you, but you must get well as soon as you can. There is no doctor or proper hospital here, but we do what we can. There's a sick bay, run by an English woman and a couple of nuns. They're wonderful, but there's only so much you can do in these conditions.'

'What are the conditions like here?' asked Evelyn.

'Terrible, just look at these beds. They're only bamboo slats and very uncomfortable, unless you have money to buy a thin mattress – then I guess they're a bit better. To eat we get a cupful of rice a day, occasionally some terrible meat and greens that are slimy and inedible, although we eat them. Drinking water is precious. We catch as much as we can when it rains. The latrines are a nightmare. They are just a hole in the ground, over there behind that shack, and someone has to empty them out every day.'

'How long have you been here?' asked Evelyn. 'Oh, you're right. This bed is very uncomfortable.'

'About three months now. I suppose we should be grateful that at least the bed is off the ground. Do you have a blanket or cover?'

'Yes,' said Marjorie quickly, opening one of their suitcases. 'Mother made it.'

Bette fingered the embroidered silk coverlet Marjorie had taken from the suitcase. 'That's wonderful. Philip and I sleep under my sarong and a skirt. Where are you from?'

Marjorie leaned over her mother. 'Could we have a drink of water please? We've had nothing for hours. We were living in Sarawak.'

'My husband was the DO, up-country,' sighed Evelyn. 'When the war broke out we thought that we could stay hidden in the jungle, but eventually my husband realised that by staying there, we were putting the Dayaks at risk, so we gave ourselves up to the Japanese authorities. The Japs put us into a house in Kuching for a few weeks with some Chinese and other people, mainly foreigners who seemed to have come from all over. The house just got more and more crowded. Eventually the Japs decided that we should move. Marjorie and I were separated from my husband and we were loaded onto the back of a truck like cattle and driven about two miles from the camp. Then we were told to get out and walk the rest of the way carrying all our things in the heat. I don't understand why they did that. They could just have easily driven us all the way.' She looked tearful.

'Just rest as best you can and try and get better,' advised Bette. She looked at Marjorie. 'How old are you?'

'Twelve.'

'You look younger. And that's a good thing. The Japs might hate us, and they do, but they seem to like children, or at least tolerate them.'

'It must be very hard for you and your son, just the same,' said Evelyn.

'Philip isn't my son, he's my nephew. We got separated from my sister on the docks in Singapore, so she got evacuated on a ship and we didn't.' She looked fondly at Philip. 'Anyway, he's my responsibility and he's the only family I have right now.'

'How terrible for you,' said Evelyn, who lay back and closed her eyes. Bette and Philip took Marjorie outside. Two more of the new arrivals were standing outside their hut looking stunned.

'How are we expected to live in these conditions?' asked one of them. 'The hut they put us in is overcrowded. There's no food and we're trapped in here.'

Bette nodded. 'It's hard. If you have money or things to sell, you can get by a little better. But there are many of us who came in with nothing so we try to share as best we can.'

'Where do you sell things?' asked the woman with bright curly red hair.

'Traders are permitted to come to the fence to sell and barter every so often, but their prices are outrageous. The sentries let it go on because they get a cut of the profits. Be careful though, and don't let people know if you have jewellery or money. Keep it hidden. You'll find out that not everyone in this camp can be trusted.'

'You seem to know a lot,' said the redhead. 'I'm Babs. This is Norma. Her husband was put in the men's camp. Is there any way of making contact with them?'

'I'm not sure how far away the men's camp is. Very occasionally we see some of them march past to go to work somewhere. When they do, we shout over to them. The Japs don't like it but we're not going to stop it. The men call back their wives' names, to let them know they're okay. Sometimes, if you've got enough money, the traders will take them a message. But that could be very dangerous. I'm sorry, but I have to go now and work with the

271

group in the cookhouse,' said Bette. 'There are lots of jobs that have to be done, cooking, keeping the camp clean. The Japs get really angry if they think that it's untidy. Anyway, I know that June and her committee will appoint you to something.'

'So, no mems here then,' said Babs with a smile.

Bette shook her head. She liked this chirpy redhead. 'We're all equal here, though some think that they're more important than others.'

'There are always those who don't want to pull their weight,' agreed Norma. 'So, is that lean-to affair over there the kitchen?'

'Yes. I'm afraid it is.'

'Well,' said Norma cheerfully, 'I'd better go and introduce myself.'

'Is there anything that I can do?' asked Marjorie. 'I want to pull my weight, too.'

'We try to keep the little kids around this area, so whoever is on kitchen detail can keep an eye on them. Marjorie, if you could watch them, or play with them as well, that would be wonderful.'

'Sounds like you have a job,' said Babs.

Bette leaned down and kissed Philip. 'This is our new friend Marjorie. She saved your elephant, and she wants to play with you, so be a good boy, won't you?' Bette ruffled his hair and then quickly turned and followed Norma into the kitchen.

By the end of the day the new arrivals had ascertained the full horror of their surroundings.

'We can't live on this,' exclaimed Babs, after she tasted the watery soup, which passed for that evening's meal.

'We do our best. Occasionally we have some protein – a scrawny chicken, if you can afford to buy one, sometimes meat, although we don't ask where it came from,' said Gloria, a tall imperious English woman who

272

had been a matron of a large hospital in Penang and now was in charge of the sick in the camp. 'Cockroaches can add a bit of a crunch,' she added with a wicked gleam in her eye.

Norma shuddered.

Marjorie noticed that Bette had put a portion of her own food onto Philip's plate and tried to entertain and distract him during their meagre meal. Marjorie did the same for her mother, but Bette noticed and spoke to her.

'Marjorie. You can't give your nourishing food to your mother. You'll get sick and then you'll be of no use to her. Your mother will get better. She just needs time and rest to get over that terrible journey.'

As time went on, food remained the greatest problem for the interned women. Those who had some money bought or traded extras from the local traders who appeared at the fence: a tough chicken, some fresh vegetables or the luxury of a few eggs. Usually these extras weren't shared, but Marjorie noticed that when any of the children were given treats, they were always happy to share the riches of an egg or banana with their friends.

A routine was established, a roster system was put in place and each woman's strengths and weaknesses were quickly known and accepted. Evelyn was still frail and unable to do the physically hard work around the camp, but she worked in the kitchen helping to prepare food. Gradually, like many of the other women, she sold pieces of her jewellery to supplement her and Marjorie's diet.

One day, Evelyn took Bette aside. 'I've managed to acquire two chickens! There's not much meat on them but we can make up a soup for us all.'

'Evelyn, how fantastic. Philip certainly could use some meat. So could you.'

'And you, Bette. You're so thin and you work so hard, and I watch how you give the best of your food to Philip. If you get sick, then where would he be?' asked the older woman. 'And I know you take a little bit of dry rice from the ration before it's cooked each day and keep it. Why do you do that?'

'Emergency supply,' said Bette ruefully. 'I've saved a couple of cupfuls. Just in case the rations get reduced or we need it sometime. It's not stealing. I take less of the cooked rice. Philip is growing so fast, he's all skinny legs and arms.'

'Well, we can all enjoy chicken soup tonight. I'll ask some of the others to share as well,' added Evelyn.

'I wish I had something to sell,' sighed Bette. 'I've sold all I had to get us a mosquito net and some clothes for Philip. And he's almost grown out of his shoes. I wish we had something we could make shoes from.'

'Rubber? I've seen kids in the kampongs and villages wearing shoes made from bits of latex,' said Evelyn. 'Surely we might be able to get someone to find some for us. It's a thought anyway.'

'Who knows what is happening on the rubber plantations? I wonder what has happened to my brother-in-law's place and its staff. If the Japs are there they won't be looking after the trees. It's all too depressing to think about,' said Bette. 'But speaking of the Japs, have you noticed that the soldiers aren't exactly treated like kings by their commanding officer, Major Sakura? He's always shouting at them and I've seen him slap a few faces. Maybe they don't like being here any more than we do.'

'I don't care about them. They live ten times better than us,' said Evelyn. 'But it's the surprise searches I can't stand. I don't know what they expect to find. As if we'd have weapons or radios, or do they think that we're digging a tunnel under the fence? And they make us stand for hours outside in the boiling sun while they do it. It's inhumane.'

Bette didn't answer. There were some secrets in their camp that were known only to a small group of the women and Bette was one. Some of them had thought it imperative that a record was kept of their imprisonment and so they kept a diary. Bette wrote small entries and added sketches to it. Paper was hard to come by but one of the women had managed to steal some from the Japanese. They kept the diary well hidden and constantly moved it to different locations to avoid it being found. All the women taking part in maintaining the diary knew that they would be severely punished if it was found, but they all thought the risk was worthwhile. Some day they would be released and the world would know what they had experienced.

'It's Marjorie's birthday soon,' continued Evelyn. 'What can we possibly do for it? She'll be thirteen and this isn't how I imagined celebrating the occasion.'

'I'll talk to Babs and some of the others. See what we can come up with,' said Bette. 'I think we should celebrate Marjorie's birthday. It's important to her and it will show the Japs that we can't be intimidated all the time.'

The women in Bette's hut embraced the idea of a celebration, and they quickly became involved in producing a surprise birthday party for her. An evening skirt of shot taffeta was produced, and a top was cut down to make a party outfit for Marjorie. Someone else produced a glamorous hair clip for the occasion.

'I know she's still a baby,' said Norma, 'but, heck, give her this.' She passed over a stub of precious lipstick. 'A sort of symbol of the fun times to come when she gets out of here.'

'Wish we could get her a cake,' sighed Evelyn. 'It just won't seem like a proper birthday party without one.'

The children got into the spirit of the party and were thrilled to receive gifts of pieces of fruit wrapped in small squares of banana leaf. But the surprise came when Bette came from the kitchen holding a bowl with a 'candle' made from a vine twisted around a small stick topped with dried grass tied onto it as a wick.

'Happy birthday, to you, happy birthday, dear Marjorie . . .' Bette sang as the others chimed in and Marjorie, decked out in her finery, blew out the improvised candle. 'Make a wish,' said Bette softly.

'What is it?' asked Marjorie. 'It smells wonderful.'

'Gula melaka pudding! A birthday pudding,' said Bette, pleased with the way the coconut and rice dessert had turned out. Small scoops of the sweet rice pudding were carefully doled out to everyone and they all ate it slowly, trying to make the treat last as long as possible.

Marjorie hugged Bette. 'I can't thank you enough. This is a birthday I'll never forget.'

'I have a little gift for you, it's from Philip and me.' She handed Marjorie a folded piece of paper. Marjorie opened it up to find a home-made birthday card decorated with a drawing of a thin young girl with long hair and a small boy eating bowls of rice with chopsticks.

Tears sprang to Marjorie's eyes. 'This is beautiful. It's Philip and me, isn't it? I'm going to hide it and keep it forever. Thank you, Bette, thank you, Philip.'

The little boy hugged Marjorie. 'You can play with Lumpy,' and he thrust his treasured toy at her.

Marjorie kissed the little blue elephant. 'Well, that's an honour. Maybe one day we can see real elephants.'

'And orangutans in the jungle,' smiled Bette.

'I'm done with walking in the jungle,' commented one of the women quietly.

'I'd rather take my chances with the wild animals than in here,' said another woman in a low voice.

'It's Marjorie's birthday and it's cheered us all up,' said Bette in a loud voice. 'Let's have a bit of a sing-song.'

As usual, the women found that singing their favourite songs lifted their spirits and because it was Marjorie's birthday, they sang even louder.

Later that night, Marjorie and Evelyn thanked Bette again.

'I need a hiding place for my card you made and my little things,' said Marjorie.

'Why don't you sew it into your pillow? The Japs won't look for it there. Here, I'll do it for you,' said Bette. So Bette carefully sewed the card into the little pillow and when she returned it to Marjorie, she whispered, 'Our little secret.'

Bette lay on her bed, Philip's warm form curled against her, sleeping soundly, his cheek resting on his elephant. She looked across to Evelyn, lying only inches away.

'I can feel his tiny frame, every single fragile bone, like a bird. His breathing seems shallow and he's so pale. He just doesn't have the energy he used to. I know he's malnourished. I just don't know how to help him.'

'But Bette, you're wonderful with Philip. His own mother couldn't have done more for him.'

'Evelyn, I feel so helpless. I can't believe how everything went so wrong and we ended up here. The surprise Jap attack, the hopeless British defence, the terrible muddle in Singapore. I couldn't even bring the most basic things into camp. At least you and Marjorie brought some things in. I only had my handbag with a bit of money and a few cosmetics. It was all so little. I've got nothing to sell and I'm almost out of money.'

'Yes, this has been very hard for you. And there are

some women who seem to have a lot of valuables and influence. Life for them does not seem as difficult as it does for you. That horrible Hannah Lampton, for instance. Just because her husband was a wealthy planter, she expects deference in this camp. I know she buys a lot from the traders, but you never see her actually doing the buying. She gets other people to do it for her.'

'I know. For all the talk in this camp of pulling together, that Hannah Lampton certainly believes that it's every woman for herself.'

The next day, before heading to the cookhouse, Bette told Evelyn that their talk last night had given her an idea, and with that she walked over to the hut where Hannah Lampton lived. Hannah was a big woman who looked to be well fed. She was fashionably dressed and her shoes looked almost new. She was sitting outside the hut, in the shade, on a handmade wooden chair, obviously procured from a trader.

'It's my veins. My legs and ankles are too swollen to work,' she said as Bette approached.

Bette nodded. 'We all have something wrong,' she said. 'But we must soldier on, right?'

Hannah frowned, sensing some implied criticism in Bette's bright remark. But she sat and listened to what Bette had to say and when Bette said she had to leave to go to the cookhouse, Hannah folded her arms and said, 'I'll talk to you this afternoon.'

The worst part about the job in the cookhouse, Bette told Evelyn, was not cooking for large numbers of women with terrible rice and the few nourishing ingredients that were their rations, although that was difficult enough, it was maintaining the fires to do the job. The rice vats required a lot of wood to keep them boiling, but obtaining the wood was always difficult. Often the wood that was delivered to the camp each day by truck was green or sometimes an entire tree trunk might arrive and then there would be the problem of chopping it up. The tools for this job consisted of two very blunt hatchets, so that by the end of the day Bette's hands would be covered in blisters.

When she returned from the cookhouse that day after battling with the firewood, Philip scampered over and hugged her, exclaiming over what he and Marjorie had been doing.

'What a clever boy you are. Now, I have to see one of the women. I'll be back shortly.'

He refused to let go of her hand. 'I want to come.' He lifted her hand and turned it over. 'Oh, hurt.' He looked at the raw blisters on her palms then put his own hand protectively over hers.

'Oh, all right. Marjorie, can you come as well? Just for a few minutes.' And the three walked over to Hannah's hut.

'Sit here and wait a minute,' Bette told Philip who obediently sat in the dirt and began playing with Lumpy, while Marjorie watched him. When Bette returned from her conversation with Hannah, she was smiling. 'Come on, tell me what you've been up to today.'

Everyone in the camp went to bed early, exhausted from the lack of food and the sheer hard work of getting through each day. Sometimes the women talked quietly among themselves sharing a rare cigarette in the darkness before the shrill voices of the soldiers signalled curfew. Sleep, when it came, was a welcome escape from the reality of their existence. After Bette settled Philip, she went to Evelyn and Marjorie and spoke softly.

'I've made an arrangement with Hannah Lampton today,' she told them.

'She's nasty, she gets things and keeps them to herself,' said Marjorie.

'Yes, I think that's true,' said Bette. 'She came into camp with a lot of assets, which is why I approached her.

I asked if I could work for her in return for payment. It's the only way I can think of to get extra food for Philip.'

'Bette! You work like a dog now! And you deprive yourself,' exclaimed Evelyn.

'Doing what sort of work? Can I help?' said Marjorie quickly.

'No, it's enough that you help me with Philip. I wish I could pay you for that,' said Bette. 'No, Hannah is used to servants and she's also lazy. I've offered to work for her. Sew, help her cook, do her rostered jobs for her. Whatever she needs. Just here and there,' she added.

'That woman will make you her slave,' said Evelyn shortly. 'You'll kill yourself, Bette.'

'I need the money.'

'I have one or two pieces of jewellery put aside,' began Evelyn but Bette touched her arm.

'Save it for yourself and Marjorie. You might need it. Philip is my responsibility and it's up to me to do whatever is necessary. I'm just asking you to keep an eye on Philip when I'm working for Hannah.'

'Of course. You know we will.' Evelyn looked at her daughter. 'Marjorie adores him, like a little brother.'

But it soon became obvious to everyone that Hannah was driving Bette almost beyond exhaustion point. When Evelyn pointed this out to her, Bette replied that she was thankful for the pittance that she got from mean Hannah, as it enabled her to buy the occasional egg or banana for Philip.

There was a blast from the watchtower and another muster was called. For once Bette was relieved to put down the heavy metal bucket and join everyone in the centre of

280

the compound as Major Sakura strutted out to inspect them.

'Why does the silly fool bother with these inspections?' whispered Babs.

'Got to justify his existence, I suppose,' said Bette.

When the short, balding man stood to attention in front of them, the women and children bowed deferentially, as was expected. But then he shouted at them in Japanese, raising the heavy riding crop which he always carried.

'He's cranky, what's wrong?' hissed Evelyn.

A soldier strode towards Evelyn and whether he had seen her speaking or thought that she had not bowed humbly enough, he was displeased and he brought the solid wooden butt of his rifle down across her shoulders causing her to fall to the ground with a short cry. Bette and the woman on the other side of Evelyn went to help her, but Major Sakura and the sudden movement from two other soldiers brandishing rifles made it clear that the women were to stay still. One of the guards elbowed Marjorie aside with his rifle and stood in front of the crumpled figure of Evelyn, his legs apart, his rifle held in front of his chest, as he shouted at Evelyn, making it clear that she was to get up.

Evelyn moved but simply could not get to her feet. There was a trickle of blood from her mouth. Marjorie started to cry. The women were silent, shaking, biting back their own tears of fright and sadness for Evelyn.

The soldier's boot shot out and he kicked Evelyn in the ribs.

'That's enough! The woman can't get up!' shouted Bette.

There was an involuntary gasp at her daring, if incautious, remark.

Defying the soldier, Bette leaned down and tried to

help Evelyn to her feet but Evelyn's legs wouldn't hold her up and she looked as though she was about to pass out.

'This woman needs medical attention,' said Bette. 'We must take her to the sick bay.'

There was no movement from anyone. Bette took a deep breath and, leaving the lines, walked to where Major Sakura was standing. 'You must see that this woman needs medical treatment. Surely the Emperor of Japan would not want this woman to die while you are in charge of her.'

Major Sakura glared at Bette, and then said, 'You take.'

With the help of one of the others, Bette half carried, half dragged Evelyn to the camp hospital. The room contained several beds made from bamboo. There was no doctor, it was run by the redoubtable former matron from Penang. There were very few medical supplies, although it was thought that the Japanese had plenty. The two women left Evelyn there and returned to the parade ground. One of the guards who spoke English told Bette that she was to go to the major's office at once.

'You break rules,' he said ominously.

'Yes, Corporal Hashimoto, I know.'

Bette knocked nervously on Major Sakura's office door. When she entered, he stood glaring at her, his arms behind his back.

'You, name?'

Bette gave an exaggerated low slow bow, every inch of her body radiating scorn. She straightened up and looked him in the eye. 'Bette Oldham. I'm from Australia.'

He stabbed a finger towards her. 'You bad. Disobey rule. You speak to me in front of other women. You are not prisoner representative.' He exploded into an outburst of Japanese that left Bette in no doubt that she was in trouble.

'You must learn, white women are not important. Only Japanese forces of his Imperial Majesty important. Japanese women know that they must obey. White women must also learn this. You will be punished. Solitary confinement, many days, maybe two, three weeks.'

Bette caught her breath. Solitary confinement. It had been threatened but the women hadn't believed it would ever be inflicted upon them. 'No. Wait. I must see Philip. Little boy. He can't be left alone. I must explain to him.'

But the major ignored her and, calling to one of the soldiers, ordered him to lead her away. The soldier shook his head and grabbed Bette's arm, afraid she was going to dash away from him. As she was marched across the ground to the building that held the solitary confinement cell, she shouted towards Marjorie, 'You must look out for Philip for me. I'm being put away in solitary, I don't know for how long. Please tell him, I'll be back soon. Make sure he gets food . . .'

'Yes, of course. Please don't worry, Bette, I'll take care of him.'

'Just tell him I have a special job to do . . . anything . . .'

It was the darkness that distressed her most, and the separation from Philip. Bette lost all sense of time, day and night. The room had no windows and was lit for only a brief time each day when a daily bowl of thin rice gruel or boiled rice was pushed through the door to her. She had no idea how long her punishment would last, so she tried to keep her mind active as well as her body. Sleep was difficult as she had only the dirt floor to lie on. Noises, deliberately made, she felt, banged and crashed at all hours to prevent any decent interval of rest. A hole in the ground in a corner served as her latrine and from this hole cockroaches and rats made their way into the cell to keep her company. In the dimness her senses were strengthened. Her eyes adjusted to the darkness and she could make out the corners of the small space she inhabited. Her hearing became acute and she strained for every noise from the tiny movement of a gecko on her wall to the sound of rain or distant voices, and she learned to recognise the differing footsteps of her guards.

With nothing to occupy her minute after minute, hour after hour, day after day, she worked out a routine as best she could. She recalled her bedroom at home in Brisbane and she chose her favourite pieces of furniture and mentally moved them in here with her. The bed with its smooth white marcella bedspread was over there. Her dressing table with its oval mirror and her collection of miniature china animals was in that corner, and every twenty-four hours, or what she thought might be that time span, she added another decorating component.

She could now move into the garden, having added French doors and a verandah to her dark cell.

Other times she recited poems she'd learned at school. She sang softly to herself. What she missed most was being able to draw, so she decided to imagine drawing. She sat on the floor and closed her eyes and drew in her mind, using first her right hand and then her left hand. Being right-handed, the challenge of recreating the images in her mind using her left hand added an extra dimension of involvement and forced her to concentrate. She drew the garden at home, the avenues of rubber trees at Utopia, the hidden waterfall she'd visited with Gilbert, the street scenes of Ipoh, and the faces of the rubber tappers. She drew Philip, hunched over his favourite game on the verandah at Utopia, or sitting in the dusty yard of the camp playing with Lumpy. And just for Philip she drew a special picture of his toy blue elephant. Maybe one day she'd write a book, titled, *The Story of Lumpy,*

284

the Blue Elephant, and illustrate it with pictures of their adventures.

There was a rattle at the door, and the English-speaking guard Corporal Hashimoto appeared, gesturing to her.

'You come. Major Sakura speak to you.'

Bette had no idea how long she'd been confined. The light hurt her eyes as she staggered out of her cell. She was aware that Corporal Hashimoto was giving her sidelong glances and she knew she smelled, her hair was tangled and matted and that she had lost even more weight. But she wanted everyone to see that she was strong and show them that this punishment had not defeated her.

Once more she bowed low before the major, straightened up slowly, put her hands behind her back, pulled back her shoulders and lifted her chin. She didn't wish to appear defiant, even if she felt it, but neither was she going to cower.

'You have been punished. You will now be model prisoner and show other women that they must be humble and obey rules. Go.'

Bette bowed her thanks and backed out of the room. The sunlight burned her eyes and she staggered, throwing her hand across her face. To her surprise, and perhaps his, Corporal Hashimoto reached for her arm and steadied her. As she walked towards her hut, there were shouts and cries as women dropped what they were doing and hurried to her and she was quickly surrounded by the women from the kitchen.

'Where's Philip?' asked Bette.

'He's with Marjorie and the other children, he's fine,' Evelyn quickly reassured her. She gave Bette a hug. 'I feel badly that you suffered this because of me. Thank you.'

'How's your head?' asked Bette.

Evelyn nodded. 'I'm all right. I think that you had

better clean up before Philip sees you. I've got a little bit of soap left that you can have.' Evelyn led her gently into the shade behind the kitchen.

'You do pong a bit,' said Norma. 'And you look thinner.'

Bette had barely finished washing, when she saw the small figure of Philip running across the yard towards her as fast as his short legs would carry him.

He flung himself at Bette and they held each other tightly. 'Don't go away any more,' he said, through muffled tears.

'I promise I won't. But I had to help Aunty Evelyn. Everything is fine now.' She unclasped his arms. 'Let me look at you. Why, I do believe you've grown a whole inch.'

He looked at her and touched her face, unable to form the words and express the strong emotions he was feeling. Instead he asked. 'What did you do? Did you bring me something?'

Bette smiled. 'There wasn't anything to bring you. But you know, I missed you and Lumpy so much I made up drawings of you both.'

'Where are they?' he asked eagerly.

Bette tapped her head. 'Up here, where no one can take them away. When we leave here and go home I'll put them on paper for you. And I'll make Lumpy the most beautiful bright blue colour you've ever seen.'

Philip looked at his faded, ragged soft toy which had been stitched up, yet again, and nodded. 'All right. Lumpy got sick. But he's better now.'

Bette ruffled his hair. 'I'm pleased.' But as they walked into their hut to wait for Marjorie and Evelyn, Bette was more worried than ever by Philip's appearance. Not only was he thinner, but he also had a pale yellow tinge to his skin and eyes which meant that he was suffering from jaundice. Somehow she had to get better food for him and quinine. How she dreaded going back to work for the imperious mean Hannah.

It was when she discovered the theft of some of her hoarded rice, that Bette had another idea.

'It's rats, I know it,' she said sadly to Marjorie. 'Little sods got into the container by eating through it. I knew I should have tried to get a tin to store the rice in.'

'They must be hungry too,' said Marjorie.

'Mmmm. I think I might have an idea,' said Bette. 'I'll have to use the last of the rice for a trap.'

'You can't outsmart a rat,' said Evelyn.

But Bette became fixated by the idea of trapping the rodents that scurried around the camp. She scratched a design in the dust and then had Marjorie and Philip hunt for the materials to make it. About a week or so later, she had a box roughly made from wood with wire mesh, some netting, a bit of a bicycle spring, and a kind of tin slide for a trap door. She oiled the slide with grease from the kitchen and set the bait.

'He'll get down and get trapped and the little door thing should close. A simple mouse trap device,' she explained proudly.

The others looked doubtful, but agreed to set the trap and see if anything happened.

Philip could barely sleep for the excitement. 'Will we hear him go into the trap? And then what are we going to do with him?' he asked.

'We'll see,' said Bette. She wasn't about to tell Philip that anything caught in the trap would be eaten. She shut her eyes. God, had it really come to this? Looking forward to eating a rat?

Philip was up early the next morning. He raced to check the trap and came back disappointed.

'Never mind, maybe tomorrow,' said Bette. 'Now off you go with Marjorie. She's going to take you weaving.'

'What's that?' he asked dubiously.

'You'll see. Maybe you can help her,' smiled Bette.

Marjorie and some of the older children were very keen to make surprise presents for their mothers for Christmas. Marjorie had spent hours unravelling old jute and hessian bags, stripping and joining lengths of fabric from worn-out clothes, strips of dried bamboo and any other material that could be wound around a carved shuttle and a loom made from a precious piece of cardboard with notches along each end. Weaving had been a keen hobby for Gloria, the former matron, so she had shown Marjorie how to do string threads then weave over and under them to produce an interestingly textured woven surface. The woven cloth was to be sewn up at one end to form a kind of handbag, with the straps to be made from braided strips. It was a long and laborious task, but one done with enthusiasm.

The next morning Evelyn, who'd woken very early, shook Bette.

'I think there's something in your trap. It's moving and banging about, I don't dare look. There's nobody up there yet. What will I do?'

Bette slid from bed, leaving Philip still sleeping. 'Don't make any noise.' She quickly checked the trap and found it certainly contained something.

'Come on,' she whispered to Evelyn. 'Let's take this to the kitchen and hope that there's no one about.'

The two of them walked calmly to the cook house, and Bette took down one of the kitchen knives.

'Are you going to kill it with that?'

'I'm not going to use my bare hands.'

Gingerly she started to open the trap, but she quickly stepped back in alarm. 'God!'

'What's in there?' asked Evelyn.

'Stand back.' Bette turned the whole contraption upside down. There was a very wild and furious rat in the bottom part of the cage where the trap door had locked it in, and in the space between it and the opening of the trap, lay a coiled snake. 'Wow, a bonus. The snake must've been after the rat.'

'How are you going to get them out?' asked Evelyn nervously. 'They both look pretty wild.'

'They certainly do. Can you see if there are any embers in the fire from last night?'

'Yes, we can get it started again, but you're not going to roast them alive? What about the trap? We'll never be able to make another,' said Evelyn.

'Smoke. Find something green or wet. We'll smoke 'em out.'

Evelyn dunked a pile of the green bamboo that was kept to sweep the floor into some water and then onto the fire. As the smoke billowed out, Bette put the trap and its occupants close to it until the animals were stunned by the acrid smoke. Quickly Bette and Evelyn pulled them from the cage and Bette killed them with the knife and swiftly proceeded to butcher the meat. Evelyn watched, with a hand over her mouth.

'Let's not tell the kids. Have you any ideas on how to cook them?'

Evelyn and Bette smiled to each other as Marjorie and Philip licked their fingers after they sucked on the tiny bones that had been chopped up and roasted and added to their rice. Bette had described the treat as baby chicken. Evelyn cleaned up and collected all the bones that could be used as bait in the trap when it was set once again. Both women realised that this was only a small taste of meat, but it was better than nothing and would help the children survive a bit longer.

No one trusted the soldiers. The women knew that the Japanese did not want to be there, guarding a lot of women, when they would prefer to be fighting for their Emperor. To relieve their resentment, the men seemed to take great delight in tormenting their captives and making life for the women as difficult as possible.

Philip had caught malaria once before, but Bette became alarmed when another attack seemed to be very serious. Clearly his resistance was weakened by his terrible diet and he became very feverish and too weak to get up. There was no point in taking him to the clinic. There wasn't any medicine there and Bette could look after him just as well in the hut. But she had no money for quinine either. Then she thought about the English-speaking guard, Corporal Hashimoto, and she remembered his kindness to her when she had been released from solitary confinement. So, with nothing to lose, she found him in the yard by himself, and bowing very low and humbly, she asked if she might speak to him.

'It's my little boy. He's very sick. Malaria. I need medicine. Quinine. Can you help me?'

Corporal Hashimoto just looked at her and shrugged his shoulders and then walked away. How Bette hated the Japanese. It was bad enough that they should make war on women, but to callously let little children die was beyond comprehension.

'I just don't understand them,' she said to Evelyn. 'You often see the guards looking at pictures of their families, but they don't want to acknowledge that we love our children as well.'

Later that day, as Bette walked back from the cook-house, with a bowl of rice which she knew Philip wouldn't eat, Corporal Hashimoto called to her.

'Hateful man,' she murmured under her breath. 'What does he want now?'

Corporal Hashimoto didn't say anything to Bette as she bowed before him, but he dropped a paper packet on the ground in front of her.

'You pick up. You not leave rubbish in camp. You will be punished,' he shouted at her.

Bette was about to protest that the packet wasn't hers when she suddenly realised what was going on. She picked up the paper and apologised to Corporal Hashimoto for dirtying the camp. Then she fled back to her hut. She opened the packet carefully, and inside lay a few quinine tablets and two boiled lollies.

Within a week, Philip was on the mend but Bette wondered for how much longer they could survive like this.

The camp had become their world. June, their leader, had rosters and committees and support groups and life was organised and running as smoothly as possible, and despite the occasional emotional flare-ups, petty squabbles and complaints, the women took pride in surviving each day. Many of them were proud to be British but Evelyn told Bette that what kept some of them going was the Australian irreverent attitude and sense of humour.

'It's an Aussie thing, I've heard,' agreed Babs. 'You never give up. You've really kept a lot of us going, Bette. Sure, we have Gloria and June, who are great leaders, but it's your spunk that fires us up.'

Bette pointed at Philip. 'It's the little bloke. I love him so much and I just can't ever let him think we're not going home. When someone has such utter belief and faith in you, what else can you do?' she shrugged.

'He's a lucky little boy. I hope your sister knows that,' said Evelyn.

Bette sighed. 'I don't know where she is, I pray she got back to Australia, but I have no idea what's happened to Roland, Philip's father, or the rest of the family. And poor Margaret probably has no idea where her son is. She must be frantic with worry. Those pathetic postcards the Japs made us fill in probably never made it home. But then, I'm not alone in this.'

Marjorie heard their conversation and came and sat next to her mother taking her hand. 'Do you think we'll ever get out of here? Will the war ever end and then what will happen to us? Can we go home then?'

The two women were silent. Evelyn was thinking of her husband. When it was all over, as surely it must end, what would they all be going home to?

'Of course we'll get out of here,' said Bette. 'I have no idea if things will have changed, but if we can adapt to this, we can adapt to anything.'

'If only we could hear some news. Know what was going on outside,' said Evelyn. 'Has anyone heard anything from the men's camp recently?'

'I hope their radio hasn't been found,' said Bette. 'And, you know, I think the Jap soldiers here are just as much in the dark as we are. This place is such a backwater in the big scheme of things. They've probably forgotten about us all.'

'The soldiers have been as much prisoners here as we have, just better conditions,' said Evelyn. 'I wonder if they think it's all been worth it.'

'I wish I knew about my father and how he is,' said Marjorie sadly.

'It's only been a couple of months since your mother had a message from him, so I'm sure that he's still fine. Do you know the best thing you can do to help your father?' asked Bette, taking Marjorie's hand. 'It's to be strong, keep your spirits up, get through this and look forward to the rest of your life. You're growing up. He'll be so proud of you.'

'Bette's right,' said Evelyn smoothing her daughter's hair.

At that moment both women looked at Marjorie and saw, for the first time, that little Marjorie was hovering on the cusp of womanhood. She was now nearly fifteen, tall and pretty despite her thinness. She'd also been forced to grow up more swiftly than she might have done. Her protected and carefree childhood had been swept away. Evelyn and Bette looked at each other, both realising the dangers that Marjorie could face as she matured in the POW camp. Bette knew that one of the Japanese soldiers, who'd arrived a few months before, was predatory and arrogant. He'd spoken to another soldier in front of Bette, leaving her in no doubt that his comments about her had been lewd. Evelyn had the same thought. There'd been wild rumours from the time the Japanese had landed in Borneo of what they would do with women prisoners and there had been talk about brothels.

Evelyn fingered Marjorie's hair, which was twisted on top of her head for coolness. It made her look sophisticated. Evelyn unpinned her daughter's hair. 'Why don't you let me plait your hair? Easier to keep clean and it's out of your way.'

'Good idea,' said Bette knowing that plaits would keep Marjorie looking more like a child. 'Damned lice and bugs have been such a problem.' There was one woman in the camp who had previously been a hairdresser, and she had used her skills to barter for goods. Bette had sometimes traded precious food for a haircut and her long wavy hair had been cropped to a short curly bob, which was easier to keep clean, especially as soap was now a very rare commodity.

Lately Marjorie had been spending more time with the adult women rather than the other children because she found them more interesting. Bette and Evelyn now decided that Marjorie should spend more time back with the children.

293

'Just a precaution,' said Evelyn.

'Why don't we all take turns to sit with the children and show them something we can do or tell them stories about our families, our growing up, that sort of thing? I bet we all have something to learn from each other.'

These sessions between the children and the women became one of the most popular events, for the children as well as the women. They all learned something happy about each other's previous life. Sometimes there was laughter, and occasionally tears, but for the children it was a reminder of a life they'd forgotten and what they had to look forward to one day, when they were free.

Time was measured in meals. The women thought only of food. They talked constantly about it, describing their favourite meals, exchanging recipes and dreaming about what they would eat when they got out of the camp. And now the rations were becoming even more meagre.

'This is disgusting. How're we supposed to live on this?' asked Norma as they faced another watered-down rice soup, helped along with a few dried beans.

'It's not right we have to trade all we have for basic food to keep us alive,' said Babs.

'If we could just grow some of our own food, it would make such a difference,' said Evelyn.

'We've asked and asked if we could use the old rice field beside the main gate to grow some food, but Sakura says that he hasn't got enough soldiers to watch us,' said Bette.

'As if we could run away in the state we're in. I think that man has been completely unreasonable. I'd love to keep a few chickens. I had them at home and they wouldn't be too hard to manage,' said Norma.

Norma's description of the chickens she had kept was interrupted by June, who had some very interesting news.

'I have just left Sakura's office. He's been transferred.

294

Actually given a promotion and he's left to go on active service.'

'I hope he gets killed,' said Babs. 'He was such a mean old git. Look what he did to Bette.'

Bette was thoughtful. 'Maybe we could ask the new commander if we could have a garden. He might be more approachable. When does he get here, June?'

'Don't ask me, but I imagine in a couple of days. And you're right, he might be more reasonable.'

'They don't know the word,' sniffed Norma.

'Well, I think that we should ask,' said Evelyn. 'Any extra food would be so welcome. Nearly everyone is out of money, even Hannah. People are getting sick so easily now, because we're starving.'

They walked over to the fence and peered at the rutted earth that had once been a rice field.

'There doesn't seem to be any water. We'd have to bring in our own or dig a well,' said Babs.

'At least the soil looks all right,' said Norma. 'Where would we get seeds?'

'That'd be worth bargaining for,' said Bette. 'Maybe we could at least get some root vegetables and let them sprout or save the seeds and plant them. Sweet potatoes, tapioca, yams, some greens.'

'Who's going to organise it and work in it?' said Norma looking at Bette.

'Everyone who's well enough,' said Bette.

Some of the women protested because they thought they no longer had the strength for any more physical effort, but Gloria stepped in.

'I agree with Bette. A garden is a fine idea. We can't just sit here and starve to death. Every bit of vegetable is helping to keep us alive because it puts some variety into our very limited diet. I suggest that we ask June to ask the new Japanese commander when he arrives, as if we've just thought of the idea, and not let on that Sakura would never let us have one. Then we can set up a committee to plan a garden.'

There was a long discussion the following morning about turning the field into a garden bed.

'We could do all the work and the Nips could end up taking it all,' was one complaint.

'Well, at least let's ask,' said Bette.

When the new commander, Captain Toyama, arrived, June and Bette asked permission to speak to him. Bette took along the half cup of rice that was now each woman's daily ration, and a miserable meal it looked. She bowed low and humbly and carefully explained that this amount of food was not adequate to live on and outlined their plan to grow some more if they could have permission to tend the disused field beside the main gate.

'You run away, soldiers will shoot.'

'I understand,' said Bette. 'But where are we going to run? There is nowhere to go.'

'You grow only for you. Women work in field every day. You work like coolies.' He looked rather pleased as he imparted this news. Perhaps he thought that if the women were more occupied, they would create fewer problems, or perhaps he thought that white women working in the fields was the correct place for them to be.

Bette and June bowed as they expressed their thanks. Captain Toyama turned his back. They were dismissed.

The women were given heavy mattocks and a few old spades with splintered wood handles and they gradually created more tools from flattened tins and heavy sticks. Once they'd prepared the garden beds, fertilised with waste from their latrines, water supply became the next problem to solve. They dug trenches alongside the beds in order to catch the rain and started digging a small pond in the hope it would also hold water.

Seeds were bartered for, and a bunch of uprooted green vegetables that no one could identify were also handed over and quickly planted. Yams that had sprouted became the first crop to be harvested.

'This garden might be providing a bit of fresh food but its wrecking my back,' sighed Babs.

'Gloria and the nuns have made up some sort of liniment,' said Norma. 'It burns but seems to help.'

'I wonder if Hannah has any of her fancy cream left. I certainly could use it,' sighed Bette. 'At one stage I thought she had brought half her bathroom.'

'She might have face cream, but you're prettier,' said Marjorie and they all laughed.

It was a relief to laugh. And the hard work was worth it. The garden struggled, like the women workers, but eventually it produced small crops of fresh food that helped to halt the outbreaks of deficiency diseases like beri-beri and general malnutrition.

It was Norma who first said something to Bette. 'There's something up with the Japs. What do you suppose is going on?'

'Don't know. There seem to be a lot of meetings. Captain Toyama took off and hasn't come back.'

'They're not paying us a lot of attention,' added Gloria.

'Hashimoto is waiting for the field gang, though. Let's go,' said Bette standing up. 'I'll have to get someone to rub my shoulders this afternoon, I feel terrible again.'

'Aren't you going to work for mean Hannah today?' asked Norma as they picked up their heavy gardening tools.

'She's conserving her assets.' Bette shrugged.

'Poor thing,' said Evelyn unsympathetically. 'Maybe she might have to work like the rest of us soon.'

It was while they were hoeing a new row, cloths wrapped around their calloused hands to protect them, the remains of any hats pulled down low over their faces, strips of cloth across the backs of their necks protecting them from the sun, that Bette thought she heard a whistle, then a shout.

Slowly, stiffly, she straightened up. The other women stopped what they were doing and looked across the road at half-a-dozen men coming their way. 'They're white. It's some of our men,' Bette shouted.

Evelyn limped closer to Bette, shading her eyes. 'What are they saying? How can they be here?'

The few times the women had seen the male prisoners marching past, the men had shouted out and sung to them despite the admonitions from the Japanese guarding them. But this time the men were waving, punching the air and smiling as they called out. And there were no guards with them.

Ignoring Corporal Hashimoto, the women ran to the road at the edge of the garden.

'What's happened?'

'The war's over. The Japs have surrendered.'

'The war is over? Is that what they're saying?' The women all looked at each other trying to absorb this news.

'What's happened?' shouted Bette to the men.

'Surrender. The Nips have surrendered. We heard on our radio that there was a huge bomb and now the Japs have given up. You'll be all right now. We came to tell you the news, but now we're going back to our camp.'

As the men turned and went back the way they had come, the women stood, silent and stunned. One woman started sobbing, dropping her face in her hands.

'Do you think it could be true?' Evelyn asked Bette. 'Could it be . . . ? How?'

She turned and looked at sober-faced Hashimoto.

'He's not going to tell us anything. I guess we'll know soon enough if it's the truth.'

'I can't believe that the Japs are surrendering,' said Norma. 'Too proud. Losing face and all that. It must have been a bloody big bomb.'

'I wish we had some way of finding out what's happening.' Bette picked up her hoe. 'Let's finish this up. Yam tops and rice for supper.'

There was a lot more chatter as they worked and later when they headed back to camp they held their shoulders back, heads held high and hopeful. The sad, weary sag of their bodies was gone.

The news the men had given them spread quickly through the camp and women gathered in groups talking and speculating. Every move by the soldiers was scrutinised. The surrender seemed too good to be true but, until it was confirmed, most women didn't want to raise their hopes. Nevertheless, Gloria told those in the sick bay what the men had told them in an effort to lift their spirits.

To everyone's surprise and growing excitement, the next morning they were called to assembly and it was announced that special parcels were to be handed out, all due to the munificence of the Japanese Emperor. Impassively the soldiers piled packages in front of the women and stood back as they rushed forward as though they were at a clearance sale, tearing the parcels open.

'It's food!'

'Tinned fruit! Oh my God!'

Bette suddenly made the connection. 'It's from the Red Cross. Something has happened.' She grabbed Philip's hand and spun him in a twirl.

'Why are you doing that?' he asked in a worried voice.

'Now I know that the war is over. We'll be going home,' sang out Bette.

Evelyn was studying the contents of one of the parcels. 'You know what? I bet this is old stuff. I think this food has been sitting in that shed for damned years while we starved and died.'

There was a stunned silence. 'Do you think so? The bastards,' said Norma.

'Now, ladies. Let's have some order to this,' shouted June. 'Let's sort through systematically, what we have and take it to the kitchen.'

'Let's have a party,' called out Norma.

After that, it was happy chaos as children ran off with chocolate bars and women sat drinking proper coffee with tinned milk. The soldiers left them to it. After a slap-up meal, a sing-song and a prayer of thanks led by one of the nuns they fell into bed.

Philip went to sleep immediately. Bette stroked his hair.

'I don't think he's gone to sleep with a full tummy for years. You know, wonderful as it will be to go home, it's all going to be a big adjustment,' said Bette, cradling the sleeping boy beside her.

'When do you think that will happen?' said Evelyn. 'My mind can't take that in.'

'Oh, I do hope it's soon,' said Marjorie, her eyes shining 'It's so exciting. What are you going to do first, Mother?'

'Hot bath. Clean clothes. Kiss your father.'

'And you, Bette?'

'I can't wait to get back to Brisbane and see my parents, and Margaret, and my home again. I've so missed them all. But I do wonder what sort of world we'll find after all this heartache. I suspect that it will be awhile before life settles down again. But I am so looking forward to it.'

'We've all changed, haven't we,' said Marjorie.

'You certainly have, you've grown up,' said Bette. 'And we must believe that this terrible time in our lives has given us strengths and knowledge about ourselves that we can use in the future.'

Uncharacteristically, the Japanese soldiers didn't appear first thing the next morning, though the sentries were still at the entrance to the camp. After the uninhibited and rather hysterical previous evening, everyone was drained, tired and still disbelieving that the end could be near. That was until there was a drone from above and everybody stopped what they were doing and looked to the sky.

'Is it one of ours?'

Once the women recognised the Allied plane, they started jumping up and down and waving to it. The plane flew low and a snowstorm of white paper fluttered to the ground, which everybody ran to pick up.

Philip scooped some up and ran to Bette. 'Letters, they're letters. What's it say, what's it say?' He jumped up and down excitedly.

Bette and Evelyn looked at the leaflet. 'It's from the Australian 9th Division. The Japanese have surrendered. It's official!' Bette leaned down and hugged Philip as Marjorie dashed towards them.

Wiping tears from her eyes, Bette read on. 'Due to your location it will be difficult to get aid to you immediately . . .' She smiled at them. 'Not to worry, they're going to help us. We're going to be okay.'

The final days were a blur but eventually the 9th Division arrived to liberate the women. For Bette, to see the cheerful open-faced Australian soldiers, to hear their familiar accents, to suddenly have strong, kind men to look after them, to play with the children, to give them rides in their vehicles and to have enough to eat was all overwhelming.

'It's wonderful how most of the women have managed to save one reasonably good outfit for this day,' said Evelyn.

'Yes,' replied Bette. 'But it hardly disguises the terrible physical state of their bodies. You can see by the look on the faces of the Australian soldiers that they think we look pretty awful. There is such a yawning gulf between their world and the three-and-a-half years we've been here. I wonder how we will manage when we get out.'

Despite Bette's fears, Philip and the other children were beside themselves with joy, and the sense of new-found freedom and opportunity. The reality of home and family, barely recalled, was of little consequence in the excitement of the moment.

Finally the day came when the women went home. Evelyn and Marjorie, arms about each other's waists, walked beside Bette and Philip. The little boy skipped as Bette firmly held his hand and walked to the smiling Australians and Americans waiting to drive them away.

Evelyn saw Bette glance over her shoulder at the emptying compound, the huts and the wire that had enclosed their world for so long. Evelyn gave a quick prayer of thanks that they had all come safely through this ordeal. She did not look back. She squeezed Marjorie's hand and led her away.

10

JULIE HAD TEARS IN her eyes. She took Marjorie's hand.

'What an incredible story. What an experience for a young girl. What happened after you got back home to the UK?'

Marjorie sighed. 'It was as wonderful as I had anticipated, and although Mother was still frail, she recovered surprisingly well. My father refused to go back to Sarawak and got a job managing a printing company. I have to say, though, that the cold weather was hard for all of us, at first. It was also difficult to be parted from so many friends. They all went their different ways naturally, but we left some of them behind, too. One of Mother's closest friends, Babs, died not long before we were freed. Her death was a great shock to us.'

'Oh, she sounded such a jolly person. What happened?' asked Julie.

'I suppose she just wasted away. A lot of people died in camp from malnutrition and various deficiency diseases. When I think back, Mother and I were very lucky to have survived.'

'Philip and Bette? What happened to them?'

'We were so focused on our lives and wanting to put the war behind us that we pressed on. Bette went back to Australia. Mother and she wrote to each other for a while, but being separated by twelve thousand miles and having nothing in common except the POW camp, the letters gradually ceased, but, as you know, Philip came back into our lives. He was at boarding school in England and he wrote a letter to Mother and me, and so my mother insisted that he come and stay with us when he had holidays. So we saw a lot of him during his school years.'

'You must have enjoyed having him around in much easier circumstances,' said Julie.

'Yes. And then years later Philip persuaded me to return to Malaysia, and I've just kept coming. The memories of the war have faded and you can't blame this country for what happened during those years. And Malaysia really is a lovely place.'

'I can see why Shane and Peter are so attached to you,' said Julie.

'Yes, and I'm very fond of them. I'm sorry that I can't tell you much more about your aunt. Looking back now, it's a shame that she dropped out of our lives. But perhaps from what I've been able to tell you, you can get a sense of how strong she was. She was also very creative. She told me that when she was in solitary confinement that time, she drew in her head as a way of staying sane. And of course there was the card she gave me for my birthday.'

'Do you know what happened to the diary that was kept in the camp?'

'I didn't know about the diary at all until after we were liberated, but I found out later that one of the women rewrote it and it was published.'

'My aunt wrote a book about the Iban, but I don't know if she continued her art. She obviously loved to draw,' mused Julie. 'Marjorie, I can't thank you enough for sharing your story. It's certainly given me an insight into my Great Aunt Bette. It's amazing what she did for Philip. You would think that when Bette returned him to his mother, she would have been grateful to have her son back alive. I find it very hard to understand why Margaret ended up hating Bette.'

They sat and chatted a while longer, then Julie hugged Marjorie goodbye, and walked from the villa along the beach, past the coconut palms and freshly raked sand. She continued along the beach to the point, deep in thought. A shout caused her to look up and she saw Aidi jumping from his boat.

'Hi, where are you off to?' she called.

'I'm collecting a couple of guests for the mangrove tour. What're you doing?'

'I've been visiting a friend here, a lovely lady, who knew my aunt when they were in a prison camp together near Kuching.'

'They were hard times. What are you doing now?'

'Just walking.'

'Be careful of broken glass and rubbish,' said Aidi, pointing to where the clean sweep of beach in front of the resort was bordered by piles of rubbish on both sides. 'This junk swills back and forth on the tide between us and Thailand over there. It's toxic.'

Julie could see that the naturalist was affronted by the garbage washed from the sea and now lying on the beach beyond the hotel grounds. 'I've noticed that away from the tourist places, the locals don't seem to care about pollution and rubbish.'

Aidi sighed. 'Yes, it's a big job to educate people not to treat the beaches and the sea as a sewer and a dumping place.'

'I've been told the east coast has wonderful beaches but the pollution is getting out of hand over there, too,' said Julie.

'That's true. The east coast of Malaysia is different from this side of the peninsula. It is the poorest and most culturally conservative part of Malaysia. In some places the supermarket queues are separated for men and women and the people all dress very modestly,' said Aidi. 'But on the island resorts, all regulations about dress codes and alcohol seem to get ignored. But pollution is a problem everywhere in Malaysia.' He glanced at his watch. 'I'd better not be late. Catch you before you leave. Say hi to everyone,' he added.

'Will do. Lovely to see you.' Julie went back through the hotel gardens to reception where she caught a taxi back to her resort.

Christopher was waiting for her.

'So, how did it go?' he took her hand. 'You look a little dazed.'

Julie laughed. 'Well, I could do with a long cold drink.'

'How about a swim and a cold beer?'

'Actually, I'd love one of those green coconuts if you can open one.'

'That's easy, lop off the top and stick a straw in the coconut water.'

'Coconut water?'

'You might call it coconut milk, but it's called coconut water here.'

'I'd love one of those, whatever it's called.'

Bobbing in the pool, she told Christopher about Marjorie's experience in the camp as a prisoner during the war.

'It's amazing that she knew your aunt, but it's not so surprising that they lost touch. You'd want to put all those awful experiences behind you. So where to now?' he asked. 'What are your plans? When are you going back to Brissie?'

'I have another few days. Work seems a forgotten country. I feel I've been away for months when I'll have been gone barely two weeks.'

'I know the feeling,' said Christopher. 'Holidays take a bit of adjustment. Sometimes I miss the routine of my job. Don't know what to do with a lot of free time, I get bored.'

'Really? Are you bored here?'

He laughed. 'Absolutely not! These few days have been a lot of fun. And I'm enjoying sharing it with someone from home.'

'It's been nice for me, too,' said Julie thinking to herself how comfortable they were with each other, how unlike it was travelling with David Cooper. As Christopher began playing with one of the cats that had come to the edge of the swimming pool, she decided he was just one of those unpretentious people who made you feel at ease. 'I'm heading back to Utopia for a couple of days and then I'll do a bit more sightseeing before I go home,' she said finally.

'I have to go back to Butterworth. But you should see Penang. It's a great place. Just about my favourite place in the whole country. If you get there, I'd like to buy you dinner.'

'That'd be lovely. Will you be flying around in your jet, or whatever it is?'

'Not at all. Mostly what I do involves a lot of paperwork and discussions with the Malaysian Air Force.'

'Is that the sort of thing that you want to do for the rest of your career?' asked Julie.

'I'm happy in the Air Force, it's a great life and the work can be very interesting and varied, but I might think about being a commercial pilot eventually. It seems the logical career path, though I have a few ideas of other things I might do one day.' He stepped out of the pool. Julie studied his lean, tanned body and he caught her looking at him. She smiled. He smiled back as they both acknowledged the moment. 'Would you like some satay? I can smell them cooking from here.'

They all flew from Langkawi to Penang airport and there were rushed farewells as everyone found their luggage. Ramdin, the Utopia driver, swept them away in minutes in the Jaguar. Once they were in the car, Peter and Shane began to talk business. Martine offered Julie some magazines to look at, but she shook her head, preferring to gaze at the passing scenery.

As the car purred along the highway, Julie looked at the endless hills covered with palm oil plantations. The immaculate, serried ranks of plump fronds marched in straight lines as far as she could see. It all looked so silent, so ordered, so militaristic. She longed for the tangle of jungle, the disorder of human habitation, the sight and sounds of birds and wild animals. Every few miles a neat billboard announced the name of the company that owned that particular plantation.

'Shane, Peter, would you mind if I asked you how you feel about the spread of the palm oil plantations?' she asked. 'I know you must think palm oil is important, because you now grow so much of it, but palm oil is a contentious issue.'

Peter turned and smiled at her. 'Ah, this is a discussion that can fill in a few hours.'

Shane drew a long breath and said, 'It's true, palm

308

oil is a part of the Malaysian economy and yes, there are problems because the jungle is being cut down to create these oil plantations, but at Utopia we are trying to be as ethical as possible. My father made the decision to plant palm oil after Grandfather Roland died. Grandfather was such a rubber man and although he had experimented with palm oil before the war, he couldn't bring himself to change the whole plantation over to it. But Dad decided that the time was right to make the move, but he wanted to do it the right way.'

'It takes a lot of investment, organisation and long-term commitment to create a properly run plantation,' added Peter. 'We try to show that we're not just after profits but want to give local people opportunities for a better standard of living. Governments also say that they want these things for their people, but it's really difficult to find the best balance between the economy and development, and the ecology and forest conservation.'

'It's such a complex issue, it's impossible to give easy answers,' added Shane.

'But what about these campaigns telling us not to touch any products with palm oil in them?' asked Julie.

'We belong to an international organisation – the Roundtable on Sustainable Palm Oil. This is moving forward to promote best practices as well as labelling products so that consumers can choose to buy products from sustainable sources,' said Peter.

'Frankly, if we don't persevere with sustainable production, then others would say that they don't care about all these high standards and restrictions, either. So they'd just clear the jungle for plantations, with no ongoing support for the community or interest in long-term viability,' said Shane.

'Lately, there has been some acknowledgment that continuing to clear for palm oil production can't go on,' said Peter. 'Governments are beginning to compensate farmers for not clearing land and giving them funds to start other projects. And, of course, this new policy allows for carbon trading, which is great, so long as corrupt politicians and other interests don't derail it.'

'It is complicated,' said Julie. She didn't doubt the sincerity of her cousins, but she could see both sides of the argument, especially after what she had learned from the Iban.

'Julie, you've had the visitor's tour of the plantation, perhaps we need to show you how the business side really works,' said Shane.

Martine lifted her head. 'Don't lecture her, Shane. Let Julie enjoy her last day or so.'

'No, I am really interested,' protested Julie. 'Our great grandfather established the plantation, so I'd better find out how it works.'

'Enough of this serious talk,' said Martine, putting down her magazine. 'Tell me, Julie, what did you learn about your great aunt from Marjorie?'

Julie told Martine briefly about Bette and her efforts to keep Philip alive in the POW camp. 'I wish I knew more about Bette,' Julie said. 'I really know very little. My mother says she remembers her aunt from when she was a little girl, but then Bette just dropped out of her life.'

'Why was that? After all she went through with that little boy, I would have thought that Bette would have been close to Philip forever. It all seems very ungrateful,' said Martine.

'My mother says that she was ostracised from the family because she married a Chinese man,' said Julie.

'Oh, I can't believe that!' exclaimed the worldly Martine. 'Shane, you told me that your grandfather had many good Malay, Chinese and Indian friends. He doesn't sound like a racist, or a person easily shocked by such a marriage.'

'My grandmother painted Bette's husband as the devil in the piece,' said Julie. 'According to my mother, Gran never got over the shame of her sister marrying a "Chinaman".'

'But the Tsangs were very influential people. According to Grandfather, they were a very impressive, warm and fun-loving family,' said Peter. 'I think he knew Tony Tsang well. They were at university together.'

Julie stared at Peter.

'What is up, Julie?' asked Martine.

Julie suddenly leaned forward. 'Tsang. Tony Tsang. Is that who Bette married?' she asked breathlessly. 'I never knew her married name.'

'Good Lord! You were kept in the dark. I'm sorry that we didn't tell you earlier, but we didn't know what you didn't know, if you get what I mean. Mind you, we have been on the go the whole time you've been here, so we haven't really had time to talk as much as we should about the family. The Tsang's house is one of the great old Peranakan homes in Penang,' said Shane.

'You could have a look at it when you go there,' added Peter.

'I had no idea about any of this. Mum did mention Tony Tsang to me when she told me about Gran's time in Malaya before the war, but neither of us had any idea about the connection. Did you boys ever meet the Tsangs?' asked Julie.

'No, we didn't,' replied Peter.

'The Tsang house is now a boutique hotel, well, part of it is, I think,' said Shane. 'Have you ever been there, Pete?'

He shook his head. 'No, it's a pretty pricey place to stay, I believe.'

Martine looked at Julie and smiled. 'Your visit to Penang is going to be interesting.'

Julie leaned back, shaking her head. 'I had no idea.'

'Perhaps you should ask Christopher to come with you,' suggested Martine. 'You're going to see him, yes? It will be quite interesting for you to see the old mansion.'

'Christopher did suggest dinner when I went to Penang, but now I have so much more to check out. Do you know the address of Bette's old home, Shane?'

'Oh, everyone knows it. It's known as Rose Mansion. Big old pink stucco place with gold trim. It used to be virtually on the water but the land was reclaimed along the seafront so there's a promenade in front of it now,' said Shane.

'At least the old home hasn't been torn down, but restored and made into a hotel,' said Peter.

'I know Gran told my mother that he was very rich. Is that right?' asked Julie.

Peter chuckled. 'I'd say so. He kept racehorses. That was the heyday of high society before the war. Even afterwards, the Chinese and the Peranakan did very well, until the anti-Chinese riots in the 1960s. Things changed after that.'

'The history of the mansion is probably well documented,' said Shane. 'In the last ten years there's been a resurgence of interest in the old days. I think some of the Tsang descendants helped with its preservation.'

'It's interesting for tourists,' said Martine.

'I guess that's what I'll be, a tourist,' said Julie quietly. 'I wish I knew more.'

Martine touched her arm. 'This is a quest. All the time you are discovering things. It will all unfold,' she said to Julie.

Julie stared at her. 'Yes. I suppose so. But I'm impatient to know as much as I can. My holiday is almost over. I have to go back home, go back to work . . . deal with my family's fight to save our home . . .' All these things seemed a world away. Here, in Malaysia, Julie felt

312

herself touching a part of her family's past that had been unknown to her. 'I wonder when I see this mansion, if it might help me understand why there was such a rift between Margaret and Bette.'

'Perhaps you may,' said Martine gently.

'Anyway, even if I don't find any answers in Penang, it will be nice to see where Great Aunt Bette lived,' said Julie, and sank back in the soft leather seat of the Jaguar.

She must have dozed off, for when she opened her eyes they were driving past the long plantation rows of Utopia in bright sunlight. A mini steam train was chugging along pulling iron buckets, each holding two tonnes of just harvested palm oil fruit. The spiky clusters of the red fruit were piled high.

'There they go, straight from the field, no trucks, less handling, those metal cages go right into the ovens, so there's less bruising,' said Shane proudly.

'Makes for better quality oil if it's direct from the field,' said Peter. 'Nothing is wasted, the by-products and effluent from the mills are collected and made into bio gas, which is then used to heat the water, which becomes the steam, which runs the refinery. Everywhere we can, we try to reduce our dependence on petrochemicals.'

'Let's get some curry puffs at the bakery,' said Martine, who had heard all this before, many times.

They got out of the car, glad to stretch their legs. As Shane and Peter walked into the bakery they were immediately greeted by a middle-aged woman and a younger woman behind the counter. While their order was being assembled the manager, a middle-aged man of Indian descent, proudly showed his bosses the food preparation area. It was spotless. Julie felt that she could have eaten from the floor. Every piece of equipment was gleaming, bench tops sterile, and the staff wore plastic gloves, hair nets and cotton coverings over their shoes.

'You can come in here any time and it is always immaculate,' Martine whispered to Julia. 'It's the same in the factories, too.'

The older woman had a big smile for Shane and Peter, and handed them both a warm curry puff. They introduced Julie to her as their cousin from Australia. She took both of Julie's hands, in what was clearly a very warm welcome.

As they walked outside Shane told Julie, 'Mrs Seeto's family has been here since our grandfather's time. Her mother suffered terribly under the Japanese, and we've always looked after her. Now her family works here too. She still likes to help out in the bakery. That's her grand-daughter behind the counter.'

Once again the mention of the war years brought back Marjorie's story to Julie. She remarked, 'Bette lived in Penang, and now Marjorie does. I suppose their time there didn't overlap, but it's very curious.'

Martine tucked her arm through Julie's. 'When you get to Penang you will see the old and the new, and understand its appeal. Now you have family connections in lots of parts of Malaysia!'

Julie had one more day at Utopia. She wanted to take photos for her mother who had lived here as a very young child, but now had so few memories of it. Peter drove her around the plantation, stopping by one of the long avenues of palms where the dried fronds were neatly cut and stacked, the harvested bunches of fruit on the ground in a neat circle at the base of each palm tree. Peter walked into the row and stopped at one of the trees pointing at the loose red fruit and seeds scattered at the base of the tree.

'When the fruit starts dropping around the tree, we know that it's time to pick the bunches. Every division has to be checked every day. There's not a season for oil palms, they produce year round.'

'Just as well with six thousand people working here. You can't have them waiting for the crop,' said Julie.

'There's always work. Shane and I come out every day, we walk around, meet the managers and assistants, and that's how we get to know our people. Our father always said the best fertiliser is the boss's footprints!'

'So how many trees are on Utopia?'

'Around five million. And each is numbered in its division, so if one develops a problem, or the R and D people pick something up, we can check the exact palm straight away.'

'What's this box?' asked Julie. 'It looks like a letterbox.'

Peter laughed. 'It's actually a pheromone trap. Our biggest pest on the plantation is the rhinoceros beetle. Here, see, an ugly brute.' He picked a beetle off the ground. It was the length of his palm and had vicious pincers. 'This box gives off the smell of a female beetle, and so the males are attracted to it. When the box is full we know there are too many beetles around this particular area and we spray. If they're not constantly controlled these beetles can kill a full-grown palm pretty quickly.'

As they got back into the car, Julie pointed to some young palms in a field covered in a carpet of green growth. 'And over there?'

'Those palms are three years old, but we don't let them bear fruit right away because we want them to grow strong first. There's no rush for crops because a strong palm will yield for up to fifty years. We plant this ground-cover around the trees to hold in moisture and to stop erosion. And the flowers look pretty.'

From the bottling plant where the rich red oil was being bottled and labelled in spotless conditions, they went into the nursery where thousands of various types of palm seeds were being hybridised. In the hothouse, Julie looked at the racks of thousands of sprouting seeds and couldn't help but be impressed by the innovative breeding program, which would produce dwarf varieties of oil and coconut palms for easier harvesting, while still ensuring that they bore quality fruit.

'The operation is so huge, it's hard to take it all in. I'd imagined a plantation being just rows of trees and that was all,' said Julie.

'That was pretty much the way it was in our great grandfather Eugene's day. I think he would be surprised to see how we've grown, too,' said Peter.

Julie felt torn as they headed back to the big house for lunch. She could see why Utopia was regarded as one of the top plantations in South East Asia, not just because of its quality produce but also because of Peter and Shane's dedication to ecological sustainability. The plantation had excellent relationships with the local people but she wished all this development didn't come at such a cost to the landscape and the wildlife. But, on the whole, Julie thought, Shane was probably right. It was better to have sustainable development than the total rape of an area with no rehabilitation at all.

Luncheon was a formal meal, laid out in the dining room in the big house, with silverware and a lace tablecloth and crystal glasses. Martine's touch was evident in the flower arrangement. The cook had prepared a superb meal – spring rolls, a light but very spicy Malay curry and fresh fruit from the plantation's garden to finish.

Shane rose and lifted his glass. 'I'd like to propose a toast to our cousin, who has been our honoured guest for too brief a time. Thank you for coming, and for reuniting our families. Julie, I hope you will come again soon, and bring your mother back to the land of her birth. Perhaps next time you come, our children will be here from school, so you can meet them as well. I hope the search for the story of Great Aunt Bette continues successfully in Penang and have a safe trip back to Australia. Bon voyage, Julie.'

Julie responded as best she could, caught unawares by the emotions she was feeling, but sincerely thanking the Elliotts for their hospitality and good company and assuring them that she would only be too delighted to return one day.

The car and driver swept up to the guest bungalow that afternoon. She hugged Siti the housekeeper goodbye, and thanked her for making her stay so comfortable and asked the driver to take a photo of them both standing in front of the bungalow before sliding into the car. The gardener straightened up and gave her a salute and a big grin, and two girls who worked in the big house waved her goodbye as the car turned into the lane.

By early evening Julie was in Penang, ensconced in her hotel. To her surprise and delight there was a message from Christopher.

'Call me when you arrive, and could you join me for dinner?'

He took her to an area known as little India, a colourful, noisy, vibrant collection of narrow streets filled with wonderful smelling eateries, temples, gold stores and bazaar-like shops selling everything from brilliant saris that hung around the doors like folded butterfly wings, to spice, brass ornaments and antique erotic statues. Braziers and tandooris sizzled in the smoky night air, outdoor eateries and long neon-lit and air-conditioned restaurants were crowded with families enjoying the many types of

Indian dishes available, from spicy vegetarian and delicate Goanese curries to fiery rendangs and roasted chillis.

In the corner of a small restaurant the two of them sat at a laminated table covered with plastic plates and tin utensils, drinking cold beer from chipped glasses. Next to them was a family eating with their fingers from food spread out on banana leaves in front of them.

'This is one of the best meals I've ever eaten,' said Julie.

'Despite the humble surroundings this place is quite famous,' said Christopher. 'And quite the cultural experience.'

They had been talking about all manner of things and it was only as they sipped their glasses of strong black coffee sweetened with condensed milk that Julie told him about discovering that Bette had married Tony Tsang and had lived in the Rose Mansion in Penang.

Christopher raised an eyebrow. 'Wow, Rose Mansion is a landmark in Penang, though I have to say I've never been there. The more you discover about your great aunt, the more interesting she seems. So after Penang, you'll go home, and back to work and that's the end of it?'

Julie paused. 'I suppose so.' She toyed with her glass. 'I just hate to let Malaysia go, though. Being here has brought me closer to another part of my family. It's not like just being a tourist and coming here for a holiday. I have a sense of connection with this country now.'

'You can come back any time. Shane and Peter told you that. So you're lucky in that respect, you could come for holidays every year! And there's a lot more to see of Malaysia. The beaches half an hour from here are popular, although, to tell the truth, they're not nearly as good as the ones on the Gold or Sunshine coasts and there are a lot of resorts.' He caught her expression and smiled. 'And you haven't been to the mountains or many of the islands. There are so many places I keep thinking I must go and see, too.'

'I know, I've just been so bound up in my own personal journey. Even my parents and brother don't know everything I've discovered, and I think they'll be pretty excited when I tell them.'

'You'll certainly have a lot to talk about when you get home. Now, would you like to take a bit of a walk? It's all quite colourful around here. Then we can grab a taxi and I'll drop you off.'

'This has been fun, thanks, Chris. Where are you staying?'

'I'm bunking down at a mate's flat. His parents have a place here. They never mind when I use it.' He linked his arm through hers as they pushed their way through the jostling crowd. 'I have tomorrow free. Could I come with you to Rose Mansion, or do you want to plough through the nostalgia there on your own?'

'I'd love you to come with me tomorrow! And it's not at all nostalgic as I've only just heard of the place, so we can nose around it together.'

Julie stood speechless as the taxi pulled away leaving her and Christopher staring at the enormous old mansion. The street was wide, and lined with similarly grand old buildings that appeared to be either consulates or wealthy private homes, although one house on the corner was a private club. Beside the ornate double doors of number 211 was a discreet sign in gold lettering indicating that this was the 'Hotel Tsang'. The building faced the sea and behind the tall fence with its security gate, a short driveway curved through formal gardens. Julie instantly noticed the topiaried shrubs, every tree and plant pruned and clipped to such perfection that they almost looked plastic. The soft peach pink stucco three-storey mansion had gold filigree trim around all the windows. The red tiled roofline supported colourful figurines, flowers and birds at the corners and on the eaves. To Julie the size of the windows suggested that the rooms would be huge.

'It's pretty formal,' said Christopher. 'I feel as though we're at some palace. It looks like it would be an expensive hotel, too.'

'It's stunning. I can't believe it was once a family home, let alone my family!' said Julie. 'It's been brilliantly maintained. I wonder what the view is like. This splendour isn't quite what I'd imagined. Do you think they'll let us in?'

'Let's say we want to make a reservation,' said Christopher, leading her to the sentry box that stood at the entrance to the driveway.

An elderly Indian security guard looked at them enquiringly. 'You wish to speak to a guest?' he asked, lifting up the phone in the security box.

'We'd like to make a reservation,' said Christopher.

The security guard pushed a number and handed him the phone.

Christopher spoke smoothly, explaining that they were interested in making reservations for a group to stay and they also wanted to organise a small reception. 'Yes, a wedding,' he said, winking at Julie. He handed the phone back to the Indian who raised the boom gate and waved them through.

They walked along the driveway admiring the gardens. Two pretty rose and blue antique rickshaws with elaborate designs painted on their sides and canvas awnings stood to one side of two rampant stone lions that were guarding the front steps.

Christopher took Julie's hand and led her up the steps. One of the huge carved doors stood open, its entrance flanked by two shiny brass pots, each holding laden cumquat trees.

They both paused, blinking in the cool darkness after the bright sunlight. In front of them was a large foyer, filled with stands of bamboo in blue and white ceramic pots. A large, ornate gold-framed mirror on one of the walls reflected the heavy, dark, carved furniture, while delicate wooden screens divided the rest of the room. The floor was covered in large old black and white tiles and edged in a gold geometric pattern. Above them, a ceiling fan turned gently.

A youthful Chinese man came to meet them, impeccably dressed in dark pants and a neat white shirt. Christopher introduced Julie and himself.

'I'm Ti Yung. You're the wedding couple?' the young man asked in a faint American accent.

'That's right. We're interested in a small, elegant reception as well as booking some rooms for the wedding guests and bridal party,' said Christopher shaking Ti's hand.

'Is it possible to look at the rooms, to see if they are suitable?' asked Julie, glancing around. 'This doesn't appear to be the usual kind of hotel.'

'You are right. It's not your usual hotel, not even your usual boutique hotel. But I'm sorry, all our rooms are fully booked at present. I can show you the function room. Could you give me some details first, please? This way.' He gestured towards two wing-back chairs, both covered in brocade, which faced a large table in the corner. It clearly served as a desk. Ti waited for them to be seated before taking his place opposite them.

He slid a silver pen and a printed sheet towards Christopher. 'If you'd like to fill in the details. What date did you have in mind?'

Christopher completed several lines of the form and handed it to Julie, who took it absentmindedly. She was distracted by a series of framed formal photographs of elderly Chinese men and women, which hung from the picture rail on thin gold chains.

'Who are those people?' she asked.

Ti didn't look up from his diary. 'They are members of the original Tsang family. For several generations this used to be their private residence, but the upkeep became too expensive. The place was left empty for some years until our parent company made an offer for it and then renovated it and set it up as a hotel.'

'When was that?' asked Christopher.

'We opened two years ago but the restoration took a few years. Many people, including the government itself, realised that the heritage buildings here in Penang, as in Malacca and other Malaysian places, can be valuable tourism assets.'

'That's so interesting,' said Julie. 'Is there a family history of this place?'

Ti took the form from Julie. 'We run tours of the house two mornings a week, but only the public areas so the guests are not disturbed. You might like to come along one morning. There's one tour tomorrow at ten am. It will give you a better idea of how things were in the old days. Now, you haven't put the date for your wedding on the form.'

Christopher looked at Julie.

'Seventh of September,' she said firmly.

'A propitious date, I have no doubt. Very well. If you would like to follow me, we'll go to the function room. There's a side entrance through to the garden so you won't have to come through the front of the hotel.' Ti waved a hand into the shadows behind the screens. 'There's a tea-room through there, as well as a small bar. We've tried to keep some of the rooms as they were originally, but updated their function. Downstairs, for example, part of the old indoor kitchen has been turned into a suite, and it still includes the old brick stove.'

'It all sounds different, even unique,' said Julie, looking

at Christopher as they walked past a dark-blue iron spiral staircase. The interior of the house was cool but Julie found its dimness unsettling. She couldn't imagine a happy, sun-loving Australian woman feeling comfortable in this. But then they walked around a corner and entered an open-air courtyard. Here, the sun poured down. A fountain splashed in the centre of it and raised cement tubs held ornamental flowers and plants. Stone benches sat against the old stone walls.

'How lovely!' exclaimed Julie. At the rear of the courtyard was an archway and beyond it stretched a corridor of doorways. Some of the private suites, Julie assumed. Ti then turned to the right and went through another archway. They saw a sweeping polished wood staircase leading to the next floor.

'The honeymoon suite is up those stairs. The function area is this way. Please follow me.'

Obediently they followed Ti.

Everywhere they looked Julie wanted to stop and spend time examining the artifacts, the antiques and especially the photographs. She thought that although the furniture was dark wood, oriental and large, it was interesting and suited the huge rooms. Richly coloured antique rugs with elaborate patterns were scattered on the decorated marble and polished wooden floors. Light through the tall windows filled the rooms.

Ti pushed opened two tall carved wooden doors. 'Here is the function room.'

'Wow,' said Christopher.

'It's called the Rose Room,' said Ti.

'I see why,' said Julie. 'It's lovely.'

The room was gracious, with floor-length windows swathed in ruched cream silk. The windows looked out onto a private courtyard garden. Ten round tables, each set for ten places, were covered in heavy cream damask tablecloths with pink linen napkins folded into the shape of swans atop each setting. Bouquets of roses and small white and pink peonies were arranged in the centre of each table, surrounded by candles and crystal goblets. The gold chairs were covered in deep rose brocade, and the cream carpet was patterned with delicate woven pink-hued roses trailing pale green leaves.

To one side there was a small dance floor and beside it a podium. The large marble fireplace had a massive gilt-framed mirror above it, reflecting the private garden. Paintings and antique embroidered Chinese silk tapestries were hung around the room.

'This room has been set for a function to be held this evening, but we can adjust to your special requirements. The garden area is very nice for photographs.'

Ti led them through the French doors to a small covered terrace and a walled garden. A brightly coloured bougainvillea arbour and a lion's head fountain were set against the cobblestone wall. Colourful crotons in tall urns framed the backdrop.

'As well as weddings, a lot of private corporations like to hold lunches and dinners here,' said Ti. 'Do you think this room will suit your needs?'

Christopher held Julie's hand. 'It's very tasteful. We both like it very much. It's a pity we can't see any accommodation.' He glanced fondly at Julie who was trying not to giggle. 'My fiancée has a special reason for wanting to stay here, don't you, darling?'

Julie stared at him, then quickly took up the cue. 'Oh, indeed. You see, I'm related to this house, to the Tsangs, that is . . . my aunt . . .'

Ti gave her a surprised look. 'Really? What was your aunt's name?'

'Bette Oldham, she was Australian and she married Tony Tsang.'

'So she would have been a second or third wife?'

'I don't know . . .' Julie stumbled to a halt, aware of the great gaps in her knowledge of the marriage.

'Julie has just found out about her aunt's connection with this house,' said Christopher, putting his arm around her. 'She's come from Australia to try to find out more . . .'

'And you just decided to get married while you're here?' asked Ti.

'I'm working at Butterworth at present,' said Christopher. 'Malaysia is a great place for a honeymoon.'

Ti nodded. 'I understand. Come inside, there's someone you might like to meet.'

Julie glanced at Christopher, who shrugged as they followed Ti inside. They crossed a landing and were ushered into a small sitting room.

'Just a moment, please.' Ti left them.

'Look at that,' exclaimed Christopher going to a large glass-fronted display cabinet that was filled with a collection of beautiful glass pieces. 'Art Deco. Art Nouveau. It's all Lalique. There's squillions of dollars worth of object d'art in there.'

Julie joined him, gazing at the carefully lit figurines, vases, bowls and perfume bottles. 'They're exquisite. How did you know what they are? Do you collect glass?'

'I wish. No, it's a period that interests me. I first saw pieces like this in a museum in France.'

Julie was slightly surprised, indeed, quite impressed by Christopher's interests. She turned back to the collection.

'There are some lovely pieces of Lalique, aren't there?' said a soft voice behind them. They turned to see a Eurasian woman, perhaps about Shane's age, smiling at them. She came forward and Julie noticed her beautifully tailored pants and her exquisite draped silk top. Her dark hair was pinned up in a smooth ponytail.

'I am Carla Wong. Congratulations on your engagement. Ti tells me you have a relative connected to Rose Mansion.' She shook both their hands.

Christopher gave her a broad smile as he took her hand. 'It's Julie who has the relative. Bit of a long story, isn't that right, Julie?'

'Please sit down.' Carla gestured to the sofa and took one of the carved chairs next to it. 'I'm the manager here, so I would love to hear it.'

'Sorry to take your time without an appointment,' began Julie. 'I would love to know if there is anything written about Rose Mansion.'

'A lot. Architect plans, the names of original fabrics and wallpapers . . .'

'No, I didn't mean that so much, actually, I meant about the family. The people who lived here.'

'Oh yes, there's a lovely book on the history of the house and the collections here.'

'You mean, other than the Lalique?' asked Christopher.

Carla smiled. 'Yes, there's a lot of memorabilia scattered about the mansion, although I have to say that it is well protected.'

'What we have seen is lovely, but what I'm really interested in is my great aunt. I was told that she married Tony Tsang and lived here after the war. She was an Australian,' she added.

Carla studied Julie for a moment, then smiled. 'I know she's Australian. Actually, you remind me a little of her. Your smile and your hair colouring. May I ask why you want to know about her?'

'I never knew a thing about my Aunt Bette's life story till very recently,' said Julie. 'I'm afraid she was one of those family secrets that's never been explained. My grandmother, her sister, refused to speak about her, so that my mother and I have known nothing about her until recently.'

'Is your grandmother still alive?' asked Carla.

Julie shook her head. 'No. But now I've found out that Great Aunt Bette lived in Malaya, was a prisoner during the war, married Tony Tsang and wrote a book about the Iban. And that's all I know. She sounds like a remarkable person and I want to find out as much as I can about her.'

Carla was quiet for a moment. 'May I ask why now? Why has no one in your family tried to find answers before this?'

Christopher spoke gently. 'It's not so unusual that members of a family lose touch. Julie took two weeks holiday and jumped on a plane to meet her cousins who live on a plantation near Slim River. Now she is trying to find out more about her mother's aunt, who apparently also lived in Malaysia for years.'

Carla nodded. 'Some families are tied together more closely by choice or circumstance. Others drift apart. I understand that you must be wanting to explore your family more, especially as you're about to be married.'

Julie gave Christopher a concerned look and he spoke up quickly. 'We're not engaged. Julie is a friend. She wanted to come here and see this house, hoping to find out something about her great aunt, so I concocted this story to get us admitted. I hope you can understand our little deception. It was my idea,' he added quickly.

Carla's mouth twitched, and she smiled. 'I see.'

'I'm sorry if we've wasted your time,' began Julie, but Carla held up her hand.

'I agreed to see you not because you said that you wanted to have a wedding reception here but because of your aunt. We have a lot of information here. Rose Mansion is still very much a family home. I live in the private apartments here.'

'So there is some information about her here?' asked

Julie. 'Did she did live here after she married Tony Tsang? Are there any photographs of her I could see?'

Carla nodded. 'Yes, there are. I know about your aunt and Tony Tsang.' She leaned forward and took Julie's hand. 'Tony Tsang was my grandfather. So I guess that makes us cousins through marriage.'

Christopher burst out laughing at the shocked expression on Julie's face. 'Geez, Julie, you've got more cousins than you can poke a stick at!'

'I can't believe it. Your grandfather was Tony Tsang? This place, the life . . . It must have been so different for Great Aunt Bette,' said Julie. This mansion seemed a long way from the house in Brisbane where Bette had grown up.

'You will have a lot of questions,' said Carla. 'This is quite something. I often wondered if anyone from Australia would be curious about us. I'd love to sit down and go through all the family things with you, Julie, but I do have an appointment that I must keep.'

'I'm so sorry to just barge in like this,' began Julie. 'Unfortunately I'm booked to go back to Australia tomorrow. Perhaps we could correspond.' She didn't want to miss this chance to learn more.

Carla leaned forward. 'Julie, I don't think you understand. All these questions you have about Por Por, you should ask her yourself,' she said gently.

'Who's Por Por?' asked Julie, confused.

'That is our name for Bette. It means grandmother and that's how we like to think about her, although she is really our step grandmother.'

Christopher leaned forward. 'Carla, are you saying that Bette, Julie's great aunt, is still alive?'

Carla nodded. 'Yes. Of course, she's no longer young but she is still very bright, alert and still drawing. We will soon celebrate her ninetieth birthday.'

'Oh my God. Where is she?' Julie looked around, as

though expecting to see Bette walk into the room. Christopher held Julie's hand as she was shaking with excitement. 'Is she here in Penang?'

Carla shook her head. 'Oh, no. As she got older she got homesick for Australia, so she went back.'

'She's in Australia?' asked Julie incredulously.

'Yes. She lives in Cairns. All our family like to visit her there often.'

'Cairns! Why Cairns?' asked Julie, amazed by this news.

'She said she liked the climate. After all her years in Malaysia, she said that she couldn't live any further south than Cairns. It would be too cold for her anywhere else, even Brisbane. She still lives independently, in an apartment. It's very nice.'

'Is she still painting?' asked Julie, her voice almost a whisper.

'Yes. She likes to paint Australian flora, especially the orchids that grow in North Queensland. I'll write down her details for you.' She rose and left the room.

Julie turned to Christopher. 'Pinch me. I don't believe this. Wait till I tell Mum. She'll be over the moon.'

He gave her a quick hug. 'I'm really happy for you. I suppose you're going straight up to Cairns when you get back?'

Julie shook her head. 'I'll have to talk to Mum. I just hope that it's not too late and Bette will see us.'

'Nonsense, I'm sure she'll be thrilled to meet you and your mother,' said Christopher.

Julie nodded. 'Maybe we'll phone her. Or send her a letter.'

Carla returned with a piece of paper and handed it to Julie who glanced at the address.

'Yes, I suppose we should write first, let her get used to the idea. I hope she'll agree to see us.'

'Por Por is a very lovely lady,' said Carla. 'You'll like

her. Perhaps you could come back and see us another time. Stay here, of course. I've written my phone and email on the paper as well.'

'How about I take a photo of the two of you?' said Christopher.

Julie handed him her camera and he took a shot of the two women with their arms around each other.

'Well, we don't want to hold you up any longer,' said Christopher. 'It's been very interesting.'

'So the wedding's off?' asked Carla with a smile.

''Fraid so. I'm going back to Australia. Christopher is here, working at Butterworth,' said Julie.

Carla shook Christopher's hand. 'Do call me and come for tea sometime. I'll give you a proper tour of the treasures of Rose Mansion. They seem to interest you.'

'Thank you. I'd like that.'

'So would I,' said Julie. 'And I'll bring my mother, next time. If that's all right.'

Carla gave her a brief embrace. 'Please do. We'll keep in touch.'

Christopher glanced at his watch as the elderly Indian opened the boom gate for them. 'Only an hour in there. It felt as though we were in there for ages.'

'I know. It seems like a dream. I can't believe that Bette is still around. I'll call my mother and tell her the news as soon as I get back to the hotel.'

'I hope you'll have the opportunity to meet your aunt and that she turns out to be all that you expect,' said Christopher.

'I'm really grateful that you got us into Rose Mansion, or I'd never have known any of this,' said Julie.

'You can buy me a drink tonight if you like.'

Julie smiled. 'Happy to, see you at my hotel around seven.'

*

When Christopher arrived at Julie's hotel that evening, he knocked on her door.

'Chris, come in. I'm talking to my mother. I have some nibbles and a bottle of wine on the table.'

Clutching the phone to her ear, Julie pointed to the wine, standing in an ice bucket, beside a small plate of hors d'oeuvres. Chris poured her some and handed her a glass before picking up an olive and gazed out the window at the city skyscrapers around them.

Julie was trying to interrupt the flow of conversation at the other end of the phone. 'I know, I know. It's staggering. I agree, we should write to her first. Listen, Mum, I have to go, I have a friend here . . . of course. Yes, I took photos of the Rose Mansion, well, the outside. Yes, and Carla. Okay, I'll call you tomorrow before I leave. Yes . . . it's extraordinary. I love you too.' She put down the phone. 'Sorry, Mum was so excited about the news and wanted details, so I told her all I knew. I'm ready for this glass of wine. Cheers.'

They touched glasses.

'Have you told Shane and Peter?' asked Christopher.

'I rang the boys, but they weren't there, so I spoke to Martine. She was really happy for me and said she'd tell them.'

'I'm pleased for you too.' He raised his glass. 'This has been quite a trip for you.' He sipped his wine. 'I hope we can keep in touch. I want to know the next episode in the saga of Great Aunt Bette.'

'Of course! I'll keep pestering you with emails.' Julie suddenly realised that she would soon be leaving Malaysia and, while she was sure that she would eventually return, she now realised how dismayed she felt about leaving Christopher. 'I suppose you'll be leaving Malaysia at some stage.'

He shrugged. 'I won't be here much longer, but your life isn't your own when you're part of the RAAF.

Occasionally you have a say in things. But you'll come back here to Penang, won't you?'

'Yes, but when? I have a job and I've used up all my holidays. But the time I've spent in Malaysia has been amazing. I never dreamed I'd find, well, so much!' she spread her arms. 'Seems surreal. My cousins, the plantation, Rose Mansion, Carla, and now Bette – alive and kicking it seems.'

'And me. Do I get a look-in as a character in this story?' he asked softly.

'Of course! It's been wonderful to share this with you and you've been so helpful and so interested.' Her voice trailed off as she saw the tender look in his eyes, the slight smile and lifted eyebrow. And in a rush, a kaleidoscope of images came to her: playing tennis with him, drifting through the magic of the mangroves, talking by the pool, sharing dinners and lunches, and now the excitement of Rose Mansion and the discovery of Bette . . . And then their heads drew close and he was kissing her. Julie had the sensation of suddenly letting go, of being swamped by a tide of feelings she hadn't realised she had held in check. If Christopher was surprised by her unexpected ardour he didn't react except to enfold her in his arms as she wound her arms about him.

Much later, dinner forgotten, they fell asleep in a tangle of sheets.

Dawn came and a distant muezzin called the faithful to prayer. Soon the jingle of bicycle bells and the clang of food hawkers setting up their stalls stirred them from their sleep. The day had begun.

'I'm going to miss these exotic sounds first thing in the morning,' said Julie.

Christopher didn't reply at first, but rolled onto his side and gently smoothed her hair. 'You look pretty first thing in the morning.'

She pulled the sheet over her face. 'I didn't even wash my face last night.'

'We had better things to do.' He pulled the sheet away and kissed her nose. 'In a way I wish this hadn't happened . . .' As she started to protest, he put a finger to her lips. 'I feel very attracted to you and now I'm going to miss you. Wonder about you . . .'

'Me too . . . But I have to go back, Chris. I'd love to stay longer.'

'I know, I know. Of course you have to. Listen, we just have to keep in touch, keep in contact,' he said. 'Speaking of contact . . .' He grabbed her and the intensity of their looming separation was dissipated as they playfully wrestled before clinging to one another, making love once more, this time the passion more tender, more poignant.

They went out to the street and sat at a street stall together while Chris watched in amazement as Julie downed a huge breakfast.

'Where are you putting all that?'

'I'm going back to Brisbane . . . It's hard to find food like this at home! I'm making the most of it.'

Before he returned to Butterworth, Christopher drove her to the airport for her flight to Kuala Lumpur.

'It won't be too long till we see each other again. I just know it. We'll work something out. Keep me posted about Aunt Bette.'

She nodded, finding it hard to speak.

He kissed her and then handed her a small package. 'Nothing sinister. You'll be right going through security,' he said, giving her a quick hug before watching her walk away.

She opened the package on the plane and found that Christopher had given her a small book of watercolour paintings of Penang including one of Rose Mansion. Later on the flight, to distract herself from thinking too much about him, she delved in her bag and pulled out the copy of Bette's pamphlet that Angie Ping from the Kuching museum had given her and read it.

Julie gazed out the window at the clouds shielding the view below. She imagined that she was far above the mist-shrouded dark jungles of Borneo and the passion of her aunt's words, written so long ago, struck a powerful chord with her.

These affable, clever, playful, loving creatures are among our nearest living relatives. The wanton destruction of their jungle home, the stealing and murder of their families, is as unnecessary as war, genocide and the worst kind of human behaviour. Let us leave the orangutans in peace and learn from them.

Almost fifty years ago, Bette had feared for the future of orangutans. Sadly, Julie reflected, her aunt had been right. Those issues that Bette had raised all those years ago had not yet been addressed, and the great apes were now critically endangered.

Julie was happy to be home. The minute she walked out of the airport into bright sunshine she realised how she'd missed the clear blue skies of Brisbane. She had not enjoyed the grey pall that hung above Malaysia so much of the time. And it was nice to be back in her neat, white, calming cottage. How quiet and reclusive her street seemed after the clutter, noise and energy of the streets in Malaysia. She then drove to her mother's house and walked around the garden with her father while her mother made tea.

'This has been quite an eventful trip,' commented Paul. 'Your mother is quite stunned by your news. Excited too, of course.'

'It is quite a story. I suppose it's not so unusual to have these kinds of secrets in a family,' said Julie. 'I'm sure we're not the only ones.'

Her father nodded. 'Your mother watches those TV shows where they find lost relatives and so on. There's always some twist and surprise and a secret revealed. As a matter of fact, I know a fellow whose wife was perfectly happy, grew up with an older sister and when her mother died she was going though some documents and found out at the age of fifty that she had been adopted. On top of that was the revelation that her older sister had known all along. It certainly rocked her and she took some time to get over that little family secret.'

'How awful,' said Julie. 'At least our secret turns out to be good news.'

'I hope so. You remember how prickly your grand-mother could be? Let's hope that her sister isn't the same. By the way, your mother missed you while you were away, so it's been good she's involved in this bypass thing.'

'What's happened with the bypass, Dad?'

'The committee has hired a lawyer and he's found out that there could have been an earlier bypass plan, but he doesn't know why it was scrapped.'

'That's interesting, I suppose, but will it give us any ammunition to fight it here?' asked Julie.

'No idea, but you let your mother handle this, she's really got her teeth into it.'

Caroline called them to the verandah where she had morning tea set out.

'This looks lovely. Didn't see any pumpkin scones in Malaysia,' said Julie.

'Did you like the food?' asked her mother as she poured the tea. 'Mother always had a fondness for spicy dishes. And she made a wonderful mango chutney.'

'I loved it!' said Julie, feeling happy as she thought of

the meals with Christopher. 'Do you remember any special dishes?' she asked her mother.

'I can't say I do,' she replied. 'I was too little. Now, fill me in on your adventures. Was David Cooper helpful? How was it living in the jungle with the wild men of Borneo?'

'Yes, he was helpful. So many people were. Especially a very nice RAAF pilot, a friend of the Elliotts. If it hadn't been for Christopher getting me into Rose Mansion and meeting Carla we'd never have found out about Bette.'

'A pilot?' asked her father.

'He's working at Butterworth. Some liaison thing with the Malaysian Air Force,' said Julie.

'What happened to David?' demanded Caroline. 'I thought you'd see a lot of him there.'

'He had to spend more time with the villagers, which I didn't want to do. It was a bit uncomfortable in those longhouses,' said Julie. 'Actually, Mum, I found David a bit, well, overkeen, a bit pushy. He irritated me.'

Her father smiled at his wife. 'Oh dear. You can forget about that one, dear.'

'Dad, he was absolutely not my type. But, I have to say that the experiences I had in Sarawak were very interesting. I think he's still very keen to help you with the bypass, Mum.'

'We could still use him, so I hope you didn't upset him too much,' said Caroline.

'Mum! It's okay. I went off to do my own thing and he had his work. You can catch up with him when he gets back to Brisbane.'

'So what's your plan?' asked Paul, to change the subject.

'I thought we should write to Bette. Break our existence to her gently, let her take her own time, rather than ring her out of the blue,' said Julie.

'Very sensible,' said her father. 'Besides, you have to go back to work, you can't go gallivanting all the way up to Cairns, just now, can you?'

'I think we should make contact with Bette as soon as we can. She is getting on,' said Caroline.

That evening with her parents, Julie went through the whole sequence of events from when she first arrived in Malaysia. She brought out her laptop with her downloaded photographs and showed pictures of Shane and Peter, Martine, the big house at Utopia and other parts of the plantation.

Caroline was thoughtful. 'I can't recall any of this. I have some vague memories, but none of this looks familiar.'

'I'm not surprised. The plantation would've been very different in your day. But we should all go there,' said Julie. 'We could stay in Penang at Rose Mansion with Carla, see Marjorie, then go to Utopia. And I'd love to show you Langkawi Island. I've made so many new friends there . . .'

'Yes, looking at your photos, I can see it all looks very beautiful, but I have to say that I would love to meet Bette first,' said Caroline.

'Yes, I agree, but really you should go to Malaysia, it's part of our family, it's your heritage,' exclaimed Julie.

'You seem pretty keen on the place,' said Paul.

'I feel I've just scratched the surface,' said Julie. 'I didn't go to Malacca, which everyone tells me is really interesting and has beautifully restored historic architecture, or to the east coast and swim in the South China Sea, or drive into the highlands.'

Her mother started putting glasses and plates on the tray. 'Let's see Bette first. Why don't we compose the letter together tonight?'

After much discussion about how much to put in the letter and deciding to keep it brief and simple, they finally posted it.

> *Dear Aunt Bette,*
> *I am Caroline, Margaret's daughter, and I have only just discovered that you are living in Cairns. I am living in the family home in Brisbane since Mother died. My daughter Julie and I would love to talk to you, if that is at all possible. Here is my phone number. With love and warm wishes – after such a long time!*
> *Caroline Reagan, nee Elliott*

'We'll give her a couple of weeks to reply and then if we don't hear from her we'll call her,' said Julie.

'She might take awhile to digest this news and my hunch is she'll send a note rather than phone,' said Caroline. 'She's of that generation.'

Julie emailed Christopher, telling him how she felt about being home, and how she and Caroline hoped to go to Cairns in the near future. But once she returned to work, she had a lot of catching up to do. She was swamped and found that she was working late – there was a marketing project in Melbourne that would take up all her time for the next few weeks.

Then all thoughts of Bette were swept away when Caroline rang Julie one evening with some very exciting news.

'It's Adam and Heather,' she exclaimed breathlessly.

'Mum, what's up? What's happened to Adam and Heather? Are they all right?'

'They're expecting a baby! At last! I'm beside myself. I'm so thrilled. I have to go and visit them immediately.'

'Mum! They've just announced it. When is it due?'

'Not for seven months. But I want to be there now, help them celebrate. I've been longing to be a grandmother.'

Julie smiled to herself. 'Mum, you can't stay with them for seven months. Make it a quick trip. I'm sure they'll want you back when the baby is due. What about the bypass? And what about visiting Bette?'

'Well, there's not much happening with the bypass since we heard from the lawyer, and you're flat out at work anyway, and we haven't heard from Bette at all, so maybe she doesn't want to speak with us. And I know, you're right, I can't stay with Adam and Heather for seven months, but I just have to go now.'

Julie was pleased that her mother was so happy about her brother's news. She shared the excitement with Christopher.

I'm very pleased that you're going to be an aunt. I bet you'll be the best aunt ever. I like the sound of your family and I know when you meet Bette, she'll warm to you no matter what happened in the past. I'm waiting for the next exciting episode. My life seems pretty dull and empty compared with yours! Have to say I miss seeing you. Chris x

II

How QUICKLY SHE SLIPPED back into her old life, and how crazy and frustrating that life suddenly seemed to Julie. She was hardly ever home. She made two trips to Melbourne to help launch a new company, she wrote reports, and she tried to spend time with her father while her mother was away in Adelaide. There just didn't seem to be time to sit back and relax in peace, with space and openness around her.

She found herself thinking about the ritual in the longhouse after the evening meal when everyone sat quietly on mats, mothers singing or talking softly to children, men smoking their pipes staring into the flames of the little fire while discussing the events of the day, and women and girls weaving by lantern and firelight. By the time the jungle night creatures stirred and began foraging, the Iban

340

were asleep. At the same hour in Australia, Julie was just getting home from work, wondering what she had in the freezer that she could heat up quickly for supper, before she sat down at her computer to look at her emails.

Having to come home by train one evening, Julie thought of the sundowners she'd shared on the verandah at Utopia as the chick blinds were raised to let in the cool night breeze and delicious smells wafted from the kitchen. Meals with her cousins were relaxed gatherings of friends and family, waited on discreetly by old family retainers, and served from silver and china dating from Eugene and Charlotte's day. The guests were always interesting and worldly, and the conversation stimulating.

She thought of Christopher, how well he'd fitted in, and yet he had been unobtrusive. His company, laughter and friendship had crept up on her. She wished that she'd paid more attention to him right from the start. Now she missed him and longed to spend more time with him.

Julie tried to work out how she could get back to Penang. She'd used up all her holidays and her job commitments were heavy as she'd taken on two new clients. But a welcome diversion came when her father rang and asked her over for tea.

'Dinner, I mean. I've made a rather good chicken soup. There's a letter here you might want to sneak a peak at. It's addressed to your mother but if we call her, she'll say to go ahead and read it, I'm sure.'

Julie caught her breath. 'Bette. It's from Cairns?'

'Yes. Just a card by the feel of it.'

As soon as Julie arrived at her parents' home, she picked up the pale blue envelope, turned it over and slit it open with her father's letter opener. Inside was a blue card with a few lines written on it in deep blue ink.

Dear Caroline,

Well, what a surprise! I am very pleased to hear from you after all these years. I recall you very well as a small child and am happy to know you now have a daughter of your own.

I would be delighted to meet or speak with you when time permits. I still dabble in my art and I am finishing off some watercolours for an exhibition, but after this month I will have some free time. I look forward to hearing from you.

Warmly, your Aunt Bette

'Gosh, she's still painting. Dabbling. How sweet,' said Julie.

'Well, there's no rush to go to Cairns,' said her father. 'She sounds quite active and together.'

'I wonder if she's still painting flowers,' said Julie. 'I have a book of lovely watercolours of Penang my friend Chris gave me.'

'That's something you can ask her. About her art, to get the conversation going,' said Paul Reagan. 'I'm relieved, I must say, for your mother's sake to get this note. Bette sounds friendly and coherent. Did you tell me that she was nearly ninety? I suppose your mother will adjust to the impending birth, sort out the bypass and then turn her attention to Bette as her next project.'

Julie gave her father a hug. 'Mum does have her projects, doesn't she? What about you, Dad? When are you going to retire and "dabble" in something?'

'I wouldn't know what to do with myself, Jules.'

'You could travel. Take Mum to Malaysia.'

'After all that you've told us, that'll be on the cards at some stage, for sure,' he smiled.

Julie felt a smile break out. 'I'd love to go back.'

'Would that be a keen interest in more research, a

holiday, sightseeing or dinner with a certain handsome RAAF officer?' asked her father.

Julie laughed. 'Can't pull the wool over your eyes, you ol' smartie, Dad. Well, hopefully, all of the above.'

'You'd better call your mother. She'll be hanging out to find out what's in the letter.'

When Caroline returned home, they agreed over the phone that Caroline should reply to Bette's note straight away. The next Saturday afternoon, Julie went over to her parents' assuming she'd stay for dinner. She wanted to hear all the news about Adam and Heather from her mother who'd taken heaps of photos of their new house. But when Julie arrived, she was dismayed to see David Cooper standing on the front verandah talking with Caroline. She waved to her father as he pottered in the front garden and then went up the front steps. Before she could greet Caroline, David rushed to embrace her, and kissed her cheek.

'Wonderful to see you, Julie! I've been hearing all about you finding your aunt! How amazing!'

'Thanks to you, David,' said Caroline. 'Come and have some tea, Jules.'

'Welcome home, Mum. Glad you enjoyed Adelaide.' Julie kissed her mother.

'Seems we all have a lot of catching up to do,' said David. 'I'm looking forward to hearing about how things developed after you left Sarawak,' he said to Julie.

Julie took the cup her mother passed her and sat down. 'Oh, the Elliott boys were great but their friend Christopher really made the breakthrough in finding Bette.'

'Jules, we wouldn't have even begun all this if David hadn't contacted us,' Caroline reminded her.

'Oh, I realise that,' said Julie quickly. 'You gave us our first clue.'

'So tell me all about it,' said David settling into his chair.

'I'm sure Mum has filled you in,' said Julie quickly. 'Anyway, we haven't talked to Bette yet. I hope your research with the Iban went well.'

'It's a never-ending process, really. I'll be going back in a few months. Do you think you will?' he asked.

'She'd like to,' began Caroline, but Julie broke into the conversation, fearful that her mother was going to say more about Christopher.

'I've run out of holidays, but we'll see. I have a lot to do at work at the moment. So, tell me, is there any progress with the bypass?' she asked.

'David is trying to find out more about the original bypass plans that the lawyer dug up,' said her mother.

'They sound interesting,' said David. 'But we have to find out more about them to see why those plans were rejected and if that information's useful to us.'

'So this is just a social visit? There's no dramatic news,' said Julie. 'Good to know you're still helping the cause, David. Now, if you'll excuse me, I'm just going to see Dad about some cuttings for my garden pots.'

Julie stayed in the garden, keeping her father company, until her mother called to tell her that David was leaving. She pulled off her gardening gloves and went to the bottom of the steps. 'Good to see you, again, David. Sorry I've been so busy with Dad.'

'That's all right. By the way, I have a lot of photos of our trip. Some good ones of you!'

'Terrific. Could you email them to me? I'm sure Mum and Dad would love to see them,' said Julie quickly.

'I'll be anxious to hear what Bette is like,' continued David, advancing closer. 'I wonder what she thinks about the continuing loss of orangutan habitat.'

Julie nodded and waved her muddy gardening gloves

at him. 'I'm not sure that she's keeping up with all that sort of thing now. She is nearly ninety. Have to go and wash up. Good to see you.' She skipped past him up the steps and, avoiding her mother, went indoors.

'You didn't have to be so rude, so brusque to David,' said Caroline as soon as he had gone.

'Mum, he annoys me. He's just too pushy. Can't he see I have no interest in him?'

'You can't blame a fellow for trying,' said her father.

'And if it hadn't been for David, we wouldn't have known about Bette and he's been very helpful with the bypass campaign,' added her mother.

'I know, but think of him as your friend rather than mine,' said Julie.

'Well, I hope he continues to help us,' said Caroline pointedly.

'I'd say that David has a thick skin,' said Paul, grinning at Julie.

Two weeks later Caroline called Julie to tell her that Bette had made contact again.

'Bette's written another short note. She says that she's still busy painting for her exhibition. Can you believe it? She must have steady hands and good eyesight.'

'Let's hope it's hereditary,' said Julie. 'Does she say anything about meeting us?'

'Only that she's glad we've made contact. I don't think she realises how interested we are in her,' said Caroline.

'Let's just take things gently. You know, we could just go up to Cairns unannounced. When's her exhibition?'

'She doesn't say. When have you got time to go north? Do you have any clients up in Cairns you could visit?' asked Caroline.

'Not really. I've been more focused on Melbourne.'

'Maybe *we* should phone her,' said Caroline.

'Why not? Say that we would like to come up for her exhibition, if we can.'

'Bette sounded lovely when I rang her,' Caroline told Julie. 'We didn't chat for long, but she told me that she lives alone, although a woman comes in each day to help with domestic things. The exhibition opens in three weeks time, to coincide with the long weekend. We could fly to Cairns for that weekend and it would be even better if you could manage to get an extra day off.'

'That's a fantastic idea. I'm sure I'll be able to arrange an extra day. It will be lovely up there this time of year. See if Dad can get time off and come up, too,' said Julie. 'Gosh, it's going to be interesting meeting an elderly Aunt Bette, when I've been reading about a headstrong adventurous young woman studying orangutans and living with the Iban in the jungle!'

Julie got a kick out of travelling to Cairns with Caroline and Paul. She couldn't remember the last time just the three of them had been on a trip together.

'What does Adam think of us taking off on this little family excursion?' Julie asked her parents, sitting across from her on the plane.

'To tell you the truth, darling, he doesn't care. I don't think he's looked at any of your photos of Malaysia. He's just wrapped up in the baby and finishing the house,' said Caroline.

'I was feeling a bit out of the loop, too,' said Paul. 'But having read Bette's book about the Iban and the pamphlet about the orangutans, you get the sense that she's a very intelligent woman.'

They checked into a two-bedroom suite in a small European-style hotel.

'All very Tuscan, isn't it. Nice pool area, and the suite is huge,' said Caroline.

'A few too many Greek statues for me,' commented Paul. 'But the urns of flowers are nice.'

'And we're very central,' said Julie. 'Let's go for a walk and see what's around.'

'Not me. I'm going to sit out here with a beer and relax,' said her father, settling himself on a lounge chair on the balcony. 'I might go to the pool later.'

Julie and Caroline browsed through shops, ate a salad at an outdoor café, walked along the esplanade, chose a bistro they would go to for dinner and walked back to their hotel.

'I'm trying to remind myself that we're on a mission,' Julie said, linking her arm through Caroline's.

'Can't you just relax? At least for the rest of today and tonight,' said Caroline.

'Right. I just don't know what to expect with Aunt Bette,' said Julie.

When they arrived back at their hotel, Paul showed them the free local magazine he'd found on the coffee table in their suite. 'Here's an advertisement for her exhibition!' It showed a picture of some of Bette's paintings.

'Wow, look at those! They're exquisite,' said Caroline.

'Is there a photo of her?' asked Julie peering over her mother's shoulder. 'Those flowers are gorgeous. You feel you can pick them off the page.'

'No photo of her but she definitely has a particular style. I thought we were going to the exhibition to see Bette, now I want to see her paintings, as well!'

'Did she suggest that you come to the opening?' asked Paul.

'Yes, she did. Just to say hello. I don't think she realises we want to sit down and drag her life story out of her,' said Caroline.

'Must you?' asked Paul. 'Isn't finding each other enough? Surely things will come out in due course.'

'You don't know women,' said Caroline.

'Oh, Dad, we'll be subtle, and gentle,' said Julie. 'We're not going to attack her!'

The art gallery was buzzing when Julie and her parents arrived.

'This place is very trendy,' said Julie.

'Look at those flowers,' said Caroline, pausing beside huge banks of tropical flowers and stands of orchids. 'There are orchids everywhere. It's quite spectacular.'

A pretty girl came towards them, holding a tray of glasses filled with champagne. They each took a glass and looked around the gallery, which was already filling with smartly dressed guests. They were ushered to a table spread with name tags, where there were ones for Julie and Caroline. Another was quickly written out for Paul.

People were still arriving when Julie nudged Caroline. 'That must be her.' She nodded towards an older lady sitting in a wheelchair and chatting to a small group of people at the far end of the room. 'Let's meander around the gallery and look at the pictures first,' suggested Julie.

They took their time, studying each of the paintings, which were all intensely passionate. Vibrant flowers bloomed amid fungi and patterned bark. Sinister shapes of strange creature-like plants lurked in dark foliage among vines and damp, lichen-covered rotting tree trunks.

'You feel as though you could walk right into the paintings,' said Julie in some awe.

'They're astonishing,' agreed Caroline.

'I'm glad you think so,' said a voice behind them.

They turned.

The woman who had spoken held out her hand. 'I'm Cyndi George, the gallery director. We're very proud of this exhibition. Would you like to meet the artist?'

Before either Caroline or Julie could speak, she gestured to the woman beside her. 'Please, may I introduce you to Mrs Tsang, or Bette Oldham – as she is known professionally?'

Mother and daughter stared at Bette and struggled to speak. For Caroline there were only hazy memories of this woman from long ago. For Julie there were the conversations she had had, the stories that had captivated her. Now, it was almost like seeing a ghost. But in Bette's smile, her direct gaze and her firm handshake, Julie glimpsed the strong and intriguing young woman she'd come to know through anecdote, and the gift of her pen and her brush.

The pause was long enough for Cyndi George to look quickly at them and consider what she should say next as this silence was unusual. Gallery guests were usually prompt to gush at the presiding painter.

'And your names are?' She looked enquiringly at Caroline and Julie, who hadn't taken their eyes off the tall, straight figure standing before them.

Bette was striking looking, her beauty transformed from the unformed clay of youth to the beauty of old age, radiating a sense of satisfaction with herself, though it was not through ego. Her presence seemed to say, *Here I am, a woman who has followed her own path. A woman who has no regrets, no recriminations and no unfinished business.*

It was Bette who broke the silence. 'I know who you are.'

A smile softened her features as she took Caroline's hand. 'What a beautiful woman you are. I always hoped I'd see you again. You were such a sweet child.' She turned to Julie. 'And you are Julie? Yes, I can certainly see the family resemblance.' She leaned forward and brushed her lips against Julie's cheek before turning to embrace Caroline.

This woman was not the frail woman in a wheelchair they'd anticipated. Bette had short cropped grey hair streaked with dramatic white strands that looked modern even though the style was inspired by the twenties. She wore tailored dark slacks and a shirt softened by a burst of lilac ruffles at her throat. On her shirt was pinned a large diamond and gold brooch of a tiger with ruby eyes. Beautiful rings on her fingers. Despite her narrow frame and slight build she wore the jewellery stylishly. The ebony walking stick with a silver head that she leaned on slightly was the only hint of any frailty.

Cyndi looked at the trio in surprise. 'You're all old friends then?'

'Yes, in a way.' Caroline smiled, her eyes filled with tears. In the rush of different emotions she couldn't help but wish that Margaret was here, too. No matter what had happened in the past between the sisters, she would have liked her mother to have been around to share in their lives once more. 'I do remember you, Aunt Bette.'

'You're relations! How wonderful,' said Cyndi. 'I'll leave you for a few minutes. But, Bette, we do have to move on with the proceedings. There's a chair beside the podium for you, if you think that you'll need it.'

'Thank you, Cyndi. Just give me the signal.' She smiled at Caroline. 'Speeches, you understand how things are. And I don't hang around after the formalities. I can only cope with so much these days.'

'Of course, Aunt Bette. I'm so pleased to see you again. This is my husband, Paul, and, as you've realised, my daughter, Julie. We're sorry to intrude on such an important occasion. This exhibition must have taken a long time to put together,' said Caroline.

'It was a while, I suppose. I finally had to rent a studio to get all my mess out of the living room,' said Bette. 'Besides I needed good light, and the studio was perfect.'

'Do you paint from specimens or photographs?' asked Julie, wondering at the detail of each flower and also its surrounds.

'About ten years ago I travelled to Cooktown and went into the rainforest and did paintings, took some photographs. I also did some of these paintings which I remembered from sketches I'd done in Malaysia, years ago. Gradually I built up a collection and the Gardens Gallery heard about my work and very kindly asked me if I'd like to exhibit.'

'That sounds like it must have been quite an undertaking,' said Julie. 'You seem a very intrepid explorer.'

'Yes. I love jungles and rainforests, but I'd like to look at the other extremes too, and see our deserts. I plan to take a trip to Alice Springs and the interior, but haven't got around to it yet.'

'Bette, you're incredible!' said Caroline. 'We don't want to hold you up, but we're so impressed with your work and we're very proud of you. If you have time tomorrow, we'd like to take you out for morning or afternoon tea. Would that suit you?'

Bette's eyes sparkled. 'And pump me with questions? Of course! And I want to know all about you. But what I'd prefer is that you come to me for tea. It's quieter and more comfortable for me at my place. We can make arrangements when the speeches are over.'

Paul agreed with Caroline and Julie that Bette was so charming. 'I was enchanted to meet her. But I think she might feel more comfortable if just you two go to her place,' he said. 'I'll be fine by the pool and you can tell me all about it later.'

Bette's apartment was on the ground floor of a large

block with a parking spot close to the front door. The other apartments had balconies, but Bette's place had a small private garden.

A young woman opened the door and greeted them, then ushered them into the large sitting room. 'I'm Suzie. Mrs Tsang has told me about you both. How lovely for her to have relatives living in Australia. Now, what can I get everyone?'

Bette was sitting on a sofa, her feet up on a footstool. Sliding glass doors looked out onto a patio crowded with pots of orchids and tropical plants. 'Tea, I think please, Suzie. Or would anyone rather have coffee or a cold drink?'

'Tea is lovely, thank you. What a sweet apartment,' said Caroline. She glanced around the room and noted the Chinese décor. There were beautiful woven rugs, embroidered cushions and silk tapestries on the walls beside framed watercolours and delicate calligraphy.

'You work here as well?' asked Julie, sitting beside Bette.

There was an easel in one corner and a small card table next to it, which was covered in tubes of paints, brushes and sketchbooks.

'Only if I don't feel like going to the studio or if inspiration strikes,' said Bette.

'Were you happy with the exhibition opening?' asked Caroline.

'Cyndi was. Apparently we sold quite a few paintings, which is good as the proceeds are going to charity. A selection is also going to the Gardens Gallery permanent collection. All this is very flattering for an old lady's hobby.'

'But surely you've drawn and painted all your life?' asked Julie.

'I did a lot, certainly. And I enjoyed writing. I once

thought of illustrating children's books. But circumstances changed and by the time I was married, life became very busy and I did other things.'

Suzie came in with the tea tray and Bette directed her to put it on the table. She smiled at them. 'Please help yourselves. Now tell me a little about you both. Are you married, Julie? Do you have brothers and sisters? Are you a career girl?'

'I have an interesting job as a marketing consultant, mainly helping companies sell themselves, so I get to travel quite a bit,' said Julie. 'And I'm single. My brother Adam is married and lives in the Adelaide Hills.'

'He's expecting my first grandchild, so I'm very excited,' added Caroline.

'And Caroline, you still live in Brisbane don't you?' asked Bette.

'Yes. In the old family house. My husband's job took him away from Brisbane for a while and when we got back we moved in with Mother. Paul was agreeable about it as it's such a lovely home and so big. We looked after my mother till she died. Julie has lived in that house for most of her life.'

'It's a lovely tradition, maintaining the links with the place where you were born and where you grew up,' agreed Bette. 'I guess I subconsciously severed my links with that house when I stayed in Malaysia. I often wondered what happened to our old house in Brisbane, with the view of the bay. Old homes like Bayview get torn down too often. That's partly why it's important to me to know that Rose Mansion is still intact. I'm very happy that it has been so lovingly restored.'

'When I found that Rose Mansion had been your family home, I thought about our house in Brisbane. They are both very different, but very special to our families,' said Julie.

'That's why we're currently involved in a fight to stop our house in Brisbane from being pulled down for a bypass,' said Caroline.

'That's just awful. It would be a tragedy for that lovely old place to be demolished!' exclaimed Bette. 'Good for you for fighting to save it. I hope you succeed. There are a lot of memories connected with that house. Do you think you'll win the battle?'

'Mum is giving it her best shot,' said Julie.

'I don't know,' said Caroline. 'We've had some encouraging news. It seems that there was a similar plan in the area previously, and it was scrapped. So if we can find out the details about why that happened, it might help us do the same thing.'

'If you could do that, it would mean that you're not living with uncertainty,' said Bette.

'Exactly. We've had help from a bright young man who's good at research and we're hoping that David can sift through the old council papers and get some clues. In fact, it was through David that we found that you had written a book about the Iban,' said Caroline. 'It was the first time we knew about your adventures in Sarawak,' she continued with a smile. 'We were terribly impressed.'

'Goodness me! I didn't think that there was a copy still in existence,' said Bette. 'That time with the Iban was a wonderful experience.'

'Why did you write the book as Oldham and not Tsang?' asked Caroline. 'I liked the dedication to Philip.'

Bette was thoughtful and sipped her tea. 'Yes. I wanted Philip to know that I hadn't forgotten him. He was such a lovely little boy. My husband's family was quite conservative and I didn't want to embarrass them so I wrote my adventures under my maiden name.' She straightened up, changing the subject. 'Could you top up my tea please, Julie?' She leaned back in her chair and folded her hands over the silk shirt she'd tucked into a colourful skirt. 'So, now that you've told me something about yourselves, what would you like to know about me?'

Caroline glanced at Julie. 'Where to start?'

Julie had thought about this. 'Well,' said Julie, 'I'd like to know how you and Margaret got separated in Singapore. When I was on Langkawi Island I met Marjorie Carter, who was Marjorie Potts when she was a POW with you. She told me a lot about the camp, but didn't explain how you got there. How did my grandmother end up back in Australia while you and Philip were prisoners in Sarawak?'

'Good heavens. Fancy you meeting Marjorie. How is she? I'm sorry that I didn't keep in touch with her. Evelyn, her mother, and I were great friends. We wrote to each other for years.'

'She's a lovely person,' replied Julie. 'She's actually bought a place in Penang and lives there a lot of the year, when it's too cold in Scotland.'

'I'm glad to know that Marjorie is well. Fancy her returning to live in Malaysia.'

'I'm sure she'd love to hear from you,' said Julie. 'She has very warm memories of you. She told us how strong you were in that camp and how devoted you were to Philip.'

'Yes. Perhaps you're right. I should contact her. I remember the first time I saw Marjorie. She was a shy, gangly girl, dragging her mother's suitcase through the camp gates. Her mother wasn't well, which the camp conditions didn't help. It was a marvel she survived. So many didn't. I remember being riveted by the sight of that suitcase. Philip and I had nothing except what we stood up in. In fact luggage was the cause of our being in that camp, now that I think about it.'

'Why was that?' asked Julie. 'Perhaps before you tell us that, what was it like in Malaya before the war? Mum has told me what Gran told her, but it would be nice to hear what you thought about it.'

'In Malaya before the war, life was certainly glamorous and social. Margaret was in with a cosmopolitan crowd. She had lots of servants. Her way of life was quite different from our life in Brisbane. In a way, I think she wanted me to visit her so that she could show off to me. I wanted to travel, climb mountains, see the pyramids but mostly I wanted to see the Far East, so I was pleased to be asked. And she and Roland certainly showed me a good time.'

'We have a photo of you at the races with my mother,' said Caroline.

'Oh, yes, Margaret loved the races. She and Roland took me to race day in Penang. That was a wonderful day, I'll never forget it. All of Malaya, at that time, seemed to be full of eligible bachelors, civil servants, planters and assistant managers out from the UK,' said Bette with a smile. 'I became very friendly with one of Roland's chums, Gilbert Mason. We had some great times together. He was a very nice man.' She looked away for a moment and then asked Julie, 'Did you enjoy your time in Malaysia?'

'I did. It's a very romantic place. And it still seems wild in parts.'

'I agree, it is romantic,' said Bette. 'And I loved the jungle. I went upriver once with Margaret, Roland and Gilbert. It was very beautiful and wild. Roland's father, Eugene, was a game hunter so I heard his stories and saw his trophies. Are they still on the walls of the big house? Rubber was fetching a good price just before the war and they lived well then. Of course no one ever thought the war would touch Malaya, except Roland.'

'So you were caught by surprise when the Japanese came down the peninsula?' asked Caroline.

'There was a lot of talk in those final months about the war, but the plantation seemed so far away from everything. I remember when the Japanese attacked the north of Malaya in early December. We were all shattered. A family arrived from the north, planter acquaintances of Roland's,' said Bette, now looking out the French doors.

Julie and Caroline knew she wasn't seeing her pretty patio but another place in another time.

'They were quite traumatised and had fled for their lives with what they could throw in the car. That galvanised Roland into action. He insisted that his father, Margaret and I, and little Philip leave for the safety of Australia straight away. I remember that Eugene refused to leave. Of course the Japanese killed him when they reached Utopia. It was so sad and so brutal. Anyway, Eugene's driver, Hamid, was to take us to Singapore, where we were to meet Gilbert who was there looking after his employer's warehouses. He would make sure that we got onto a ship as quickly as possible.'

'Weren't some of the passenger ships sunk?' asked Caroline.

'Yes,' said Bette. 'But we didn't know about that then. Anyway, there were so many rumours flying around.' She took a sip of tea. 'We had planned to leave Utopia first thing in the morning, but after hearing what had happened to the planter family, my sister was adamant that she should pack up as many valuables to take as she could.'

'You mean jewellery? Personal things?' asked Julie.

'Roland and I persuaded her to bury some of her valuable things. She took all the cash they could round up and all her and Philip's clothes. I took all of mine, but I didn't have much since I was only visiting. You have no idea what Margaret crammed into the car, which was so full there was scarcely room for us all. I remember that she even had hat boxes. Philip and I were perched on top of bags in the back seat of the Oldsmobile when we finally set off later that day.'

'I suppose the trip was pretty frightening. I read Roland's account of his drive,' said Julie.

'Did you read that? How very interesting. Yes, it was very frightening. The roads were crowded as everyone was heading south towards the Johore Causeway, hoping to get across it before the Japanese cut it off. As we drove towards Singapore, we passed burning cars and buildings, people fleeing on bicycles and carrying what they could or just running blindly, with no idea where to find safety. The worst part was seeing dead and dying bodies along the road. We came upon a horrific scene of mutilated bodies where a bomb had hit a bus. There was a child, about Philip's age, right in front of us and before we could prevent it, he saw this headless body lying in the road. Everywhere there was smoke and the smell of petrol fumes. It was very frightening and Philip clung to me in the back of the car. Margaret was shouting directions at Hamid, but he was magnificent and stayed calm. When a group of people blocked the road and started hammering on the car, I'm not sure whether they wanted a ride or were telling us to go back or were just frightened, it was very unnerving. Margaret told Hamid to get out of the car and get rid of them, and she shouted through the window at them. Philip was sobbing, but Hamid kept nosing the car forward. Suddenly he accelerated, and drove onto the footpath, sending people flying. They certainly got out of his way – I think he would have run them over if they hadn't.'

'It sounds awful,' said Caroline.

'When we got to Gilbert's place, which was in one of the better areas, a bit out of town, the sky was a strange orange-yellow,' continued Bette. 'We fell inside, so glad to be out of the car. There were groups of people wandering rather aimlessly along the street, and a lot of shouting and crying. When Margaret saw them, she thought that the luggage might be stolen, so she made Hamid and Gilbert's houseboy unload the car and store everything inside for the night. I held Philip who was still terrified. Gilbert explained that we'd have to go in person to the city the next morning to get tickets on one of the ships leaving Singapore. We did, and on the drive into the city, we could see that parts of Chinatown and many city buildings had been bombed. We also saw a lot of Australian soldiers. They seemed pretty cheery about the whole thing. How sad that just days later they would end up as POWs in Changi. We were lucky that Gilbert had so many contacts in the shipping industry because he managed to get us tickets on a boat that was to sail for Perth the next day. That night we had a light dinner and tried to sleep but the bombing started up in earnest. We took cover under the dining room table. At times it sounded as though the bombs were falling right next to us.'

'So what happened the next day?' asked Julie.

'We found ourselves in another country. A country at war. When daylight came, we realised that although Gil's house had not been hit, the Oldsmobile on the street had. It was crushed, and completely undriveable. Margaret kept saying what a good thing it was that she'd insisted on unloading it.

'All that morning, the Japanese planes continued their bombing runs and the city and docks were in chaos. We were very worried that we would miss the boat, but Margaret would not leave her possessions. So Hamid packed them all into Gil's car, which was pretty tiny. Gil insisted that Hamid drive Margaret and he would look after Philip and me. This was fair enough because Margaret's ankle still worried her from an earlier car accident and she couldn't walk any great distance on it.

So Margaret went off with Hamid and the luggage, while Gil, Philip and I walked until we could find some transport. Eventually, Gil persuaded a trishaw driver to take us in his little vehicle by offering him a wad of money. The driver was obviously frightened by the bombing, but business was business. There were people running everywhere, ambulances and army trucks, but they couldn't do much as it was so crowded, smoke billowing from burning buildings, sirens going off, and everything was just in chaos. Philip was terrified and so was I. By this time Hamid was well ahead of us. Just as we were squeezing our way past a bomb crater, there was another raid and the Japanese dropped a bomb just ahead of us. A building came down right across the roadway. We couldn't get around it on the trishaw, so Gil just grabbed Philip, held my hand and we started running, pushing our way through the crowd. Gil took us back up the street looking for a laneway or some way to get through to the wharf. But it was impossible. The next thing we knew there were soldiers, British and Australian, telling us to go back. Gil took no notice of them and, still carrying Philip, he doubled back and found a laneway that led to the wharf. But the ship we were to sail on wasn't there.'

'But Margaret had made it on board,' finished Caroline.

Bette rubbed a hand over her eyes. 'Yes. Poor Margaret. She told me later that it was an absolute disaster on the docks and when that last bombing raid occurred, the captain decided that it was too dangerous to wait any longer and the gangplank was raised and the ship sailed. Margaret had no idea where we were and when she looked at the horrific scenes on the docks she didn't even know if we were dead or alive. Of course it was years before I found out that Margaret's ship had made it safely to Australia.'

Caroline and Julie just stared at Bette.

'How did you feel when you realised that the boat had sailed without you and Philip. What did you do?' asked Julie.

'Well, in a way we were lucky, thanks to dear Gilbert.

As we ran down to the burning docks Gil took matters into his own hands.'

'He sounds very resourceful,' said Caroline.

'He was. He saved us,' said Bette softly. 'Gil found a Malay with a small trading vessel. He had his wife and three children on board with him and when Gil gave him a fistful of money he let us jump on board. We were among the flotilla of small boats streaming away from Singapore in every direction, trying to escape the Japanese. We headed south towards the Dutch East Indies, hoping to land in Java. None of us had any idea just how far the Japanese would spread and Gil thought that we would find a way to get from Java back to Australia.

'The first night we pulled into a tiny island that seemed to be uninhabited. We tried not to use any lights, though Gilbert and the boatman waded ashore with torches and caught us several good-sized crabs, which we boiled on a paraffin ring on the stern of the boat. I often recalled that delicious meal during the lean times in the camp. We anchored in a mangrove inlet and the mosquitoes were ferocious. Philip and I rolled together under some canvas and Gil sat up and kept watch. In the morning Philip was tired and cranky and very weepy. Gil took him aside and told him that he understood just how he felt, but that he had to be a little man and do everything I said until we got home to his parents. That man-to-man talk from Gil seemed to do the trick and I was forever grateful as Philip tried so hard after that not to be difficult, and he wasn't.'

'It must have been like a bad dream.' Caroline shook her head. 'I wonder how I'd have managed, if I'd been thrown into such a terrible situation.'

'You don't know what reserves of strength you have within yourself until you need them,' replied Bette.

'But you didn't get to Java before the Japanese, did you?' said Julie.

'No. We were trying to travel among these little islands in the hope of not being spotted. Several planes flew over us and the next thing we knew there was a large powerful gunboat coming towards us. Gilbert made everyone except the Malay hide below and Gil lay under the canvas on the deck. He and the Malay boatman had concocted some story that they were only poor fisherman or something like that. Gil spoke Malay quite well.'

'Did that work?' asked Julie. She and Caroline were transfixed by Bette's story, imagining what they would have done in such a ghastly situation.

'They pulled alongside, shouting in Japanese, which of course the boatman didn't understand. Then one of them jumped onto the bow of the boat and fired through the deck and the little windows down below. The Malay man started shouting and his wife started screaming and the children scrambled up on deck, one of them bleeding quite profusely. I was too frightened to stay below, in case they fired again. Gil jumped out and started shouting. Then another Japanese soldier signalled that Gil, Philip and I should get onto the Japanese boat.

I looked at Gilbert and he nodded. 'Do as they say, and don't argue,' he said.

'So Philip was passed up and then it was my turn. Philip, I could see, was clinging to the railing and sobbing for me. Gilbert helped me scramble onto the Japanese boat. I remember the touch of his hand as he squeezed my arm. "You'll be right," he said.

'At this point, the Malay suddenly jumped up shouting "Allah Akbar" and waved one of those big parangs, knives, at the Japanese. Well, the soldier on the gunboat fired at him and the poor man was riddled with bullets and fell onto the deck of the boat. The soldier then turned his gun on Gil. Gilbert made a wild dash to jump overboard and then I saw everything as if in slow motion.

362

As he went over the side, the soldier fired at him, I don't know how many times, but the sea went red. Gil didn't have a chance.'

'That's terrible,' said Julie, tears springing to her eyes. 'Poor Gilbert.'

'What a horror for you and Philip. How do you recover from something like that?' said Caroline.

'You have to learn to live with it,' said Bette simply. 'Later I learned to live and love again, but the scars are still there. Still part of you.'

'What happened to the Malay woman and her children?' asked Julie.

'I don't know. The Japanese just left them there. I don't think they were interested in making anyone else, except Europeans, prisoners. Philip and I huddled in their boat as they headed across to Sarawak. The Japanese had already established a POW camp near Kuching, some distance out of the town. We were driven and then marched to it. Through all this I managed to keep my bag slung over my chest. In it were Philip's blue elephant and some money. I had nothing else. And so began our sojourn at the Emperor's pleasure.'

Bette reached for a glass of water on the tray.

'When did my grandmother find out that you'd both survived the bombing of Singapore and were interned in a POW camp?' asked Julie.

'Not for years. Twice in the camp the Japanese gave us special postcards and we were allowed to write two lines on them. They were supposed to be sent to our families, but we never knew if they got through, and they hadn't. It was only after the surrender that a full list of names of those interned in our camp was made known, so neither my parents nor Margaret knew that we were alive until the war was over. I find it difficult to forgive the Japanese such cruel indifference.'

'Internment must have been hard on Philip,' said Caroline.

'Yes. He kept asking where his mummy was, and why she wasn't coming back to get him. For a while I was angry with Margaret for fussing with all the unnecessary stuff and getting separated from us, but I realised that I couldn't really blame her. Everything was in complete chaos, so it was no one's fault. I promised myself that I would protect Philip and see us through whatever was ahead.' Bette straightened up and gave a small smile. 'It was a tough three and a half years. But he came through it. We both survived.'

Julie looked at Caroline. This was her mother's brother that Bette had been talking about and Caroline had been quite ignorant of these terrible experiences he had been through. She wondered how much Shane and Peter knew about this episode in their father's life. For a moment all three women sat in silence.

Finally Caroline spoke. 'And when my mother knew that her son was safe and that you'd protected and looked after Philip, got through this incredible, horrible ordeal, surely she must have fallen on her knees to give thanks,' said Caroline.

Bette was noncommittal. 'I have no idea how she reacted when she first heard the news. But certainly, when we were all reunited, it was very emotional.'

'I can't imagine how it must have been for you all. The days sailing back to Australia, what was that like?' asked Caroline.

'Wonderful in many ways. Everyone was so kind and generous to us, especially the Red Cross and there was plenty of food, I could see Philip's health and spirits improve day by day. Children can be very resilient. But we'd all been through rough times and were still fragile and finding it hard to adjust, even to a soft bed, and terribly anxious just to be home, well, it was still a bit stressful.'

'And when you arrived back in Brisbane?' asked Caroline.

Bette closed her eyes briefly and sighed, then returned to her story. 'My mother Winifred, my father and Margaret were at the dock to meet us. It was very crowded. The injured servicemen were taken off first. I was so focused on Philip and making sure that he wasn't lost or crushed among all the people on the wharf that I was unprepared for how overwhelmed I felt when I saw my own parents. I just wanted to rush into their arms and be held, like a small child. Margaret was crying and she held Philip so tight, smothering him and I'm not sure that the poor little boy even recognised her. I'd talked constantly to him about meeting his mummy and being home again, and he was excited when the moment came, but he was also quite bewildered because no one on that wharf was familiar.'

'I suppose you were surrounded on the wharf by other emotional reunions, too,' said Julie.

'Very much so. But my father was great. He picked Philip up and sat him on his shoulders, showing him all the boats on the river and letting him sit in the front seat of the car so that by the time we got back home, Philip seemed to be very happy. But I soon realised that if I was out of his sight he'd become very shy and he'd come and look for me. Mother kept cooking her wonderful meals to build us both up. We were still painfully thin and she would tell Margaret not to expect the boy to sit on her lap and cuddle her all the time. "Let him come to you gradually," she would say. But it was hard for Margaret, of course. She'd missed three and a half years of Philip's life and she wanted their relationship to resume straight away. But I was so happy to be home. I remember that I took a walk around the garden and couldn't help crying.

I'd lived with the memory of this house, my room, the garden, recreating it all in my mind as a means of staying sane while I was in the camp. And now to find it all as I'd remembered, but more peaceful, the garden more beautiful, the song of the birds, well it brought me undone a little. Everything I'd bottled up all those years, the constant fears I'd had for Philip, just came gushing out. My father finally found me sitting, crying on the swing and he just stood there, his hand on top of my head, until I settled down a bit and then we took another stroll around the garden together. He made small talk, about his vegetables, news of neighbours, and how he planned to paint the house. When Philip came outside, calling for me, Dad patted my shoulder and just said, "I'm proud of you. I know that the rest of your life will be happy and good." And it was.'

'My poor brother. How did he finally adjust to his new life?' asked Caroline.

'It took some time. The first few nights he crept out of his room to curl up in bed with me as we'd done for so long, and I put him back into his bed early each morning so Margaret wouldn't know. It was my father who suggested that I go away for a holiday. I needed a break and it was a chance for Philip to get used to his mother and new surroundings without me. Then I tried to start my own life again. I went to art school and then I moved to Sydney for a while. You can see the product of those classes, all these years later,' said Bette, with a smile.

Julie was about to ask another question, but Caroline put a hand on her arm.

'Bette, thank you for telling us all this. It must have been difficult for you. Of course we want to know more, but you look tired.'

Bette waved a dismissive hand. 'Nonsense, I'm fine and after the war there were good times. Many good years. I'd like you to know about those. As you can imagine, after the war it wasn't easy to pick up where everyone had left off. Philip and I weren't the only ones who'd had tough times. Roland had served through the war under extremely difficult circumstances and he had returned to his home to find it in a very poor condition and his father dead.

'At the beginning of 1946 Margaret and Philip sailed for Malaya to join him and to pick up the pieces of their life on the plantation. It was difficult for Margaret as the house had been occupied by the Japanese. Eugene was tragically gone and life was not the long party that it'd been before the war. But Roland refused to leave the plantation that his father had worked so hard to establish and a lot of the loyal staff had remained and so they battled on to rebuild it.

'And then you came along, Caroline, and then, when you were about three, Margaret wrote and asked me to come up and visit again. I was in two minds. I was enjoying my life and had an interesting job and a nice circle of friends, but Roland wrote to me privately to say it would be helpful if I could come and he offered to pay my fare. He said that Margaret was lonely and, reading between the lines, I suspected that she was unhappy. So I agreed and I returned to Malaya.'

As she said this, Suzie appeared. 'Suzie, could you clear away the tea things, please? I think we're done.' Stiffly Bette stood up. 'If you both don't mind I have to go out for a while. Cyndi wants to talk to me about the sales of my paintings.'

'I hope we haven't been pests,' said Caroline quickly.

'Not at all. You've opened a floodgate of memories I haven't thought about for a long time.'

'You mentioned the good times after the war. It sounds like you had a wonderful life. We'd love to hear about those, as well,' said Julie, taking Bette's thin but strong hand in hers.

'Jules, please, I don't think that we should ask Bette too many questions about her personal life.'

Bette smiled at Julie. 'Nonsense, Caroline, I'd be delighted to tell you both, if you're interested. Perhaps tomorrow. You've been to Rose Mansion, Julie, and you've met one of my granddaughters and you've visited the Iban, so we seem to have a lot in common. I think I'd enjoy telling you more about my life.'

'I'd love that. From the little I know about you, it sounds really interesting,' said Julie smiling.

'Tomorrow then.' Bette lifted her cheek for Julie to kiss and they embraced warmly as Caroline did the same.

Back at their hotel Caroline and Julie recounted Bette's story to Paul who shook his head and stood up. 'What a remarkable person. I need a stiff drink after what you've told me. Anyone else like one? What's on the agenda for tomorrow?'

'We thought we'd ask Bette if she'd like to go somewhere nice, just a social thing, no draining conversations,' said Caroline.

'You might find that once you open a door to old memories she might want to keep talking,' said Paul. 'It's probably quite cathartic. And I've heard that old people like to pass on their story, so that it's known, and their life with all its triumphs and tragedies doesn't disappear when they do.'

'That could be true,' agreed Caroline. 'It's also important for me. Look how little I know about my parents.'

'Margaret always seemed to be holding something inside her,' said Paul. 'When I first met her I thought she was a very straight-laced lady. I thought she disapproved of me.'

'Never! She loved you,' exclaimed Caroline. 'Especially after we moved in with her and she could boss you around.' Caroline smiled and gave her husband an affectionate kiss. 'You were so patient, so kind and easygoing all those years.'

'Shame you've turned into a grumpy old man, Dad,' joked Julie affectionately.

That night after Caroline and Paul had gone to sleep Julie sent an email to Chris, telling him that they'd met Bette and how amazing she was, not just because she was nearly ninety, but because she was an artist and a warm and vibrant woman.

> She told us how she and Margaret became separated and how she ended up in a POW camp with Philip. She also told us that the man she loved and was probably going to marry was horribly killed. And yet she says she has had a full, good life. Mum and I are curious about her marriage to Tony Tsang. She seems quite happy to tell us about it. Dad thinks that now she's started reminiscing, she'll want us to know everything. I'll write more tomorrow. Julie.

Julie lay in bed trying to read but she kept putting her book down and thinking about Bette. Then to her surprise her mobile rang. She grabbed it, wondering who would ring her at this late hour. When she saw the name on her mobile, her heart leapt.

'Hi, Chris! What's up? This is a nice surprise.'

'Hi, Jules, I got your email and figured you might still be awake. Is it okay to talk?' His voice was warm and familiar and she found she couldn't stop smiling.

She spoke softly. 'I'm curled up in bed trying to read, but I can't stop wondering about my aunt. How are you?'

'Nothing new this end, for the moment anyway. It

sounds as though Aunt Bette is something out of the box. Are you happy you found her? No nasty surprises, skeletons in closets?'

'No, nothing like that at all. Even without knowing anything about her life, she's a personable woman. She's quite different from my grandmother, even though they were sisters. Bette seems very open, warm and giving. Gran was a closed sort of person.'

'You mean bitter?'

'No, more a private person. Not at all outgoing.'

'On another topic, you haven't mentioned the battle of the bypass lately.'

'A glimmer of light. David Cooper is going through some old records. There was a similar plan for a bypass a few years back which was abandoned and David wants to know why.'

'And how is the good Doctor Cooper?' asked Chris, and she knew he was smiling.

'The same. He's rather like an uncontrollable puppy dog, desperate to be loved but actually rather irritating. But I feel bad thinking that about him, he's doing a terrific job on this bypass and Mum really likes him and appreciates his efforts, so I'm being mean.'

'I have to admit I'm rather pleased you feel the way you do, though,' said Chris. 'I'm jealous that he's in and out of your house, involved with your family, helping you. I wish I could see more of you. I was hoping you'd have time to come back up here.'

Julie cradled the phone against her pillow. 'I wish you were here too.'

There was a brief silence. It was as if Chris was going to say something then changed his mind. Then he said, 'How's your job going?'

'It's fine. I'm keeping busy, which is good. Mum enjoyed Adelaide.'

'Well, enjoy the bright lights of Cairns. Will you keep me posted about Bette's story? Now we've been to Rose Mansion, I want to know all about her life in Penang.'

'Me too. Thanks for the call, it's been great hearing your voice,' said Julie. 'I miss you, Chris,' she added suddenly.

'I'm pleased about that. I miss you too. Sleep tight.'

Sleep didn't come easily despite the late hour. When she finally did fall asleep, Julie kept her phone under her pillow as if through it, she could reach out and touch Christopher.

12

As Julie's father had surmised, Bette was enthusiastic when Julie and Caroline arrived to spend the next day with her. She was settled comfortably in a chair and her eyes sparkled.

'Suzie has made us lunch and left it in the kitchen, so we won't be disturbed at all,' said Bette. 'Suddenly it seems important to me that you, my Australian family, my blood relations, know *my* story.'

1950

The white house glowed with a mellow warmth as yellow light spilled from its windows onto the verandah. Ted Oldham watched as his daughter Bette walked up the hill from the bus stop. She called out to him as she came through the garden.

'Now, how'd you know I was out here?' he said.

'The red glow from your cigarette,' she answered, knowing he'd been watching and waiting for her.

'Pleased to be back in Brisbane?' he asked as she came up the steps. 'You could stay here and get a job, you know. Why don't you do a secretarial course?'

'Mum's been in your ear again, has she? I don't think she wants me to go back to Sydney. Mmm, something smells good.' She followed her father down the hallway to the kitchen.

Winifred looked up from the flour-covered tabletop where she was rolling out pastry. 'Glad you got back safely, dear. Dinner won't be long. It's lovely cooking for more than just your father and me. I'm so glad that you've come back for a holiday. It would be even better if you could get a nice job here, at home.'

'Mother, we've been through this. Brisbane is such a backwater. I know that Sydney is not the centre of the universe, either, but there are more opportunities there than there are here.'

'Let her be, Win,' said her father. 'What's for tea?'

'Steak and kidney pie,' said Winifred flattening the circle of pastry with a firm bang of the rolling pin.

Bette wandered out of the kitchen. She knew her parents worried about her future. It had taken some time for her health to return after the years of deprivation in the prison camp, but she had been determined to catch up on life. She enjoyed Sydney, mixing with the bohemian artists, while she worked in several jobs. But Bette felt that she had lived for so long minute by minute, day by day, that she still couldn't bring herself to make long-term plans. Maybe Winifred was right and that she was indulging herself by doing only what interested her and gave her pleasure. Art seemed to fulfil her. She was content losing herself in the images she could paint, which replaced the ugly scenes that haunted her sleep.

'There's a letter for you from Margaret. I put it on your bed,' said Winifred. 'I do hope she's sent some photos of Philip and our dear little Caroline.'

Margaret and Philip had returned to Malaya three and a half years ago. Eventually Margaret had given birth to a daughter, whom they'd named Caroline, while Roland tried to rebuild Utopia after the devastation of the war. But clearly life was difficult. In her letters home, Margaret described things as being tiresome, nowhere near as glamorous as the pre-war years had been.

Bette skimmed through the opening niceties of the letter, before finding the real reason her sister had written:

And while I understand you're absorbed in whatever you do in Sydney, it would be very nice, and very helpful, if you could come up and visit us. Roland agrees with me and, indeed, is very keen to have you here again. Unfortunately, you must realise that things won't be as they were. Sadly many of the wonderful men like Gilbert are no longer around. As you know, the estate was a disaster at the end of the war and it's a big job for Roland to get things turned around, especially without his father, although some of the old staff are still here to help. I'd like the opportunity to get out and about a bit, and if you were here I'm sure Roland would be more amenable to the children and me taking a few little trips. I'd also like Caroline to meet someone from my family and it would be nice to have you here to brighten our dreary social calendar! I know Mother and Father are getting on a bit and, anyway, they're not travellers, so I don't expect them to visit me. You don't have a proper job to speak of, so it's easy for you to leave. It would please us both if you could come. I've enclosed some current photographs of Caroline for you.
Love, your sister, Margaret

There was little mention of Philip in the letter. Bette had kept in touch with her nephew and sent him illustrations of things she thought would interest him, as well as a good supply of Australian storybooks. His thank you notes for these gifts were short and revealed little about himself. Bette wondered how he was getting on. Children were resilient, she told herself, so she hoped that he had put all the horrors of the war behind him and was now a happy, normal boy.

Several days later another letter arrived from Malaya. Bette realised at once that it wasn't from her sister and hoped that nothing had happened to cause the invitation to be withdrawn. To her surprise, the note was from Roland.

. . . I'm pleased to hear you are doing well, Bette. I know Margaret has written inviting you to visit and I just wanted to add that it is also my sincere hope that you will come. I'm a little concerned that Margaret is rather restless and dispirited by our current situation. Young Caroline is a delight and Philip, well you wouldn't know him from the child who arrived back here after the war, he has grown so. I will always be in your debt for caring for him. I know you saved his life and I'm sure that your actions were at a cost to yourself. I think it would do us all good to have your company here for as long as you wish, and to that end, I insist on providing you an airline ticket. You'll find the country is going through troubled times at present, and life at Utopia is not as it was. Those carefree days have gone and what is yet to come remains unsure. However, putting these troubles aside, there is no doubt that we would very much enjoy your company. It would be a very welcome distraction for your sister, and I need not tell you how much your presence would mean to Philip. I look forward to welcoming you back to Utopia.
Warmly, Roland

Bette was slightly surprised, even a little concerned, at this gentle pressure from Roland and she wondered about Margaret. She had vaguely heard about the political problems in Malaya, and Margaret and Roland's letters had confirmed it. Still, there was no question in Bette's mind. This was a wonderful opportunity to return to Malaya and she was going to take it.

But her parents questioned her decision.

'You must have so many unhappy memories of that country, and there's a bit of trouble brewing there, according to the newspaper,' said her father.

'Of course, it would be lovely to visit with little Caroline,' said her mother. 'And I suspect Margaret might be a bit lonely, not having the social whirl she was used to before the war.'

'I'm sure there's still some social scene,' said Bette, fondly recalling her previous visit with the Elliotts. 'But I suspect Roland is less inclined to party and hunt since he's working so hard to build the plantation up again. And it does seem that he doesn't like Margaret going out and about by herself. But I'm a free agent these days. I'll have to go back to Sydney and resign from my job. I can always get another one when I get back.'

'A free spirit, indeed,' said her father. 'I just hope that Malaya doesn't disappoint you again.'

Because she was flying, Bette found herself packing very carefully. She put in her art materials, added her favourite book, and photographs of her parents and their garden to show Margaret, and she gave a lot of thought to presents for Philip and Caroline.

She was amazed that it took so short a time to fly from Sydney to Singapore and then on to KL, especially compared with her sea voyage ten years ago. Aeroplane travel was the future, the man seated next to Bette told her. Long sea voyages were now just for the young or the elderly with plenty of time on their hands, he added.

Bette was momentarily taken aback by the impact of her emotions when Margaret met her at the airport in Kuala Lumpur.

'Margaret, I can't believe that it's more than three years. You look wonderful. Motherhood obviously suits you.'

'You look very well yourself,' said Margaret. 'I guess having no responsibilities suits you.'

Bette was disappointed that Caroline and Philip weren't there as well, but she was touched when she realised that Margaret wanted to share a few days in KL, just the two of them.

Bette was also delighted to see Hamid again.

'Is everything well with you, Hamid, and your family?' asked Bette shaking his hand warmly.

The driver nodded, his eyes moist, clearly pleased to see Bette. Then he was once again his smiling, deferential self. For Bette, seeing him again in such normal circumstances, the wild nightmare drive to Singapore all those years ago seemed like a strange dream that had happened to someone else.

'It is very good to see you again, mem. You will see many changes. Tuan kechil is grown up now. He is learning many things at Utopia.'

Margaret sniffed at this comment. 'Following his father around, trying to boss the workers and messing in the rubber factory with the latex. And he keeps pestering Roland to take him flying. We have a plane now, an Auster. Roland flies around as much as he can because he says some of the roads aren't safe.'

'I suppose that now he's twelve, you'll be sending him to boarding school?' asked Bette.

'Roland put Philip's name down at his old school in England before he was born. I'd much rather he went to school in Australia, it's much closer. Going to school in England means he'll never really know or visit our parents in Brisbane. But Roland insists that that's the way it's to be and his mother backs him. I wish she'd keep out of it.'

Bette nodded. She realised at once that Margaret was not looking forward to losing her son and she thought this was quite understandable. 'I'm so looking forward to meeting little Caroline. I can't wait to see her.'

'She's running around and becoming very independent. You may recall how the servants indulge and spoil the children. Caroline will be princess of the estate while I'm away,' said Margaret.

'Yes, she'd probably have a better time there than getting bored shopping and dining out with us,' said Bette, who wasn't especially looking forward to doing these activities either.

Nevertheless, as she and Margaret spent the next few days travelling about the city, Bette found that being back in bustling Malaya was exhilarating. All signs of wartime austerity were gone. She would have liked to explore more of KL, but Margaret flatly refused to venture into Chinatown or the seedy areas, preferring to wander through the new department stores.

Margaret was pleased with her purchases and enjoyed her break away in the city. She was a lot more relaxed as Hamid drove the two of them to the Selangor Club for tea. 'We'll have to do this again, or we could take another trip. I was thinking of going to the Cameron Highlands or Fraser's Hill. I could take the children, Caroline's old enough to enjoy that,' said Margaret.

Hamid glanced at them in the rear-vision mirror of Roland's new Oldsmobile. 'Tuan says that it's not so safe to travel in the countryside, mem,' he advised. 'The communists are making trouble for everyone.'

'Those wretched Chinese communists. It's all a lot of fire in the belly and shouting, as far as I'm concerned,' said Margaret. 'They want the British out of Malaya, but these people aren't ready to rule themselves.'

'Be independent, like India? I don't know about that, Margaret. Surely the most important issue is for all the different races to live together in peaceful harmony and then decide what sort of an independent Malaya they want,' said Bette.

'Really, Bette, you've been so far removed from all of this. Speak to Roland before venturing an opinion, though frankly I think some of the planters are being rather alarmist. We've had no trouble on Utopia.' She nudged Bette and nodded her head towards Hamid. 'It's rumours and innuendo flying around that start the trouble.'

In spite of Margaret's comments about the communists, when they left KL, their car was escorted by two special constables armed with submachine guns. Margaret admitted to Bette that Roland would not allow her to travel to KL and back without such an escort.

As they approached Utopia, Bette began to recognise the once familiar countryside. As soon as the car slid under the portico, two people appeared at the front door. Bette gasped as she realised that one of them was Philip. She saw he was now a young man, not yet as tall as his father, who looked, Bette thought, rather careworn. Hamid opened Bette's door and she leapt out of the car and raced to the steps as Roland came down to embrace her.

'Welcome, welcome. Wonderful to see you again, Bette. Hello, darling,' he said, turning to Margaret as she stepped from the car.

Bette stood at the bottom of the four steps staring up at Philip. They looked at each other curiously. Then slowly a smile broke out on Philip's face and in one leap he was down the steps, standing before her.

Bette couldn't speak. The physical memory of the thin body she'd held in her arms night after night in the camp was imprinted on her mind and on her body, but this strong, firm frame was almost unrecognisable. As was his voice, which had lost its high, childish tone.

'Bet-Bet.'

She laughed and hugged him. 'I haven't been called that in a long time. You look wonderful. I can't believe how tall you are.'

'Goodness, Bette, remember how we hated people saying that to us when we were young?' Margaret leaned towards Philip, offering her cheek to be kissed. 'Where's Caroline?'

'Asleep,' said Philip taking Bette's arm. 'Can I show Bette to her room?'

'Good idea, take Bette's small bag. Ho and Hamid can bring in the rest,' said Roland.

'Ho is still here! That's wonderful, he must be very old,' said Bette. 'And Ah Kit? That was the name of your houseboy when you were in the other house, wasn't it?'

'He no longer works for me,' said Roland.

Philip took Bette's small carry bag. She wanted to say that she was travelling with more luggage than the last time the two of them had travelled together, but she wasn't sure how a flippant remark about the past would be received.

'I'll go and check on Caroline,' said Margaret.

'I can't wait to see her,' said Bette, following Philip up the stairs.

'She's a bundle of energy. A bit of a tomboy. Mother put you in this room. It has a nice view.' He put her bag down.

'I'm so pleased to see you looking . . . so well,' said Bette.

'You look different too. I think you're very pretty,' said Philip shyly. He paused awkwardly. 'Thank you for the letters, the books and pictures.'

'I'm glad you liked them.'

'Yes. I wrote to you,' he said.

'Thank you. I enjoyed receiving your notes. I'm hoping to do some more drawings while I'm here,' said Bette. As they left the bedroom, Bette asked, 'Are you looking forward to boarding school?'

'Yes, lots. All my friends have been going for years. I can't wait to play cricket and rugby with them. I'm starting next term.'

Bette didn't pursue the subject. She had thought that perhaps Philip would not want to go to school so far away from home but clearly he was eager to. 'So what do you do with yourself here, when you're not studying?'

'I'm learning the plantation business. I like to watch the tappers working, but it's most fun to mess around where the latex is drying. Those sheets remind me of spooky ghosts.' He grinned. 'And we've got a fast boat down at the river so I drive that.'

'You'll have to take me out in it,' said Bette.

Margaret appeared in the hallway. 'He's not supposed to take that boat out alone.'

'Is the pagar still there? Maybe we could go on a picnic,' suggested Bette.

'Father says it might not be safe there,' said Philip.

'Really?' asked Bette. 'Why not?'

'The communists,' said Margaret.

'They're guerillas in the jungle,' said Philip.

'We seem to be quite safe at Utopia. But just the same Roland says we mustn't go anywhere unsupervised. And that definitely means you, young man. Now please go and tell Ho to bring the tea outside onto the verandah, and ask Ah Min to bring Caroline out when she wakes up.'

'Tea sounds lovely,' said Bette. 'It's wonderful some of the staff are still here – Ho, Ah Min, Philip's old amah, Hamid. What happened to Ah Kit?'

'According to Roland, he fought with the communists during the war. Hard to believe that he would do something like that, after living here at Utopia and everything we did for him,' snapped Margaret. 'Talk about ingratitude!'

With that the subject was dismissed, and at that moment their attention was diverted to a small blonde rocket propelling herself across the verandah to stand next to her mother. The little girl chewed her finger and looked at Bette.

'Caroline, this is your Aunt Bette. Now what do you do? Take that finger out of your mouth. Come on, curtsy.' Caroline bent one of her knees, giving a brief bob. 'Where's your skirt, hold out your skirt,' directed Margaret.

'Oh, that's all right, you did very well,' said Bette. 'What a clever little girl you are.'

'Yes, butter wouldn't melt in her mouth, but she can be an imp. She has to be watched all the time,' said Margaret smoothing the little girl's blonde curls. 'Ah Min has a full-time job chasing after her. Philip simply won't spend time entertaining her.'

'I don't imagine Philip has much in common with her. Ten years is a pretty big age gap, but they will get closer when they're older,' said Bette.

'Boys change once they go away to school,' said Margaret.

'They have to grow up, Margaret. And Philip seems to love the plantation. I'm sure he'll come back and work with Roland,' said Bette.

'I don't know how long rubber is going to be profitable. Times are changing. Some plantations are trying other crops. Roland was experimenting with palm oil before the war. But the workers don't seem as dedicated as they were in Eugene's day. There are always strikes somewhere. I've heard that some of their wage demands are quite outrageous. They'll send the plantations broke if they get them. It's all very destabilising.'

'Yes, war has a way of changing things,' said Bette quietly.

'I might have been out of the fighting, but it wasn't easy in Australia, either,' said Margaret testily.

Suddenly Caroline wanted attention and Ho brought in the cake and tea, and the war was not mentioned again.

A few days later a group of Roland's old friends, mainly planters, were relaxing on the verandah, stengahs in hand, and the discussion of the current political situation resurfaced. Bette was shocked to see that each guest arrived with a Malay special constable, and stacked his gun in a corner, before shaking hands with Roland. She sat in the shade by the steps watching Caroline play and listened with interest to their conversation.

'Don't know why they're calling this communist insurgency an Emergency. It's looking like a bloody war to me,' grumbled an old friend of Eugene's.

'Because,' explained Roland patiently, 'our losses won't be covered by Lloyd's if it's declared to be a war. And you wouldn't like that.'

'Insurgency, Emergency, it's still a bloody anti-British war,' replied the old planter. ''Cause we didn't think much about it two years ago, when Chin Peng's lot murdered those plantation managers in Perak. Nasty business. But now it's really getting out of hand. These terrorists tell the workers to go on strike, or they'll attack their villages, so we have trouble with our labour, as well.'

'There aren't the jobs there used to be, and food is

expensive so that's been part of the problem,' said Roland. 'But the administration is trying to get Malaya's economy on track.'

'It's all a load of rubbish this propaganda that the commies are putting about. High wages and independence for everyone, what rot,' said the planter. 'We've got floodlights, dogs and guns at the ready on our estate, so just let them try something.'

'I'd prefer it if it was an out-and-out fight,' said another, younger man. 'These terrorists have hit-and-run raids out of the jungle, sneaking around the villages, blackmailing the locals into giving them food and help. It's all very underhanded and difficult to control.'

'It's highly unstable and I for one won't venture too far afield without these security force fellows in tow,' declared another of Roland's neighbours, pointing to the Malay special constables sitting below the verandah. 'I think the army and the police chaps are doing a fine job.'

'They've re-formed the special air service I worked with in India during the war,' said Roland. 'Specialised reconnaissance, counterinsurgency, intelligence, that sort of thing, taking the fight to the communists in the jungle.'

'You thinking of joining them, Roland?'

'No, I have enough to do protecting my family and the plantation. Mind you, I worked with some of those communists during the war and there is no doubt that they are determined to make Malaya a communist country.'

'Let's hope they put a lid on it all quick smart. I'm tired of travelling in convoys, always carrying a gun, and being careful to alter my travel route every day I go out on to the estate. And as for having a curfew! Having to be at home between seven pm and six am means that you can't go anywhere much at all. Good thing I could get here for the afternoon, Roland. And, you know, there can't be more than eight to ten thousand of the commie blighters out there, just making our lives a misery,' said another neighbour.

'That's quite true. There aren't so many, so we should get things sorted out fairly quickly,' said Roland. 'Righto, who's for a top up before you have to leave? Ho! Another round.'

Now that Bette had spent a little more time exploring the plantation with Philip, she noticed the changes and the subtle shift in the workers' demeanour and attitude. Ah Min, Caroline's amah, whispered to Bette that things were not good outside the plantation. She said that there was a lot of suspicion in the kampong about who was or wasn't helping the communists and there were lots of stories of atrocities and torture. Ah Min assured Bette that most of the staff on the estate were against the communists and very afraid of them.

'I only feel safe here. I do not want any more war. I have had enough of war. We all suffered badly at the hands of the Japanese. When the Japanese lived here, the workers had to fling themselves face down on the roads whenever a Japanese drove past. I do not want this to happen again.'

'I see,' replied Bette. 'It must be hard for everyone, recovering from the war, and now having to face this communist insurgency.'

That evening, Bette repeated what Ah Min had said to Roland.

'Yes, it is a difficult situation, as you must realise by now. The government is trying a new tactic to protect the vulnerable from being intimidated, while at the same time preventing the communists from getting food supplies. People are being moved from the sparsely settled rural areas close to the jungle, where they can't be protected from the communist guerillas, into settlements.

New Villages, they call them. The communists say that they are concentration camps and I suppose they look like them with their barbed-wire fences, big lights and guards. But they keep people safe. The government also provides services, like health clinics and schools, so that the people want to stay in these villages.'

'Is it working ?' asked Bette.

'It's a very slow process, but it is having some success.'

'Here, at Utopia, you wouldn't know all this was going on,' said Bette.

'We're quite safe, as I've told you, and the British and the Malayan auxiliary patrols are everywhere,' said Margaret. 'I think we should take that trip up to Fraser's Hill, Roland. I'd like to see the boarding school there again. We have to think of Caroline's future. We could meet some of our friends up there, too. Have a bit of laugh, what do you think?'

Bette could see that Roland wasn't particularly enthusiastic about the idea, but Margaret continued to make plans. Eventually, Roland agreed that if they could organise an escort, they could go.

'I've heard that there's a Malayan auxiliary police unit up there and a company of Gurkhas. We'll probably be invited to a dining-in night and that will mean a white monkey jacket,' he said as a way of agreeing to the trip.

'Oh, wonderful, we can dress up,' said Margaret.

But just before they were due to leave for Fraser's Hill, a machine in the latex factory broke down and Roland told Margaret that he would have to organise a spare part for it. This would mean that the trip would have to be postponed. Margaret was furious and flatly refused to abandon her plans as several other families had agreed to join them for a long weekend of social activities which would be a welcome respite from the suffocating strictures of the Emergency.

'All right, Margaret. You take Bette and the children with Hamid and drive up. The escort has already been arranged but I'll notify the garrison at the Gap that you're coming. I'll join you as soon as I can.'

Margaret smiled at Bette. 'There. We'll be looked after and I'll get to show you the Hill. Of course, we're sorry you won't be with us, Roland, but do the best you can to get up there.'

Philip sat in the front of the new Oldsmobile with Hamid, while Bette sat in the middle of the back seat with Margaret and Caroline on either side of her. They were on the last stage of the journey, Caroline was bored and Philip was pale and quiet. When they reached the Gap rest house, they all piled out of the car to join the other travellers waiting for the boom gate that would change the flow of traffic from down the hill to up. Two army tanks would travel with the convoy through the mountain pass and up the final climb to Fraser's Hill. While they were waiting they sat down to tea and sandwiches. Caroline raced around expending energy and Margaret caught up with several of her friends.

Bette glanced at Philip. 'You're very quiet, are you all right?'

'I get car sick. I hate the winding road.'

'You'll be fine,' said Bette. 'Keep looking straight ahead. Your mother says that we're on the last leg now.'

When the boom gate was finally raised, the sisters found that they were the last in the line of vehicles on the narrow one-way road to the peak. One of the tanks brought up the rear.

Hamid drove carefully and slowly, as the road twisted and turned. But even Hamid's careful driving became too much for Philip and he suddenly gulped and called to Hamid to pull over.

'I'm going to be sick!'

'We can't stop here. Just wait a few minutes,' said Margaret.

'The tank is behind us, Margaret. We'll have to let Philip out, or he'll be sick in the car.

Hamid braked, stopping in the middle of the road and Philip scrambled out onto the side of the road, which dropped down into a sheer ravine. He stood there retching, coughing and spluttering. Bette got out and stood beside him as Caroline clambered out of the car too. Margaret took a handkerchief from her handbag to wipe Philip's face. The heavy tank came up behind them and a soldier leaned out.

'You can't stop here. It's too dangerous. Please get back in the car.'

'We have a sick child. We'll only be a few minutes,' called Margaret.

'We have to stay together in the convoy,' said the soldier.

'You just go around us and we'll catch up as soon as we can. Hamid, move the car, please. Caroline, come here.'

'Yes, mem. I will go ahead, where the road is wider, and I can pull over to let them past and then I will come down here to you. Just a few moments.' Hamid then drove around the hairpin bend just ahead of where they stood.

The women heard the tank pick up speed as it overtook Hamid and then they saw the Oldsmobile inch back around the corner and reverse down the road towards them.

'Do you feel better?' Bette asked Philip.

'For goodness' sake let's get back in the car and catch up to the others,' said Margaret.

Hamid stopped the car a little ahead of them. As Caroline ran ahead of the others, Hamid got out to open the doors in readiness, but something made him glance up to the thickly forested hillside. A different shade of green and a glint of metal suddenly sent him spinning around and he shouted as he ran towards the little girl who was racing towards the car.

'Get down, mem!' Hamid flung himself at Caroline, pinning her to the ground while bullets screamed around them.

Margaret heard the whine of bullets, she saw Hamid cover her daughter and, as she turned, she saw her son rush not to her but to Bette, tackling her sister, wrapping his arms about her, and covering Bette's body with his own as they fell to the ground. Margaret started to run, stumbled, but ran on – despite the continuing gunfire – to where Hamid lay, his blood spilling onto the road.

'Caroline!' she screamed. She pushed Hamid's limp and bleeding body to one side and was dimly aware that there was now more heavy gunfire, this time coming from the direction of the hairpin bend.

Caroline was covered in Hamid's blood.

'Get into the car, quickly. Lie on the floor,' said Bette, pushing Caroline and Margaret towards the car. Staying low, Philip opened a door and they all scrambled into the back seat and lay flat. The firing from the hillside continued.

Suddenly a spray of bullets hit the car, shattering a window and pinging into the metal. There was a small explosion and then all was silent. Caroline whimpered but they still didn't move. More gunshots were fired and then they heard running footsteps.

'Are you all right? You, in the car, it's all right.'

At the sound of the British soldiers, they all began to move. Margaret sat up and Philip lifted himself from Bette and glanced at his mother. Then he jumped from the car and ran to where the tank had stopped. One of the soldiers was standing over Hamid's body. The other soldier lowered his machine gun and looked at the now deserted hillside.

'They've gone,' he said.

'Is Hamid dead?'

'If you mean your driver, yes, I'm afraid so, son. Is anyone else hurt?'

'I don't think so. My sister is covered in blood but I think it's Hamid's. He saved her life,' said Philip tearfully.

'You have to get out of here. Can anyone drive?'

'I can,' said Margaret, holding Caroline and clearly shaken and distressed.

'So can I,' said Bette. She looked at the bloodied body of Roland's driver and shook her head. 'Poor Hamid.'

At this Philip burst into tears, he was once again just a frightened boy. He reached for Bette who put her arms around him, and held him close. 'It's all right, Philip. It's over. We're all right.'

'We'll have to put the body of your driver in the boot, ma'am. If you're all right to drive, follow us.'

Bette smoothed Philip's hair. 'Go and help your mother.'

Bette spoke briefly to the soldier and then returned to the car and got in behind the wheel. Philip sat beside her while Margaret, in the back, held Caroline who had stopped crying and was now asking where Hamid was.

No one answered her as Bette cautiously manoeuvred the big, bullet-riddled car around the tight bends, following the tank to the safety of the holiday township at Fraser's Hill.

They were all deeply distressed. Margaret was quickly surrounded by her sympathetic friends and arrangements were made for them to return to Utopia straight away.

*

390

When they arrived home, Margaret was still extremely upset. Roland kissed his wife, embraced Bette, and hugged Philip and Caroline.

'Thank you, Bette. That couldn't have been an easy drive for you to manage from Fraser's Hill,' said Roland as the children went to find Ah Min. 'I've broken the news to Hamid's family. It's been a terrible shock for them.'

'It must be. Philip kept me company and wanted to talk about Hamid and all the memories he had of him.' She looked at Margaret. 'I'll never forget the time he drove us to Singapore.' Seeing her sister's set and angry face, she said no more about Hamid. 'I'm glad that Caroline's all right.'

'She's still too little to articulate her feelings. Unlike Philip,' snapped Margaret. 'All those years you had with my son. All those years. Now it seems you are still trying to come between us.'

'Now, dear,' began Roland, looking distressed.

'Don't be naïve, Roland. Philip had a choice and he chose to save Bette rather than his mother,' cried Margaret.

'Margaret! What do you mean? Philip . . .' Bette wanted to remind Margaret how brave Philip had been on the Fraser's Hill road, but she realised that Margaret didn't want to hear about that. 'He's a young man now. I was just closer to him . . .'

'Than I was because I wasn't there! That's what you're trying to say. It wasn't my fault that you missed the damn boat!'

'I didn't mean that. I was just saying that on the mountain road, Philip was closer to me than he was to you, so that's why he tried to protect me. Anyway, you were rushing to Caroline,' Bette said, trying to calm Margaret who was now looking wild-eyed.

'Bette, I've watched you ever since you came and you've done nothing but try to take my son away from me,' screamed Margaret.

'Margaret! That's enough,' bellowed Roland.

'That's not true! I was not trying to steal your son. I did all I could to look after him – for your sake!' cried Bette, feeling wounded that Margaret could harbour such ill feeling and jealousy. But no accusations could alter the fact that Bette and Philip did share a special bond.

'Margaret, Philip's feelings towards me are different from how he feels about you. He loves you and needs you, too. He's your son, for God's sake! I was always so glad you weren't the one in the camp . . .'

'You had him to yourself all those years. You put ideas into his head,' shouted Margaret. 'It should have been me with him.'

'If it had been you, how do you know if both of you would have survived?' asked Bette heatedly.

'I insist that this argument stops, immediately,' said Roland. 'Bette, I must apologise for my wife's uncalled-for remarks.'

At this Margaret turned on her heel and hurried from the room, slamming the door.

'There's no need to apologise, Roland,' said Bette miserably. 'I shouldn't have come. I should have realised that Margaret still has a lot of anger and a lot of guilt about what happened in Singapore. In a way that's also true for me. I lost the man I thought I would marry and my life was on hold for three and a half years. Every day I prayed we'd survive the POW camp so I could bring Philip home to his parents.' Tears sprang to Bette's eyes. 'I thought Margaret would love me for doing that.'

Roland sighed. 'Margaret is a very complicated woman.'

'I'm sorry I've caused such . . . distress. I had no idea how deeply she's been affected by what happened.'

'Yes. I knew there was something troubling her, and I hoped your visit would help.'

'I'm so sorry my being here is making things worse.'

'Well, it's certainly brought matters to a head,' said Roland ruefully. 'But at least I know now what the cause of her unhappiness is. She feels very guilty for having been separated from Philip. She's full of remorse, although it obviously wasn't her fault. Now she doesn't want him to go away to boarding school either. I don't believe that her attitude is doing him any favours, but it seems that she's afraid to let him out of her sight.'

'That's not going to bring him closer,' said Bette sadly. 'I think the best thing is for me to leave. I just want to make sure Philip understands why I'm going and the reasons I think that it's best if I don't make any contact with him again, at least until things improve with Margaret. Maybe if I stay right out of the picture, relations between the two of them might get better.'

'I'd hate to see you leave, Bette. I know how fond you are of Philip and I'd hoped you'd be able to enjoy staying with us. I'm not sure that your leaving will improve things for Margaret, because I know that the current situation with the communist terrorists, the curfews and the constant violence is not helping matters either, but I can't take Margaret away from here because this place is our future, and our children's.'

'It's not your fault, Roland. You've been wonderful. Perhaps I'll travel a little, go where it's safe. I'm not ready to go home just yet.'

'Then let me help you. Go to KL for awhile, or to Penang. It's far safer there than in the countryside. We have good friends there. I'm sure you'll remember some of them and they would enjoy your company. Remember the good times we had there when you first visited? Or you could go to Malacca, it's such an interesting old place. Use that artist's eye of yours, see new things. Meet new people.'

'Yes,' she said. 'I think that would be for the best. I

hope Philip will understand the situation better and the reasons why I've decided to leave when he gets older.'

'I'm sure that he will,' said Roland firmly.

'I'd like to speak to him and explain about this change of plan. I don't want him to know about the problems between his mother and me.'

'You're a very loyal and kind person, Bette. I'll give you our friends' addresses in Penang and send them a note asking them to look after you.'

Before she left, Bette took Philip aside and spoke to him quietly.

'Philip, I'm leaving early in the morning. I'm going to travel a bit and see some of your parents' friends. Some of them I know from my first visit. I think that my being here has brought back memories of a painful time for your mother.' Bette looked at Philip and smiled. 'I know it was tough and horrible and awful at times for us in that POW camp, but I also remember laughter, friends and a lot of love and caring, and we had each other. Your mother was quite alone.'

Philip nodded, hardly trusting himself to speak but managed to say, 'I still have Lumpy. My elephant.'

Bette took his hand, the tall boy on the brink of adolescence suddenly looking like the insecure little chap she'd loved through those terrible war years.

'I'll be going to England, soon, to boarding school.'

Bette nodded. 'Yes. But, Philip, your mother needs you now. Before you leave, let her know that you love her. She will miss you so much while you're away. I know that we'll always have a special tie between us, but we have to get on with our own lives now.'

'She'll have Caroline,' said Philip pragmatically.

'Yes. And your father.' She dropped his hand. 'Be generous, big-hearted and work hard. As I know you will. And think of me sometimes.'

'I'll never forget you, Bet-Bet.' He looked stricken, tears filling his eyes.

'I know I'll always be proud of you, Philip. Give Lumpy a cuddle from me.' Bette smiled and turned away, relinquishing the boy she loved so deeply.

As the driver turned the car into the laneway outside the garden of the big house, Bette glanced up at the solid colonial home Eugene had built so many years ago, and knew that behind a curtain a young boy was watching her leave.

Although Roland had suggested that the driver take her all the way to Penang, Bette insisted on taking the train, even though it was very slow. She loved the jungle-clad hills, the stretches of plantations, the villages and rivers as they wound through the countryside.

Bette was happy to be in a city. The threat of insurgents and attacks on remote estates seemed far away. She indulged herself, wandering through the places she'd missed on her previous visit. She found that in spite of the circumstances, she enjoyed travelling and visiting Roland's friends, many of whom remembered her from her previous visit. They were all delighted to entertain the pretty, charming woman in their happy-go-lucky social circle.

But behind the laughter, the drinking, the dancing and the sports, there was always a shadow. All had been affected in one way or another by the war and now they had to live with the uncertainty of the Emergency and the push for independence. Sometimes it seemed to Bette that there was a tinge of desperation to their gaiety. But Bette thanked them for their hospitality and the opportunity they provided for her to have a bit of adventure and the chance to sketch and absorb something of the rich culture of this interesting country. And she told them that she was, of course, in regular contact with Roland and Margaret who continued to make so many wonderful introductions for her. This wasn't quite the truth, for Bette sent the occasional note to Roland only. Margaret had made it very clear that what Bette did and where she went were of no interest to her at all.

Being on her own, Bette felt a great sense of freedom and fun. She booked herself into the E&O Hotel where there was no Margaret frowning at her, no parents to worry about and no demands on her in any way. It was a heady time. There were many single men and a dearth of attractive, unattached women, so Bette was whirled from dances to dinners. There were social sporting events, picnics, house parties and tour trips. She accepted an invitation from some friends of Roland's, Lori and Andrew Pike, to stay in their summer house on Penang Hill. Other friends of Roland's, Nancy and Beau Gideon, asked her to join them for a weekend party at their beach house at Batu Ferringhi.

She travelled to the Pikes' summer house on the pretty funicular railway, with its two carriages that stopped at tiny stations on the way up Penang Hill. Bette felt the temperature cooling and the humidity dissolve as the train gained altitude. At the little viaduct station she was met by Andrew with his driver but no car.

'Can you carry your small bag? Lim will take the rest. The house is a bit of a hike from the station,' Andrew told her. 'The other guests are already there.'

In single file, they followed a jungle path that ended at some rough steps leading to a large bungalow on the edge of a cliff. It had commanding views.

'Bette, we've given you the sunrise room, so you'll see the morning light first,' said Lorraine as she came over to greet her guest. 'The housegirls will unpack your things. After that walk from the station you'll need refreshments,

I expect. Come along, we'll all meet on the lawn for tea. I think you already know some of our other friends, Harold Mitchum and Tony Tsang. They are old friends of Roland and Margaret.'

'Yes, I did meet Tony Tsang and his wife, years ago.'

'Did Roland and Margaret tell you that Mai Ling was killed in the war?'

'No, they didn't. How very sad. She was tall and very beautiful. I do remember her,' said Bette. 'He must miss her.'

'I'm sure he does. She was caught in the street during a bombing raid. Anyway, Tony has a big family, four children, and what seems to be lots of other relatives. We thought he needed a bit of time away from business and his family, so we asked him up,' said Lorraine. 'See you downstairs on the lawn when you're ready.'

Before joining the others for tea, Bette decided to walk around the grounds. She discovered a flourishing kitchen garden and some well-tended fruit trees, and was entranced by the view of the valley below. Terraced slopes were cut into the hillside, the gardens on them beautifully laid out.

'There are a lot of secret paths down there. They make lovely walks,' said a friendly voice behind her. 'I'm Tony Tsang. I believe we met at the races before the war. You were with the Elliotts.'

Bette turned and was immediately struck by how exotically handsome he was. She recalled Roland telling her about his old university friend. She returned his smile. 'That's right, we did.' She hesitated. 'I'm sorry to hear about your wife.'

'Yes. But that was a long time ago now. The war was hard on many of us. But then you'd know about that,' he said. 'I heard you were interned in a POW camp. Roland was full of praise for the way you looked after their son.'

'It wasn't easy. Even though it was years ago, it's not something that fades from one's memory.'

Tony looked away and said slowly, 'I know what you mean. I find it difficult to be in the street where . . . the bomb fell. It was as if Mai Ling was an exquisite porcelain vase that just . . . shattered into fragments.'

Bette nodded. 'My friend Gilbert Mason died, too, so horribly, trying to save Philip and me. I always thought I'd marry Gilbert, if he asked me. There just seemed to be an understanding between us without our saying anything.' In a rush she blurted the words she'd never said before, 'I wish I'd told him I loved him.'

'I remember Gilbert. I'm sure he would have known how you felt. You just do, you just know . . .'

Bette nodded, tears in her eyes. 'He touched my hand before he was shot and I felt everything in that moment, and that it was not to be.'

Tony took her hand and held it as they stood gazing across the valley.

'I can't believe I said that. I've never told anyone that before. I hardly let myself think about it,' said Bette finally.

'I think we have a lot in common,' said Tony.

After a few moments, Bette withdrew her hand and turned back to the garden. She took a breath, trying to steady herself and regain a sense of normalcy. 'I try to think about the good times, the times I shared with Gil.'

'Yes, those years before the war were a lot of fun. I doubt such carefree times will return soon. I remember you that day at the races, very well,' he added.

'I know this decade will be different. There's certainly a lot of talk of change,' said Bette as they began to stroll through the gardens.

'So it seems. What plans do you have for the 1950s?' he asked with a quizzical smile.

Bette shrugged. 'I don't really have any plans. I've

been studying art and working in Sydney, and then Margaret and Roland asked me to come and stay. I was glad to come back to Malaya. Roland is devoted to Utopia and has a big job to re-establish the plantation after the Japanese occupation.'

'Yes, I can imagine. I know a lot of planters are turning to new crops. I think Roland experimented with palm oil before the war, didn't he? And there is the problem with the communists and the push to independence,' Tony said.

'The communists? Do you really think the British would be forced out?' asked Bette.

'The insurgents are a tiny minority. I'm sure when and if independence comes, it will be through co-operation and agreement with Britain. We need each other. But in the meantime, areas of the country are quite unstable,' said Tony and he glanced at her. 'It is fortunate that my business can spare me for a bit so that I could accept this invitation. I'm glad I did.'

'I remember Roland and Eugene telling me something about your business, but apart from saying that you are an excellent businessman, I'm afraid I don't recall anything else.'

Tony smiled. 'After my father died I diversified, but at the end of the war it was difficult to export to our traditional markets – Siam, Burma and Sumatra. But being Chinese I was able to overcome these problems through the kongsi.'

'I'm sorry,' said Bette. 'What are kongsi?'

'When the original Chinese immigrants came to Penang they formed associations, or clans, and built clan houses. These were like clubs, in a way, where newcomers could stay, be introduced to important people, given employment and helped to settle into their new city, so they became places to honour the achievements of the family clan. Some of the kongsi are very elaborate. Would you like to visit one?' he asked.

'I'd love to, it sounds fascinating. Is there a Tsang kongsi?'

He smiled. 'Yes. My family has been here for many generations. My father's ancestors fled persecution from the Manchus and came here not long after Penang was settled.'

'You have a very colourful family story, Tony. Mine seems very bland in comparison.'

'I think that all families are interesting. They are made up of individuals and although the family might present a united front to the world, scratch the surface and you'll find the dominant and gentle, the weak and strong, and people with different talents, tastes and desires,' he said.

'Yes, that's for sure,' said Bette, laughing. 'That sounds just like my family.'

They reached the front lawn where people were gathering for the lavish tea and cakes set out on rattan tables covered with embroidered cloths.

Tony held out a chair for Bette and she sat down as Lorraine announced plans for croquet and tennis for those who were interested.

'Will you be playing?' Tony asked her.

Bette shook her head. 'No, I'd like to explore a little. This is such a pretty and unusual setting, and cool enough to go hiking.'

'Don't get lost, Bette. Stay on the paths,' advised Andrew.

'I'd be happy to go with you,' said Tony. 'I know the area, my family have a bungalow up here, although I don't seem to have much time to use it.'

'Thank you, but I don't want to take you away from a game,' said Bette.

'Nonsense, a good walk will do me good. And Andrew is right, you can get lost quite easily in the hill country,' said Tony. 'Besides I think I'll enjoy your company more than I would those frenetic tennis players.'

'You always were quick to corner the prettiest girl at the party,' Andrew said cheerfully.

In sensible shoes, Bette set off with Tony. In no time at all they were deep in the thick forest.

'Is this jungle? These trees remind me of what I imagine an old English forest to be like,' said Bette.

Tony stopped and gazed up at the trees. 'You're right. Not all of these trees are native. Some would have been planted here when the first Europeans came – to remind them of home, I expect. You'll find more original jungle as we go in further.'

'Are these the secret paths where you brought your girlfriends?' teased Bette.

Tony laughed. 'No, I was too shy. When I was young we used to come and stay here in the hot months and the caretaker's son, a Malay boy, showed me all his favourite places.'

The path soon narrowed, so Tony took the lead. They didn't talk. Occasionally Tony held back an overhanging branch, or pointed out obstacles like roots and rocks that might trip Bette up, especially as she was constantly craning her neck upwards, looking for monkeys, butterflies, birds, and unfamiliar plants and flowers.

'Look at those strange plants,' she said.

'Pitcher plants.' Tony took one of the long, hollow, tubular flowers from the vine. 'See how they hold water. Monkeys have been seen drinking water from them, so they're sometimes called monkey cups. See, this one is half full.' He tipped it up and sipped the water. 'Mmm, sweet. Try some. Actually this flower looks a bit like a saxophone. Do you like dancing?'

Bette nodded, suddenly aware of their closeness as he held the strange plant to her lips to drink the raindrops. She hadn't been so affected by the physicality of an attractive man for a long time.

'Good. I'd like to take you dancing. I think I need to put a little fun and laughter back into my life. I haven't felt inclined to . . . until now. Would you help me out?' His dark eyes were warm, a hint of a mischievous smile in their depths.

'I'd like that. Thank you,' said Bette.

They stopped by a small pool where water from the peak trickled down the hillside.

'This trickle is a torrent when the rains come,' said Tony. He held out his hand and helped her across. 'We can circle around and come out above the bungalow.'

They continued to meander along the hidden pathways. Once back on the wider, smoother path Tony took her hand again, and Bette was very aware of the smoothness of his skin and the touch of his fingertips.

While it appeared to their hosts, and other guests, that Tony and Bette had an easy friendship, both of them realised that there was a powerful attraction between them. Neither acknowledged this chemistry, but in moments of physical closeness, the brush of an arm, sitting together, both felt as if electricity had crackled between them.

Bette and Tony seemed to like the same things. They were the ones who were up very early sitting on the terrace in the crisp morning air to watch the day begin, sipping hot, sweet coffee. When the group gathered on the terrace after dinner for nightcaps to watch the lights of George Town twinkling below them, Tony and Bette sat side by side, talking softly, looking more at each other than the view.

Tony cheerfully flirted with her, sometimes teasing her to make her laugh. Although he was at least ten years older than she was, Bette found him an interesting combination of youthful exuberance and energy, yet with the wisdom and thoughtfulness of a mature man.

At breakfast one morning, Andrew asked Bette, 'So what are you two planning for these last days? Anything you'd like us to arrange?'

Bette liked the way he assumed that she and Tony would spend their remaining time together. 'Andrew, you've been so hospitable, I can't thank you enough. It's been great.'

'You're charming company,' said Andrew. 'I do hope we see more of you while you're here in Penang, Bette.'

'Me too,' said Tony. 'Tell me where you'd really like to go, what you'd like to see while you're here. I was planning to go back to Penang tomorrow but apparently we're all expected at Batu Ferringhi, so I've changed my plans.' He smiled at Bette.

'We've all been invited,' said Andrew.

'The Gideons' beach house? I'm looking forward to a swim in the sea,' said Bette.

'You might not find it ideal for swimming. But there are some nice spots. Personally I prefer swimming off the islands,' said Tony. He gave Bette a smile. 'I now feel I have a special project.'

'A project?' she asked.

'Yes. You. I'm going to show you some of my favourite places. And I'm going to enjoy every minute of it,' said Tony firmly.

Bette was surprised that the Gideons referred to their home as a beach house. It looked more like an English stately home with its gothic windows, a coat of arms above the entrance and stone lions standing on either side of the terrace that overlooked the coastline.

The Gideons' house party was really enjoyable, made more so for Bette because of Tony's company. They took long walks along the beach, sat by the pool, or just talked at length. Once Tony asked Bette when was she returning to Australia.

'I'm not sure. I haven't made a lot of plans and I left everything open ended.'

'Bette, when we go back to Penang I'd like you to visit my family home sometime, and meet my children. Would you come?'

Bette looked into his eyes and nodded. Tony leaned towards her as Bette's eyes closed, waiting for the touch of his lips on hers. A fuse had been ignited and Bette had no idea whether it would surge brightly and explode or simply fizzle out, but there was no stopping the consequences, nor did she want to do so.

By the time Tony drove Bette back to Penang and to the E&O Hotel at the end of the short holiday, there was an unspoken bond between them. The passion between them was restrained. Bette didn't like to think too far ahead to the time when she'd be leaving Malaya. Now was the time to enjoy herself, not to wonder what her future held.

Tony courted Bette assiduously. He arrived at her door at the hotel with gifts, sweets and flowers. He took her to lavish restaurants and clubs. When she said that she had no suitable clothes for such occasions, he insisted on buying her a beautiful gown to wear dancing. He drove her around the city in his Allard K2 sports car. She'd never ridden in a convertible before and she loved the red two-seater. Tony assured her that she could drive it any time she wished. Bette could never remember a more glorious time. He showed her the backstreets, the temples and the markets, and, wherever they went, Tony introduced her to his friends.

After a week he announced, 'You've met my friends, now I'd like you to meet my family. My mother-in-law has invited you to tea, with the children.'

Even after the Gideons' stately beach house at Batu

Ferringhi, Bette was unprepared for the grandeur of the Tsang's large rose-hued mansion, set back from a wide boulevard amid formal gardens. Tony possessively took her arm as they approached the entrance and entered the elaborately carved front doors with coloured glass lanterns that hung on either side. Bette was aware of shadowy figures in the cool dark rooms and the sweet smell of incense. She heard children's laughter as Tony guided her into a large open-air courtyard surrounded by stone walls, where water splayed from a fountain as though it was dancing in the sunlight.

Two children came running towards them, abandoning their amah in her black trousers and starched white jacket. Everyone was smiling. The younger child, a girl of about ten, flung herself into her father's arms, the other, a young boy about Philip's age, smiled at Bette as Tony introduced her to them.

'This young man is Toby and the little miss is Connie.'

'I'm so pleased to meet you both,' said Bette. 'Thank you for having me to your house.'

'James and Eunice are both at boarding school in England. Toby will be heading there shortly, as well,' said Tony.

Both children greeted Bette warmly. Their manners were impeccable and any curiosity they had about their father's friend was carefully hidden, but Bette thought that they seemed to be kindly disposed towards her. Then she became aware of another woman walking slowly into the courtyard. She was dressed in a batik sarong topped by a richly patterned silk batik tunic fastened with carved buttons and a jewelled clip. Her hair was pulled smoothly, tightly, into a bun, which was pinned with a jade ornament.

'Bette, I would like you to meet Madam Chang, my mother-in-law,' said Tony.

'Thank you for inviting me,' said Bette, taking the fingertips of the hand the older woman held out.

'You are welcome to the house of Tsang.' She turned and spoke swiftly in the baba patois of Malaya and Hokkien to the servants standing behind her. Then she said to Bette, 'Tea is ready upstairs.' Her English was clear and very precise. 'You are the first Australian lady we have had to tea.'

'I am honoured. What a beautiful house,' exclaimed Bette as the two women followed Tony and the children up the carved staircase.

'Tony's parents, his great uncle and grandfather have all added to the original home. There is a lot of history in this house,' said Madam Chang.

'Did you come to live here when Mai Ling married Tony?' asked Bette.

'Yes. I was a widow and I came to help Mai Ling with the children, and of course I stayed when Mai Ling was killed.'

They entered a pretty room with tall windows where a long table was set in a formal English style for afternoon tea. Chinese rugs, porcelain vases and dark carved furniture contrasted with the silver tea service and the gold-edged china. Jellies, cakes and delicate triangle sandwiches were spread along the table. Two amahs and a young nyonya house girl were there to serve them. When everyone was settled, Madam Chang lifted the large silver teapot and poured the golden tea into a fine bone china cup, which she handed to Bette.

Bette unfolded her linen napkin and caught Tony's eye as he gave her a warm smile. Soon she was relaxed and laughing as the children giggled and told stories about each other. Connie explained to Bette that she had just received her first bicycle, a dark green Raleigh. She couldn't ride it yet but after tea would Bette please come and watch her practise?

The time passed quickly. When tea was over, they

went outside into the garden and Connie showed Bette her bicycle. When Bette showed them that she could ride it, they all clapped in appreciation of her talents. While Bette had an idea of what the rest of the large house might be like and the treasures it contained, it was clear to her that, above all, it was a boisterous, happy family home.

'You were a big success. The children enjoyed you,' said Tony as he drove her back to the hotel.

'They are delightful, and a credit to you.'

'I must share your compliment with Madam Chang. She is very conscious of her position,' said Tony. Then he added, with a grin, 'But she is old now, and she would never have ridden that bicycle!'

'I hope it wasn't too unladylike!' joked Bette.

'No. And they want you to come again. Perhaps we could arrange an outing?'

'That would be lovely,' said Bette and she meant it. Despite the formality and opulence of the Tsang mansion, it was filled with laughter and a sense of co-operation. The atmosphere was very different from the mood at Utopia.

By now Bette was utterly in love with Tony Tsang, and it seemed that he was fascinated with her. But while their passionate embraces held a promise of mutual longing, Tony made no moves to take things further.

Seeing Bette looking rather wistful and thoughtful one morning, Tony asked if everything was all right.

'I have a letter from my parents. They are concerned about my frittering away my time here. It seems Margaret has told them about my relationship with you.'

'And they disapprove. Do they say that our friendship would be inappropriate in your society?' asked Tony.

'No, not at all. They make no mention of anything

like that. My father, however, is concerned about the communist insurgency and the news of attacks on Europeans. There seems to be a lot about it in the Australian newspapers,' said Bette. 'He wants me to come home before things get out of hand, as he puts it.'

'That's understandable,' said Tony calmly. 'Fathers worry about their daughters. Has he suggested that Margaret returns also?'

'I have no idea. I imagine that he is leaving the decision about what is best for her to her husband.'

'Then it's very clear what you should do, my sweet Bette.' As she gave him a curious look, he said, 'You must marry me so I will look after you.' He took her hand. 'I've been wanting to say this for some time. Would you marry me?'

Bette stared at the gentle, loving and humorous man she adored. She'd just loved being with him and tried to live for every moment they were together, not daring to think past each day. She had never dreamed that Tony would offer to be by her side for all the days of her life. But now that the words were there, hanging between them, she knew this was very right. And very wonderful. She flung her arms about him.

'Oh, yes, Tony. Yes, yes.'

13

Penang, 1950

THE WEDDING WAS INTIMATE, fifty guests at a reception at the E&O Hotel following a ceremony in St George's church and then an offering at a Buddhist temple.

Tony had explained that traditionally, Straits Chinese weddings were hugely elaborate twelve-day celebrations.

'I don't expect to follow the baba custom,' said Bette. 'And your family may consider me to be an outsider.'

'Don't think that,' said Tony. 'My family and friends are so happy for me. They adore you. But times have changed since the war and large ceremonies are not as common as they once were.'

Bette wore a beautiful white silk dress, with a veil held by a tiara of jasmine buds. Her shoes were made by the family cobbler, small-heeled silk shoes in the Malay slipper style, heavily embroidered with beads. She carried a breathtaking bouquet of Singapore orchids.

Madam Chang told Tony that some of the old customs should continue to be observed, and so she decorated the bridal chamber in the traditional manner. The carved, canopied bed in the master bedroom was hung with embroidered curtains and lengths of silk, which were held open by gold filigree clasps. The bed cushions and bolsters were covered in specially embroidered silk and satin covers, and decorated with silver and gold threads. Special pots and jars holding fragrant potpourri, incense and lucky talismans were hung in the room.

'I'm pleased she passed on some of the other old customs, especially the rooster and hens under the bed,' said Tony when he saw Madam Chang's efforts.

Bette wondered how many other customs Madam Chang might insist on observing and she raised the matter with Tony. 'I'm concerned about my relationship with Madam Chang. She has lived here a long time and I don't want her to feel uncomfortable about my being here.'

'Madam Chang is very fond of you, but I think she's worried that your mother might want to move in and run the household,' said Tony reassuringly.

'There's no chance of that! Anyway, Madam Chang organises everything so well I wouldn't want to interfere. But what will I actually do?' asked Bette.

Tony kissed her. 'Make me happy and be a friend and adviser to the children. Does that suit you?'

'It certainly does,' said Bette. 'But I don't want Madam Chang to feel like a servant, waiting on me.'

'There's no question of that,' said Tony. 'She takes her position of matriarch very seriously. And you can always ask her about some of the old baba customs and ways, even if we decide not to observe them.'

*

Bette decided to follow one of her own traditions at her wedding by carrying something old, something new, something borrowed and something blue. For the something blue she tucked an aerogram letter from her mother, which had arrived several days beforehand, into her handbag. While it made Bette sad, it was a bittersweet reminder of her family. In it Winifred had written:

> *While I can't say that I approve of your choice of husband, you are my daughter and I pray for your happiness and wellbeing. Margaret has told me that she is very shocked by your flouting of society's conventions and the way we've raised you, but she says that things are done differently in Malaya. She tells me that this man is very rich so I hope you will always be comfortable. I worry about any children you might have from this union. They would have a hard time being accepted here in Australia. But you have always been an independent girl, Bette, so I shouldn't be surprised by your decision. Your father also prays for your happiness. I don't understand why you want to live there with people whose lives and customs are so different from our own, but I will hold my tongue. We are very happy to have Margaret and Caroline here on a visit.*
> *Your loving mother, Winifred*

For their wedding, Tony gave Bette a beautiful gold filigree necklace of delicate flower stars and he wore a single matching star on the lapel of his suit. He had already given Bette several pieces of elaborate jewellery, but Bette liked the simpler pieces better. So her wedding ring was a plain engraved gold band. Her engagement ring was a cluster of diamonds set in a shape that, Tony told her, was called bujur kana, meaning oval-shaped olive. Bette loved it, not just because the diamonds were so pretty and she liked the shape of the ring, but because Tony had given it to her.

The wedding was joyful and Tony's children genuinely enjoyed the occasion, welcoming it as a way of recognising that Bette was now part of their lives. Before the event Bette had spoken privately to each of them, explaining that she would never be able to take their mother's place, but she hoped that they would see her as a friend and someone who could make their father happy.

On their wedding night, in the silky shadows of the great Chinese bed, Tony and Bette made love. It was gentle and tender, and wild and passionate. They found themselves joined in an embrace in which they cried out and clung together, releasing and sharing pleasure, grief and joy. Afterwards, as they lay together in each other's arms, Bette knew that they would be happy forever.

She didn't need to fret that she might not be able to fill her days because Bette found every day to be wonderful, filled with interesting people, places, activities, all reinforced by the knowledge that marrying Tony was the most fulfilling thing she had ever done.

She was fascinated by everything that went on in the new society she had joined. She began to notice the jewellery worn by the women, and she began to learn more about its significance. Jewellery was a woman's inheritance, worn on special occasions to show wealth and standing. Even the amahs had gold earrings and jade bangles and special pieces given to them by employers for their long-term security. Bette had no desire to display her wealth, thinking that this Chinese custom was somewhat vulgar.

But her attitude to jewellery was in sharp contrast to her thoughts about the treasures that surrounded her in Rose Mansion. As she explored the house, she was entranced by the antiques and collections of objet d'arts. She decided to catalogue them and she even thought of writing and illustrating a small book about Rose Mansion, its history and its contents.

The years slid by. Periodically she fretted about the lack of contact from her parents and the complete silence from Margaret, but Bette was making a life of her own. She had been completely accepted by Tony's children, who loved her, and apart from the pointed lack of enthusiasm for her marriage from her own family, the only sadness in her life was the knowledge she could not have children. She had been to all the best specialists but they all told her the same thing. The years of malnutrition, illness and deprivation in the POW camp had taken its toll on her body. Still, she was very happy to involve herself in the lives of the four Tsang children. She continued painting and began to study Chinese ceramics. She was very happy when Tony, who'd seen Roland in KL, told her that Philip was loving his boarding school.

While she and Madam Chang could not be considered close, they respected each other. Bette always put one day a week aside to play mah jong with Madam Chang and her friends. They played in a special games room, where the shutters were closed to the noise from the street. Tables were set up for one or more groups of four, and laughter, shouts, and the constant clacking and banging of the mah jong tiles echoed in the room. Madam Chang was a ferocious player, set in her rituals designed to bring her good luck, and she was a heady gambler. Bette found the game challenging, but she enjoyed it as much for the energy, enthusiasm and sometimes ribald humour of the women, who all spoke English so that she could join in, as she did for the gambling. Madam Chang always organised a lunch of numerous dainty dishes, which could be eaten quickly so as not to interrupt the games. Before the women departed, exclaiming over their wins and losses, afternoon tea and cakes were served.

Bette and Tony travelled a lot. Tony shared details of his business with her, and Bette accompanied him on trips to Europe as well as to the neighbouring countries in South East Asia. They had a busy social life with an eclectic circle of friends. While things were different from the prewar days, Bette still enjoyed the expatriate camaraderie as well as the company of the locals with their different ethnic backgrounds. British, Malay, Indian, Chinese, and their many combinations, made for a richly diverse circle of friends. Occasionally she met an Australian, but discussed neither Australia nor her family with them. As far as everyone was concerned, Bette was Mrs Tony Tsang, one half of an exotic, wealthy, charming, Penang family.

Strangely, in spite of the neglect from her family, Bette never felt that she was completely cut off from them. She thought it was just a state of hiatus. She had suggested to her parents a couple of times that she could visit them, but they always seemed unenthusiastic about the idea. And then time had a way of slipping by without her noticing and now she rarely stopped to dwell on what changes might have taken place back in Brisbane preferring instead, if she did think of them, to recall happy childhood memories. So it came as a shock to receive a letter from home, written by Margaret, telling her that their father had died.

> I did try to telephone your house but the language problem was difficult. I understood you were away, so we presumed you would not have been able to get back in time for the funeral. Mother is weepy but coping, and Caroline and I are here to help her. It was a short illness, and unexpected, though he wasn't a young man. But the main thing is he

didn't suffer. He left everything to Mother, naturally, so I presume that is all right by you. Mother will continue to live in the house, and sends her best wishes. She hopes you remember your father as the good man he was.
Margaret

Bette felt tears trickle down her cheeks. Sadness for her father, then guilt that she had never been back to see him, and then anger and hurt at learning about his death and funeral in such a casual manner.

She showed the letter to Tony. 'Can you believe Margaret?'

'I am sorry, darling. I know that you wanted to go home for a visit.'

'This is my home!' said Bette vehemently. 'I wonder who Margaret spoke to?'

'Does it matter who it was? At least she and Caroline are there in Brisbane, so your mother is being looked after. But you're right. She should have tried harder to contact you when it happened,' said Tony.

Bette nodded. 'I wonder if she told Philip. Not that he ever knew his grandfather.' She pushed thoughts of Margaret aside and sat down to reflect on her father. Tony asked one of the servants to bring them some tea and then he sat beside her, ready to listen.

'He was a quiet man. That generation didn't talk a lot. You had to get them on their own. Mother could be a bit bossy. She called the shots, around the house anyway, but Father had the final word on outside things, like spending money, going away, making the big decisions. I remember one holiday we had, we rented a holiday cottage and he let us go out with him prawning and fishing at night. We lit a little fire on the beach. Mother was convinced we'd get washed away in the surf in the dark, or that a shark would grab us by the ankles, and she refused to go down to the beach at night. Margaret didn't like the dark, so she went back to the cottage. Father caught a couple of small fish and we cooked them on the fire and picked them clean with our fingers. Tasted wonderful. We pretended we were castaways.' Bette smiled. 'I sometimes thought, even when I was older, that I'd like to go back to the beach with Father but we never got the opportunity again.'

'So you have happy memories. He was kind and loving and proud of you,' said Tony.

Bette straightened up. 'Yes. I think he was. He once told me that he was proud of what I had done for Philip. He used to say, "You'll be all right in this world, Bette."'

'Hang onto that,' said Tony softly.

'I know I should have made more of an effort to visit, but I can't forgive the offhand way Margaret has told me. As though he's not my father, too. As though she deliberately wanted to hurt me.' She looked at Tony, her eyes filled with anger and pain. 'You know, I don't think that she will ever forgive me for being the one to save her son, strange as that sounds.'

Tony put his arms around his wife. 'Bette, I'm sorry that you weren't there for your father's passing or the funeral, but you know that he admired you. Remember that.'

Bette buried her head in Tony's shoulder and the tears fell. She looked up at him. 'You won't ever leave me, will you?'

'No.' Tony kissed her. 'You are more to me than every breath I take.' He stroked her hair. 'I will always be here for you and when I'm not, my spirit will watch over you, be close to you.'

Bette felt calm and a warmth spread through her. She drew a slow healing breath. 'Is that a Buddhist thing?'

'No. Just a Tony Tsang thing. Because you and I are one,' he said lightly.

Bette smiled. She felt a great sense of peace and comfort. No matter what happened, Tony would always be there for her.

Changes began to sweep through the country. In 1957 Malaya gained independence from Britain and became the Federated States of Malaya. Bette and Tony's marriage continued to be happy and harmonious, and Tony's business interests continued to prosper.

One evening three years after independence Bette sat alone in the cool twilight of the side courtyard and heard Tony returning home. She burst out laughing when she saw him trot along the pathway in white baggy shorts, a white T-shirt and soft tennis shoes. His hair was awry and his face shiny with exertion.

'What have you been doing? Trying to look like Marlon Brando?'

'I've been talked into joining the Hash House Harriers. They've restarted a club here. They go for runs around the waterfront.'

'Who are the Hash House Harriers?'

'The group was started in KL before the war by a group of crazy British officers. The idea was to run to get rid of a hangover while building up a thirst for the next one.'

'It sounds insane, darling, running for miles in this hot climate, but if it makes you happy,' Bette said laughingly as she looked at her enthusiastic if somewhat unfit husband.

'I've come home to change and to take you out for dinner with some of the harriers and their wives.'

'That's fine, and remember we have dinner plans for tomorrow night,' said Bette.

'As if I could forget.' He sat beside her and put his

arm around her. 'Ten years together. And every day a joy.'
He kissed her. 'What would you like me to give you for
this special milestone?'

'No more expensive gifts,' said Bette. She looked at
him, and suddenly her eyes filled with tears.

'Is everything all right?' he asked softly.

'Yes. It's just that before you came in, I'd been sitting here and thinking . . . about the camp. I think that I
would like to go back to Sarawak and see what has happened to the POW camp.'

'Settle a few ghosts, perhaps?' said Tony.

Bette nodded. 'Sort of. I can't explain why, I just feel
drawn to it.'

'Then we must go. I will make arrangements,' he said
firmly. 'We shall make it our wedding anniversary trip.'

Bette wasn't sure exactly why she wanted to return to
Sarawak. Part of her wanted to revisit the place where the
prison camp had been just outside Kuching. But as they
flew over the dense jungle canopy and she saw the broad,
brown, snaking sweep of the Sarawak River, its protective mangrove wetlands stretching inland, and the pretty
township of Kuching strung out along its banks, she felt a
great sense of delight.

'Thank you, darling. This is very special,' she whispered to Tony,

They settled into the comfortable Aurora Hotel and
walked into the centre of Kuching along the riverfront,
exploring the township on the way. Bette spotted the Sarawak museum and told Tony that she would like to spend
time visiting it. Tony agreed, as he wanted to see someone
recommended to him by a business associate in Penang.

When they met later that afternoon by the river,
Bette's eyes were alight. 'I met the curator at the museum,

Tom Harrisson. An extraordinary fellow! And very interesting. I told him I was going to visit the old camp and we got talking about the war. He recognised my Australian accent and told me that he had been parachuted onto a hidden plateau in Borneo with seven Australian special operatives from Z force,' said Bette. 'He said that not only did they provide intelligence reports, but they managed to recruit a thousand blowpiping headhunters who killed or captured about one and a half thousand Japanese soldiers.'

'That does sound interesting,' said Tony. 'I've heard of this fellow. He's regarded as being a bit eccentric and very colourful.'

'He's lived here since the war and says he's made some amazing archeological discoveries in the Niah caves. He's found fossils and skulls which he says date back more than forty thousand years. I would so love to go there and see them. He says the caves are huge.'

'You would? I'll look into it if you like. What about visiting the camp? Is tomorrow morning all right with you?'

Bette nodded, her bubbling enthusiasm about the museum curator subsiding at the thought of revisiting the internment camp.

It wasn't as she remembered, for which she was glad. It was now a peaceful place. Green fields surrounded the original barracks, which were now part of a teacher training college. Grass had replaced dust. There were neat signs, a monument, a flagpole, and some of the occupied buildings were cleaned up and open to the public. There was no sign of the barbed-wire fences or the watchtowers. But the faces of the women and children Bette had seen every day, came clearly to her mind.

She walked alone towards the buildings she remembered as being her world, her home and her prison for nearly four years. When she walked back to Tony, who stood smoking a cigarette in the shade of a tree, she was smiling.

'Are you all right?' He embraced her and she clung to him, resting her head on his shoulder.

'Yes. At last I really am all right.' She looked up into his face. 'You are my life now, Tony. Everything that happened before I married you, means very little to me any more.'

He kissed her softly. 'Then we shall make every day ours.'

Back in Kuching, Tony took Bette's idle remark about visiting the Niah caves quite seriously. But when he talked to the museum curator, Tom Harrisson told him that the caves were quite isolated and difficult to reach, and the area was off limits because it was a dig site. Nevertheless, Tom invited them both to come to his house in Pig Lane for a drink and to discuss the possibility of visiting other parts of Sarawak.

Bette was fascinated by the cluttered, ramshackle home that Tom shared with his anthropologist wife Barbara, who was currently making a documentary about their work at Niah. The house was like a museum. Walls and surfaces were smothered in the artifacts that Tom had collected over the years he'd been in South East Asia. native woven baskets and hats, ornamental knives, krises, blowpipes and mats were hung everywhere, while the walls were decorated with magnificent, boldly coloured murals. Tom explained that the paintings and carvings in the house had been done by various orang ulu – upriver natives. Bette was intrigued by his collection of pottery pieces and shards of Chinese and Siamese porcelain, which were very much older than the perfect porcelain on display in Rose Mansion.

'This is amazing,' said Bette. 'These artifacts are such

a contrast to the things that we have in Penang. Just look at those paintings. Fantastic.'

Seeing her enthusiasm and interest, Tom suggested that since they couldn't go to the caves, they might like to visit a longhouse, where he had Iban friends.

'Leonard is one of the assistants working at the museum and he's Iban. I'm sure he'd help you, if you'd like to go,' said Tom.

Tom also introduced Bette and Tony to his 'children', and Bette was fascinated. Kept in cages out the back of the house and roaming around inside, demanding constant attention, were several baby orangutans. Tom explained that they had been rescued from illegal traders trying to smuggle them out of the country. Barbara was rearing them and trying to prepare them to be released back into the wild.

'Can they look after themselves if they've been hand reared?' asked Bette, as a small orange-furred creature took hold of her hand and swung into her arms, its saucer-shaped eyes studying her face closely, before it rested its head on her shoulder.

'We've created a small, sheltered camp where the orangutans live in cages for a month. After that we leave the cage doors open so that they can come and go as they like. Hopefully, when they get used to their surroundings, they will mate and live with the wild orangutans,' said Tom.

'They are amazing. Aren't they lovable creatures, Tony?' said Bette.

'Yes, at this age, but an adult male might be a different matter,' said Tony.

Tom was a boisterous, boastful, heavy-drinking, entertaining, knowledgeable raconteur. Bette was not surprised when he was able to arrange for them to go upriver with Leonard to visit the orangutan camp.

Tony was not comfortable roughing it and he was amused at how well Bette took to travelling in the canoe with its clunky outboard motor driven by Leonard at a high incautious speed. They drew up at a small landing on the edge of the jungle. From here they walked through the swampy river fringe into the jungle to Camp Salang. The small clearing contained tents, a hut, cages and a feeding platform for the orangutans. Two Iban women brought fruit each day for the apes. A young German woman was on field duty, making notes, taking photographs and keeping a record of the comings and goings of the primates.

'This is pioneering work,' Leonard told Tony and Bette. 'But it is also sad for me, because I believe that one day these orangutans will have nowhere to live.'

'But look how much jungle there is!' exclaimed Bette.

'It's being eaten up every day,' said Leonard. 'The timber industry and land clearing are destroying it.'

Bette looked at him. 'Surely the government will protect the forests?'

'The government and businesspeople see more dollars in wood than in orangutans,' said Leonard.

'It's true,' said Tony. 'There is very big money to be made from tropical rainforest woods like ramin, and I don't believe there are enough restrictions and regulations in place, yet. You know the meeting I had in Kuching the other day? It was with a man who wanted me to go into the timber industry with him.'

'But you're not, are you?' said Bette.

'No. I told him that I preferred to pursue other opportunities,' said Tony.

'I'm glad. I'd hate to think we were party to hurting these wonderful animals,' said Bette.

Once Bette and Tony became familiar with the area, they were left to their own devices. They liked to walk quietly through the jungle staring into the trees, waiting to spot the orangutans, eating, playing and courting. Bette spent hours quietly waiting and watching, occasionally making quick sketches in her notebook.

Tony watched her and smiled. 'I'm so pleased that we made this trip and you have laid to rest the ghosts of the war. All I want is your happiness. Will you be okay on your own for a while? I want to go to the village and talk to the headman.'

'Of course. I'm sorry if you're bored. I could stay here for hours. We'll have to come back for a longer visit. Leonard says we can go to his village upriver and stay in their longhouse.'

'Would you like that?' asked Tony. 'I could never have imagined that you would be so swept up by this very different culture. I know that you enjoy studying Chinese and Peranakan history and culture because that's my family background, but your thirst for knowledge seems prodigious. You want to explore all around you and I love you for that.'

'Thank you, darling. I'll meet you back at the boat in, say, an hour or so?' She glanced at her watch.

'Fine. Leonard will take me to the headman and come back for you.'

But later, as Tony talked with the village chief at the river landing, Bette came hurrying towards them looking distraught. She pulled Tony aside and quietly told him what she'd seen. As soon as Tony had finished speaking with the headman, he found Leonard and said, 'My wife says there are two men with guns trying to shoot the apes.'

'Poachers. The orangutan camp is a target for them because the apes are tame. Quickly, can you show us where you saw them?' asked Leonard. Bette pointed to the direction where she had seen the men, and Leonard set off at a fast jog, with Tony and Bette following him.

*

The subsequent events were defining moments for Bette. Her heart ached, and she tightly held Tony's hand as the boat sped back down the river towards Kuching. The death of the mother orangutan and the disappearance of its infant had shocked and saddened her, and she vowed that somehow, one day, she would try to teach people the value and uniqueness of these gentle creatures.

When Bette and Tony told Tom about the poachers, he was furious.

'Things are changing so rapidly around here, it's difficult to exercise control over poaching and illegal logging,' he said.

'I expect that things will be better if Sarawak becomes one of the Federated States of Malaya,' said Tony.

'I don't know,' replied Tom. 'I know that the communist Emergency has ended on the Malay peninsula, but they are still causing trouble for us on the Indonesian border.'

'On the peninsula, independence has changed things, and I think for the better. Malayanisation is taking place rapidly as the British move out and their places are being taken by the locals,' said Tony.

'I don't think everyone is happy about it. Three years ago my Chinese friends were upset at the British going and leaving a Malayan government in their place. I kept out of the way when the flag came down,' commented Tom.

'We went to the padang, the open space on the Penang waterfront on the eve of independence and there were thousands of people of all races celebrating,' said Bette. 'I was amazed. It was quite moving and very respectful.'

'Yes,' said Tony. 'My hope is that the different races will work well together. The ruling Alliance Party is made up of Malays, Chinese and Indians, and they want to spread the wealth and responsibility among everyone.'

'Well,' said Tom, 'when things change here, I think I'll try to stay out in the jungle and at the caves as much as possible,' he grinned.

Tony nodded. Later he told Bette that he didn't imagine there'd be a lot of opportunities for the hard-drinking, bossy, sometimes arrogant Englishmen for much longer. To Tom he said, 'The British have left behind a lot of goodwill, and I think that the transition has been quite well organised.'

Bette glanced at her husband, knowing that already his company had taken advantage of Malayanisation to buy into big, former British industries and trading houses, and especially the tin mines. The house of Tsang seemed to be doing well under independence.

When they thanked Tom for his hospitality, he said, 'Come back any time. I'm not going anywhere.'

Several years later, Tony's optimism about the future direction of Malaya changed. For Bette, Tony was his usual loving self, but he spent long hours at work and often people came to see him at the house, where he closeted himself in his study with them. Bette noticed that frequently the cars that came belonged to high-ranking government officials and even to the sultans. Finally she asked Tony about what was going on.

'It's to do with this Malayanisation,' he said. 'The government is insisting that Malays have preferential treatment. This policy has created power struggles between the Malays and the Chinese, and, to a lesser extent, the Indians. Now that Singapore has chosen to become independent from Malaya, many Chinese businessmen have decided to move there, but I have decided to stay here in Penang and adjust. I have promoted Malays onto my board.'

'What do you think will happen?' asked Bette.

Tony sighed and kissed her cheek. 'We have to hope commonsense will prevail, and all this ethnic rivalry will eventually stop and everyone will work in the best interests of the country. Unfortunately, a lot of these problems are to do with the control of the rich natural resources of this part of the world. It always comes down to power and money and who can manipulate others for their own ends.' He rose and drew her to her feet. 'The children are all away, we have no appointments. Let's take an afternoon rest before we go out to dinner.'

May 1969

Bette's life continued to be busy and happy. Even though the two eldest children, James and Eunice, were married, she was still involved in their lives as well of those of Connie and Toby, the younger ones. Bette cherished the closeness they now all shared. Madam Chang was ageing, but not gracefully. She still played mah jong each week, and she insisted on running the household in the same disciplined manner she always had. She went to the market each day to haggle for fresh produce, taking the young kitchen maid with her to carry her basket. Although she took to sleeping each afternoon, first she did a tour of inspection of the house and woe betide any servant if she found dust in a corner or a dead leaf on the ornamental trees. When Bette quietly tried to manage things behind her back, giving discreet instructions to the staff, Madam Chang chose to ignore it all.

The joy Bette found in sharing every day with Tony never diminished. She often thought that their love was like a beautiful gem that sparkled on the outside while glowing with inner fire. Tony's tenderness and humour, his integrity and kindness, his passion and devotion often left her breathless with wonderment that her life had turned out this way. Australia, and her family, seemed to belong to childhood experiences that had happened and passed while she was waiting to begin her life. She was saddened but not particularly surprised when Margaret notified her of Winifred's death with a telegram that arrived after her mother's funeral had taken place. For Bette her life and family were here around her in Penang.

'Are you ready?' Bette asked as Tony walked into the airy downstairs passage that ran between the two wings of the house. Bette sat in a carved seat on silk cushions watching the sunbeams sparkle on the water of the old lion fountain.

Tony stopped in the shadow of the spiral staircase that led down from his study and looked at his beloved wife. She was dressed in the loose silk pants she favoured topped with an embroidered lace-edged tunic. She now wore her hair swept up on her head for coolness and had taken to securing it with one of his mother's collection of jewelled hair combs. A book lay on her lap. He looked at her face, he knew every inch of it, and caught his breath at the rush of love he felt for her. 'I am,' he said. 'I'm sorry I have to be away for this weekend's elections. Are you sure you won't come up to KL with me? There's bound to be all manner of celebrations after the election on Saturday.'

'So the Democratic Action Party is feeling very confident then?'

'I believe so. I had hoped that the Alliance Party would deliver what is best for everyone, but it hasn't worked out that way, as far as I'm concerned. The constitution is set up to favour the Malays, and while there's no denying they are way behind the Indian and Chinese communities economically, I think that they have too much political power and there is now an undercurrent of racial intolerance towards us.'

'I know, and you think that they should share their political power more,' said Bette.

'Well, we Chinese are the main source of the country's wealth,' said Tony. 'I believe that our Democratic Action Party might just give the ruling Alliance a fright. We shall see. But it's a pity we'll be apart.'

'Madam Chang is tired and I promised Eunice that I'd look after little Carla while she went to a tea party.'

Tony kissed her. 'You're wonderful. Enjoy our grandchildren. I'll be back on Tuesday.'

'That's the thirteenth – it's an unlucky number. Come back on the twelfth.'

Tony chuckled. 'You've been listening to too many of Madam Chang's superstitions.'

'I hope it all goes well. I love you, Tony.'

He kissed her fiercely. 'I'll get through my business and be back to you as quickly as I can. Just a few days.'

The calmness at Rose Mansion was disrupted when some of Tony's friends called by to see Tony, elated at the result of the general election.

'Tony's in KL on business. He'll be back as soon as he can,' Bette told them.

'We've heard how well the Chinese vote has gone in Selangor! The state could be run by the Chinese!' they told Bette.

But Bette's elation at the election results were quickly replaced by apprehension when Tony's elder son, James, told her that violence had broken out in Kuala Lumpur.

'What has happened, James?' asked Bette.

'It seems that some Indians and Chinese started celebrating the election results on Sunday afternoon by parading through the streets in a Malay area. They carried brooms, apparently, to symbolise the sweeping out of the Malays.'

'That was a silly thing to do,' said Bette.

'And dangerous. I have heard that the Malays began attacking both the Chinese and the Indians. Apparently this violence is spreading around the city.'

Bette was immediately alarmed. 'Do you know where Tony is? I hope he is safe in his hotel.'

'I'm trying to find out. I've been talking to friends in KL and they have told me that there are rumours going around that this violence wasn't spontaneous. Some young Malays, many from out of town, are armed with knives, spears and parangs, and they are out looking for Chinese, to teach them a lesson, they say. And what's more, there are plans to hold a political procession. Talk about provocative! And even though the police have vetoed such a foolhardy plan, the chief minister has said that he will give the okay for it to go ahead. I'm sure Father will lie low in his hotel until this all blows over and sanity prevails.'

Bette paced through Rose Mansion, waiting to hear news of Tony.

What she did hear caused her much disquiet. The political procession had turned into a riot. Cars and buildings were being burned and the Malay police were firing indiscriminately into Chinese shophouses. The Chinese were being attacked all over the city, although, as she found out later, many were hidden by their friends. Their homes were being ransacked and burned and many were brutally murdered. The city had descended into chaos.

*

429

Wednesday morning, the fourteenth, came and Bette lay in her canopied bed feeling as though her legs and body were made of lead. She heard the jangle of the bell at the gate and willed herself out of the bed. Calmly, she smoothed her hair, wrapped her silk flowered robe around herself, put her feet in her beaded slippers and began to walk downstairs slowly. One step after another. She could hear, as if from far away, hurrying servants, voices calling and a motor vehicle in the driveway.

It was Madam Chang's long shrill shriek, 'Aaaeeeie,' that jolted Bette and she broke into a run to the front foyer. She saw a police inspector standing at the door talking to James. His face told her what she already knew in her heart.

According to the police inspector, Tony had been shot by a passing band of youths as he was getting into his car to drive back home to her. The police officer told her that the army had now moved into Kuala Lumpur, and a state of emergency and a curfew would soon be declared. But it would all come too late for Tony. Bette listened, eyes closed, her face white, hands clenched.

'Where is my husband?'

'At the hospital, Mrs Tsang.'

'Please arrange to bring him home.' She cast an anguished look at James, who nodded. He would be the one to bring his father home because he was now the eldest male in the family.

There was silence in the bright room as Bette finished speaking. Julie and Caroline glanced at each other hoping the other would speak first.

Julie said, 'Thank you for telling us what happened, Bette. It was such a tragedy. You obviously loved each other so much.'

Bette turned to her great niece, her eyes misty. 'I still do. I feel him beside me every day of my life.' She straightened and smiled. 'So that's my story. Naturally my life didn't end after Tony was killed, though it felt like it at the time. I remained at Rose Mansion helping the children and after Madam Chang died I kept the house running.'

'The book you wrote, about the Iban, how did that come about?' asked Julie.

'After Tony's and my trip to Sarawak, I became intrigued with the orangutans and the Iban. Orangutans are remarkable animals, but the Iban are people I could talk to and I wanted to know more about their way of life. So, thanks to Tom Harrisson, who'd introduced us to Leonard and his village, I returned to Sarawak to spend time in the jungle with them.

'But when I returned to Kuching, Tom had been blacklisted. He wasn't allowed re-entry into Sarawak. Apparently a jealous woman colleague had made false allegations about his work. I didn't believe them, but Tom's wild behaviour had offended many people, so the charges stuck.

'Even without him, I was happy to travel upriver with Leonard or Bidui, which was his Iban name, and I stayed with his family in their longhouse. I was also able to observe the orangutans and I realised that the destruction of their habitat would create a perilous situation for them.'

'Hence the book and the pamphlet you wrote,' said Caroline.

Bette smiled. 'There are a lot of people who are trying to raise awareness about the situation now.'

As Bette and Julie chatted on about the Iban and orangutans, Caroline was thoughtful, appearing a little distracted. 'Bette,' she said. 'I've learned a lot about the rift between you and my mother and a lot about you and your life in Penang, and the POW camp. But the person I don't know much about is my father. I still don't understand why I grew up in Brisbane with my mother while my brother stayed on in Malaya with him.'

Bette took her hand. 'Roland was a lovely man. Tony had a lot of respect for him. Actually, the last time I saw Roland was at Tony's funeral. He died from cancer not long afterwards. But he never said an ill word about your mother. Whenever I had asked how Margaret was, all Roland said was that she was spending time in Australia. I think that after the war Margaret never settled back into life at the plantation. But more than that I cannot say.'

'And you never spoke to Philip after you left Utopia,' said Julie. 'I think that's so sad.'

'I suppose I could have made contact, but I always thought that if I stayed away, then Philip and Margaret would become closer. I might have written to Philip if Margaret had died, but he was the one who died first. Now, of course, I regret our separation, but it's all too late.'

Julie looked at her mother and realised that Caroline also had a lot of unanswered questions that went right back to her childhood. She turned to her great aunt. 'Bette, is there no one you can recall who knew Roland and Margaret and who might be able to shed some light on what happened between them?'

Bette was thoughtful. 'There could be someone. Give me a minute to think.'

'I'll make a fresh pot of tea, shall I?' said Julie.

Over tea they talked about Brisbane and all of the changes that had occurred there since Bette had left nearly sixty years before, but Julie could see her mother was anxiously watching Bette. Then, in the middle of a conversation about something quite unrelated, Bette's eyes lit up and she broke into a smile.

'Bill! Excuse me, Julie. Bill Dickson. Roland had an

old army friend he fought with in Malaya. I think Tony knew him as well. He said he met him a couple of times. I wonder if the boys at Utopia would know of him, and whether he's still alive.'

'He'd be very old,' said Caroline doubtfully.

'Grandfather Roland wrote about him in his war memoir,' exclaimed Julie. 'I'll email Shane and Peter and ask if they know anything.'

'Thank you so much for having us, Bette,' said Caroline as she rose to leave.

'Not at all,' replied Bette. 'I can't tell you how happy you have made me. Knowing that my Australian family are interested in me and care about what has happened to me means more than I can possibly say. My ninetieth birthday will be on me soon and I know that the Tsangs are planning big things. I do hope that you can get back to Cairns to join the festivities. I would love you both to meet my other family.'

Caroline and Julie hugged Bette goodbye, and assured her that they wouldn't miss her birthday party for anything.

'It's a lot to take in,' said Caroline in the taxi going back to their hotel. 'I'm sorry Dad missed hearing about it all. What an extraordinary life she's led.'

'Now you're anxious to know what happened between Roland and Margaret, aren't you?' said Julie.

'I am. It's something I didn't think about all my life, it's just how it was. Now of course I want to know what the relationship between the two of them actually was. I have a million questions.'

'Gran was not very forthcoming, was she?' said Julie.

'No. She was a good mother, but when it came to family matters, she wasn't approachable and I grew up knowing that it was a forbidden subject. I suppose it seems silly and unbelievable now.'

'I don't think so, Mum. I'm sure there are a lot of families who have mysteries,' said Julie. 'I'll send the email to Shane and Peter.'

That evening while Caroline was recounting Bette's story to Paul over drinks, Julie received a reply email from Shane.

'Mum, he says that they know about Bill because they've read Roland's memoir, too, but that's all they know.'

'How disappointing,' said Caroline.

But Julie was not to be deterred. She fired back another email asking her cousins if they would mind looking through Roland's papers to see if they could find out anything more about Bill Dickson.

'He's probably dead,' said Paul pragmatically.

Caroline and Paul were happy to get home to Bayview where they were flung back into the drama of the bypass. Julie felt as though she'd hardly had time to unpack when Caroline rang her.

'David says he's found out something important! We should call a meeting of all the interested parties. He sounds quite excited, can you come around tomorrow night?'

Julie debated with herself about dancing attendance on David's little dramas, but she didn't want to let her mother down. He really might have found out something useful. After all, he was an effective researcher. When she turned up at her parents' house the following evening, she was surprised to see a large number of cars parked outside.

'Jules, so glad you're here. David is being so mysterious.'

A group of neighbours, several local councillors and representatives of the council were spread out along the verandah. David had set up a large board on an easel and had a lot of papers in front of him. He gave Julie a wave as she headed down the hallway to the kitchen to find her mother.

'I hope he has something worthwhile, there are a lot of people out there. Can I help you with the drinks and tea things?'

'Thanks, darling, but my friend Erica is giving me a hand. I wish Paul was here. I asked him to come home early. We have some nibbles, but I'm sure people will leave to get home to dinner.'

David took command of the gathering, asking the council representatives to sit at the front. He paid special attention to Fred Louden from the council who was look-ing smug and, as David began speaking, adopted a bored expression.

David thanked the Reagans for opening their home. 'A home that, like so many in this area, represents what this battle has been about. A building in surroundings that have been here for a long time and represent a beautiful and historic part of this city. This is an area we do not want to see ripped apart for a large road bypass.'

'Hear, hear.'

'We know all this,' interjected another of the council's representatives.

David ignored him. 'Perhaps we don't know every-thing. We know that there was a similar plan for a bypass in a slightly different area some years ago. But the plan failed to go ahead. How fortunate for those living in that area.' He paused and looked around the attentive group. 'I'd like to show you all where that original bypass was going to go.'

'That has nothing to do with the current situation,' said Fred Louden in an irritated way.

David paid no attention, but unfolded a large picture that he pinned on the board for all to see. Like everyone, Julie craned forward, staring at the photograph. It was a picture of a large, extremely expensive modern house: a mish-mash of soaring glass, steel and fantasy castle components that illustrated the saying that money can't always buy good taste.

'Imagine having that monstrosity next door,' muttered a neighbour.

'What's your point, young man?' demanded a councillor.

'I think you might know where I'm going with this, Mr Louden,' said David affably.

'I'm not staying. You have no right to use my home as some point of reference, and hold it up to ridicule. I'll have you know that my house was designed by a top-notch architect, built by a master builder and featured in several magazines,' snapped Fred Louden.

'Is it *your* place, Mr Louden?' asked Caroline.

'Whatever you may think of the design, this is Mr Louden's house, which was plonk in the middle of the original route for the bypass. And he didn't want to see his home demolished for a bypass,' exclaimed David. 'Isn't that so, Mr Louden?'

Fred Louden, red-faced and angry, glared at David. 'You are right. Fortunately that route was changed and no houses were demolished,' he answered.

There was a sudden murmur among the group.

'Yes and no doubt very convenient for you. But may we know how you were able to avoid having your home demolished, while the heritage homes in this area are now earmarked for such a fate? Would it be because you used your influence to change the route of the bypass?' asked David.

Fred Louden jumped to his feet. He could feel the open hostility directed towards him. 'You can't prove that! It's outrageous for you to impugn my reputation,' he began.

'Before you threaten me with legal action,' said David calmly picking up a sheaf of papers, 'you might want to read the minutes and motions moved in Council two years ago when the bypass was originally mooted. It makes for some very interesting reading.'

There was now a surge as people grabbed the documents from David and shouted questions and sharp comments at Fred Louden and the startled councillors.

'Outrageous.'

'What a damn cheek.'

'Were bribes paid?'

Fred Louden stood up and pushed his way through the group. 'I'm not listening to this garbage. You'll be hearing from me.' He was hurrying down the steps into the night just as Paul pulled into the driveway.

'What's going on?' asked Paul as he kissed Caroline.

Julie filled him in on the evening's events and her father smiled.

'Sounds like we should break out the good stuff. Well done, David.' Paul pumped David's hand as the academic joined them, looking rather pleased with himself.

'I'll see how the champagne stocks are going. Everyone will want a celebratory drink,' said Paul as he and Caroline headed indoors.

'Congratulations, that was quite a coup. A great piece of detective work,' said Julie.

'Thanks. I wonder how he assumed it would never come to light. I don't think that we can prove anything untoward happened, but the fact his house was in the middle of the original bypass plan, which was changed and that he was part of the decision-making process puts a rather unpleasant cloud over him,' said David.

'So what will happen now? Do we get a reprieve and some other neighbourhood suffers?' asked Julie.

David shook his head. 'I don't think so. I have heard,

although it's still unofficial, that the council is now considering a tunnel. Seems your campaign has stirred things up.'

'You mean you and my mother! You've been doing all the stirring. Thank you, David,' added Julie with feeling.

He nodded. 'Least I could do. I like a challenge. And, it's been nice to get to know your family. And you.' He smiled at her. 'Julie, I owe you an apology, I guess I blew it with you. Came on too strong. I didn't read you correctly. I can be a bit of a bull at a gate. But I hope we can be friends.'

A great feeling of relief, and warmth, rushed through her. 'Of course we can. We are friends. And my mother adores you.'

'I think my stocks went up a bit after this,' he said as Caroline came out bearing a bottle of champagne and glasses.

'You were brilliant. Well done, David. I wish I had a photo of Fred Louden's face when he saw his home up on the board!' said Caroline. 'Here's to you, David.'

Caroline poured them each a champagne and they touched glasses.

'So, what's next, David?' asked Julie.

'Plugging on. I'll be going back to Sarawak. Y'know, I'd love to meet your Aunt Bette before I go. Is that possible?'

'I'm sure she'd love to meet you,' said Julie. 'After all, if it wasn't for you, we wouldn't have found her.'

The bypass meeting transformed into a neighbourhood party to celebrate with people rushing home and bringing food and children back to the Reagans for a barbecue dinner. It was late when Julie headed home, but after a shower she curled up on her bed in her pyjamas to send a long email to Christopher filling him in on all the news about Bette and the bypass.

As she was brushing her teeth she heard the ping of an incoming email and hurried to her laptop, hoping it was a reply from Chris. But it was Shane, answering her email at last about Roland's friend Bill.

Found him! He used to send Christmas cards to Grandfather Roland years ago, but the last address we have for him is 6 Park Place, Goondiwindi, Queensland. Best of luck and stay in contact. S. xx

Julie stared at the screen then burst out laughing. 'Goondiwindi! I don't believe it. Well, that is a turn up! Bill, I hope you're still out there!'

14

Caroline walked through the garden of Bayview to the letterbox and found a letter addressed to her in a spidery hand, from Goondiwindi.

'It's from Bill!' she called to Paul.

'Well, Shane and Peter were on the money with the right address,' said Paul.

Caroline skimmed the letter and said, 'Actually, he's moved from that address. Listen: "I've moved into a retirement village, still in Goondiwindi. Mrs Peterson, who bought my house, was kind enough to bring me your letter when she received it. I remember Roland very well. We were very good friends, especially during the war, and I would love to meet his daughter, if you can get to Gundy."'

'I think we should contact the staff at the retirement

village to find out how strong he is,' Caroline said later over the phone to Julie. 'We don't want to race out west and find that he's really not up to visitors.'

'Mum, he sounds as sharp as a tack, but I will ring, just to check,' said Julie.

When Julie finally spoke with the manager of the retirement village, she was assured that Bill Dickson was brilliant for his age. 'He still plays bridge and does the crossword puzzles in the daily paper, and his mind is quite active. Mind you, he's a bit slow to get around these days. His arthritis can be a problem for him at times. But I can assure you that he certainly loves visitors. In fact, I can guarantee that he'll give you a warm reception. Bill likes a chat.'

When Julie spoke to Bill on the phone she found him to be as alert and strong as she expected.

'What a surprise, lass. You're related to Roland, you say? Let me get this straight, you're his granddaughter? Are you Philip or Caroline's child?'

Julie explained that she was Caroline's daughter, and that she and her mother would love to drive to Goondi-windi and meet him.

'So, you're little Caroline's daughter. That makes me feel like an old-timer. Where do you live? You're welcome to drop by any time.'

'Both my mother and I live in Brisbane. How long have you been there, Bill?'

'In Gundy? Or this retirement place? We came out to Australia in the late fifties and my wife Vera and I had a nice little house down the road. Vera died a few years ago, so I moved in here. Our kids are all scattered to the winds, all over Australia, but they like to visit me. They're good kids.'

'You didn't stay in Malaya?' asked Julie.

'Only for a time. After the war I went back there. It

was great to catch up again with Roland. I took up my position again in the Civil Service, but once Malayanisation started, I found that there was no place for me, so I went back to the UK. No place for me there either and I couldn't take the blasted cold weather. I was married by then, and so Vera and I decided to emigrate to Australia.' He paused as if waiting for her to say something. 'You're probably too young to know about the ten-pound Poms,' he laughed.

'I do know. After the war, people from the UK could emigrate to Australia for ten pounds, right up till the seventies, I think,' said Julie. 'A friend of mine's parents did that, too.'

'Some didn't settle in and went back to the UK, but most did, like Vera and me.'

'Why Goondiwindi?' asked Julie. 'It seems a long way for an Englishman to come.'

'Bit of luck, really. I'd been in the Civil Service in Malaya and when I got to Australia I saw an ad for a job in council administration in Gundy. I applied and got the job and moved here. Loved the place from the start. Raised our family here and never wanted to leave. When are you coming to see me, did you say? Friday, is that right?'

'That's right, Bill. Next Friday, if that suits you. Mum and I will make a long weekend of it. Is there something I can bring you? Are you allowed a beer?'

''Course I am. But I tell you, lass, I wouldn't say no to a decent glass of red.'

'It's a deal. I'll see you at the end of the week,' said Julie.

Julie and Caroline cruised in to Goondiwindi the next Friday. The town was typical of Australian country towns, with palm trees dividing its broad main street. They drove past the classic Victoria Hotel, its upper storey fringed with iron lace, and past the statue of the beautiful grey racehorse, Gunsynd, which was the town's claim to fame in the seventies. They found Bill's retirement village close to the Macintyre River, and pulled in to the reception area.

'You're friends of Bill's?' said one of the admin staff as she showed them the way to his suite. 'He still gets visitors because he has lived in Gundy for so long, but they're getting on, too, so there aren't as many as there used to be. Some of his family come by every few months, so this will be nice for him.'

'We won't tire him out,' said Julie.

'Oh, Bill chugs along like a steam train,' she said. 'He plays bridge twice a week, and takes his daily constitutional around the garden. Wish I knew what his secret is.'

'He asked us to bring him some red wine. Is that all right?' said Caroline.

'Perfectly. Bill doesn't smoke, but he does like a tipple now and then. There's his room, number six. He has a bell in there to call for anything if he has a problem.'

They heard the scuffing of feet as Bill called out, 'Door's open.'

When they opened it, they found a sprightly, smiling man, a thin scattering of white hair over his pink scalp, bright blue eyes, a silver moustache and skin that sagged in folds but had few wrinkles. He was straight-backed, but moved with the aid of a walking stick. He smiled at both women and held out his hand in a friendly manner.

'Welcome, dear ladies, to my humble abode. Would you care to sit outside in the sun?'

'That sounds lovely. I'm Julie, and this is my mother Caroline.'

'Yes. I remember you, Caroline. You were just a little girl when I saw you last. A bundle of energy, as I remember. Kept that amah of yours on the hop,' he chuckled to himself. 'I can make us tea or coffee and I've ordered some sandwiches.' He led the way through the large bright room which served as the sitting room. It contained a little dining table, as well as a small lounge and two chairs, and it had a kitchenette in one corner. Folding doors evidently hid his bedroom and bathroom. There were no steps, and Julie noticed that where the sliding glass door opened onto the tiny patio with its seats and small table, there was no ledge or strip for Bill to trip over. The patio looked out onto the communal garden, while the unit next door was screened from Bill's by a hedge which was low enough to chat over. The area was decorated with flowerpots and a small bird bath. Through the distant trees, Julie and Caroline could see the glimmer of the river.

'This is pretty. Very peaceful.'

'Make yourselves comfortable. The birds are noisy. They love that bath. I feed them scraps. I shouldn't, but they entertain me. It's lovely to be visited by two such delightful ladies and to be presented with such a nice bottle of wine. I know I shouldn't look a gift horse in the mouth, but why are you here?' His eyes twinkled.

So Caroline and Julie told him the story of Bette's book and how that had led Julie to visit the family plantation in Malaysia and meet Peter and Shane and then how they'd finally tracked down Bette, whom Caroline had not seen since she was a toddler.

'Mum and I are still sorting it all out in our heads. It's been quite a revelation to us. The more we learn, the more questions we seem to have,' said Julie as they reached the end of their story.

Bill nodded. 'I can imagine.'

'From my mother's point of view, she always . . .' Caroline began.

'Ah, Margaret . . .' interjected Bill.

'That's right, Mother told me about her life in Malaya

444

before the war, but never wanted to talk about her sister, or about her marriage, after the war. And we know that Bette and Philip were in the POW camp in Sarawak, but Mother told me nothing about that at all. Now I wonder if maybe Roland changed as a result of the war, as well.'

'As so many did, but not Roland,' said Bill.

'So what happened after the war was a closed chapter. My grandmother seemed content in her big old house in Brisbane while grandfather Roland stayed on in Malaysia with my uncle Philip and contact between the two parts of the family has been rather sparse, especially after Philip died,' said Julie.

'Now you must think that it's rather strange for me to want to know what happened between my parents after all this time. Until we met Bette and found out what my mother had told me about my aunt's marriage was not exactly the truth, I really hadn't questioned my parents' relationship. I had accepted that it was just the way things were. Now I want to know if you have any idea what the real reason was for my mother's return to Brisbane?'

'Yes, actually I do. It was all very unfortunate.'

'What do you know, Bill?' asked Julie softly.

'I kept in contact with Roland after the war, when we both returned to Malaya, and after I came to Australia, too, for that matter. We'd shared some experiences in the war, and we knew things that very few people knew. We were in intelligence, you know.'

Julie nodded. 'I've read Roland's account of his war service, so I have a good idea of the work you two did behind the lines. I know that it was very, very dangerous. But I can't see how that would affect Roland's and Margaret's relationship after the war.'

'Yes, I always assumed my mother wasn't happy in Malaya after the war, because of all the changes. It wasn't the grand life any more,' said Caroline.

Bill nodded. 'I suppose that was part of it. The communist insurgency made things uncomfortable for people living in the rural areas, but attitudes were changing as well. There was talk of independence, which would mean a big shift in political power. It was clear that things would not return to the way they were before. But I think, at the bottom of it all, was that Roland found it very hard to forgive Margaret.'

Julie stared at him. 'Forgive Margaret? For what? What happened?'

Bill paused as if deciding whether to say more. Then he shifted in his seat. 'Julie, why don't you make us some tea? All the makings are in the kitchen. The lassie will be around with the sandwiches any minute.'

'Of course.' Julie got up. 'So you can get your meals provided, or do you make something for yourself, Bill?'

'I usually eat in the dining room, but I can make up a brew or a bit of toast if I want to. Never did get into the cooking caper. There's the doorbell. That'll be our sandwiches.'

A smiling young woman came in carrying a tray. 'You want it out there in the sun, Bill?'

Holding mugs of tea and triangle sandwiches, Julie and Caroline looked expectantly at Bill.

After he'd settled himself he turned to them. 'It's quite a story. I don't wonder that Margaret never told you the real reason she left Malaya, it doesn't surprise me at all. I know that she would not approve of my telling you what happened, but I feel I owe it to Roland to tell you, Caroline, the truth about your parents' relationship.'

'Thank you,' said Caroline. 'I would like to know, for better or worse, what happened.'

'I'm glad that you feel like that, lass. I was there, as it happened, when the whole thing blew up. But it's so late in the day now I know I'm not breaking any confidences by telling you about it.'

'When this happened, was Bette married to Tony Tsang?' asked Julie.

'Yes, now that you mention it, I think she could have been, or the same year at any rate. Margaret told me that her sister had gone to Penang and had been seen with Tony. Roland and I thought that was wonderful, as Tony was a friend of ours, but Margaret didn't approve.'

'And was Philip there?' asked Julie.

'No, he'd gone to boarding school by that stage. He was a fine boy. I heard that when he finished school and university, he came back and worked with his father on the plantation. After Roland died I didn't hear much about Utopia, but I did learn, via the grapevine, that Philip and his wife were killed in a car accident. That upset me, I can tell you.'

'Philip's sons Shane and Peter are running the plantation now. They are certainly committed to making it a modern operation. They're doing a great job. But Bill, we are dying to find out why Gran brought Mum back to Australia,' said Julie.

'As I said before, I know what happened but I don't suppose anyone else ever knew the story. Maybe it's time, Caroline, for you and your family to know the truth.'

Utopia, 1950

Margaret was clearly pleased at the welcome distraction of Bill Dickson's visit. 'Bill, I'm delighted to see you. It's always so dull around here these days – a friendly face is a cheery sight. I know that you and Roland want to spend time reminiscing about the war and your adventures, so I'll leave you two here on the verandah with your whisky and water so that you can talk.'

Later that evening, while Roland was dressing for dinner, Margaret joined Bill and asked him his views on the present Emergency.

'Roland doesn't like to discuss it with me. But what are these communists doing? The war is over, the country should be grateful that the British are back in control. These Chinese are troublemakers,' said Margaret. 'All these murders, arson attacks and strikes. You know we were all nearly killed on the Fraser's Hill road, don't you?'

'Roland told me about that. You lost your driver, didn't you? The experience must have been very frightening.'

'I never thought we'd see the day when people would try to push the British out of Malaya. What I can't stand is the disloyalty from some of our workers, after all we've done for them,' said Margaret. 'Several of our staff have disappeared and haven't come back. It's shocking that there are still communists in this area. I worry about our safety.'

'I wouldn't worry. Utopia seems to be quite safe,' Bill said soothingly.

'And,' continued Margaret, 'that Ah Kit is one of those communists. He was our houseboy. I think I've seen him around the district, but Roland won't talk about him.'

Bill seemed quite interested in Margaret's claims. 'You saw Ah Kit? Whereabouts?'

Margaret smiled at Bill. At last someone wanted to listen to something she had to say. 'I was driving back from Slim River a couple of weeks ago. We have a new driver, of course, although he's not as good as Hamid, and there was a young Malay police constable in the front seat with him. He's been assigned to protect us. We passed a rice field where there were several farmers in large straw hats talking to a man with a bicycle. I know that the car was speeding past, but I'm sure that the man with the bicycle was Ah Kit. It shocked me.'

'Are you sure that it was Ah Kit? You couldn't have been mistaken?'

'No, Bill, I'm convinced that it was Ah Kit!' she exclaimed. 'The new driver told me that he's often around, talking to the villagers, asking them questions, helping them. Bill, those communists killed Hamid and they nearly killed me and my children. They're getting very brazen,' said Margaret.

Bill was shocked by how angry Margaret was about the communists, but he supposed that under the circumstances it was understandable. At least Philip was safe in England. Both Margaret and Roland had told him how happy Philip was at school, enjoying the company of other boys his own age, although Margaret said that she missed him.

'I do wish he could come home for holidays, but Roland says that it's too dangerous at present. He thinks that Philip is better off in the UK. I expect that he's right. He visits Roland's mother, or stays in Scotland with some people that he knew in the POW camp.'

'Have you thought of going away for a while?' suggested Bill. 'You could take Caroline to your parents, and you would probably feel more relaxed in Australia.'

'Roland made the same suggestion,' said Margaret non-committally.

'So you're happy here?' asked Bill.

Margaret paused and looked away. 'Sometimes I miss my home in Australia. Nothing here has been the same since the war. Many of my friends have gone and we can't get about very much. I wonder how much longer this guerilla war will go on for. No one seems to be winning.'

'How do you occupy yourself?' asked Bill, thinking Margaret sounded lonely.

'I spend a lot of time supervising the gardeners.'

'I noticed. The grounds are looking very spectacular,' said Bill.

'I wish I could travel around more, but it's not safe, although I always travel with a policeman. I meet my friends in Ipoh every few weeks, and Slim River isn't too far away. In fact I'm going there tomorrow to do some shopping.'

'Perhaps you and Roland could take a trip when things settle down,' said Bill comfortingly, though he doubted that would be any time soon. He felt sorry for Margaret, the current situation had made things difficult for everyone, but especially for people on isolated plantations.

When Margaret returned from her outing to Slim River the next day, her cheeks were pink, and she seemed quite buoyed, almost agitated. She came straight out to the verandah where Roland and Bill were settled, and called Ho to bring her a drink. Almost as an afterthought she asked, 'May I join you?'

Roland and Bill jumped to their feet as she collapsed into a rattan chair.

'You look somewhat frazzled, dear. A big day?' asked Roland solicitously.

Margaret opened the sandalwood fan she always carried and fanned her flushed face. 'It's been quite a day of excitement for a small town,' she began. Ho placed her gin and tonic beside her and Margaret took a sip before continuing. 'I met Anne Farquar in Slim River, and she brought along another friend, Shirley Fielding, who is staying with her. Shirley was still quite shaken up. Her husband manages an estate in the north and it was set alight a week ago. The communists, of course.'

'I've met Thomas Fielding,' said Bill.

Margaret ignored the interruption and continued her story. 'We had a pleasant time in the little shops and the bazaar, then Anne Farquar insisted on going to those smelly markets. Anyway, after that, we went for a nice lunch at that Tip Top Tea House.' She took a sip of her drink as the men waited politely for her to continue. 'My

450

driver and the Malay policeman were right outside, waiting for us, thank goodness.'

'Why was that?' asked Roland.

'I'll tell you,' continued Margaret. 'I said goodbye to the other women, then I decided to pop into that small general store next to the tea house for some items, and when I came out, there was a man looking at something at the front of the shop. I had to squeeze past him, you know how cluttered those little places are, and then he turned around, so we came face to face. Do you know who it was?' She looked at them in horror. 'It was Ah Kit. When he saw me, he was as shocked as I was. He turned away without a word. But it was too late. I'd seen him. So I shouted to the Malay policeman, "Quick, quick, that man's a communist!"'

'And what happened then?' said Roland curtly.

'I told the policeman to arrest Ah Kit.'

Roland leapt to his feet. 'Margaret, what have you done? Where is Ah Kit?' he demanded.

'Goodness, Roland, there's no need to get upset. The man is a communist. You told me so yourself. Anyway they took him to the police station in Slim River for questioning.'

Bill and Roland exchanged a look.

Margaret stared, wide-eyed, at her husband. It seemed that neither Roland nor Bill were sharing in her triumph. 'Really, Roland, I know that you fought with him in the war but he was a Chinese houseboy! Is he more important than your family, your friends, your country?'

'I'll go and telephone the station,' said Roland, hurrying from the room.

'Whatever for? Why on earth do you care so much about Ah Kit?'

'Margaret, it's not just that Ah Kit fought with us in the jungle, but he *saved your husband's life*!' said Bill. 'Mine too, if it comes to that. Neither of us would be here, sitting on the verandah, if it had not been for Ah Kit.'

451

'But he turned against us once the Japanese were defeated,' said Margaret. 'I have no sympathy for him, or any communist.'

'That's unfortunate,' said Bill tersely. 'Because not only did Ah Kit save our lives but I believe the reason there have been no communist attacks on Utopia is because Ah Kit has prevented them out of respect for Roland. Ah Kit has made this place safe for all of you.'

Margaret shrugged. 'I don't believe that. And even if it's true, it's the least he could do, after all Roland has done for him.'

'Margaret, Ah Kit could be in a lot of trouble.'

Bill turned as Roland walked back out to the verandah. Roland's face was set and his eyes were cold.

He spoke to Bill. 'They got him.'

'You mean they arrested him?'

'No, shot him.'

'Shot him? How bad?' asked Bill.

Then Roland looked at Margaret and said quietly, 'He's dead.'

'Oh, bloody hell,' said Bill.

'He was shot trying to escape. That's what I was told.' Roland's voice was filled with anger.

'So they say,' said Bill.

Margaret jumped up. 'Well, that's not my fault! He was trying to run away. He's guilty!'

Bill and Roland ignored her.

'What do you want to do?' asked Bill.

Roland rubbed his eyes. 'There's little we can do for him now. I'd like to help his family, if I can. Margaret, how could you have done this? You know what Ah Kit and I went through during the war!'

Margaret looked at Roland and, without a word, turned and left the verandah.

'Roland, you can't entirely blame Margaret,' said Bill.

'The war and then the communist insurgency, especially after the incident on the Fraser's Hill road, have made life here very difficult for her.'

'Bill, you're a good friend, but what you say doesn't entirely wash with me. Ah Kit was not responsible for what happened on Fraser's Hill. First her sister and now Ah Kit. Margaret only seems to care about the way people and events affect her personally. She isn't concerned about anyone but herself,' said Roland bitterly. 'I have to speak to her, please excuse me.' He strode from the room.

Bill sat on the verandah with his whisky. He could clearly hear the raised voices.

'What do you mean – you can't forgive me? You should thank me!' snapped Margaret. 'One less communist to worry about, who won't set fire to our place, or kill our children. Really, Roland, it's your attitude that I find shocking.'

'And I yours! You are wrapped up in yourself. Everything revolves around you, Margaret. I know it's difficult at present but I have tried my best to provide for you, make you happy, indulge your wishes, but it never seems to be enough.'

'Roland, I think you spend more energy and time worrying about those damn trees than me! The war was hard on me too, yet you make such a fuss about Bette. I bet you encouraged her to go off with that wealthy Tony Tsang, just to annoy me!' Margaret's voice was rising.

'You're being hysterical, and that's ridiculous. I have no control over Bette's decisions. Anyway you should be grateful to Bette for looking after Philip in that POW camp, but you want to turn her heroic actions into some sort of fight for Philip's affection. It's as though you can't forgive your sister for saving our son's life.'

There was silence for a moment, then Margaret's voice was filled with fury. 'I will not stay under the same roof as you any longer, Roland. I think it would be best if I returned to Australia and leave you to your precious plantation! I'll take Caroline with me because I don't want her to be endangered by your communist friends any longer.'

There was another silence and then Roland spoke in a resigned voice. 'They are not my friends, but perhaps that is a good idea given the precariousness of our security here, now that Ah Kit is gone. It won't surprise people that you are returning to the safety of your family in Australia.'

'That's not the reason I'm leaving,' said Margaret in a dull tone.

'I know.'

Roland walked slowly back to the verandah where Bill was still sitting. 'You heard, I suppose,' he said as he slumped into his chair.

Bill nodded. 'Might be the best solution, for the time being.'

'No. She won't be back. Nor will I chase after her. Utopia hasn't been the right place for her since she came back in forty-six.'

'You'll be all right, old man,' said Bill awkwardly.

The morning Margaret and Caroline left the plantation, it was not yet fiercely hot, but the sky was clear and blue, a soft wind rustling through the garden, shaking frangipani and bougainvillea flowers to the ground. Later, the gardener would sweep them into piles with his twig broom and scoop them into a large bamboo basket. Margaret always liked the gravel driveway to be hosed clean, and the earth in the garden beds and the dusty road to the gate to be raked and smoothed, marked with straight lines by the sticks of the broom, and with no leaf or petal despoiling the lawns. The perfect garden would go on, even without her.

There was a lot of busyness as the luggage was

stowed, though her many trunks had already been sent ahead. Margaret's and Roland's parting was perfunctory and unemotional, although it might have seemed from a distance that Roland held his wife more tightly than usual, lingering for a moment so he could remember the softness of her body, the smell of her hair, the familiarity of her. But Margaret didn't seem to notice.

Roland swung his daughter into the air, but she was eager to be in the car, heading off on an adventure in her best dress. In the car, Margaret rolled down the window and gave a final wave to the staff, hovering by the portico, before Roland touched her fingertips.

'Travel safely.'

'Of course, Roland.'

'Be a good girl for your mother, Caroline.'

He stood in the driveway until the car was out of sight, then slowly turned and walked up the steps into the house.

'And Roland never wavered. As far as I know he never tried to get Margaret to return to Utopia,' said Bill.

'Do you know why they never divorced?' Julie asked.

'I don't suppose Margaret ever asked him for one, so Roland saw no need. He was old-fashioned in that sense. But he never saw her or Caroline again,' answered Bill.

'She must have felt very ashamed, because she never mentioned the Ah Kit episode to anyone,' said Caroline. 'She led everyone to believe it was her choice to return to Australia because the East no longer suited her, and Roland had acquiesced in her decision. I used to tell people that my father was too busy running a plantation in Malaya to come to Australia. Because my parents had never got divorced, I always hoped that one day they would get back together and we'd be a family once more, but I realise now that I was just trying to suppress the reality of the situation.'

455

'Mum, she kept everything secret. No wonder she never wanted to talk about Malaya after the war,' said Julie.

Caroline twisted her hands together. 'Do you know what really makes me upset about all this? My mother told everyone that Bette's decision to marry Tony Tsang was the reason that the family were disgraced but now it turns out that it was her actions that were the problem. It is terrible to think that although Bette saved Philip's life, my mother made my aunt the scapegoat for all her troubles.'

'I'm sorry to upset you. Maybe I shouldn't have told you everything that happened,' said Bill, looking concerned.

Julie took her mother's hand. 'No, Bill. It's fine. It's what we came to find out. You've answered a lot of questions for us. Maybe they're not what we were expecting.' She looked at her mother. 'Mum, you can't blame your mother for everything. The war changed things for Gran. It did for a lot of people. Some adjusted and some didn't.'

'That is very true,' said Bill. 'And while Roland knew the marriage was over, I believe that he never stopped loving the woman he had married, and there was never anyone else, until the day he died.'

On the drive from Goondiwindi back to Brisbane, mother and daughter reviewed Bill's story. They felt they'd come to know and understand Margaret much better.

'If only she'd shared what had happened with me,' said Caroline. 'I'd have tried to understand.'

'Maybe in this day and age family would have been more accepting, but there's no way Gran would ever have told anyone that her husband essentially banished her because she'd betrayed the man who'd saved Roland's life in the war!' said Julie.

'But that secret deprived me of a relationship with my father and my brother,' said Caroline sadly.

'I wonder if Philip knew about all this?' said Julie.

'It's no use speculating, because it's all too late now, anyway.'

Julie glanced at her mother. 'I think you've done pretty well with the family you've got, Mum. You've helped find Aunt Bette, you're about to dash to Adelaide and become a granny yourself. You've won the battle of the bypass. Now all you have to do is to take Dad up to Malaysia, and reconnect with your family there.'

Caroline smiled. 'Actually, I've been thinking about that. I'm going to ring those boys at Utopia and discuss a visit, but not till next year.'

'No! You'll be hard to drag away from that baby in the Adelaide Hills,' laughed Julie.

'And what about you, Jules? Are you planning another trip? Maybe to Penang to see a certain RAAF officer?'

'That would be nice,' said Julie. 'I hate this long-distance social networking. A kiss and a cuddle would be far better. But I don't think that he'll be at Butterworth much longer. He's told me that the operation there is nearly finished.'

Paul had the barbecue going and a salad made when they arrived back at Bayview.

'So are you going to tell me the story over a glass of wine?' he asked Caroline as he gave her a kiss and then hugged Julie.

'Dad, open a bottle. It's quite a saga,' said Julie.

He looked at Caroline. 'You all right, sweetie?'

She nodded. 'Bill was amazing, especially for his age. His memory was better than mine, I felt! What is it with these ex-colonials? They seem to go on forever. His story explains a lot about my mother. In a way I do feel sorry for her, but she did some very unjust things, and not only to Roland and Bette,' said Caroline suddenly feeling teary.

Paul put his arms about her and held her. 'It's probably best to know the whole truth, darling. Tell me about it, when you're ready.'

Julie went out onto the verandah, leaving her parents together. What good, kind, loving people they were. Suddenly, she felt lonely. She missed Christopher. She went to the car and found her phone, and sent a text message to him asking when he was available to Skype and chat. Although she wanted to share Bill's story, what she really wanted was to hear Christopher's voice. But when she read his reply to her message, she let out a gasp and raced inside. Her parents were sitting close together on the lounge, sipping a glass of wine.

'You're never going to believe this!' shrieked Julie, dancing and waving her phone about.

'No more surprises, please,' begged her father.

'Darling, what is it?' asked her mother.

'It's Christopher. He asked for a transfer and it's come through! You'll never guess where he's been transferred . . . Amberley Air Force Base.'

'Amberley, here in Brisbane? That's great,' cried Caroline. 'I'm so happy for you.'

Paul beamed at his daughter. 'He must have had a reason to want to transfer to Amberley, and I think I can guess what it is.'

'Now we'll get to meet him,' said Caroline.

Paul stood up. 'I think it's time to open a bottle of my best champagne.'

The End